THE DEVIL'S BIBLE

Steve Berry is the *New York Times* and #1 internationally bestselling author of twenty Cotton Malone novels, six stand-alone thrillers, two Luke Daniels adventures, and several works of short fiction. He has over twenty-six million books in print, translated into forty-one languages. With his wife, Elizabeth, he is the founder of History Matters, an organization dedicated to historical preservation. He serves as an emeritus member of the Smithsonian Libraries Advisory Board and was a founding member of International Thriller Writers, formerly serving as its copresident.

ALSO BY STEVE BERRY

The Amber Room
The Romanov Prophecy
The Third Secret
The Columbus Affair
The Omega Factor
The List

THE COTTON MALONE SERIES

The Templar Legacy
The Alexandria Link
The Venetian Betrayal
The Charlemagne Pursuit
The Paris Vendetta
The Emperor's Tomb
The Jefferson Key
The King's Deception
The Lincoln Myth
The Patriot Threat
The 14th Colony
The Lost Order
The Bishop's Pawn
The Malta Exchange
The Warsaw Protocol
The Kaiser's Web
The Last Kingdom
The Atlas Maneuver
The Medici Return

WITH GRANT BLACKWOOD

The 9th Man
Red Star Falling

WITH M.J. ROSE

The Museum of Mysteries
The Lake of Learning
The House of Long Ago
The End of Forever

THE DEVIL'S BIBLE

STEVE BERRY

HODDER &
STOUGHTON

First published in Great Britain in 2026 by Hodder & Stoughton Limited
An Hachette UK company

The authorised representative in the EEA is Hachette Ireland,
8 Castlecourt Centre, Dublin 15, D15 XTP3, Ireland (email: info@hbgi.ie)

1

Copyright © Steve Berry 2026

The right of Steve Berry to be identified as the Author of the Work has been asserted by him in accordance with the Copyright, Designs and Patents Act 1988.

Cover design by Eric Fuentecilla
Jacket images © Shutterstock
Cover copyright © 2026 by Hachette Book Group, Inc.

All rights reserved. No part of this publication may be reproduced, stored in a retrieval system, or transmitted, in any form or by any means without the prior written permission of the publisher, nor be otherwise circulated in any form of binding or cover other than that in which it is published and without a similar condition being imposed on the subsequent purchaser.

All characters in this publication are fictitious and any resemblance to real persons, living or dead, is purely coincidental.

A CIP catalogue record for this title is available from the British Library

Hardback ISBN 9781399738910
Trade Paperback ISBN 9781399738927
ebook ISBN 9781399738934

Typeset in Aldus LT Std

Printed and bound in Great Britain by Clays Ltd, Elcograf S.p.A.

Hodder & Stoughton policy is to use papers that are natural, renewable and recyclable products and made from wood grown in sustainable forests. The logging and manufacturing processes are expected to conform to the environmental regulations of the country of origin.

Hodder & Stoughton Limited
Carmelite House
50 Victoria Embankment
London EC4Y 0DZ

www.hodder.co.uk

For Yvonne Governor,
Travel expert extraordinaire

*I have fought the good fight,
I have finished the race,
I have kept the faith.*

—2 Timothy 4:7

PROLOGUE

ATLANTA, GEORGIA
JULY 23, PRESENT DAY
2:10 P.M.

COTTON MALONE NEVER LIKED RAIN. SOME FOUND COMFORT IN ITS monotonous pitter-patter, the consistency, the calmness. But he preferred the warm sunshine of a bright clear day.

Nothing better.

His childhood, up until he was ten, had been spent moving from one naval base to another, following his father who'd commanded submarines. But when that sainted man was lost at sea, he and his mother settled permanently on her family's onion farm. Vidalias. Acres and acres of them. Called that because they were grown in and around the town of Vidalia, in middle Georgia. One of a kind. Valued. A whole host of state laws protected the brand from counterfeits. Protection was good. For both onions and people.

He stood coatless, holding no umbrella, Cassiopeia Vitt beside him, his right hand gently embraced with her left. Rare they showed any PDA. Neither of them was much for that. But he liked her touch. Always welcoming. Inviting. Signaling that she derived as much pleasure from the contact as he. They loved each other. A fact they'd both come to accept.

Especially now.

They'd been in Georgia for a week on an unexpected trip across the Atlantic. There'd been duties and obligations that he would have preferred not doing. Having Cassiopeia here, with him, helped. He'd even spent some quality time with Gary, his seventeen-year-old son, whom he hadn't seen since last Christmas. No longer a boy. Now a young man. With a driver's license.

And big plans.

"I'm going to join the navy."

"No college?"

"It's not for me. I want to serve."

That had been hard to argue with. But *serving* was a big word. Being a member of the United States Navy made you one of 350,000 personnel. A small fish in a really big pond. He'd once been one of those fish, an inexperienced lieutenant with a Georgetown law degree, who was poached for a new position. One that took him from the navy's Judge Advocate General's corps to the United States Justice Department's Magellan Billet. All thanks to Stephanie Nelle. She changed his life. And he went from one in 350,000 to one in twelve.

A big fish in a small pond.

Through his dozen years with the Billet agents came and went, but he stayed and made a career. Even after retiring out early at age forty-seven he continued to work for Stephanie from time to time, drawn back into a world that he'd thought behind him. It seemed his life was all about taking chances. Pushing the envelope. But what had he heard once? *Good health is merely the slowest possible rate at which you can die.* And another piece of wisdom, *Health nuts are going to feel real stupid one day, lying in a hospital, dying of nothing.* Did the end justify the means? Or, more important, did the means justify the end?

Hard to say. Especially now.

"Are we leaving tomorrow?" Cassiopeia quietly asked.

Though the sky remained packed with heavy gray pillows of storm clouds, the rain had slackened to more of a mist. Not a hint of a breeze disturbed the warm, humid air. Cassiopeia looked lovely. Her face devoid of anything other than a few touches of makeup. Her dark wet hair was tied back with a silver silk scarf that matched the one at her neck, her knit suit a dove gray, tailored and elegant.

Like him, though, she seemed vulnerable.

Being in Georgia had brought back memories. Some good. Most not so. He'd lived in Atlanta during his entire time with the Magellan Billet. But once he'd retired out, he divorced his wife, sold his house, moved to Denmark, and bought a rare-book shop. A complete 180-degree change that he never regretted.

Until two weeks ago.

"How did we get here?" he muttered.

"We had to," she said.

He asked the only thing that mattered. "Was it worth it?"

She did not answer.

So he thought back.

And tried to answer the question himself.

TWO WEEKS EARLIER

CHAPTER 1

STOCKHOLM, SWEDEN
TUESDAY, JULY 8
4:15 P.M.

COTTON MALONE WAS ON HIGH ALERT.

His Ice Station Zebra condition.

The reference was to the Alistair MacLean novel, where nothing was as it seemed and everything, and everyone, was suspect. His senses were focused on the hustle and bustle of the major metropolitan area that surrounded him. So many different and confusing signals. Totally unlike *Ice Station Zebra*, which the author had set in the isolated Arctic. Earlier in the day he and Stephanie Nelle had completed their business in Italy and flown direct from Florence, arriving in Stockholm three hours ago.

"*I have a problem, Cotton. A big one. I hate to ask. But I need your immediate help.*"

His answer to Stephanie was never in doubt.

"*You got it.*"

And the problem?

The only sibling of the king of Sweden, sixty-eight-year-old Princess Lysa, had been kidnapped off the streets of Stockholm near her apartment. She'd been walking her dog, something she did every day when in town. The dog had returned to the residence still on the leash, but without its owner. A hasty search had revealed nothing. But a message, delivered shortly afterward to the palace, had identified the crime and specified the demands.

Definitely *a problem*, to say the least.

They were expected at the royal palace at 4:30, so they'd taken the time to eat an early dinner. The coming night promised to be a long one. Luckily, they'd both grabbed a little sleep on the flight.

Unfortunately, the weather was not cooperating. A leaden sky hung low, enveloping Stockholm in a premature dusk. A storm had arrived, the humid air bringing down a drenching moisture. Both he and Stephanie wore raincoats and carried umbrellas. Around them other pedestrians were similarly attired, all hurrying in their quest for drier havens.

He'd always regarded Stockholm as one of the world's great cities. It owned a Viking past and a cosmopolitan present. A beguiling mixture of culture and nature, built on a series of islands, which meant you were never far from the water. Unlike other major cities, he knew all that water was clean and swimmable.

They were walking across the Strömbron bridge onto the island that had first been settled over a thousand years ago. Now it held Stockholm's old town, Gamla Stan, a charming maze of cobblestone streets, archways, and stairways that recalled a bygone era when Sweden reigned as a world power. Today it hosted an impressive collection of pastel-colored stone buildings filled with souvenir shops, bars, restaurants, and, his personal favorite, bookstores. It all had grown up around the medieval fortress of Tre Kronor, Three Crowns, that had been surrounded, as was customary in its time, by a great stone wall. Today a royal palace occupied that site. One side faced the water, the opposite a plaza that accommodated the main visitor entrance. Streets lined the other two sides, one private, the other public. They were headed for the public one.

Slottsbacken.

"Considering all that happened in Tuscany," Stephanie said, "you coming here with me is above and beyond."

"Where else would I be?"

"Home in Copenhagen. Running your bookshop."

"My business is fine. I'm exactly where I need to be."

And he meant that.

"I appreciate it. I truly do," she said. "Princess Lysa and I are friends. We met ten years ago. We're the same age and even share a birthday."

He knew that age was a sore subject for Stephanie. She never talked about or revealed her own. His best guess before today? Late sixties, but that was based on her employment history and not her looks, which were of a woman much younger. On every government form where it asked for age she always wrote N/A, which had caused more than one bureaucratic problem. But everyone had their quirks. Even his former boss.

"The king is a friend too," she said. "I've known him for nearly thirty years. We first met when I was with the State Department."

"Is that why he called you?"

She nodded. "One reason."

"And I assume that at some point, you plan to tell me all the others?"

"Don't I always?"

He opened his mouth to point out that this was not the case, but she silenced him with a raised hand. So he shook his head and surrendered. "Never mind."

They came to an intersection.

The eastern waterfront of old town stretched to their left, where more rain crept in off the choppy Baltic Sea under a dome of stained clouds. The wind freshened, gusting in long dark streaks that swept over the inlet. A bronze statue of the famed King Gustav III, dressed in the uniform of the Swedish Navy, dominated a small park. The king stood with his back to the water, an arm outstretched, supposedly offering a twig of peace to the burghers of Stockholm. They'd called him the charming king, but he was assassinated in 1792 by his own nobility, who resented his reestablishment of absolute monarchal power. Tolstoy was right. *Power is a word the meaning of which we do not understand.*

They waited for the traffic signal to change, then crossed the intersection onto Slottsbacken, a wide cobbled street that inclined sharply upward. Originally it had been a slop of sand and gravel, deliberately left unfinished for defensive purposes. But eventually a paved route was formed, along with a moat that protected the palace's southern side. The moat had been filled in centuries ago, but the street remained. Cars moved up and down in a sporadic procession. The palace's most attractive façade, with entry to the treasury and the royal chapel, faced this way to his right, everything soaked from the rain.

"No Swedish police or security forces have been involved," Stephanie said to him. "Just a few of the palace guard, who are closest to the king."

"Is that wise?"

"That's not for us to judge. The king and the government both want this handled quietly."

Odd. Especially for a supposed kidnapping of a royal.

They walked up the wet incline, headed for the highest point of old town. At the top stood the Storkyrkan, the seven-hundred-year-old national cathedral. Once Catholic, now it was a monument to Protestantism, central to the Church of Sweden. Little to no curbing existed, just a double layer of cobbles that formed a line between the walkway and the street. A series of concrete pedestals connected by sloping chains created a barrier on the right where there was a sharp drop-off down to a small parking lot. Most likely for palace employees. The looping chains ended about fifty feet ahead, where a driveway up from the lower lot drained into Slottsbacken. A gate blocked the entrance.

He was tired. The past few days had taken a toll. He'd definitely done some things he thought he would never do. No longer could he go full speed ahead without a few aches and pains. But he wasn't dead yet. He could still run with the big dogs. As Italy had shown.

Two cars eased past them on the street headed down toward the water and the traffic signal behind them. Stephanie walked with her eyes fixed forward, her mind seemingly off somewhere else, as if the distance between herself and some ill-defined past was closing with each step she took. She held her umbrella steady in the breeze. All was okay. He was here. And it was his job to stay alert. She'd tell him everything. When ready.

They passed the last of the chain and concrete pedestals. Ahead on the right stood a triumphal arch for the entrance to the royal treasury. A uniformed palace guard manned a post outside, standing at attention inside a small weather enclosure.

A white Volvo turned onto Slottsbacken at the top of the hill and headed their way. What caught his attention was its speed. Accelerating down the incline, unlike the other cars that were allowing gravity to carefully ease them down the wet cobbles.

The engine gunned.

Stephanie walked closer to the street. The Volvo was about fifty yards away, the distance between them evaporating fast. A quick glance back and he saw that Slottsbacken all the way down to the intersection was clear.

He refocused ahead.

The Volvo was thirty yards away. Still in the middle of the wide street. Not a threat. He realized European drivers were more aggressive than their American counterparts. Driving fast was not unusual. Was he being paranoid? Maybe. But if someone was really after you, then it wasn't paranoia.

Damn right.

Suddenly, the Volvo veered left.

Straight toward them. Twenty yards away.

Coming fast.

He reacted by tossing his umbrella aside and wrapping his left arm around Stephanie, sweeping her off her feet and pushing them both to the right, toward the palace's outer wall.

The Volvo kept coming.

Right behind them was the beginning of the ramp that led down to the parking lot. He was gambling that the Volvo was not going to head through the pole gate into a dead end. So he took them both to the ground, absorbing most of the impact with his right shoulder, and rolled over. Stephanie let go of her umbrella, and it launched out into the wind. They passed beneath the barrier that blocked the ramp. The Volvo could not now get close enough to them without colliding with the gate, then heading downward.

A gamble? For sure.

But it was the only move on the board.

The Volvo's tires wobbled at the road's edge. The driver seemed to realize the quandary and, at the last moment, swerved right, rubber screaming across the wet cobblestones as they grabbed traction and reentered Slottsbacken. Cotton sprang to his feet and darted out, searching with his gaze for the license plate, which was hard to see in the rain. The Volvo was a good forty yards away and receding fast. He could only make out the first three letters—FJB—before the car turned at the intersection and disappeared.

What the hell?

He helped Stephanie to her feet. The guard rushed their way, spewing out something in Swedish.

"We're fine," Stephanie said. "Really, we are."

"This should be reported," the guard said, switching to English.

"Are there cameras out here?" Cotton asked.

The guard nodded.

"We are on our way to meet with palace security," Stephanie pointed out, grabbing hold of her composure. "We will speak to them about this."

The guard seemed satisfied and retreated to his station, but not before retrieving their two umbrellas and handing them over.

"What was that?" she quietly asked Cotton as the guard walked away.

"Three possibilities. That car was after me. Or you. Or both of us. My guess?"

"Me. Since nobody knew you were coming."

"Seems like the correct answer."

"I feared this whole thing may turn personal."

"Is that another reason why I'm here?"

She nodded. "I was afraid me being involved would escalate an already bad situation. I told the king that, tried to beg off, but he insisted I come."

He waited.

"And it's all thanks to a man named John Westlake."

CHAPTER 2

JOHN WESTLAKE COULD NOT BELIEVE HIS GOOD FORTUNE. ONE MINUTE he was home, enjoying the glorious English countryside, about to begin another uneventful day. Less than twelve hours later he was in Sweden.

Back for the first time in many years.

He'd once routinely entered the royal palace through the official diplomatic entrance, a portal reserved for heads of state and foreign ambassadors, uniformed guards always at attention atop a red carpet. Today he'd gained access through a lesser side door used only by staff. No honor guard. No welcome. Nothing.

That was okay. He hadn't been hoping for much.

He remained a royal consort, husband to Princess Lysa and thus a senior member, by marriage, of the Swedish royal family. Twenty-six years ago there'd been a grand wedding here in the palace televised to the nation. The king and queen had both attended, along with over a thousand invited guests. The festivities had consumed four full days. A bit of a fairy tale. It was customary for the royal family to wed other royalty, either from within Sweden but more often from the outside. Lysa had broken with that tradition and married a wealthy British businessman. The king had never considered him anything more than a commoner, telegraphing his distaste every chance he could.

Like today.

And the entrance he'd been told to use.

"The king needs to speak with you. In person. Please come to the palace with all speed."

There'd been no explanation from the royal secretary beyond that the matter was important and discretion was advised. Lysa was here, in Stockholm, on a previously scheduled visit and he'd tried to call and speak with her, but she'd not answered her mobile phone. He'd stopped by her apartment, but there'd been no answer there either.

He stood for a moment and took stock of his surroundings.

He'd always been impressed with the royal residence. Long ago the famed Vasa kings had turned the ugly Tre Kronor fortress into a beautiful Renaissance palace, but that building burned to the ground in 1697. Its replacement—which took sixty years to complete—had an Italian exterior and a French interior, all muted by a mundane Swedish influence. One thousand four hundred and thirteen rooms across fifty thousand square feet. A daunting edifice that served as the official residence of the king, housing his and the queen's offices along with the royal administration. Used only during official duties, though. Otherwise the family lived three miles away at the much smaller Drottningholm, which allowed the main palace to serve as a tourist destination, many of the rooms open for viewing. Summer was the busy time, but he noticed little activity today. The place seemed deserted save for the bureaucrats that, he assumed, remained in perpetual foot-dragging mode.

He grabbed his bearings and found the administrative offices, still located where they'd always been, and was told he was expected in the Jubilee Room.

He nearly smiled.

Another message?

For sure.

Its decorations were a gift a decade ago from Sweden's parliament and local municipalities honoring the king's silver jubilee on the throne. The overall theme and design was the embodiment of a Swedish summer. Its carpet a reminder of wildflowers, the watercolor walls like open fields, the ceiling a blue sky dotted with light clouds.

Everything airy and upbeat.

Belonging exclusively to the king.

He climbed an impressive staircase of Swedish marble and porphyry to the second floor and followed another familiar path to the palace's north side. The rooms ran into one another in the French way, making corridors sparse. Two plainclothes security men waited outside the Jubilee Room. He told himself to be mindful. Be gracious. Conciliatory. The king was old school. A traditionalist who'd sat on the throne going on fifty-one years. Married to the same woman since he was twenty-nine years old. Father of six children. Grandfather to nine. Educated first privately here at the palace, then at boarding school, serving three years in the Swedish Army, rising to the rank of captain before his accession to the throne. A learned man trained in history, sociology, political science, and economics. But also stubborn and arrogant, with myriad rigid opinions, many of which had been sore spots between them.

None of that disagreement today, though.

Thankfully, over the past nine years, he might not have acquired any resolution or ease of manner, but he'd at least gained a comfortable self-confidence.

So embrace it.

He'd dressed appropriately. Clothes were important. He loved what Coco Chanel once said. *In order to be irreplaceable, one must always be different.* For him suits were like tools. Navy was the hands-down top choice. And rightly so. It worked with every skin tone, suitable for work, weddings, and everything in between, screaming class. Gray was just as versatile but generally connoted business, used more often as the go-to option when navy seemed too relaxed. Formal events and evenings demanded a black suit, as did funerals, but vibrancy could be added through colorful accessories like a bright silk tie, pocket square, or bold socks. Today, for this royal audience, he'd chosen a gray windowpane check, tailor-fitted on Saville Row. The ensemble was, as Chanel would have loved, one of a kind.

He stopped before the Jubilee Room.

The door before him was old, weathered, its grain-raised, fine walnut surface glowing a rich red-brown. The two security men clearly knew who he was as neither asked for any identification.

One reached for the handle.

Curiosity screamed within him at the prospect of being face-to-face with the man he'd hated for so many years. He told himself to project the relaxed awareness of someone who lived his life in the open, free of guilt.

Okay.

Here we go.

CHAPTER 3

Stephanie remained shaken. Thank goodness Cotton had been there. As usual, he'd handled the situation. That ability to do the extraordinary was what made him special. She'd known this was going to be complicated.

But an attempt on her life? Right off the bat?

That changed things.

There were few people in the world she truly trusted. Danny Daniels, of course. The two of them had cemented their relationship, and they both seemed happy. Her husband had died decades ago, and she'd never thought love possible again. But Danny had changed that. He was a good, decent man who led the United States for eight years as president. Now he served in the Senate, first appointed then elected to a full term from Tennessee. He remained a political force. Not much was done in Congress that did not make its way through him. He had friends on both sides of the aisle and knew the workings of the American republic better than probably anyone in the country. He was also immensely popular, which provided a Teflon coating from his enemies. He and the current president, Warner Fox, did not see eye-to-eye, and that animosity had spilled over to her on more than one occasion. A truce now existed between them. Not an unconditional peace and an end to all hostilities. More a cease-fire that everyone was trying hard not to break.

Her son Mark was also on the trust list. An Oxford-educated historian who'd once taught at the University of Toulouse in southern France. Long ago he was supposedly lost in the Pyrenees during an avalanche. But he'd risen from the dead, found alive and well, living in a cloistered French monastery, where he was today, and they remained close.

All thanks to Cotton.

Who was the third person she trusted unconditionally.

They'd met a long time ago. She'd been pointed his way by admirals who thought Cotton better suited for intelligence work than being a navy JAG lawyer. She'd been skeptical, particularly considering his youth and brashness. Their first encounter had been a memorable one in Florida. But those admirals had been right. There was something there. A boldness, tempered by reason, that sprang from an ability to independently think, assess, and act. He simply got things done. A true pragmatist, taking the world as it came, dealing only in facts or inferences that could be reasonably made from them. No guessing. No seat-of-the-pants. Few mistakes. She'd never regretted the decision to hire him, and he remained her go-to man when the chips were down.

She and Cotton walked to the top of Slottsbacken, umbrellas back in hand, and left the rain, entering the palace through the tourist doors. Waiting for them was a woman in her mid- to late fifties, pleasant-faced, well dressed in a charcoal-colored business suit, her brown hair piled serenely in braided coils.

Simone de Ciutiis. The current prime minister of Sweden.

Not someone Stephanie had ever dealt with, so she'd been briefed by those in the know who offered two pieces of advice. First, pronounce her name correctly: *Simona de Chootis*. She was peculiar about that. The foreign press loved to screw it up. And second? Tread carefully. Her talent was being herself—easy, natural, giving, accepting—but all that hid the mind of someone who, she'd been warned, always thought beyond the moment. *She likes to be underestimated.* But who didn't? The prime minister was in her eighth year in office, only the second woman to ever achieve the top political spot in Sweden.

"It is good to meet you," Stephanie said in English. "I wish it were under different circumstances."

"As do I."

She introduced Cotton. "He worked for me a long time. He's now retired. Out of the official loop. But there is no one better qualified to help with this matter."

"Then it is good you are here," de Ciutiis said to Cotton.

They left their wet coats and umbrellas at the counter and were led into the palace.

"Has John Westlake arrived?" Stephanie asked their host. She'd been told the Brit had been summoned.

"He is with the king. His Majesty wanted to speak with him alone, first, before we became involved."

Cotton showed no reaction to the mention of the name, and being a pro, he made no further inquiry. He knew the pecking order, realizing that he was the low man on the pole. As he loved to say, you learned a lot more with your ears open and mouth shut.

They climbed an ornate staircase to the third floor.

"The building will be closed for the next few days," the prime minister said. "Nothing unusual there. It is often shut for official functions and state visits."

"Has this been contained?" Stephanie asked.

"So far. Beyond the king and queen, no one else in the royal family knows anything."

They made their way into what was identified by a placard as the Council Chamber, a beautiful room with gilded walls, crystal chandeliers, tapestries, and stunning oil portraits. Four curtained windows opened to the outside. Once the king of Sweden's principal dining room, now it served as a meeting space, where the cabinet council occasionally met to inform the monarch on the affairs of government. A long table dominated the space, solid and graceful, placed with respect according to some official instinct, catty-cornered in the middle of the room. It was sheathed in a green cloth with ten red velvet chairs down each side. A single chair sat at the far end was reserved for the king. Two guards waited at the entrance. Once they were inside the doors were closed, leaving the three of them alone.

"Let me start," the prime minister said, "by saying that I personally am sympathetic to this situation, as is the government. This is awful. And totally unexpected."

"Is the cabinet council involved?" Stephanie asked.

"They have been informed."

And she knew why. Sweden's government was focused on the cabinet council, comprising twenty-five ministers who oversaw the various government departments. Similar to the United States with the president's cabinet. But unlike back home, none of these ministers were autonomous in their various areas. Instead, everything was decided collectively. Which, more often than not, resulted in too many cooks in the kitchen.

Stephanie noticed a file folder atop the table. "Is that it?"

De Ciutiis nodded.

She stepped over, motioned for Cotton to come close, and opened the file. Inside was a single sheet of paper with a few lines of plain English print.

```
We can trade. The Devil's Bible for your
sister. If there is agreement, fly the flag
on the palace roof inverted. You have until
noon tomorrow to do that. If not, your
sister will not be coming back alive.
```

A door seemed to open in Cotton's mind, and he gave her the look. One she'd seen many times before.
Which said.
Really?

CHAPTER 4

Lysa's nerves were on edge.

She'd agreed to all that had happened but had not realized, at the time, just how out of place the whole experience would be. She was a creature of the familiar. Change was not something she actively sought. But John had assured her that everything was okay. This would be short-lived and vitally important. And though she had reservations she sincerely believed that her husband would never mislead her.

They met nearly thirty years ago at a social gathering held at Stirling Castle in southern Scotland. She'd been there on behalf of her philanthropic foundation that dealt with dyslexia, an affliction she herself suffered from. They dated for nearly three years before he proposed, and they were married inside the royal chapel, in Stockholm, at the palace. Her brother the king had not been thrilled but, to his credit, he'd not been an obstacle either. She'd worn a fabulous gown made at Märthaskolen, the famed Stockholm couture school where, in her youth, she'd been a student. Everything had been perfect.

What a wonderful day.

And her life changed.

Long ago, prior to her brother marrying, she'd acted as First Lady of the realm and hosted events at the palace. So being in the spotlight was not foreign to her. But when Queen Ingrid came along, she was relegated to a different role.

Which was okay.

The king needed a wife, the nation a queen, and Ingrid took her position seriously.

That was the way of the monarchy.

As was another long-standing rule.

Once she married a commoner she lost her title as Her Royal Highness. Now she was Princess Lysa, Mrs. Westlake. An odd designation that Wilhelm himself had created. But she never minded. She was old school. And liked being called Mrs. Westlake. She was also, like her mother, a strict believer in the Bible.

Ephesians 5.

Wives, obey your husbands as you obey the Lord. The husband is the head of the wife, just as Christ is the head of the church people. The church is his body and he saved it. Wives should obey their husbands in everything, just as the church people obey Christ.

Which was why she was here. Doing what God instructed.

Pleasing her husband.

A soft knock came at the door.

She'd been sitting alone in the third-floor bedchamber for several hours. Waiting. An hour ago the staff had provided her cookies and tea. Perhaps they had returned to retrieve the cart?

The door opened and a woman entered. The same one who had been there yesterday. In her early forties. Shimmering ebony hair and skin. Trim and fit. Definitely British. Introduced with a double surname as Monica Butler-White.

"How are you doing?" Monica asked with a smile.

"A bit bored, but comfortable. Have you heard from John?"

"He is here, in the country. At the royal palace."

"Meeting with my brother?"

She nodded.

Really? That was most unusual.

Her brother and husband did not get along. For years she tried to bridge the gap, but neither of them seemed interested.

"It was the king himself who summoned Mr. Westlake," Monica said.

"Can you tell me what is happening?"

"Truthfully, I do not know. I work for your husband, but he has not made me privy to his plans. All I know is that it deals with his business, in some manner, and is vitally important. I was charged with getting you out of Stockholm. I am sure he will explain it all when he comes here. In the meantime I wanted to make sure all was good and that you are comfortable. You are going to need to stay here until tomorrow afternoon. I trust Mr. Westlake explained that as well."

"He did, and I am glad to help out. I must say, all that intrigue with me leaving from Stockholm was exciting."

"I can imagine. A far cry from the usual social gatherings."

"What is it you do for John's company?"

"I am more a consultant that assists him from time to time on special projects."

"From England?"

Monica nodded. "Based in Oxford."

"John has a great many stores scattered throughout Great Britain and Russia. A large presence, you know. So many employees."

"You sound proud."

"I am. He is quite successful. Sadly, and you may not know this, but my brother never approved of my marriage. He never thought we would last. But we have. Twenty-six years next month."

"That is a wonderful accomplishment."

"We are planning a trip to Bora Bora. One of those huts over the water. Just the two of us for a week. It should be wonderful."

"He must love you dearly."

Husbands, love your wives, just as Christ loved the church people. He gave his life for the church. So husbands should love their wives, as they love their own bodies. The man who loves his wife loves himself.

"He truly does, and I him. I do want to know, though, is my precious Christina okay?"

Her dog. A purebred Pomeranian. Black and tan fur. Her *baby*, as she and John had never had children of their own.

"I took her back to your residence myself, and she is safe."

"I miss her. Could she be brought here?"

"I am afraid not. But you will be back with her tomorrow afternoon. Now I must handle some other matters. If you require anything, just let the man outside the door know. He is there to assist."

Monica left.

Lysa sat alone by the window and admired the forest outside. A steady rain peppered the long narrow glass. She was north of Stockholm, on Björkö Island in Lake Mälaren. Nearby, on other islands, the first town in all of Scandinavia was founded in the eighth century, by the king of Svea, which was now central Sweden. The islands back then played home to craftsmen and merchants who lived in modest houses overlooking jetties where boats rocked at anchor. From there the king's warriors, Vikings, had headed out to sea on their maundering expeditions, which had brought fame and fortune. Christianity also first came to Sweden somewhere nearby in the eighth century. Björkö itself was full of cliffs, trees, and juniper-covered slopes. She'd once visited an archaeological dig here that had been fascinating. All in all a lovely place.

Where she would wait until tomorrow.

As a loving wife did.

CHAPTER 5

A.D. 1295

THE MONASTERY HAD STOOD IN THE ROCKY CANYON NEAR PODLAZICE since 1159, now in its 136th year. At its center sat a church, an elegant pointed arch structure with a bell tower. Grouped around it were other buildings, each long, high, and narrow, that housed dormitories, a refectory, barns, storehouses, and workshops.

  The Black Monks of the Benedictine Order were a strong presence in Bohemia with abbeys at Ostrov, Sázava, Opatovice, Labem, and Hradisko. Their rule came from Saint Benedict of Nursia, who lived in Italy during the sixth century. Uniquely, they did not operate under a single hierarchy with a central command. Instead, they were organized as a collection of autonomous monasteries and convents, each a place in the world but not of it, filled with a disproportionately large number of doddering old men. The abbey at Podlazice ranked low in regional priority. Others were endowed with ample lands and wealth, so no princes, ecclesiastical dignitaries, or land-rich lords were its benefactors. Many called it the poorest and least known monastery in all Bohemia.

But Brother Jeffery Stieglitz called it home.

And had for the past forty-three years.

His introduction to the place, though, had not been voluntary. He was born the younger son of a petty noble, thrust into the monastery at age sixteen by his father who'd offered him to God in return for salvation. How generous considering his father was not the one who would spend his life behind a wall. Yet Jeffery discovered that his fate was not unusual. A few of the brothers came on their own out of genuine piety, but most, like himself, were left merely to dispose of an unwelcome heir and save the cost of raising a child. Wise abbots sifted out those outcasts carefully and rejected most. Lesser abbots never cared. His father had found one of the latter at Podlazice, who accepted any and all who were presented. Those unwise acts, by many indifferent abbots through the years, had combined to allow Satan to enter Podlazice.

And that demon had never left.

It was All Hallows' Eve and the first evensong of the festival of All Saints had been sung to end the compline service. A departure, for sure, from their usual solemnity, but it was the feast of All Saints and those souls should be appropriately honored. The air was redolent with the breath of incense, the notes of their chant echoing through the lofty church as the Benedictine brethren passed in procession toward the doors. Jeffery was at peace with not only his life but also his piety toward God and love of his fellow man. He'd even forgiven his long-dead father for conscripting him into a life that had not been of his choosing.

The procession filed out into the cloister and the cold night.

One of the lay brothers halted Jeffery's progress toward his cell and said in a low voice close to his ear, "The abbot requires thy presence. Now."

Talking was not forbidden, but neither was it encouraged. The fact that the message had been delivered orally conveyed a sense of urgency. So he followed the laic as he threaded the dark passages and reached the abbot's private lodgings. The messenger knocked on the door, then retired, leaving Jeffery alone to obey the summons to enter.

The abbot, the latest in a long line of incompetent mitered men, sat near the window in the plainly furnished room. The old adage was that if the abbot was a practical and efficient man then the abbey would be happy and prosperous. If the reverse be true, then debt came, prosperity was wasted, the monks either living evilly or deserting, and the abbey was eventually ruined. The current abbot was a weak and infirm old man, small in stature, the countenance dignified with a modest manner. He applied a loose hand to the brethren that had further created a nest for scandal, utilizing one simple rule.

No silly luxuries, but no absurd austerities either.

Which had taxed the abbey's treasury to the point that it was now empty. All knew that they were in danger of being shuttered by their larger, more influential neighbors.

The abbot was not alone. Another man stood in the room. A stranger. Wearing a lighter-colored frock in stark contrast with the Benedictine black. He was younger, the complexion pale, with short brown hair, thin lips, and a nose that was slightly aquiline. Jeffery knew where this man had come from. The Cistercians. A strictly centralized branch of the Benedictines who'd been summoned into Bohemia to bring order and encouraged to establish their own abbeys. They lived by different customs, all designed to offer an alternative to lax Benedictine rule. Their abbeys were plain. No mosaics, stained glass, silk hangings, or floral carvings. Nothing to distract the monks from thinking about heavenly mysteries. But most avoided Cistercian severity, considering the monks nothing but trouble. Yet there was no denying that their abbeys flourished while places like Podlazice withered.

"This is Brother Chyth from the monastery in Sedlec," the abbot said.

Jeffery bowed in greeting. Which was not returned.

"Clouds are gathering thick around our devoted house," the abbot said. "The shelter thou hast long received may fail you and all others here. It is no secret. We are in need of funds. So we must do the unthinkable."

Jeffery felt his spirits sink within him at the words of his protector. One thing the abbot had always excelled at was dealing with the outside world. Few of the brethren understood much of what lay beyond the walls. For this old man to be so cynical meant that the problems were severe indeed.

"Please draw the bolt on the door," the abbot said.

He did as told.

The abbot pointed. "We must go below."

He understood and pressed the rose among the carvings in the cornice, the fourth in order from the door, third from the floor. A bookcase, which seemed a fixture in the wall, popped open to reveal a flight of circular stairs winding downward.

The abbot lifted a bowl of oil with floating wicks and descended the thirty steps to the underground below the foundations. Ahead, through the cool darkness, the lamp's ambient glow revealed an iron door. The abbot found a key in his cassock and handed it to Jeffery, who opened the lock. The room beyond was empty save for a stout wooden table.

The abbot motioned. "This was once filled with precious jewels, gemmed reliquaries, golden chalices, parchments, and, above all, books. But as you can see, they are all gone. Save one."

Jeffery's gaze locked on the table and the single tome it supported.

When his father offered him to the Benedictines, he'd come with something rare. The ability to both read and write. That ability had made him valuable and had been put to good use. Thirty years ago another abbot had a grand idea to create a single volume with all the world's wisdom recorded inside, both the word of the Lord and the knowledge of man. A one-of-a-kind book that no one else possessed. A grand, large manuscript complete with colorful images. Jeffery had labored for three decades, writing day and night, to create what was surely the largest, most expansive book in the world.

The Cistercian stepped close to the table. "It does exist. Many thought it a myth. It is so large."

"It required five of the brothers to bring it down here," the abbot said.

Jeffery had not seen the book in several years, wondering what had happened to it. But dutiful as he was, never had he asked about its whereabouts.

It was not his place to do so.

"We call it the Codex Gigas," the abbot said. "A fitting description, would you not say?"

"Giant Book. That it is," the Cistercian said.

"Tell him about it," the abbot said to Jeffery.

"It tells of the relations between heaven and earth, cosmology, education and its instruments. God and the world. Macrocosm and microcosm. Profanity and sacrality. Sinfulness and piety. Medicine and law. The church and mathematics. The elements, the human body, minerals, flora, fauna, wars, divine and human histories, time organization, and more. Not to mention the Word of God himself. All in one place."

"But is the story about what is inside also true?" the Cistercian asked.

The abbot motioned and Jeffery knew what to do. He stepped to the table and carefully opened the heavy binding. The vellum on the pages had remained bright and soft, all created from the skin of several hundred donkeys back at a time when the abbey was more prosperous. The ink itself remained clear and unblemished. The vibrant colors still there. It was good to see. He'd penned every word from his own hand, without error.

He found the folio he was looking for and displayed the page. The abbot brought the lamp closer so the illustration could be seen in all its colorful terror.

"It is the devil," the Cistercian said, crossing himself. "So the stories are true."

"It is part of the knowledge of man and the Word of God," Jeffery said.

"Why so frightening?"

"To convey that the demon is one to avoid."

The stranger continued to admire the book, gently turning a few of its pages. Jeffery knew how the Cistercians loved books, but not embellishments. Works of art to them were idols that led away from God and were good, at best, to edify feeble souls and the worldly. But books were different, and they maintained extensive libraries.

"It is yours now," the abbot said.

Jeffery was shocked. "You intend to part with it?"

"I do. As collateral for a loan so that we may acquire the funds we need to survive."

He could not believe what he was hearing. Canons required, before taking any important steps, that the abbot consult with the older monks. Pawning this book, which was the abbey's greatest remaining treasure, definitely fell into that category.

"Has this been approved?" he asked.

"This is but temporary," the abbot said. "Once we recover, we will reclaim it."

Not an answer to his question. He opened his mouth to speak, but the abbot silenced him with a raise of an arm. "This is not open for discussion. We either grow or dwindle. I prefer the former. Prepare the book to be transported."

He knew what was expected and simply bowed his head in consent.

"I have a cart and men outside the walls," the Cistercian said.

"Excellent. You will need both. And the funds?"

"I have those too."

"Then we shall conclude our business tonight."

CHAPTER 6

COTTON HAD LOVED BOOKS HIS ENTIRE LIFE.

It started long ago when, as a teenager, he visited the Carl Sandburg house in western North Carolina. A national historic site. Every wall in every room had been lined, ceiling-to-floor, with shelves that held countless books. He'd admired that dedication. Sandburg had definitely been a bibliophile. Years later, as an adult, Cotton's home in Atlanta had been similar, displaying thousands of first editions that he'd gathered. A lot of those had formed the basis of his new bookshop in Denmark, more of that out-with-the-old-in-with-the-new stuff. Others he'd given away. Only a precious few he'd kept, and they were back inside his Copenhagen apartment above the bookshop. He too was a dedicated bibliophile. Unashamed and unabashed. Books were both his passion and his profession. What had the ransom note said?

WE CAN TRADE. THE DEVIL'S BIBLE FOR YOUR SISTER.

He knew all about the Codex Gigas.

Measuring three feet tall, nearly two feet wide, and nine inches thick with 320 vellum folios. It carried the distinction of being the largest and heaviest medieval illuminated manuscript in the world, weighing an impressive 165 pounds. Best guess? Created sometime in the early thirteenth century in Bohemia, the modern-day Czech Republic, inside one of its many monasteries. Each page had been penned with impeccable precision and relentless attention to detail, all with colorful illustrations, precise borders, and highly stylized letters. It supposedly contained the then-world's volume of knowledge through authoritative, ancient, and commonly recognized texts. Which included the Vulgate Bible, both Old and New Testaments, Josephus' *Antiquities of the Jews*, Isidore of Seville's encyclopedia *Etymologiae*, the chronicle of Cosmas of Prague, an early version of the *Ars medicinae* compilation of treatises, and two books by Constantine the African. There were also some smaller works dealing with exorcism, magic formulas, and a calendar with a list of saints and people of interest, along with the days on which they were honored. The Swedes bestowed upon it a more popular label thanks to a highly unusual, nineteen-inch color drawing of Satan.

"The Devil's Bible?" he said. "That's an odd request for a ransom."

"Not really," Stephanie noted.

He waited for more.

Which the prime minister provided.

"The Czechs approached us five years ago about returning the codex to them," de Ciutiis said. "We refused. But to appease that request, we loaned it to them. It was displayed in Prague for nearly a year."

"Why didn't they just keep it?" he asked.

"We thought they might, so we took a simultaneous loan of one of their treasures for the same amount of time as collateral. The Saint Wenceslas Crown. They decided the crown was more important than the manuscript, so both were returned. But they have now seized another opportunity that came their way to get the codex back. A much more effective one. Two years ago Sweden made an application to join NATO. The vote was thirty-to-one to allow us in. The Czechs blocked our admission."

He knew that any new NATO member had to be approved unanimously and recalled reading about Sweden's failed effort.

"They have continued to block our admission," de Ciutiis said. "Publicly, they have expressed reservations about not wanting to provoke Russia and other weak excuses. The same concerns that were raised by others when Finland joined the alliance. But privately they proposed a solution to the impasse. Return the Devil's Bible and they will drop their objection."

He said, "Russia would not want Sweden in NATO."

"No, they would not, and they have made that position quite clear both publicly and privately."

He pointed to the ransom note. "You think the Russians took the princess? To get the codex and stop the deal?"

"They are the most likely candidate," the prime minister said. "Our Office for Special Acquisition thinks they want to acquire and return the Devil's Bible to the Czechs as a goodwill gesture. In return, of course, for a continued veto of our membership."

The Military Intelligence and Security Service was a division of the Swedish Armed Forces Central Command. The Office for Special Acquisition came under the Military Intelligence and Security Service, the most secret part of the Swedish intelligence network, tasked, like the CIA, with espionage abroad, including human intelligence and interagency relations as well as clandestine activities. If anyone would know, it would be them.

"Your intelligence people are briefed on all this?" he asked.

"They are. We need good information in order to make good decisions."

He agreed with that, but he was also skeptical. "This whole thing seems a bit off-the-cuff to me? And overly dramatic."

"I agree. Nonetheless it is happening, and that note is rather specific," the prime minister said. "The Devil's Bible for the princess."

"And you're saying," Cotton said, "that the government, after refusing to return the codex out of any sense of moral obligation, was going to trade all that for a ticket into NATO?"

"We believe that being in NATO is more important than keeping that book. If that is what the Czechs want, then we give it to them. We can also publicly exploit the situation with much fanfare and goodwill—returning national treasures and all that—without, of course, revealing the deal. For the past two weeks we have been in the process of preparing the codex to leave."

"When?" Stephanie asked.

"Tomorrow. We have a plane set to fly the crate south."

"All this has some curious timing," he pointed out. "Interesting the Russians waited to the end to act. This ransom note came to the palace?"

"To the king's personal email. Which Princess Lysa would know."

"No way to trace it?" Stephanie asked.

"Efforts were made. To no avail."

He checked his watch. "The deadline is less than nineteen hours from now."

De Ciutiis nodded. "Obviously, we would prefer not to concede to any demand, but we will not allow the princess to be harmed. If need be, we will trade the book for her and find another way to deal with the Czechs."

"Do the Czechs know what has happened?" he asked.

De Ciutiis shook her head. "Not to my knowledge, and there is no reason to tell them. As yet."

Now he realized why he was here. "So I have until noon tomorrow to find the princess."

"Correct. Do that and our problem is solved."

"Cotton," Stephanie said, "if the Russians are involved, which is a real likelihood, then John Westlake could be our best conduit to them."

"And why is that?"

"Because he is Princess Lysa's husband—and was once, and may still be, a covert Russian asset."

Really? That was something new.

"It all happened nine years ago," Stephanie said. "He was never prosecuted because we did not have enough evidence. And publicly acknowledging that the husband of a Swedish royal princess may be a Russian spy? The king would not allow that to happen."

"So it was all handled quietly?"

Stephanie nodded. "The king wanted things kept secret, so that is what we did. Westlake was isolated in England and placed on a watch list, which made him useless to the Russians."

"And your connection to Westlake?" he asked.

"I was the one who exposed him."

CHAPTER 7

JOHN FACED THE KING OF SWEDEN.

Gustaf Oscar Wilhelm I.

An aristocratic-looking man. Tall. Stout. His face clean-shaven and even-featured. Mid- to late seventies in age, the hair, long ago gone to silver, trimmed short. The king wore a tailored black business suit with a white shirt and pale-blue tie. If there was concern over the two of them being alone for the first time in years, not a muscle in the face betrayed any anxiety. Careful of the eyes, though. A brittle blue, boyish at first glance, disconcertingly mature on further acquaintance, able to both intimidate and penetrate to the core. All that marred the man's perfect composure was a slight limp in his gait, always controlled, as though he was determined that no one would notice.

Sweden's national government was an anomaly. It consisted of a prime minister, appointed and dismissed by the speaker of the Riksdag, and cabinet ministers, appointed and dismissed at the sole discretion of the prime minister. They functioned as a collegial council with collective responsibility to govern the realm, accountable only to the Riksdag. The monarchy was vested with no real power. But the king remained the foremost representative of Sweden. Head of state. Commander in chief. There had been kings for more than a millennium. At first they were elected, but the role became hereditary in the sixteenth century. Like other kings around the world, Wilhelm attended special events and official openings, and marked anniversaries. He also made regular visits abroad representing the soul of Sweden. Personally he championed the environment, which endeared him to Swedes. Queen Ingrid focused on children, especially their early education.

Today the royal family was broken down into three groups. Those with titles who performed official engagements, which was primarily the king, the queen, and their offspring. Those with titles who performed no official engagements, like a sister, aunts, uncles, cousins, and grandchildren. Then, finally, the extended family of other relatives who never represented the country in any way. Lysa had fallen into the second category, and John, as her spouse, was also included. No laws delineated the rules of membership in any of the three categories. All of that was left to the sole discretion of the king.

"How are you, John?" the king asked, but the politeness had the virile courtesy of a man who could not care less.

"I am quite fine, Wilhelm."

He intentionally avoided using *Your Majesty*. True, the omission might normally be disrespectful and antagonistic, but nothing about this was normal, and he owed this man not a single gram of respect.

"Have you spoken with Lysa today?" the king asked.

"I have not. I tried, but she did not answer her phone. I will find her when we are done. I must confess, I am curious why you want to speak with me."

"I have some disturbing news."

He waited.

"Lysa has been kidnapped."

"Kidnapped? What in the world are you talking about?"

"She was taken yesterday and is being held. To get her back, the government must agree to a specific term."

He listened as the king told him about Sweden's application to NATO, the Czech Republic's opposition, and the deal made to trade its vote for the return of the Codex Gigas.

"Give the kidnappers the Devil's Bible," he said to the king. "Do it immediately. What are you waiting for?"

"It is not that easy."

Wilhelm had a reputation as a fair, honest, hardworking monarch, as did his wife, Queen Ingrid. But to him? They were two sanctimonious souls who'd readily believed the worst about him without much in the way of evidence at all. But he told himself to forget all that.

The past no longer mattered.

Stay focused.

He asked, "How could this even happen? There were no security people?"

The king shook his head. "She refused any, said she was unimportant and did not want to waste the subjects' money. We believe the Russians have her."

And there it was.

Dropped quite quickly into their conversation.

Up until he met Lysa he'd led a successful but fairly mundane life as the son of a Liverpool shopkeeper. Business coursed through the family blood going back four generations. He was twenty years old when he started his own discount retail chain selling health and beauty products, groceries, and toys, maximizing his margins by acquiring inventory at a discount from companies trying to off-load unsold stock. Through the years he rebranded the stores several times while constantly expanding. By the time he and Lysa married he owned seven hundred stores across Great Britain, employing nearly forty thousand people. His current net worth was around £2.05 billion. His reputation was one of an intrepid entrepreneur and dedicated philanthropist, well regarded in British social circles. Both the royal family and the government courted his favor. He remained high on everyone's social registers. No one outside of the Swedish king, along with a few within various intelligence agencies, knew any of what had happened nine years ago. All of it had been stamped highly classified to appease Wilhelm. For nearly a decade he'd kept his end of the bargain and lived a quiet, solitary life as the seldom-seen husband of a popular Swedish royal.

"John."

He stared at the king and decided to be a little testy. "It is Sir John."

"You cannot be serious. You want me to use that title."

The British Crown had bestowed him a knighthood five years ago. Further proof that no one knew a thing.

"They have no idea what you did," the king said.

"No idea of what?"

The king shook his head. "I was hoping, praying, that you might put your wife above yourself and be able to open a back channel for us to negotiate with the Russians. Something. Anything."

"You are convinced they took Lysa?"

The king nodded. "It seems clear. They are the only logical suspect."

The tone seemed serious and sincere, but with a shading of benevolent mockery, one used when chastising an old friend who was behaving like an idiot.

"Give them the codex," he told the king again.

"We shall. If need be. But first we want to try to find her."

"You have people working on it?"

"I have asked the Americans for assistance. We need to keep this contained."

"Why? It seems going public could be to your benefit."

"I have been told that that would accomplish nothing, and could further endanger Lysa."

"So you thought I, as some sort of supposed Russian spy, could help?"

"I was hoping. You still do business there."

"I do. But none of the men I associate with are spies. Far from it in fact. None are fans of the current Russian government."

"But they might be able to speak to the right people. Are you not in the least concerned that your wife has been kidnapped?"

"Of course I am. It is horrible. Which is why I said give them the codex. And I should have been told this yesterday, after it happened."

A few moments of strained silence passed between them. He decided to allow the older man the latitude to steer the conversation. But Wilhelm said nothing else. Instead, the king walked over and opened the door.

Three people entered.

Two women and a man.

One of the women was the Swedish prime minister. He knew the face. The man was unknown. But the other woman. He knew her.

Stephanie Nelle.

"He says he cannot help, since he has no ties to Russia other than through business," the king said to them.

"For a man with no intelligence connections, there were an awful lot of SVR agents swirling around you," Stephanie said. "People went to great lengths to protect you."

No handshaking nor even a murmur of the usual pleasantries. No hello, how are you. Just more accusations that rang with arrogance and self-satisfaction.

"You were wrong then," he said. "And remain wrong today. So we are clear, I sell overstocked retail merchandise at discount prices. I have fifty-three stores in Russia, so I am forced to deal with them. But only on that level. Nothing more."

"You seem to have greatly profited from your relationship," Stephanie said.

"All of that was sanctioned through the British government, with their active help and assistance, per British law. There were, and are, no secrets."

"We heard the same thing nine years ago," Stephanie said. "*Yes, you have business contacts with Russia. The retail markets there are virgin territory. There is money to be made. But to open up that opportunity it is necessary to play ball with the government. Corruption is not only the norm, it's expected. Many businesspeople from around the world profit from the Russian markets, but they are not spies.* Did I forget anything you said back then?"

Nelle looked about the same as nine years ago. Petite. Blond hair streaked with waves of silver. The features not unattractive, but not all that noteworthy either, the face one you could easily forget. Then she'd headed an American intelligence agency. So he ignored her question and asked, "Do you still run the Magellan Billet?"

"I do. Someone just tried to kill me."

"A shame they failed."

"A car tried to run us both over," the unknown man said.

"And you are?"

"Cotton Malone."

"You work with Stephanie?"

"I once did. Now I just help out."

"How gallant."

"I like to think so."

He'd learned more than enough. Time to go. "This is pointless." He stepped toward the door, not waiting to be formally excused.

"John," the king said.

He noticed the repeated omission of *Sir*.

"Just for the sake of argument. What would it take for you to contact your Russian business associates and make inquiries about Lysa?"

He stopped but did not turn around. Excitement grew warm in his veins, and he clamped his teeth over the words he truly wanted the man to hear.

Instead he said, "A sincere apology."

And he left.

Outside, in the hall, he kept walking until out of sight of the guards. Then he found his phone and sent a text.

I was right.

CHAPTER 8

OLOF PALME SERVED AS PRIME MINISTER OF SWEDEN FOR ELEVEN *tumultuous years. He was pivotal and polarizing, steadfast in his non-alignment policy toward China, Russia, and America. An advocate for Third World countries, he despised imperialist ambitions and authoritarian regimes. He voiced harsh and emotional criticism of the United States over the Vietnam War. Expressed vocal opposition to the crushing of the Prague Spring by the Soviet Union. He campaigned against nuclear weapons proliferation. He supported the African National Congress, the Palestine Liberation Organization, and the Polisario Front. He openly called the Franco regime in Spain murderers, opposed apartheid and supported economic sanctions against South Africa.*

All of that ensured that Palme had plenty of friends and enemies.

His outspokenness led to three cooling-off periods with the United States when diplomatic relations were temporarily suspended.

Domestically, though, he was immensely popular. By his own admission he considered himself a "revolutionary reformist." A social progressive. He favored unions over business, reformed the nation's childcare and health systems, and revamped public education. No friend of the wealthy, he supported some of the highest tax rates Sweden ever imposed.

Like nearly all other Swedish officials at the time, Palme went about his day without security or bodyguards. On February 28, 1986, near midnight, he was walking home with his wife when he was shot in the back at close range. A local drug addict was convicted of the crime, but was unanimously acquitted on appeal. Many investigations ensued afterward, none of which ever led to another suspect.

But nine years ago a break came.

A Russian defector provided intel that the KGB had orchestrated Palme's death. Unfortunately, that defector died before he could offer any further testimony.

Cotton listened as Stephanie explained about Olof Palme.

"That's where Westlake comes in," she said. "We learned from that defector all about Olof Palme and the Soviet involvement with his death. Before he was killed we also learned that the SVR had a source inside the Swedish royal family. No name was provided, but enough was learned that we began to suspect Westlake. So we ran a canary trap."

He knew about those. A way of exposing an information leak by providing different versions of sensitive information to each of several suspects and seeing which version ultimately was leaked. He liked the more colloquial description. *Send something stinky up the pole, then wait to see where the scent leads.*

"We fabricated some specific intel and made sure only Westlake became aware of it. And sure enough, that information subsequently surfaced in Moscow. Pretty fast, actually."

"And once you had that connection, you kept exploiting it?"

"We did. And we would have—"

"I stopped it," the king said. "I stopped it all. The entire matter was unseemly. A disgrace to Sweden and the royal family. An insult to my sister."

"Washington went along with that," Stephanie said, "so long as Westlake was cut off from any further contact with the royal family and isolated, making him essentially useless to the Russians."

"And the Brits?"

"They know nothing."

"They made the man a knight of the realm," the king muttered, his distaste evident.

"I'm surprised the SVR didn't take him out," Cotton said.

"The only thing that stopped them," Stephanie said, "was that the whole thing remained secret. Which made it easy for them to walk away. Making a move would have only confirmed our suspicions."

"Does Princess Lysa know any of this about her husband?" Cotton asked.

"She does not," the king made clear. "And it will remain that way. It would break her heart. My sister is smart, but she is from the old school. She is deeply religious and fervently believes that it is her duty to support her husband in every manner, no matter the situation. She also loves the man. I have no idea why, but she does."

"And how does Westlake feel about his wife?" Cotton asked.

"He has stayed with her a long time," the king said. "Even after all that happened with the SVR. From all appearances he treats her with respect. I have never heard him speak an ill word about her."

Not exactly an answer. "How have you explained his lack of presence here in Stockholm?"

"My sister knows I do not care for her husband. She thinks it is because he is a commoner. Out of respect for me she kept him away unless it was absolutely necessary that he be here. Thankfully, those situations have been few and far between."

Made sense, but he wanted to know, "You think the SVR kept Westlake on a leash by allowing him to do business in Russia?"

Stephanie shrugged. "It's possible. They do play the long game. But he hasn't turned up on anyone's radar since the incident. Nothing at all. Of course, Westlake and the Russians know we're watching him."

"*Herre* Malone," the king said. "My sister chose to marry a British commoner. I was not in favor, but she would not bend, so we had no choice but to accept him. Once we learned of his duplicity, though, we had to act. True, he has been here at the palace from time to time, but always under a careful eye. There was nothing for him to see or report."

He did the math. Both the king and Stephanie knew Westlake would never admit to a thing. He'd refused nine years ago, so why would he now? Which begged the question. Why summon him here? Easy. "You and the king just jostled the barrel. Right? You don't want Westlake's help. You just want to see what spills out."

Stephanie smiled. "Seemed like a smart play. My guess? He's going to go straight to a Russian operative."

"I hope that is correct," the king said. "I did exactly what you asked. But it was truly difficult for me even to speak to the man."

"We have until noon tomorrow," the prime minister said. "After that, this situation will take on a new complexity."

"What a benign way to say my sister may die."

Disgust laced the king's voice.

"Your Majesty, that will not happen," de Ciutiis said. "We will do all that is necessary to ensure the princess is not harmed. If that means trading the book, then we shall do that. But we would prefer not to be blackmailed or coerced. Let us hope we can make progress before the deadline."

Cotton weighed his options. This was definitely a tricky problem with equally tricky solutions. Right up his alley, though he'd never been much of a fixer. Not his style. He learned long ago that the single worst thing someone could do for someone else was try to fix things. Instead, he always preferred the scene from *Frozen* when Anna was in trouble and Kristoff came to her aid. Instead of trying to fix things he simply asked, *What do you need?* Her reply? *I need to get to the top of that mountain.*

So Kristoff made that happen.

"What do you need me to do?" he asked Stephanie.

"Check it all out," she said. "See where things lead. Obviously, with what happened on the way here, someone wants me eliminated. I'll work on that partial license plate and see where it leads. In the meantime visit where the kidnapping happened. There's been no investigating to this point. There could be people who saw things. And remember, you're not associated with anything Swedish."

He got it. "Just a nosy American."

"What about Westlake?" the king asked.

"Not to worry," Stephanie answered, finding her phone. "I have that covered."

CHAPTER 9

CASSIOPEIA VITT WAITED OUTSIDE THE SWEDISH ROYAL PALACE. According to the clock another Scandinavian day was waning, but the sun remained in the western sky, masked by a thick shroud of clouds. Summer here meant days when sunlight lingered until long after midnight. All in stark contrast with winter, when the sun barely made it above the horizon before disappearing midafternoon. She'd received a call yesterday from Stephanie Nelle, who explained the situation, then said, *"We're going to push John Westlake. Hard. Once he leaves the palace, I need you to stay with him and see where it leads."*

"And Cotton?"

"He's going to try to find Lysa. I need you both on this one. Just on different angles."

So she'd booked a private charter and flown to Stockholm, arriving hours before Westlake made his appearance. Stephanie had emailed a photograph. Five minutes ago a text came that told her Westlake was leaving the palace along with, **You're on.**

She surveyed the square with an even stare, standing before a colonnade at the southern entrance. The last changing of the guard for the day was happening, which had drawn a crowd of camera-toting spectators. The wind whistled past and whipped the remaining light rain that filled the air. In the distance she caught the steady, strong, somehow reassuring tone of a bell.

Cotton had told her all about what happened in Italy. She'd not been pleased with the risks he'd taken in the Palio, but he was a big boy and could take care of himself. That was the beauty of their relationship. Neither crowded the other. True, they worried. But both understood what they were capable of doing, and neither one of them was foolish.

She was in love.

For the first time in her life.

With *her* person.

She'd never really been close to anyone. In every relationship that had ever meant a commitment, she'd been the one who'd ended things. When nothing they gave was returned, they always moved on elsewhere. A vicious self-destructive cycle that Cotton finally broke. A few years ago admitting that would have seemed a weakness. Not anymore. Instead, she'd come to understand that having him was a strength. One she no longer wanted to live without. And the best part? Cotton felt the same.

A few months ago they had a long talk, unfettered, unrestrained, everything on the table. For two people who found it hard to express their emotions the discussion had been difficult at first, but easier as they opened up. Would they marry? Hard to say. Both seemed content in the current state of the relationship. But it was not out of the question. Not anymore. She would follow him anywhere, anytime, and he would do the same for her. They were a team.

Like here. Both working the problem from different sides.

Fifty meters away John Westlake exited the palace, back out into the rain. He'd been purposefully directed to that exit as it was busy and crowded outside, no way for him to notice her among the umbrella-toting throng watching the changing of the palace guard. It was also meant as a parting shot of disrespect, hammering home the points the king had made.

Westlake turned left and avoided the ceremony, heading for the building's east side. He wore a raincoat but carried no umbrella. She moved that way too, giving him a wide berth. No need to crowd him.

Just stay back, nice and easy.

She loved Stockholm. Its name meant "island cleared of trees," which was precisely how the original settlement had been created. Many called it the Venice of the North and it was easy to see why. The city occupied fourteen spits of land surrounded on the north by the clear waters of Lake Mälaren and to the south by the Saltsjön, a brackish inlet of the Baltic. One of Europe's great locales, filled with a sprawl of buildings and churches that formed a protective girdle around narrow lanes and hairline-like alleys. She'd spent time here on both business and pleasure. She wished she was here now under better circumstances.

Though she would never admit it openly, in private she was a bit of a royal fanatic. She loved to read about the various families across the globe. The Windsors in the United Kingdom, the Grimaldis in Monaco, and the Borbón-Anjous of Spain, along with other fascinating monarchies in Africa and Asia. Like Japan's Emperor Akihito, who broke twenty-six hundred years of tradition by marrying a commoner instead of choosing an aristocratic bride. More recently his granddaughter Princess Mako had followed his example and given up her royal status completely so she could marry the man she loved. She knew about Princess Lysa of Sweden, who also chose love over duty, which had been relatively easy to do considering she stood little to no chance of ever being queen.

Westlake turned a corner, now headed down an inclined street labeled Slottsbacken toward the water. She stayed back, keeping her target in sight. The rain had devolved into more of a drizzle, her head and hair protected by a hood from her coat. At the bottom of the incline Westlake crossed the street and turned left, walking parallel to the water across a long bridge toward the mainland. The summer air had cooled. Back at her castle rebuilding project in France the weather was hot and muggy. When she'd left there earlier today, work was progressing on not only the outer walls but several of the interior buildings. It all took time, since they only used tools, materials, and techniques from the thirteenth century. It also drained money. But she had that part covered. Her parents had left her with enormous wealth, along with ownership and control of one of the largest corporations in Europe. Business was not her forte, though. Luckily she employed competent people, paid them generously, and allowed them to do their job.

Westlake made another turn at the end of the bridge and walked toward the famed Grand Hôtel. A Stockholm landmark. A place she knew. Five-starred. Built in the late nineteenth century. One of several that populated Scandinavian capitals with the label *grand*. It sat next to the national museum, facing the royal palace across the water. Famous as the place where Nobel Prize laureates and their families stayed, as well as countless world leaders. The hotel was enormous, with something like three hundred rooms. Easy to lose him in there.

Westlake entered through the front doors.

She hustled ahead and made it inside the main lobby just as

Westlake left the front desk, a bellhop in tow pushing a cart with two pieces of Louis Vuitton luggage. She slipped off her wet coat and drifted to the other side among people coming and going. Westlake entered the elevator, and the doors closed. She approached and watched the indicator. The car rose and kept going until reaching the top.

The Flag Suite.

She'd stayed there before. A spacious room in the Old World style with high ceilings, delicate moldings, and comfortable furniture. It also came with access into the glass cupola that topped the building, which offered spectacular views of Stockholm. To her? Finest room in the house. Okay. Westlake liked the best. But the man *was* wealthy.

Time to settle down.

And wait.

CHAPTER 10

Lysa considered herself blessed.

Life was good.

Her marriage was both happy and solid. She wanted for nothing and was appreciative of everything. Her approval ratings among the Swedish people were high, and her standing in British society seemed beyond reproach. Overall, she possessed an unblemished reputation as a good, decent person. Micah 6:8 was correct.

He has shown you, O mortal, what is good. And what does the Lord require of you? To act justly and to love mercy and to walk humbly with your God.

She was also a senior member of Sweden's current royal family, which started long ago with King Charles XIV, a non-Swede born in southern France as Jean Bernadotte. He served both as division general and minister of war during the French Revolution, and as marshal of the empire under Napoleon. He also had the great fortune to be adopted by the elderly King Charles XIII of Sweden, who had no other heir and whose line through the House of Oldenburg was soon to be extinct. With the death of Charles XIII in 1818, a new house came to power.

Bernadotte.

Every Swedish king since that time was a direct descendant, in a straight line, from Charles XIV. Oscar I, Charles XV, Oscar II, Gustav V, Gustav VI, Carl XVI, and the current king, Wilhelm I.

Her older brother.

She came into the world on a snowy night at Haga Palace outside Stockholm, the second child of the then-king of Sweden, given the name Elisabeth Helena Lysa, after three of her ancestors. She was educated at the palace, then at private school, and came to love the theater. She attended the Royal Dramatic Training Academy and worked for a short time as an actress. Twice Ingmar Bergman directed her onstage. That had been an exciting time. She loved performing. Occasionally, she'd harbored thoughts of doing it again, but realized that was impossible, royal princesses simply did not do that. She had, though, kept up her association with the arts by raising money for scholarships awarded to students of music, design, and art, enabling them to develop their talents early in their careers. That had brought her both notoriety and more public appreciation. But it had also provided a great measure of satisfaction. John was so proud of her accomplishments.

I Peter 3:7 said it all.

Likewise, husbands, live with your wives in an understanding way, showing honor to the woman as the weaker vessel, since they are heirs with you of the grace of life, so that your prayers may not be hindered.

She was likewise proud of John. A few years ago the British Crown had bestowed on him one of the highest honors in the United Kingdom, granted only to those who made a significant contribution to the nation. She'd been there when the king of England had tapped John's shoulders with a sword and granted him the title of Sir. What a moment. They'd celebrated with dinner at one of London's finest restaurants, toasting the day with champagne. Even now, just thinking about that evening brought a smile to her lips.

Reading was one of her passions, though it came with difficulty thanks to her dyslexia. The room she was occupying had shelves lined with books. Mainly the classics, along with some Swedish histories, which she'd perused.

But she knew all about her homeland.

Three hundred years ago Sweden had been the dominant power in northern Europe, the Baltic then little more than a Swedish inland sea. What a glorious time. But by the early nineteenth century all that power had faded. Militarism ended. The country assumed a more benign stature, withdrawing into itself, becoming famously neutral on the world stage.

Politics had never interested her. She'd only been second in line to the throne until her late twenties. Once Wilhelm married and birthed children that option ended. Fine by her. She had no desire to be queen. She much preferred her current life as a wife and royal princess. The press treated her with a light hand. She'd been called warm, engaging, and funny, with an impressive ability to disarm her listeners. A description she liked. She was always relaxed when it came to protocol, greeting people with a light handshake and a *pleased to see you*. Pretentiousness had no place with her.

She caught her reflection in the window.

How elegant she looked in a blue-and-red floral dress and matching jacket. Just a hint of red highlighted her thin lips, and the lightest dusting of face powder brought color to her pale cheeks. Wisps of gray flecked her chestnut hair, and her complexion remained flawless. She wore sensible flat-heeled shoes, but her legs and slender frame remained the physique of a former actress.

Ephesians 2:10 said it all.

For we are his workmanship created in Christ Jesus for good works, which God prepared beforehand, that we should walk in them.

Her floral gardens back home were her passion, their beauty and delicacy unparalleled in central England. She missed that tranquility. But her husband was dealing with something of great importance. He had come to her and sincerely asked for help. She readily agreed to cooperate, no questions asked, though he'd assured her all would be explained.

So she would sit and enjoy the view.

Maybe read some of the books. Eat a few cookies. Have some tea.

Like Monica had said.

All would be over by tomorrow afternoon.

CHAPTER 11

JOHN HAD NO IDEA HOW LONG HE WOULD BE IN STOCKHOLM. A FEW hours? A day? Hard to say. He was just glad to be here. Thankfully, the Grand Hôtel management had made sure he was comfortable. Before boarding his flight from England he'd called to reserve a room and they'd assured him that the Flag Suite would be available, the bar stocked with his chosen brands, including a rare bottle of expensive yellow Chartreuse, his favorite.

He decided to take a few moments and unpack, sorting the clothes his valet had chosen. The Irishman had worked for him over two decades and knew exactly what he preferred. He hung the clothes on the hotel's wooden hangers, then changed, losing the suit and donning corduroy trousers and a pale-blue button-down, open at the collar.

What was about to happen? Hard to say. He might be going out, or he might be staying around the hotel for the evening, dining in the famed Veranda, a favorite meeting place for Stockholmers and tourists alike. It also offered a wonderful view of the waterfront and the palace, with its flagpole high atop. He was craving some fresh Baltic fish and companionship. But he was careful about outside women, usually paying for proven professionals who understood the value of discretion. He used a high-end European escort service through a private app, which had indicated that there were several prospects in the area he could choose from.

Maybe later. Depending.

He slipped on a pair of Italian loafers and climbed the spiral staircase up into the cupola. Stockholm stretched out before him from ten stories in the sky. Through the thick glass the sounds from the rush of the city were muted. Like a silent movie playing out in all directions. A line from Shakespeare came to mind. *There is no art to find the mind's construction in the face.*

How true.

One could not judge a person's true intentions, or thoughts, based solely on their appearance. Humans were deceptive beings. Faces were masks. The real person remained hidden. Actions alone revealed people. Words, pictures, impressions, the fragmented history of behavior? All were tools used to work from what was, to what might have been. He'd thought a lot about the past of late. Memories that had lain dormant for years had become more prevalent. A struggle had long been raging within him, and he'd found it increasingly difficult to grab hold of anchors that rooted life. He had little family. No children. Few close friends. Just Lysa, work, and other women. A wave of cold apprehension passed through him, along with a dose of righteousness that ripped at his soul, always leaving him empty and weak. He hated the feeling. It was time to change things. Thankfully Wilhelm had called. Ironic that he was back. Here. Where it all began. With another chance. A story his father told him long ago had lately come to mind.

As a man was passing some elephants, he stopped, confused by the fact that the huge creatures were being held by only a small rope tied to their front leg. No chains, no cages. The elephants could, at any time, break their bonds. But for some reason they did not. He saw a trainer nearby and asked why the animals just stood there and made no attempt to escape. "When they are young and much smaller, we use the same size rope to tie them, and at that age it's enough to hold. As they grow they are conditioned to believe they cannot break away. They believe the rope can still hold them, so they never try to be free." The man was amazed. The elephants remained captive only because they thought there was no way out.

He'd been one of those elephants for nine years. A pawn in the chess game of ministerial pursuits. With no way out.

But not anymore.

His visit to the palace had been productive. He now knew that the Americans were involved. Stephanie Nelle and a man named Cotton Malone. Here to handle things quietly, exactly as Wilhelm would want. He'd anticipated just such a move. Good to know his instincts were still spot on. The text he'd sent from the palace had surely set things in motion.

A knock on the door below disturbed the silence.

He reined in his emotions and re-formed his own facial mask. He descended the stairs and headed into the main salon, opening the suite's exit door. One of the bellmen from below stood outside.

"A message for you," the young man said, handing over a small, sealed envelope.

"From who?" he asked.

"A man appeared in the lobby, handed me one hundred kroner, and asked that I deliver it to you."

He accepted the envelope.

The messenger left, hustling back down the stairs before he could offer more of a gratuity. He closed the door and opened the envelope to find two items. One was a ticket for admission to the Moscow Circus, which indicated that the performance was in Stockholm this evening at 6:00.

He checked his watch. Less than an hour away.

The other was a small piece of card stock upon which was printed, in English, *Use the ticket, Tomte.*

Okay. Things were in motion.

CASSIOPEIA FOUND A SEAT IN ONE OF THE LOUNGES THAT FILLED THE Grand Hôtel's main lobby. The vantage point offered a view of both the elevators and front doors. She'd texted Stephanie and reported what Westlake had done after leaving the palace and that she was in position, ready to go wherever he led.

Which might be nowhere.

A quick recon had refreshed her memory that, of the two elevators, only one reached to the top of the building and the Flag Suite. The other stopped short a floor below, a set of open stairs in between. To better fit in she ordered a glass of rosé champagne, which always reminded her of home in France. That was one difference between her and Cotton. He did not like alcohol, having never acquired the taste in his youth. She loved a good champagne but was not obsessed enough to spend obscene amounts of money on rare bottles. An excellent recent vintage, moderately priced by the glass, would more than suffice.

She sat alone and sipped from the flute.

Here she was again in the middle of something. What that was?

Who knew. Just something. For Stephanie Nelle getting involved was part of her job as head of an American intelligence agency. But for her and Cotton? It was just a matter of helping out a friend. Somebody once said, *Friendship is like money, easier made than kept.* So true. She could count on two hands the number of true friends she had. Several were within the upper management of Terra, her family's corporation. Another was the woman who'd long maintained her château. Of course Viktor, who oversaw the castle rebuilding project. They'd been friends since university. Henrik Thorvaldsen had definitely been close, but he died a while back inside a Paris church. Then there was Stephanie and, of course, her best friend in the world, Cotton. Whatever either wanted, she would do. And vice versa. No questions asked. It was comforting to know that she had two friends like that.

She'd watched a few minutes ago as one of the bellmen, holding a small white envelope, entered the elevator and rose all the way to the Flag Suite floor. Less than five minutes later he returned minus the envelope.

A message for Westlake?

Hard to say.

But her senses came alert.

JOHN LEFT HIS SUITE AND DESCENDED THE ELEVATOR TO GROUND level. The use of the label *tomte* had wrested his attention.

Nice touch.

A *nisse* and a *tomte* were similar mythical characters. The former was Norwegian, the latter Swedish. Both were solitary, mischievous, domestic sprites responsible for the protection and welfare of a home. *Tomte* literally meant "homestead man." Described as an older person, stunted in size, wearing ragged clothes and sporting a long beard and bright red cap. Americans would call it a gnome. Always male. They usually resided in the pantry or barn and protected the household.

"You are my Tomte," Lysa said to him.

"Is that a compliment?"

"Much so. They watch over things, making sure all is good. They tolerate no mischief. That seems you completely."

"And I only want a bowl of porridge with butter at Christmas? So I will not cause any problems?"

She laughed. *"Like you,* tomtes *can be easily satisfied."*

During the twenty-six years they'd been together Lysa had always used the nickname Tomte for him. But only in private.

Among the two of them.

Which now seemed the perfect way to send a message.

CASSIOPEIA ENJOYED ANOTHER SIP OF CHAMPAGNE.

People were coming and going through the hotel lobby in a steady procession. No one else had ventured up to the top floor. She was hungry, and had no idea how long she would be there, so she ordered a bowl of chowder loaded with chunks of haddock, crabmeat, scallops, and clams.

Her phone vibrated. She checked the display.

Cotton.

"You having fun?" he asked, when she answered.

"I'm sitting in a five-star hotel, drinking champagne, and eating some wonderful chowder. Living the dream." She kept her voice low.

"You sound like me."

"You're rubbing off. Where are you headed?"

"I decided to start at the scene of the crime."

"It's as good as any other place, considering how little information we have to work with."

"Tell me about it."

She listened as he reported all that had happened inside the palace with Westlake.

"He's definitely been pushed," Cotton said to her. "But to where? Who knows."

The elevator door opened across the lobby and Westlake emerged, changed out of his suit into more casual clothes, a raincoat draped over one arm.

"I have to go," she said. "He's on the move."

"Stay with him."

She ended the call, dropped fifty euros on the table, and headed off in pursuit.

CHAPTER 12

COTTON LEFT THE PALACE.

Evening had arrived, the sun lower in the western sky, but far from setting. He navigated the nearly empty main courtyard and passed the cathedral, eventually finding the Stortorget, a bustling square that sat in the heart of old town.

He knew its history.

In medieval days people came here to draw water from a community well, to trade, to jeer at those confined in stocks as punishment, or to simply amuse themselves. Today it was dominated by shops, cafés, and the Alfred Nobel museum, the entire area pedestrian-only. His gaze searched the streams of people flowing in every direction, trying to assess the presence of any threat.

Which was proving difficult.

Three streets had their origin off the square. Köpmangatan, Svartmangatan, and Skomakargatan, each lined by elegant seventeenth- and eighteenth-century Germanic-style buildings. Princess Lysa's apartment sat just to the east among a block of multistory residences.

The building was owned by the Crown but was situated outside the official palace grounds. According to the information he'd been provided, when in town, Lysa walked the side streets and alleys of old town regularly with her dog. That fact was well known among Stockholmers, whom she loved to greet. Certainly her house staff knew, by now, that something was wrong, and they were definitely a possible security breach, but the prime minister had said that they were all being closely monitored and should not be a problem, noting that *Swedes know their duty.*

He found Köpmangatan and started walking away from the main square on wet, worn cobbles. Voices swept by in gusts all around him in a variety of languages. More shops lined the way. He smelled spices, baking bread, and brewing coffee. It seemed another busy summer evening, even though the rain had yet to fully stop. He concluded that there was way too much activity here for anything nefarious to have occurred. Too many witnesses. And cameras, which he saw everywhere.

He located the princess' apartment building. Four-story. Nondescript. Ordinary in every way. And kept walking, his soles meeting the street in half slaps that echoed off the walls around him. The path steadily narrowed, making it only accessible to foot traffic. Quiet too, with no visible cameras. Definitely a possible locale now. He came to a small courtyard between the buildings. A tall tree, erect and richly leafed, dominated the space in a grassy patch with pavement all around, along with something curious. A small iron table, only a few inches high, that supported an iron sculpture. A figure, a little boy, maybe six inches high, sitting with his arms wrapped around updrawn knees. A sea of coins surrounded him. Like some sort of monument or memorial.

He looked around.

The buildings were all brightly colored and dotted with windows, the symmetry marred only by a wrought-iron spiral staircase that wound its way up one side and acted as an escape route. A screened cage at the bottom locked off access. He stepped over and examined the gateway. It required a key to open from the outside, but a knob did the trick from the inside. Made sense. If there was a fire, no time to find a key to get out.

There were two ways into and out of the courtyard. The narrow street he'd just traversed and another opening through an archway in the building to his left that led back toward the palace and a street bustling with traffic. He spotted the ornate entrance to the state treasury in the distance and the small guardhouse. Had to be Slottsbacken. Where the attempt had been made earlier on his and Stephanie's lives. He stepped beneath the archway, out of the rain, and noticed something else. In the passageway there was another iron gateway with no lock. Beyond, a metal staircase led down into the earth.

He stared back out to the courtyard. Not a good place to stage a kidnapping. He counted fifty-four windows across four stories from what were surely apartments. No way for the bad guys to know if anyone was watching, and that was assuming the princess had even come this way. Every door to every apartment needed to be knocked on and the occupants interviewed. That was the only way anything meaningful could be learned. But he knew that was not going to happen.

He walked out into the open, beneath the bushy tree, and stood before the monument. The number of coins seemed to suggest this was a place people sought out. Why? That was unknown. He was about to leave when, in one of the fourth-floor windows, he caught sight of a face. Older. Male. Watching intently, though trying hard not to be noticed. He was immediately reminded of the busybodies back in central Georgia. Every street had them. They missed little. Like the classic Mrs. Kravitz from *Bewitched* screaming for Abner to come and see what was happening at the Stevens' residence. He wondered if this gentleman was equally nosy. Since it was the only face he'd seen in any of the windows, and he had precious few other leads, he decided, *What the hell, give it a try.*

He stepped back beneath the archway.

A staircase led upward and he climbed to the fourth floor. The hallway before him was so narrow that two people could not pass each other without one having to turn a shoulder. Doors stretched every twelve feet or so. He found the one that should be the correct apartment and knocked. He heard footsteps and noticed the peephole, an eye most likely pressed tight to the little brass circle. The door opened to reveal a stolid, bland-faced older man with a shock of brilliant silver hair and eyes dwarfed by round horn-rimmed spectacles. One hand rested on a shiny walking stick.

"I saw you watching me," he said to the man in English. "Could I ask you some questions?"

"About what?"

Be clever. "That little iron sculpture. Do you know what it is?"

"Of course I do."

He caught a hint of British in the English. "I'm new to town. Could you tell me about it?"

"He is Järnpojke. Iron Boy Looking at the Moon. Some call him Olle."

"And his significance?"

"He represents the young citizens of Stockholm, the children that had to work hard back in the old times. You leave a coin, or a treat, or just clap his head to find your good luck. Stealing the coins means bad luck, as the child sees everything and forgets nothing."

He decided to give it a try. "Did you see anything unusual yesterday? From your window?"

"I saw nothing."

He doubted that. "This is important."

"I am sure it is. But it does not involve me."

"My name is Cotton Malone. Yours?"

He was trying to establish a rapport, hoping that his instincts about this old man proved correct.

"I am Lars."

He noticed that no surname was offered, so he left that alone and went with the truth. "A woman was kidnapped yesterday. We think it happened around here, but we are not sure."

"It was Princess Lysa."

"You saw?"

The old man nodded.

Though the place smelled stale and uninviting, he had to ask, "Can I come in so we can talk more?"

Hesitation. He waited. *Don't rush him.*

Finally, the old man gestured.

And he stepped inside.

CHAPTER 13

STEPHANIE EXITED THE PALACE A FEW MINUTES AFTER COTTON LEFT. The weather remained awful. The rain had slackened but tendrils of mist still groped down from the dark clouds. Her body felt a fundamental fatigue, deep and lurking, easily capable of becoming exhaustion.

But she had to keep going.

And do her job.

The king had lingered for a few minutes after Westlake left, angry and agitated, but also concerned. Having Westlake back in the country was not something he liked. He preferred his brother-in-law to stay in England, which had largely been the case for nearly a decade. When the king contacted her yesterday and explained the situation, her first instinct was that the Russians were involved. So it had been her idea to involve Westlake. Worth a try. Now she had to determine if that effort would be feast or famine, and Cassiopeia would provide those answers.

Finally, Wilhelm had been hustled along by staffers. He was due at an event outside the palace. The idea was to maintain the established schedule, drawing attention to nothing out of the ordinary. Luckily, the Swedish monarchy was not subjected to the same array of public scrutiny as their British counterparts. The press here was also far less aggressive. Few negative stories were ever written, and no major scandal had ever been attached to the royal family.

She was grateful for Cotton's and Cassiopeia's help. No way to officially involve any intelligence agency, her own included, as the ramifications would be enormous. If the Russians were behind all this, President Warner Fox and the other NATO leaders would never stand idly by. The whole thing could escalate out of control. Of late, everyone seemed itching for a fight, each side nibbling at the other. Tensions were high across the board. There'd been a similar rise in anxiety, years ago, when Finland joined NATO. Russia had pushed to stop it. Hard. But had not crossed the line. Here? To kidnap a royal and use extortion? Even for the Russians that seemed a bit much. But desperation often spawned foolishness. Unfortunately, she was still flying blind. Intel on the situation was virtually nonexistent. Just bits and pieces. The king was counting on her to find out more, so she'd sent Cotton out in the field. If there was anything at all, he would find it.

Yesterday she'd called in another favor with Derrick Koger, the CIA's European station chief. That man owed her big time. She'd stuck her neck out for him repeatedly as of late. Koger also cared little to nothing about chain of command or kissing his bosses' asses. Normally that was a problem. But here? Definitely an asset. They'd talked on the phone again right after the king left and she'd explained what she needed. A text came a few minutes later that told her where to go and when to be there.

Past the palace she hailed a cab and was driven through the commercial heart of modern Stockholm to the T-Centralen, Stockholm's main underground metro station. Sixty miles of track crisscrossed beneath the city, serviced by a hundred metro stations scattered around three rail lines. Red, Blue, and Green. Ninety of those stations were decorated with a bold blend of art and expression, earning the metro system the title of the longest art gallery in the world. T-Centralen had been carved from the bedrock then decorated with bright white and blue tiles that created lifelike vines that spread across the rough, rocky walls and ceiling.

Impressive.

She approached the turnstile and purchased a ticket, then stepped through and headed down to the platform. The station was busy. Clots of commuters merged in and out, none aware of the danger a member of their royal family was in. She'd long ago become accustomed to working in the shadows, without acknowledgments or accolades. The only reward? Getting the job done. Which fit her. But it wasn't for everyone. Some needed a pat on the back. An *atta boy*. Or a medal. Something to say *good job*. But the shadows suited her just fine. As they did Cotton. Which was another reason the two of them had always seen eye-to-eye.

She made her way to the Red Line and waited for the train, which arrived a few moments later. She stepped on board, the car brightly lit and sparkling clean. The subway extended from central downtown north, south and west, a vital transportation loop that millions utilized every year.

She rode for less than ten minutes, two stops north, to the Tekniska Högskolan station. This one cast a different vibe with a cave-like ambience that came from the earthy walls and a low ceiling, all covered with more swirling patterns of blue and white. Dangling below the ceiling was a large glass polyhedron. A placard on the wall said the sides represented Plato's five elements. Fire, water, air, earth, and ether. Other bows to technology came from depictions of Leonardo da Vinci's efforts in creating a flying machine, Polhem's mechanical alphabet, and Newton's three laws of motion. Not many people here. Only a few stepped off with her, and they all quickly moved away. She'd been told to wait under the polyhedron.

The train left the station with a sustained clattering, heading farther north. A woman turned a corner and approached from the far side of the station. Stephanie's pulse began to quicken and anticipation caused her to fidget. She was not a field officer. Never had been. Never wanted to be. The woman came close and asked in English, "Excuse me, have you ever seen the Silvertåget?"

The proper question. Delivered in a calm, quiet voice. A reference to an urban legend about a Silver Train that supposedly rode the rails beneath Stockholm and carried dead people to the afterlife.

"That's a myth," she said, uttering the correct reply. "As is the Kymlinge ghost station."

Another urban legend about an actual metro station which was built but never taken into service. Supposedly, no one living debarked at Kymlinge, only the dead. Both were rather obscure Stockholm tales, though not out of place for the surroundings. Which was the whole idea. Sign/countersign. Old-school spy craft. She'd expected no less from a CIA operative come to provide direct intel, per Derrick Koger's orders.

"Shall we walk and talk," the woman said.

"And you are?"

"Sandra Koss."

Her contact was an older woman, gray hair coiled tightly in a bun to the back of her head. She wore a simple blue blouse and a long skirt. Everything ordinary. Non-memorable. Unnoticeable. More old-school craft.

They strolled the empty station.

"It's an honor to meet you," Sandra said. "The Magellan Billet is a top-notch agency."

"I appreciate that. And you are?"

"Derrick's right hand."

She understood. "He's keeping this one close?"

"To say the least. He sent me here yesterday, after you first called. So I would be on-site, ready to go. The Russians are definitely on high alert. They have a number of assets currently deployed in Sweden."

"More than usual?"

"Definitely more. But it's understandable, given how they feel about Sweden's admission to NATO."

"Who's in charge?"

"A woman named Monica Butler-White. She's a British citizen who once oversaw SVR sleeper cells. Lately, she's been used where needed. And now she's here. As is Westlake."

Russia was notorious for embedding covert assets in foreign countries. Sleepers. Who slumbered for years, sometimes decades, before being awakened. Nine years ago Stephanie had mobilized the Magellan Billet and helped uncover a network of agents that had been planted by the SVR across the United States, posing as ordinary American citizens. For years they built contacts with academics, industrialists, and policymakers, all to gain access to usable intelligence. The investigation, carried out jointly with the FBI, called Operation Ghost Stories, culminated with ten arrests in the United States and an eleventh in Cyprus. There would have been a twelfth in England, if not for the death of their confidential source and the intervention of the king of Sweden.

By definition a sleeper never drew scrutiny. He or she would acquire a job, an identity, preferably one that could prove useful in the future, then blend into everyday life. The best sleeper agents were those who were financially solvent, able to support themselves, not requiring any payments from abroad. Those who gained social status, political power, or positions of influence were the most coveted. The higher up the pole, the better. A British billionaire with connections throughout royalty and government? He would be perfect. So she wanted to know, "And to the main question I posed to your boss?"

"We checked. Deep too, I might add. No question, Westlake makes millions from his Russian stores. His business is thriving there. He also has direct contact with many oligarchs and the government. But all of that is fully known to the British. He's filed every report and disclosure required by law. In fact, the Brits encouraged him to diversify there. We think he even might be providing them some useful intelligence."

Which might be why they knighted him.

Another way to toss everyone off the scent.

"But there is nothing indicating that Westlake is, or was, a Russian intelligence asset," Sandra said. "No proof. Nothing, but a singular accusation from a dead source."

"Which was confirmed with the canary trap," she made clear.

"A onetime test, which could have been compromised. You know that. It's not foolproof. But we do agree with your suspicions, and Koger wanted me to say, and I quote him, that *'this whole thing stinks like a fish frying in the hot sun.'* He's also skeptical the Russians would make such a radical move as kidnapping a Swedish royal. The potential for blowback is enormous."

"Maybe we should expose this whole thing to the world and put Moscow under the spotlight."

"He told me you might want to do that. He says no or, more

accurately, 'No way in hell no.' That would accomplish little to nothing. Moscow would just deny any involvement, and the princess would be killed and buried where no one would ever find her."

She knew all that too. But she just needed to hear the denial. "The prime minister told me that the Czechs are not aware of the situation. Is that true?"

"As far as we can see, the Swedes have told them nothing."

"And neither should we?"

"There's no upside to doing that. Also, Langley is not looped in here."

She smiled. Typical Koger. But, "You okay with that?"

"I do what my boss tells me to do and ask few questions."

"If this takes a bad bounce, your career could get hurt."

"But if the ball finds nothing but net, we all win."

"Spoken like a true field officer. Were you one once?"

"Nearly fifteen years. I've been posted all over the world."

"And now you're the girl Friday to the loosest cannon on the American deck."

Sandra smiled, reached into her shoulder bag, and removed a flash drive. "Here is what you wanted on Westlake. Remember it's all classified. Your eyes only."

"I'll handle it with care."

"Do you need any additional ground help?"

"Tell Derrick I appreciate the gesture, but Captain America and Wonder Woman have this. For now."

She knew the nicknames Koger liked to use when referring to Cotton and Cassiopeia. Which were not necessarily compliments.

They stopped at the long escalators that led up to ground level. Sandra reached back into her bag and removed a soft-covered glossy book, which she handed over.

Codex Gigas, The Devil's Bible: The Secrets of the World's Largest Book.

"My boss thought this might come in handy," Sandra said.

She accepted the offering. "Tell him I appreciate it."

"This is your party," Sandra said. "We respect that. But please know we are here to help, if you need us. You have my direct contact information. Just call and I'll be there with what you need."

"You're staying here in Stockholm?"

"Until the pigs fly."

She watched as the older woman stepped onto the escalator and headed up. Stephanie was violating every rule in the playbook by keeping this quiet. Washington should be told the situation. But the king had asked her not to do that, at least not until tomorrow at noon. So she'd called in the two people in the world she knew she could truly count on. Still, doubts continued to nag at her. Things that did not add up.

What was really going on here?

CHAPTER 14

JOHN WAS FIRST ALERTED TO A WOMAN FOLLOWING HIM WHEN HE was walking down Slottsbacken, in the rain, from the royal palace. He'd utilized an ear fob connected by Bluetooth to his phone. When he'd crossed the street at the bottom of the incline, he'd been told a possible minder was about fifty meters back, hood up over her head in the rain. A basic description of her shape, her size, and the color of her coat had also been relayed. Thankfully, he'd come prepared with people to keep watch as he entered and exited the palace. Always before he'd been followed by agents when in Stockholm, so this visit would not be any different. Only this time he needed to keep track of any and all shadows.

He'd stayed to the sidewalk and resisted the temptation to seem anything other than a man stepping smartly about town in the rain. He'd calmly walked to the Grand Hôtel, checked in, retrieved his luggage, then caught a glimpse of the woman, as described, in the lobby just before the elevator doors closed. Which made him wonder about everything that happened at the palace. Was it all a show?

Designed to fluster him. Cause him to do something? Which this woman would now discover? Intriguing. Had to be Stephanie Nelle's idea. Only this time he was two steps ahead.

He stood inside the Flag Suite, staring out the windows, noting that the rain had yet to abate. The ticket for the circus rested safely in his pocket. He liked what Thoreau once said. *Never look back unless you are planning to go that way.* And Darwin. So wise. *It is not the strongest of the species that survive, not the most intelligent, but the one most responsive to change.*

He grabbed his raincoat and left the room, descending to ground level in the elevator. He told himself not to appear anxious or obvious. Be casual. Indifferent. The doors opened and he stepped out into a busy lobby. His gaze quickly raked from right to left and he caught sight of the woman inside the Cadier Bar, sitting at a table alone with a flute of champagne and some food.

He kept walking toward the main entrance and noticed she rose from the table. Outside, beneath a covered sidewalk, he told the attendant that he needed a cab. One was flagged and eased up to the curb. He tipped the attendant a hundred kroner and climbed inside. Through the tinted window he saw the woman emerge from the glass doors and stole his first look at her close up. Attractive, with skin the color of amber, features dainty, face flawless, unmarked by even the slightest blemish. Long dark hair cascaded past her shoulders, the strands damp from the rain. Fit too. With plenty of curves.

A looker.

Who would need a few moments to acquire a cab of her own.

"Turn here," he told the driver, and they made the first right, rounding to the north side of the Grand Hôtel.

"Slow down," he said.

Which should allow time for her to catch up.

Cassiopeia moved fast, grabbing a cab and heading off in pursuit. She'd never hear the end of it from Cotton, or Stephanie, if she lost Westlake.

She'd noticed Westlake had changed clothes. More casual. A bit unusual for a man of his wealth and status. For her that meant Savile Row suits, leather brogues, and silk cravats. Images of Cary Grant, Sean Connery, Michael Caine, and Daniel Craig came to mind. And a tweed jacket. A caricature? Probably. But the look *was* classic.

"Turn here," she told the driver, mimicking the path Westlake had taken.

The car negotiated the corner.

"I need you to stay with that cab three cars ahead," she told the driver. "But not too close. There's a thousand kroner in it if you do not get noticed."

That should be enough incentive.

She settled into the seat and watched through the windshield. Westlake's cab made a series of turns, heading north through a succession of traffic signals until finally stopping in front of one of Stockholm's many event arenas. Placards and decorations out front announced that the Moscow Circus was performing inside.

Westlake emerged from the cab.

And walked toward the entrance.

CHAPTER 15

COTTON TRIED TO ASSESS LARS.

Ironic, as the older man shared a name with Stephanie Nelle's late husband. He'd never met that man, who died about a year after Cotton joined the Magellan Billet, at a time when he and Stephanie were just getting to know each other. But he'd subsequently read all of Lars Nelle's books, which were a mixture of history, fact, conjecture, and coincidence. Nelle had been an international conspiratorialist who'd thought the region of southern France, known as the Languedoc, harbored some sort of great treasure. He'd supposedly taken his own life, found hanging from a bridge, a note in his pocket that merely said GOODBYE, STEPHANIE. For an academician who'd penned a multitude of books, such a simple salutation had seemed almost an insult. Though she and her husband had been long separated at the time, Stephanie took the loss hard. Eventually, years later, Cotton had helped her work through it all and discover the shocking truth about her husband and his death.

Which was what friends did for each other.

The apartment for-the-alive-Lars seemed a statement to order. An upholstered sofa, tapestry chairs, flat beige walls, and a brick hearth. No signs of neglect anywhere, everything in its place. Lars appeared to be around Cotton's mother's age, mid-seventies, with a mouthful of crooked yellowed teeth. He apparently lived alone save for an annoying short-haired cat that kept patrolling with a wary eye.

"Is Princess Lysa in trouble?" Lars asked.

"She has not returned home."

"I hate to hear that. She is a fine lady. We have spoken on several occasions."

"She comes by often?"

Lars nodded. "Twice every day when she is in town. She always stops by Olle to leave a coin."

"It seems a lot of people do the same thing."

"As I told you, it is a way to find good luck. For her it was also a chance for her dog to answer nature's call in the grass around the tree."

Apparently this man was quite the watcher.

So he asked, "What happened yesterday?"

"While her dog satisfied himself, two men and a woman approached her."

"Did you see their faces?"

Lars shook his head. "My eyes are not as good as they once were."

He doubted that. "Young? Older? Skin color?"

"The men were young. Pale-skinned. The woman was dark-skinned. They left no coins for Olle. But they did talk to the princess."

"Was she upset? Frightened?"

"Not that I could see. They just spoke to one another. Then the woman took the dog and went one way, the two men and the princess the other."

That was odd. "And then?"

"They all walked away."

"Why did you not call the police?"

"I saw no reason to involve the authorities. It was none of my business."

Except that he watched it all. "She's a member of the royal family."

"But I had no idea what was happening. It could have been nothing."

He changed tack. "There's a screened gate below in the archway. Where does it lead?"

"Down to the tunnels beneath the old town, where the rainwater and the melted snow go before returning to the sea."

It made sense that anyone taking the princess would find a concealed way to make their escape. Cameras were everywhere these days, though he'd noticed none on the buildings outside in the courtyard. Back toward the palace and busy Slottsbacken, there would be a multitude of electronic surveillance devices and lots of people. Not a good escape route. But a subterranean path? That seemed perfect. "Are there many ways in and out of that underground area?"

"Oh, yes. They are all over old town. Is the princess all right?"

"That's what I'm trying to find out."

"You did not ask me about the other man."

Do tell. "What other man?"

Lars stood, gripped his cane, and shuffled across the wood floor to the window that opened to the courtyard below. He stopped, though, before standing directly in front of it. "Stay to the side and look past Olle and the tree, to the alley beyond, the one you walked down."

"You saw me approach?"

"I have been watching since yesterday."

Which further begged the question, why had this man not called the police?

Cotton stepped to the curtains and carefully peered out through the dingy glass. A man was visible where the courtyard ended and the narrow street began, wearing a clear wet poncho. He was moving back and forth, disappearing past the corner, then returning, as if on guard.

"He has been there since yesterday evening."

"Same man?"

Lars nodded.

A twinge of alarm passed through him. "Thank you for your time."

And he stepped for the door.

CHAPTER 16

JOHN KNEW A LITTLE ABOUT THE MOSCOW CIRCUS, WHICH WAS originally a generic title for the various Soviet troupes that traveled abroad. It started back in the 1950s as a way for the secretive Soviet Union to reveal a tiny part of itself through the artistry of its talented performers. *See, we are a fun people.* All that changed, though, in 1990 with the fall of communism, which spurred an exodus of performers. A decade ago there'd been a revival by the Russian Federation, *See, we are a fun people too,* and once again the troupes traveled the world.

And here one was in Stockholm. How fortunate.

The arena before him was round and attractively modern with a domed roof and plenty of glass walls. It was set back from the street on a broad, paved plaza where squares of grass alternated with the concrete.

He walked toward the entrance.

Through the glass walls he saw people buying food, drink, and souvenirs, readying themselves to be entertained. More patrons streamed in through the entrances. He checked his watch. The performance began in less than half an hour. He'd noticed another cab that had driven past the arena and deposited his female minder a little way down the street. She'd need a few moments to catch up, so he slowed his gait.

Someone suddenly bumped into him. Which caught him by surprise. A young man, dressed in jeans and a pullover shirt, wearing no rain gear.

"Pardon me," the man said in English. "My fault entirely."

He grabbed hold of himself.

"Look in your coat pocket," the young man whispered before heading off in the light rain toward the arena.

He patted his left side. Nothing.

Then the other.

Something was there.

He reached inside and removed a piece of paper folded around a laminated card. Some sort of admission pass with writing that was a mixture of English and Cyrillic. On the folded paper was written in English, USE THIS AT THE PERFORMERS' ENTRANCE AT THE REAR. ROOM 9 INSIDE.

So he rounded the building and found a two-story appendage faced with rough-cut gray stone that connected to the arena. What was labeled the performers' entrance was set back from the street. Three paved driveways led to loading docks, each wide enough to accommodate the heavy paneled trucks that were backed up to them, the area teeming with activity. Large folding doors were open, allowing access in and out for all the equipment. Lightweight aluminum gates closed off the driveways. Performers and workmen streamed in and out of the back entrance. A lone uniformed security guard stood watch, checking credentials that appeared like the laminated card he held.

He stepped around one of the gates, walked up to the loading dock, and showed the card.

The guard gave it a quick look, then waved him inside.

CASSIOPEIA WAS PUZZLED.

Westlake had come to a performance of the Moscow Circus?

But had not gone inside.

Instead he'd made his way to the rear of the building. That was after a young man had bumped into the Brit and she'd seen a hand go into Westlake's coat pocket. Clear from her wider vantage point.

But not to Westlake.

Who'd been surprised with what he'd found in the pocket.

Something was happening here.

JOHN ENTERED THE BUILDING AND BLENDED WITH THE CHAOS. THE note had said Room 9. So he found a corridor lined with a series of closed doors, each one numbered starting with 22 and working their way backward. He came to the one labeled 9 and lightly tapped.

No answer.

People moved back and forth in haste, unconcerned by his presence. He checked his watch. The performance was set to begin in fifteen minutes. He turned the knob and entered what appeared to be a small dressing room with a table abutting the wall before a lighted mirror, a small settee, and two vinyl chairs. It seemed unused. On the table lay a pair of folded yellow coveralls, a mask, a bowler hat, and a holster with a toy gun. Like something for a clown. The door behind him opened and he spun around.

"*Dobryy vecher*," Monica Butler-White said, closing the door.

"I received your message," he said in English, ignoring her use of Russian.

"And we have company," she said. "American?"

"Hard to say. But she definitely is working with Stephanie Nelle. She has been with me since I left the palace. Nice touch with using *Tomte*."

"Such a lovely term of endearment. Adorable. Though I have never thought of you as a pudgy little troll."

"How is my wife?"

"Placid and happy. Like always. She worships you. Like always. But, for the life of me, I do not see why."

He'd first met this woman, who carried herself with confidence and spoke with a quaint British accent, ten years ago. Her given name was Monica Butler-White, hyphenated with the surnames of her birth and adoptive parents. Now in her mid-forties, she still had a narrow waist and an always elaborate styling of radiant ebony hair. The face carried a few more fine lines—the net of age, his mother would have said—than a decade ago. Her mind, coiled thin and strung tight like the mainspring of a watch, was her strongest attribute. Little escaped her. She was also bold and unabashed. Afraid of nothing. Which was both attractive and scary. She was dressed in a Russian version of an American cowboy costume, complete with oversized shoes and, of all things, a blunderbuss, which seemed more apt for the Pilgrims than for the Wild West. He'd already caught the swell of her breasts from the buttons that remained open at her collar. He'd known since yesterday that there'd be a moment when he'd be tested, when he'd come face-to-face with the new reality, when his actions would either reaffirm or deny the past.

Now here it was.

"You ready?" she asked him.

"Absolutely."

He stepped over and examined the costume on the table.

"What do you have in mind?" he asked.

"Illusion is always better than reality, provided the illusion is convincing and complete."

He asked, "Can we achieve both here?"

"I think we can. We have just the audience we wanted to see what we want them to see."

The circus had always been part of the plan but, as always, Monica had made the necessary adjustments to take advantage of the opportunity offered by the woman following him. Louis Pasteur had been right. *Chance favors the prepared mind.* Still, "This will be extremely risky."

"Just the way I like it."

That she did.

"Now, please," she said, "put on the overalls, holster, and mask. The show is about to start."

CHAPTER 17

COTTON HUSTLED DOWN THE STAIRS. AT GROUND LEVEL, OUTSIDE, he caught better sight of the man he'd seen skulking around from upstairs. Dark-haired, sporting a beard with shaggy locks, the face pocked and swarthy, wearing a poncho soaked from the rain. The guy was beneath the archway, opening the gate, the hinges squealing from resistance but yielding. The man then shed the wet poncho and disappeared into the portal, descending the stairs underground.

He hesitated before following.

Was it foolish? Probably. But he received his fears from his mother and his audacity from his father, and never had the former consumed the latter. He was here to investigate. To do whatever was needed to get answers. That's what field officers did. He'd also learned that in every mission there were moments when the only course available was blind risk. Where you placed your trust in something that might otherwise be regarded as foolish and hoped for the best.

He'd once lived for those moments.

And still did, to some extent.

He crossed the breezeway, opened the gate, and descended one metal riser at a time, the air progressively becoming close and stale, like it had been breathed to exhaustion. A sense of trepidation dug deep into the pit of his stomach. A familiar uncomfortable urge started to sweep through him, one he knew might surface.

His Achilles' heel.

He carried no love for enclosed spaces. In fact, he hated them. A flaw from his mother who likewise was severely claustrophobic. His father had been the polar opposite, a submariner in the navy who spent years underwater. So he liked to think there was a balance inside him.

He reached the bottom and faced the semi-darkness surrounding him.

A heavy iron-bound door hung open, supported by two buttresses. A rumble of water echoed off walls hewn from the rock, the floor damp and gritty. A sickly smell of decay lay heavy in the air. He was standing in some sort of subterranean spillway, the bleak place dimly lit by meager bulbs within metal cages that cast a jaundiced glow across the moving water. The ceiling was only a few feet above his head. Rainwater rushed down from drains above and filled a center canal that ran quickly away, most likely out to sea. Apparently this was some sort of common construction that reduced the chance of flooding. He wondered how long this system had been in place. A long time, he concluded. A narrow ledge stretched before him down one side of the canal. No sign of anyone. The waterfalls raining down drowned out all other sounds. He heard a rustling noise ahead. Then he saw a light. Off in the darkness. On for a moment, then off again.

He moved toward it.

After about a hundred steps the floor began to angle downward. The ceiling became lower, barely leaving room to walk erect. A cold sweat formed in the hollow of his back. It wasn't enclosed spaces that got to him. It was *tight* enclosed spaces that always triggered panic. He wanted to flee back up to ground level, but he knew he had to check this out.

Suck it up. Keep going.

He came to a crossing where a second tunnel with another spillway shot off at right angles, its water moving even faster. The shadows here were long, blurring into one another like a growing stain. He was watching for the slightest movement, sound, or feeling, his primal senses honed. The tunnel to his left hit a dead end about fifty feet away where more water drained down. To his right the path kept going. He left the main shaft, turned the corner, and brushed all the disturbing thoughts from his brain.

He passed several other connecting tunnels.

A cold calm settled over his nerves.

His claustrophobia eased, but his fears seemed unrelieved.

Suddenly, the darkness moved and a form sprang from the shadows, a knife momentarily casting a sharp glint in the weak beams of light.

Long, wide, serrated.

He'd been expecting something, so he was ready, keeping agile on the balls of his feet, the knife sweeping in a circular motion of readiness.

He resisted the impulse to back away. Bad move. Never give your opponent more room to maneuver.

Instead, close in. Attack.

He brought his right elbow up and jabbed at the throat with a sharp blast. In the same motion he caught the knife arm in a tight grip and brought it over his hip, twisting and flipping the guy in a somersault. The man pounded the floor and the knife clattered away. The guy sprang back to his feet and swung a fist but the punch missed. Cotton threw his whole weight at his assailant, using his shoulder as a ram, taking them both down to the wet floor.

They rolled.

The man jolted Cotton with a left-hand blow to the side of the head that momentarily stunned him, allowing a few seconds for the knife to be found and the man to climb atop him, forcing the blade down toward his throat. Cotton fought hard to keep the tip away, pushing back. It came within an inch of his neck and kept edging lower. He swung his whole body and vaulted the guy off him. Blood pounded in his head. His pulse leaped through his body.

His opponent came to his feet.

The same bearded face from upstairs.

Cotton heaved forward, spun on his spine, and clipped the man's legs out from under him, sending the guy pounding back to the wet stone. He readied himself for a final punch.

A shot rang out. Loud. Echoing.

A bullet pinged off the rock wall.

They had company.

He stayed low and crawled forward, taking refuge inside another tunnel that opened off the main shaft. He was unarmed. Guns were illegal in Sweden. Of course, as an intelligence operative, here with the government's blessing, he could certainly carry a weapon. But he hadn't requested one.

Big mistake.

He stayed on the floor and carefully peered around the corner where the two tunnels joined. The guy with the knife was gone. But not the danger of a gun off somewhere in the dark. The sound of rushing water screamed in his ears.

"Malone," a male voice called out.

Interesting his name was known. "I'm here."

"Come to me."

"No way."

"Mr. Malone, I need your help."

A new voice. Older. Weaker. Fear lacing the tone.

"Who are you?" Cotton called out.

"They took me from my apartment."

He slowly rose to his feet.

A light came on about fifty feet away. An image took shape and dimension, then meaning. The man who'd attacked him was holding a cell phone with a light. The uneven wash caught the face of another man standing behind an older, third man, a gun to his captive's head. The older face was the color of bone, sallow, bloodless with an expression of fear and panic stamped into the features. Cotton stayed in the semi-blackness and shifted position, easing into another of the tunnel entrances, out of the line of fire.

"Help me," the older man said, with a plea in his voice.

"Who are you?"

"Lars Olsson. These men took me."

Which meant he'd been led here by a fake Lars above.

His surprise turned to consternation.

He risked another peek around the corner. Too far away to rush them. He'd be shot long before he got there. Nothing lay around him that he could use as a weapon.

"Let the old guy go," he called back. "This is between you and me."

"Okay, I'll let him go."

And the old man was shoved off the ledge and into the black of the center canal.

The body hit the water with a splash.

Three rounds came his way.

CHAPTER 18

CASSIOPEIA HAD TO GET INSIDE THE BUILDING, BUT THAT WAS GOING to be a challenge considering the arena door was manned by a security guard checking credentials. She'd watched from a distance as Westlake had produced a badge and gained admittance.

Interesting.

She noticed performers coming and going, those in costume not being hassled for any badge. They just walked right in. And the workers. Toting props and equipment. They were not bothered either. The rain had finally abated, but both her coat and her hair were wet. She hopped the gate and hustled down the ramp to one of the large trailers backed to the loading dock. Inside was an assortment of wooden and plastic crates filled with props and equipment. She decided the easiest way in was the most obvious, so she ditched her coat and grabbed one of the crates just as two men entered the trailer and scooped up a container of their own.

Perfect.

They headed out and she followed, holding the box up blocking her face. The two men approached the guard, who did not give them a second look. She fell into line behind them and made it past without a problem. Inside, an ancient gray-haired woman sat behind a wooden desk, eyeing everyone who streamed past. When people flashed their ID cards, she motioned for them to proceed. It worked outside. Why not here? So she kept in pace with the two other men, and the woman waved them through.

They passed a ramp that led down into the arena. Music played. On the right were animals in their cages. Bears, tigers, monkeys. Scantily clad women of all shapes and sizes were lining up for the opening production. A group of muscular acrobats loosened up on mats.

To her right stretched a labyrinth of rooms with closed doors.

Where was Westlake?

JOHN SLIPPED THE YELLOW COVERALLS ON OVER HIS CLOTHES AND zipped the front, which was decorated in colorful swirls and designs. The mask was a happy clown face with a broad smile along with a bright-red bowler hat. Quite the opposite of his mood. The holster and gun seemed an accompaniment to the costume Monica wore. The gun was made of plastic. Not real.

"Put on the mask and follow me," Monica said.

She opened the door and stepped out into the corridor. He followed, donning the mask as he stepped from the room. Monica walked to a ramp that led into the arena, and they moved down to its end. In the style of the old Soviet and European circuses there was but a single ring with all the seats around it slanting steeply upward in a circle, like a modern version of a Greek amphitheater. Three other runways led into the ring at various points around the arena, but the one where he stood was the widest.

"The big stuff comes in and out of here," Monica said. "Back up there, then out of the building. It will be kept cleared."

Good to know.

She told him exactly what she had in mind. He was a bit surprised but knew better than to question. One thing he'd learned. She knew what she was doing.

"Just run with it," she said. "Of course, all this is dependent on your shadow cooperating. If not, just bail out and leave."

A band struck a loud chord of a Russian folk tune and the crowd broke into applause as performers ceremoniously filed in. A metallic voice announced in Swedish and English that the show was about to begin. He and Monica stayed back and mingled with a group of performers lined up along the runway. Mini-skirted dancers pranced by. A whip-cracking animal trainer, blond and bare-chested, entered the main ring from one of the other runways with leopards. One of the animals leaped atop a horse and rode around the ring. The audience clapped in rhythm to show their approval.

Then John saw him.

Wilhelm. Grinning and gesturing to Queen Ingrid. They sat mid-arena across from the runway in prime ringside seats. Men in dark suits flanked the royal couple on either side. Two more security men, similarly dressed, sat behind them. Interesting how loose the protection. If that had been the British prime minister, or the American president, they would have been encircled by agents. Even more would be stationed backstage and across the arena. But he knew the Swedes prided themselves on a lack of violence.

Big mistake.

CASSIOPEIA CAUGHT SIGHT OF WESTLAKE AS HE EMERGED FROM ONE of the rooms down the corridor. She still held the crate and used it to shield herself from him. He'd appeared with a woman dressed in some sort of cowboy costume, Westlake wearing a bright-yellow coverall and slipping on a clown's mask with a bowler hat.

She held her distance but kept watch.

Thankfully, everyone was concentrating on the performance, with people and animals moving in and out through the runways.

The music continued to blare from inside the arena. Then it dulled and the lights dimmed. She set the crate aside and ventured farther down one of the runways, closer to where it drained out into the ring. Westlake and Cowgirl were gone, disappearing into one of the other runways. A female aerialist in red tights was climbing up a rope to the top of the domed ceiling, all eyes on her. She began her routine. Spotlights formed shadows of her body on the ceiling. She methodically worked through her performance, timed to music, without a net. When she finished, the lights came back on as applause erupted.

An elephant lumbered into the ring.

Monkeys dressed as children cavorted in too.

Another monkey rode a pony in circles.

With great fanfare from the orchestra performing bears came tumbling in, dressed as musicians. Their trainer acted as conductor and the bears began to play the accordion, cymbals, balalaika, and tambourine. The audience offered another rhythmic clapping.

She studied the crowd.

And saw the king and queen.

CHAPTER 19

Cotton caught a glimpse of the old man sweeping past in the quick current of the canal. More shots came his way, which kept him pinned in the side tunnel.

But he had to move. And fast.

So he leaped into the water.

Freezing. So cold it momentarily sucked his breath away.

The drainage channel was also surprisingly deep. He could not stand. The current rushed him along. He inhaled a deep breath and propelled himself forward with broad strokes, trying to find Lars Olsson. The chilly water grabbed at his body and sucked him under. He swept his arms out and in, swimming hard. Eventually this water had to emerge somewhere. Which probably meant the inlet that surrounded Stockholm's old town. Its levels were obviously high and active thanks to all the rain.

He pushed off the rough rock wall.

If the cold was affecting him, what was it doing to the old man's body?

He again pivoted off the side and swam with the torrent. His right biceps began to cramp. Suddenly he was not in a partially lit open channel any longer. The spillway entered a closed tunnel, the blackness absolute.

He found a foothold and wedged a knee, bracing himself against the pressure, which threatened to spit him along. He needed a breath and resisted with all his strength from being swept ahead, heading upward and finding a nose-width sliver of air between the water and the rock at the top of the channel.

Reality hit him. He was enclosed. Totally.

Trapped in water.

Don't think about that.

His mind reduced to its most basic function, that of keeping the body alive and the brain focused. He dropped beneath the surface. No way to swim back the way he'd come. The current was too strong. *Keep calm. Think.* He worked his way back to the surface and managed another long sniff of air. Careful not to choke. That could be fatal. No choice. Go forward. Use the current. But how long was this tunnel?

He grabbed for the walls, pressed harder, and searched for a grip finding none. He moved back toward the surface, but no air pocket existed. His lungs burned, teeth chattering from the cold. He fought the rising panic of his phobia and struggled to gain control of his limbs. Then, a break. Light leaked down from the surface. Had the tunnel ended?

He pushed upward and broke the surface.

Yes. He was out. Thank God.

He searched and found a hold in the rock wall. A good one this time that provided leverage. He leaped up and planted his right hand on the upper ledge. Then his left. He pulled himself out of the water, chilled to the bone. His arms shook, rivulets of water dripping from his face, clothes soaked. A sour smell lingered in his nostrils. He raked a hand across the stubble on his face. Dammit. Lars Olsson was gone. Probably out into open water by now. He checked his pocket. His cell phone was still there. Magellan Billet issued and totally water- and pressure-proof. His hands, feet, and face were cold past pain and into numbness. The muscles in his shoulders and thighs felt as though they were hauling huge chunks of stone.

He shook his head.

Somebody was way ahead of them. They, whoever they were, knew his name, and they'd readied a trap. The intelligence leak was so accurate that the real Lars had been taken and a substitute dropped in place, ready and waiting. Like that Volvo back out on the street. Its driver had known he and Stephanie would be there. This wasn't a leak. It was a gusher.

Cassiopeia? Was she in jeopardy?

And Stephanie?

He inhaled more of the rank odor, stretched his cramped limbs, then rose to his feet.

He had to get out of here.

STEPHANIE TYPED IN THE ACCESS CODE THAT KOGER HAD PROVIDED and opened the encrypted flash drive. She'd asked for the FBI's classified file on John Westlake. A quick perusal revealed little she did not already know. Surprisingly, though, she learned that the initial intel source had also revealed other sleepers across Europe, but their identities had been kept secret. Surely the idea had been to use them to send more false intelligence back to Russia in a one-way ticket to confusion. But there was no indication what, if anything, had been done.

She was back at the hotel. A moderately priced establishment not far from the elegant Grand Hôtel. Cotton was off working for information. Cassiopeia was with Westlake, wherever that might be.

For the moment all was fine.

She found her cell phone and called Koger.

"I appreciate the information," she told him.

"We're here to serve."

"I need to know what happened after Operation Ghost Stories ended. The file says there were other sleepers who were not arrested."

"I wondered the same thing. So I found out."

"I'm listening."

"There were a lot of dead people in its wake."

"Those sleepers?"

"Yep. Moscow discovered, or already knew, that we knew about them and eliminated the conduits."

"That did not raise red flags."

"Plenty. But the trail went cold All dead ends. Literally. Westlake was sent into exile, and everyone moved on."

"And now he's back, along with more SVR agents. I'll be in touch, if I need more."

"I can hardly wait."

She ended the call.

They needed to switch from defense to offense. But they still did not have the ball. In fact, they didn't even know where the damn thing was located on the playing field. Seeing Westlake again had brought back a lot of bad memories. Reading the file only reinforced those. She felt empathy for Princess Lysa. From all past appearances she'd genuinely cared for Westlake. Nothing she'd ever heard nor witnessed had telegraphed problems. But of course, she'd only been around them on a handful of occasions, always with others present, and people could, as her mother liked to say, *put on a show*. True, the evidence of Westlake's duplicity was weak. But doubt was not uncommon in the intelligence business. Suspicions were many times the only thing you had to work with, but more often than not, those hunches meant the difference between life and death.

When in doubt, go with your gut.

That was advice she'd been given long ago, when she first organized the Magellan Billet. And she'd passed that advice along to all of her agents.

Here? Something was nagging her gut.

Big time.

Earlier, she'd watched Westlake with a fresh eye. Plenty of time had elapsed since their last encounter, but old self-protective reflexes were coming back to life. She kept telling herself that Westlake was, at a minimum, an accomplished liar. He'd repeatedly beat a polygraph. But that had not said much. They simply did not work, beyond measuring someone's initial reaction to a particular question. Were they lying? Impossible to know. The best liars were skilled at blending a careful measure of fact and fiction. Just enough to make you believe. Still, when Westlake had said those two words—*an apology*—earlier, a chord was struck. She'd hoped a rereading of the FBI's file might refresh her recollection and quell the pangs of doubt that now rattled in her head.

But to no avail.

All she could do now was wait.

And see what Cassiopeia learned.

CHAPTER 20

John stood with Monica at the end of the runway, ready for what came next.

"When do I act?" he whispered to her through the mask.

"You will know when and how. Take the opportunity, as it comes. Is that not the story of your life? Hopefully, your minder is inside."

"She is here. Somewhere."

A bear on roller skates glided past him down the runway and into the noisy arena. You did not see that every day. Two more bears came roaring past on motorcycles. The arena dimmed and the colored lights on the bears' motorcycles came to life as they circled the ring.

No engine noise. Apparently the cycles were electric.

"Time for the clowns," Monica whispered.

They approached a small, shiny yellow car with brightly colored flowers painted all over it. A Moskvitch. Four doors. An older model from the Soviet era, parked inside one of the runways. Four more clowns appeared and joined them wearing outfits identical to his, including masks, bowlers, holsters, and guns. But he noticed their weapons were not plastic. All real. The six of them wedged into the car. Three in front. Three in back. He sat in the center of the front bench seat, Monica's blunderbuss in his lap, while she drove. She'd donned a mask of her own.

"Here we go," she said.

And they sped down the ramp and roared into the ring, horn tooting, screeching to a stop near the center.

Monica grabbed the weapon from his lap. "Stay close to the car. Be ready."

Then she and the other four tumbled out.

He stayed inside, the audience laughing and cheering at all that was happening. Loud music kept the pace active. With an exaggerated gunslinger's strut Monica, blunderbuss in hand, flapped over to a makeshift bar that prop men had rolled into the ring and feigned ordering a drink. John spied Wilhelm and Ingrid enjoying the performance. They were here for one reason. To keep up appearances. Not alerting the media, or the public, that something was seriously wrong. He knew this outing had been planned for some time.

Which Monica had used.

To their advantage.

CASSIOPEIA WAS SHOCKED TO SEE THE KING AND QUEEN.

And Westlake was here too? No way that was a coincidence.

A boxy yellow car popped out of the runway.

Five clowns and Cowgirl exited. Westlake was surely one of those, but she noticed that all five were dressed the same and of a similar height, shape, and build. Impossible to know which was Westlake.

Cowgirl stood at a counter with a bartender, a young man with large red freckles pasted on his face who poured a foamy beer into a huge glass, the head overflowing. She feigned anger and pointed her blunderbuss at the man, who ducked behind the bar, emerging a moment later with a fireplace bellows that he used to blow the foam off the beer.

The audience howled at the gag.

The clowns had fanned out around the ring, except for one who stayed near the car. Westlake? She eased her way to the end of the runway, mingling among the next group of performers waiting to enter. A cage full of anxious poodles provided cover. She had a clear line of sight to the car and the king and queen. One of the yellow-clad clowns bellied up to the bar in macho style and drew his six-shooter. Cowgirl shouted something then pointed to the ceiling. The clown looked up and Cowgirl "shot" him with the blunderbuss. The blank cartridge in the gun made a loud bang, and a cloud of smoke poured from the muzzle.

Down he went.

One by one the other clowns challenged Cowgirl to a shoot-out and she eliminated each one with more loud shots, the clowns feigning death and collapsing to the dirt floor.

A sixth clown appeared from the right. Dressed the same as the others. Also of a similar height and build.

He called out and grabbed Cowgirl's attention.

She whirled around and aimed her blunderbuss.

JOHN STAYED NEAR THE CAR.

The clown act was playing itself out with Monica winning each of the feigned challenges. Now a new clown had entered the arena.

Standing bowlegged in his yellow overalls, face masked, both hands out and ready to draw his fake six-shooter. Drums rolled. Lights dimmed. Spotlights focused on the coming gunfight. The "dead" clowns on the ground began to move, each stuffing a hand into one of his costume's pockets and removing a small black cylinder, which they rolled out onto the sand. Smoke began to plume outward. Thick. Gray. Filling the ring in an enveloping fog.

Part of the show?

The four clowns rose from the ground, drew their six-shooters, and began firing into the air.

Monica strutted toward him, then suddenly grabbed his mask and removed it, exposing his face.

"Go for it," she whispered.

CASSIOPEIA AT FIRST THOUGHT THE SMOKE WAS PART OF THE FUN. But when the clowns sprang to their feet and started firing, the situation escalated.

Her senses came to full alert.

Then the new cowboy drew his six-shooter and aimed it not at Cowgirl or even to the ceiling. Through the smoke she watched as he pointed the gun straight toward where the king and queen sat.

She rushed forward.

The distance between her and the cowboy was about ten meters, his back to her. The soft sand in the ring slowed her gait. Smoke was everywhere, her vision obscured. Cowboy fired one shot. Then a second. She glanced past where the clown stood and saw one of the security men rise up. Another of the protective detail had fallen atop the king and queen from behind, shielding them.

She leaped off her feet and slammed into the cowboy. Tackling him to the ground.

JOHN WATCHED AS THE WOMAN WHO'D BEEN FOLLOWING HIM appeared from one of the runway entrances and took down the sixth cowboy with the gun.

This was it. All could see him.

The Moskvitch's engine still idled, the car in park with all four doors wide open. He slid behind the wheel, jammed his left foot on the clutch, and shifted into first. He loved a manual transmission. His own Lotus Exige came with a five-speed, 177-horsepower engine that he enjoyed driving around the English countryside.

He floored the accelerator and whipped the steering wheel hard left, tires spitting out sand. The maneuver caused the doors on one side to slam shut and, on the other, to pop outward then recoil inward. The rear end came around and smacked one of the clowns off his feet. The smoke was blinding. He could barely see anything. He kept turning the wheel. Another clown went down. The other two managed to get themselves past his reach.

One of them leveled a weapon his way.

And fired.

CHAPTER 21

LYSA HAD BEEN PLEASED TO FIND A BIBLE ON THE SHELVES IN THE bedchamber. Reading from it had always brought comfort. Thankfully, her dyslexia had become a manageable affliction. She'd been diagnosed early in life and worked with a trained specialist who taught her new reading and comprehension skills. She'd never considered it a disability, more a challenge that she'd learned to master. She paged through and found some of her favorite quotes.

Jesus said to him, I am the way, and the truth, and the life. No one comes to the Father except through me.

For the wages of sin is death, but the free gift of God is eternal life in Christ Jesus our Lord.

Do not be conformed to this world, but be transformed by the renewal of your mind, that by testing you may discern what is the will of God, what is good and acceptable and perfect.

So much wisdom. And truth. She was a devout member of the Church of Sweden, faithful to its evangelical Lutheran core. The archbishop of Uppsala, its head, was a close personal friend. His predecessor had married her and John. But for all its fundamentalism she also liked its progressive leanings, allowing women as priests and sanctioning same-sex marriages. Love was love, no matter the form, and a priest was just a person close to God no matter the sex. That made sense to her, and on those points, she and her brother differed. He was much more of a traditionalist, but few knew how he felt as, like a good king, he kept his opinions to himself.

Many Swedes lived by the mantra of *lagom*. Middle way. Moderation. Along with *lagom är bäst*. Enough is as good as a feast. The right amount was best. Doing something the *lagom* way meant not taking risks, not overindulging, not standing out from the crowd. Intertwined with *lagom* was *jantelagen*. A maintaining of modesty and humility. Where no one was more special than anyone else. She lived her life more by *jantelagen* than *lagom*. She detested those who wanted to be noticed or be special, or who spoke highly of their accomplishments.

Thankfully, John was none of those.

He was quiet and modest, avoiding the spotlight. True, he was enormously wealthy and lived a lavish life, but never was it flaunted. Instead he dutifully practiced philanthropy, generous with his contributions. There was no question that tension existed between her brother and husband. She'd known that from the start. Nothing uncomfortable or threatening, though. Just an aloofness that she assumed came from one being royalty and the other not. Wilhelm was unbending on that point. But that was surely generational and she could forgive him. She and John had discussed the situation and, true to his nature, he'd told her that he understood the king's coolness and that it was okay, he was not offended. He would just stay out of sight. Their lives were pretty much centered in England, so that had been easy to accomplish. Only she ventured to Stockholm on a regular basis.

And she loved her visits.

Always good to be back home.

She approached one of the bedroom windows and glanced out at the looming night. She'd always enjoyed the Swedish summers, arriving around late May or early June and lasting until mid-August. The time of the midsummer festivals. Full of joy, togetherness, and renewal. She recalled dancing around a maypole adorned with flowered wreaths and indulging in a smorgasbord of herring, new potatoes, and fresh strawberries. Her childhood had been a happy one. Unlike other royal families hers had not been dysfunctional. Her father had been warm and loving, her mother the same. She and Wilhelm were blessed with two good parents. The one true regret she had with her life was the inability to have children. She'd been told in her twenties that conception for her was not possible.

Again the Bible had brought comfort.

Rejoice in our sufferings, knowing that suffering produces endurance, and endurance produces character, and character produces hope, and hope does not put us to shame, because God's love has been poured into our hearts through the Holy Spirit who has been given to us.

For you formed my inward parts. You knitted me together in my mother's womb.

I have said these things to you, that in me you may have peace. In the world you will have tribulation. But take heart, I have overcome the world.

That he had.

No matter. She had John. Her brother. Her nieces and nephews.

And the Swedish people.

She was a wife and princess.

Life was good.

What more could anyone want?

CHAPTER 22

COTTON EMERGED FROM THE UNDERGROUND CISTERN IN STOCKHOLM'S old town amid an array of busy shops and cafés. His clothes were soaked from the icy water. The rain had stopped, but the air remained cool and damp. He needed to return to the hotel and change, but first things first.

He grabbed his bearings, then headed for the Stortorget, making his way across the bustling square and walking back to where he'd met the old man who'd called himself Lars. Being wet had not drawn a lot of attention given the rain. The steady drizzle and streetlamps had turned the path into a gleaming black mirror. He found the courtyard with the Iron Boy sculpture. Three people were standing beside it, taking pictures. One left a coin. He walked past, climbed the stairs, found the same apartment door from earlier, and carefully jiggled the knob.

Unlocked.

He lightly rapped on the wood. No answer.

He turned the knob and gave the door a little push. It swung open, but he stayed on his side of the threshold. No alarms went off. No cat prowled about. Only a warm sickly smell greeted him.

Not unfamiliar.

A quick search revealed that the apartment was empty except for the fake Lars from earlier, who lay on the kitchen floor with two bullet holes in the chest. He crouched down to check for signs of life and was shocked to see the old man breathing, the eyes opening, alight with pain and fear.

"Take it easy. I'll get you an ambulance."

The fake Lars grabbed his right arm and tried to say something, but blood seeped from the lips.

"Don't talk," he told him. "Save your strength."

The old man shook his head. "Get…them. Bastards…shot me."

"Who shot you?"

More blood spewed from the mouth with each gargled exhale.

No way he would make it to a hospital.

"Adv…" the old man tried to say, but he began choking.

Cotton lifted the head up to help clear things. The vise grip remained on his arm. He stared hard into the old man's eyes. "What are you trying to say?"

"*Advokat*…Jakob…Elmore."

Then the body went limp.

He checked for a pulse. None.

He swallowed hard, an empty feeling shooting up from his gut. He'd seen a lot of death as a Magellan Billet agent and in the years after he retired. Most recently he'd held a woman from his past in a similar embrace, someone he'd thought never to see again, and watched her die a gruesome death. She hadn't deserved that, and neither had the fake Lars, who was most likely a loose end.

But when you play with a snake, expect to get bit.

He decided to search the apartment. In one of the cabinets he found an assortment of framed family photographs, seemingly stashed away in haste, depicting a harmless, innocent-eyed, benevolent-browed old man. The same one he'd seen down in the cistern. Not the corpse in the kitchen. He'd been played. There was no other way to view the situation.

He found his phone and dialed Stephanie.

"This is far more complicated than you imagined," he told her.

And he explained.

"There's a lot of planning going on here," she said. "This was all thought through, and by someone with some smarts. It might be time to confront the Russians head-on."

"That's your call. But flushing the birds from the bushes does make it easier to shoot 'em."

"Another of your quaint sayings?"

"My grandfather's. But good advice to live by."

"What now?" she asked.

He stared at the corpse. The cat from earlier appeared and seemed unaffected by the situation. "I keep going. Where's Cassiopeia?"

"She's tailing Westlake. I haven't heard from her."

"She needs to be told to watch herself."

"I'll take care of it. What do you need from me?"

"See about finding that old man's body, and this one here needs some attention too. I'll be in touch."

He ended the call and typed JAKOB ELMORE into the phone's browser. To help narrow the search he included STOCKHOLM.

And got a hit.

For an *advokat*. Lawyer.

With an address in the city.

STEPHANIE SAT IN HER HOTEL ROOM THINKING.

Cotton was right. This whole thing was more complex than they'd anticipated. Cassiopeia needed a warning. So she sent a text advising extreme caution and hoped all was good.

Here she was again embroiled in someone else's problems.

That seemed the story of her life.

She spent the majority of her time alone, both at work and home. Only when Danny Daniels came to town, or she traveled to DC from Atlanta, was her solitude interrupted. She loved Danny. And he loved her.

Odd to hear that in her thoughts.

His marriage had ended right after his second term in the White House, when he was ready to retire from politics and enjoy life. His wife had other plans as she'd fallen in love with another man, whom she ultimately married. They now lived in California, far from Tennessee where Danny was still regarded with the adoration of a rock star. In an age when politicians seemed to embrace fear, flamboyance, and deceit, Danny forged a reputation from the exact opposite. He was both tough and fair. But nobody really cared about ex-presidents. They were expected to live quietly, build their libraries, and write a memoir. Not serve in the United States Senate. But there was nothing conventional about Danny.

God love him.

At present she had six of her twelve Magellan Billet agents in the field, working a variety of operations. The Billet's services were utilized by both the Departments of State and Justice, sometimes by the White House, and occasionally in joint operations with the CIA and NSA. She'd never employed a second in command and no one at the Billet carried the title of deputy. Only three people worked upper management, each autonomous in their realm, reporting directly to her. She preferred that simplicity, but also realized it made the agency too dependent on one individual. She'd seen evidence of that organizational flaw during her recent suspension when her three subordinates had shouldered all the responsibility and floundered a bit. Left hand not knowing about the right hand. No matter. That was the way she ran the Billet. She'd been the one who first envisioned it. The one who created and organized it. And she'd been the only one to head it over the past twenty-plus years. Good and bad both belonged to her. Was her time coming to an end? That possibility had invaded her thoughts more and more of late. She'd always said that she would not stay around past her prime, but that was a much younger Stephanie Nelle talking. One who had not, as yet, faced the prospect of becoming irrelevant. Which was not a pleasant thought. Age brought wisdom, right?

No. Age just brought age.

She and Danny had talked retirement and marriage. A part of her longed for both. But another part hated the prospects. Danny was not dissimilar. Eight years as president of the United States had forged him a solid reputation worldwide. A few years as the junior senator from Tennessee had kept him in the game. Did he want to give that up? *Just say the word and I'll tender my resignation and book a wedding chapel.* His words from a few weeks ago. She'd said she would think on it.

But not now.

Her mind returned to the present problem and the Russians.

Time to make some calls.

CHAPTER 23

CASSIOPEIA WRESTLED WITH THE CLOWN, THE TWO OF THEM ROLLING across the sandy floor. The man was built solid and used his weight and muscles to free himself from her embrace and spring to his feet. But she was not unmindful of the gun and swung her right leg up, kicking the weapon from his grasp with her boot. The clown did not stay around to retaliate or even look for the gun. Instead he disappeared into the smoke, which was rising fast, masking the audience. She heard a lot of coughing, and the level of noise inside the arena was increasing by the second. She stood and searched for Cowgirl through the smoke.

No sign.

She caught sight of the yellow car laying down doughnuts in the sand, emerging in and out of the smoke. She found the gun, which she gripped in her right hand, finger on the trigger, ready.

The car swung around and propelled—

Straight for her.

John was having trouble seeing through the dense cloud that engulfed the car. One of the clowns emerged from the fog and aimed his weapon straight at the car. John reacted in two ways. First, he floored the accelerator, increasing speed, and second he ducked to the right just as a bullet smacked the windshield.

Spiderwebs sprouted from the impact point.

He pivoted back up just in time to see the clown dive out of the car's path. He whipped the steering wheel to the left, downshifted to first, and brought the front end around, trying to get his bearings. Before him, through the shattered windshield, stood a woman. His minder. Closing fast. Holding a gun.

Opportunity. Finally.

He slammed the brakes and skidded to a stop.

She rushed around to the passenger side.

"Who are you?" he asked through the open window.

"A friend."

"I have precious few of those."

"Those people out there your friends?"

And she pointed forward.

He spotted two of the clowns and Monica heading for him, the clowns brandishing their weapons. "Hardly."

"Then let's leave."

He shifted into first and floored the accelerator. The car responded and shot forward. Monica and her acolytes stood their ground, aiming weapons. The woman inside with him extended her gun out the open window and fired twice. The bullets had the desired effect, as they all dove out of the way. He roared past them, navigated toward the correct exit runway, and sped up.

As promised, there was nothing in the way.

At the top he slowed and turned right, angling for an outer door.

He drew close, saw no ramp that led from the dock down to ground level, and decided to just go for it, increasing speed and vaulting off the platform, the tires slamming the pavement after a couple of meters' drop. The suspension held and they rocketed off between two of the long trailers. A gate loomed ahead, blocking the way. He hit it at a solid fifty kilometers an hour, blowing the plastic bar apart, and kept going out to the street that bordered the rear of the building.

"We need to be away from here," she said to him.

He agreed and kept driving.

"You realize that this car is not the most inconspicuous," he said.

"Maybe not. But it's all we have."

CASSIOPEIA SAT SILENT AS WESTLAKE MANEUVERED THE STAGE CAR across Stockholm. From everything she'd seen, Westlake had not participated in what had happened. Just the opposite, in fact, as he'd taken down a few of the clowns who'd definitely been shooting at him. The windshield before her bore the spiderwebs of those impacts. It also appeared that at least one of the clowns had fired directly at the king and queen. Hard to know who had been hit with all the smoke. The audience had seemed confused, unsure how the mayhem should be taken.

"You handled yourself like a pro in there," she said to him.

"Long ago, in my youth, I was part of the British Army Special Air Service. That training never leaves you."

Interesting. No one had mentioned that little tidbit.

"Who are you?" he asked.

"Cassiopeia Vitt. I'm here helping out Stephanie Nelle."

"Following me?"

"Something like that."

"I have to admit, on this occasion I am thankful. Maybe now they will believe me. I was tricked into being there. They told me they had Lysa and wanted to speak to me. They threatened her with harm if I did not cooperate. I was simply trying to get her back."

"They?"

"The Russians."

"I was told you denied any involvement with them."

"I have no involvement. But just like years ago, they simply will not leave me alone."

"It did not appear that you were being forced to do anything."

He turned a corner, downshifted, and gunned the Moskvitch's engine. "I assure you, I was pressured." He reached into his pocket and handed her a slip of paper. "That was delivered to my hotel room."

She read the one-line message.

"The use of *Tomte* proved they had Lysa. It's a nickname only the two of us know."

Which explained the bellman who'd ventured up to the Flag Suite. "What about the guy who bumped into you outside the arena?"

"He left an entrance pass and instructions where to go in my pocket. They went to a lot of trouble to get me there, so I went. Once there, Monica said they would harm Lysa if I did not cooperate."

"Monica?"

"Monica Butler-White. She is an SVR asset."

She was impressed. "You speak spy language fluently."

"Believe me, I learned all I want to know nine years ago. She was the one who framed me."

"Why would she do that?"

"To protect her real asset."

They kept going, the traffic light in both directions. A petrol station appeared ahead. Westlake eased the car into the lighted space, parking off to one side.

"Ms. Vitt," Westlake said, "I assure you, I am not a Russian spy. Never was. Never will be. But I can understand why Stephanie Nelle and the king think otherwise. The SVR made a point to implicate me so that whatever real assets they had in place would be protected. I was their diversion. Now they have dragged me back in." Westlake went quiet for a moment before saying, "You saw what I did back there. They were threatening the king and queen. I want to help. Truly, I do."

"Then you need to be honest."

More silence.

Finally, he nodded. "Okay. It is probably time for that."

She was skeptical. "I am told that you may not be the most truthful person in the world."

"Stephanie Nelle and the king are going to have to decide if they want my help or not. Clearly, the Russians want me in this."

Both good points.

Any decisions here were, as Cotton would say, way above her pay grade, so she found her phone and noticed a text from Stephanie that had arrived half an hour ago. She'd silenced the unit before entering the arena.

Russian involvement confirmed. Be careful.

She sent her own text to Stephanie.

Things happening. Westlake wants to talk. He has something to say.

The reply came fast.

Head for the palace.

CHAPTER 24

COTTON MADE IT BACK TO HIS HOTEL AND CHANGED CLOTHES, THEN stopped by Stephanie's room. She was on her way out, back to the palace to meet Cassiopeia and Westlake.

"Something is happening there," she told him. "I'll keep you posted. You do the same."

He left the hotel and found a cab that took him to the address for the lawyer Jakob Elmore. Stephanie had reported the deaths of the two Larses and requested that the Swedes handle it quickly and quietly. The body of an elderly man had already been found floating in the inlet. Unfortunately the partial license plate that he'd seen on the Volvo that tried to kill them had led to nothing. So he had no choice but to keep following the breadcrumbs, however meager they might be.

Stockholm had lapsed into a nighttime state, restless and brooding. Cars and cabs rumbled along, headlights sparkling on the wet pavement. He decided this time to stay back and bird-dog the site instead of rushing right in. He was hoping that whoever double-tapped the fake Lars assumed that the old man had died. What was the saying? *Dead men tell no tales.* True. So they would have no idea that any information had been passed on, which he intended to use to maximum advantage.

A cab deposited him about a quarter mile from the address, a nondescript office building on the city's west side. The streets here were twisty, dimly lit, and quiet, only an occasional car jolting past. He approached on foot with caution, staying out of sight. The building was single-story. A sign out front identified the occupants as ADVOKATS. Jakob Elmore one of the names listed. James Elmore in English. Some kind of office-sharing arrangement. Not uncommon. It had been a long time since he'd actually practiced law. Not since his short stint with navy JAG had he stood before a judge or jury. In the beginning Stephanie Nelle wanted her agents to possess advanced degrees in areas like law and accounting, but over time that preference had waned. He wondered about James Elmore. Was he another Russian asset?

Lights burned behind several of the windows. Three cars were parked out front. The time was approaching 9:00 P.M. Apparently people at this firm, like most, worked late.

He debated his next move.

Reveal himself? No way. That would take away his hard-won advantage. Better to focus on the *advokat* and see where he led. He had about fifteen hours left to make progress. He wondered what was happening with John Westlake that seemed, at least to Stephanie, promising. Hopefully that would prove more fruitful than the path he was now following. Stephanie was convinced Westlake had Russian SVR connections. Her instincts were usually spot on. So hopefully Cassiopeia had hit pay dirt.

He stood about two hundred yards from the building, concealed by the waning twilight of another long summer day. He decided, *What the hell*, to take a chance and hustled forward, rounding to the back side of the building looking for a rear entrance, which he found. More cars were parked in a paved lot that abutted the building. He looked around and saw no cameras. But that did not mean there were not some concealed. He approached the metal door and tried the latch.

Which opened.

Was that good or bad?

Who cared.

He turned the knob and entered the building.

He'd never practiced law in the civilian sector. But he'd visited many law offices. Most were warrens of spaces connected by corridors that led to conference rooms and the obligatory library. This one was no exception, everything brightly lit from recessed fluorescent fixtures, the décor minimally modern Swedish. He heard no voices, no tap-tap of a keyboard, no phones buzzing. Nothing.

Which raised alarms.

The first few offices he passed were empty. He came to an intersection and noticed that the door to one of the conference rooms hung open, lights burning inside.

He approached and peeked around the doorjamb.

Three bodies lay inside. Two men in leather chairs, bullet holes to their heads, the other, a woman, sprawled on the laminated hardwood flooring amid a pool of blood.

More loose ends?

He decided to complete his reconnoiter and checked out the remaining rooms, ending with a small reception area near the front door. He found James Elmore's office. Large and airy, the exterior walls glass, the space filled with a variety of plants and ferns. The furniture was Scandinavian modern, the desk a rectangular slab of oak with lots of drawers. He gave what was on the desk a quick once-over, then opened the drawers and found nothing substantive. He noticed the wall of fame. Every lawyer seemed to have one, himself once included. Two certificates were in black frames. One was from Trinity College. An Irish law degree. Another was from the Advokatsamfund. He was fluent in several languages, thanks to his eidetic memory, but Swedish was not on that list. Best guess? A license to practice law from the Swedish Bar Association. He noticed the dates. It seemed Elmore had been around awhile. Was one of the bodies in the conference room him? He looked around and found no photos on display. Okay. Time to report to Stephanie. He stepped from the office and turned left in the corridor, heading back toward the rear of the building.

"*Anhalt.*"

He jumped at the sound of the unexpected voice. He spun around to see an older man, standing, with both hands on a gun.

Aimed straight at him.

CHAPTER 25

Stephanie had reacted to the attack at the Moscow Circus, along with the scant information Cassiopeia had provided, by leaving her hotel and heading back to the royal palace. The king and queen were unharmed, as was their security detail. Good to hear. Reports indicated that all of the attackers escaped the building, two inside a bright-yellow stage car that drove off the premises. The press was clamoring for a statement, but the palace had maintained a silent approach.

For now.

"We have some screenshots from cameras in the arena," one of the palace security men said to her.

They were back inside the Council Chamber with the doors closed. The king was present, along with the prime minister. The time was approaching 10:00 p.m. The queen had been taken back to Drottningholm Palace. She'd been unnerved by the incident, and a doctor had been called. The king, on the other hand, was furious.

"Who are the attackers?" Wilhelm demanded to know.

"They were dressed as part of the circus troupe," the security man said. "Clowns. The organizers are at a loss to explain what happened. Five men and one woman. We are currently investigating and have the local police involved."

Stephanie approached the long table that stretched diagonally across the room and examined the photos taken from the many cameras. The images lay side by side, blowups of varying quality, blurred by both the enlargements and smoke. The clowns were clearly armed, each of them brandishing a weapon and aiming toward the audience. Another image showed a second woman not in costume taking down one of the clowns, then climbing into a yellow car. The face familiar. She was both pleased and concerned.

Cassiopeia had done her job.

"Madam Prime Minister," the king said, "I demand the Russian ambassador be called in and our official displeasure shown over this incident, along with protesting the kidnapping of my sister."

Stephanie felt for Simone de Ciutiis. She was in an impossible situation. The media would be pressing for answers, which was not unexpected considering the gravity of what had happened. An attempt on the king's life? Not something that occurred in Sweden. But they could not compound the situation by revealing the kidnapping, as that would entail exposing the deal Sweden had made with the Czechs, which could immediately evaporate. Surely one of the conditions of the whole thing had been total secrecy. The Czechs would not want it known that their NATO vote was for sale, and the Swedes would not want to admit that they'd paid the price.

"We cannot do that, Your Majesty. Moscow will simply deny any involvement, and the Czechs will withdraw from the arrangement. That not only complicates our NATO membership but could also place the princess in a difficult situation."

"Let the Russians deny all they please. They need to know we suspect them. And I frankly do not care what the Czechs think. Only Lysa matters."

De Ciutiis stared over at her with a look that said, *Please help*.

"We have to have more facts before either the Russians or the Czechs can be confronted," Stephanie said.

"What more do we need to know?"

"Quite a bit, actually. This whole thing is filled with questions. I have two operatives in the field, right now, trying to find answers."

"And what of *Sir* John Westlake?" the king said, bitterness in his voice. "He was there. In the arena. There's a photograph."

She found it. Grainy. But clear enough. "He is on the way here. Right now. Supposedly, he has something to tell us."

"Really?" the king said. "He was dressed in costume and working with them. Right there when they tried to kill me. Is it wise that he comes here?"

"That may not have been the case," Stephanie said. "I had an operative there too. She saw everything. We should wait and hear what she has to say."

"This entire situation is untenable," the king said, disgust in his voice. "They tried to kill me, Stephanie."

"We do not know that," she made clear. "To assassinate the reigning monarch of a neutral country? In such a public way? It makes no sense."

"The Russians killed Olof Palme," the king said. "That made no sense either, but we now know it for a fact. It is how we discovered Westlake was a spy in the first place."

"That was the old Soviet Union who did that, and it took decades for that information to come to the surface," she pointed out. "It also came from a defector trying to save his own hide, who died before we could learn more or verify much of anything. There is no way

Russia risks world retaliation for kidnapping your sister and killing you. Your Majesty, there is something about this that is not right."

And she meant every word.

She possessed over two decades of experience in the intelligence business, dealing with some of the most explosive and sensitive situations in the world. Along the way she'd acquired a skill set that allowed her, as Cotton would say, to sift through the crap to get to the grass beneath.

And there was a lot of crap here.

"I am out of patience," the king said. "Sweden is a gentle place that bothers no one. We simply want to be a part of NATO for our common defense. And why would we not? What harm could that be? My family is likewise harmless, all living exemplary lives. All except for a British commoner who has caused us nothing but trouble. I need something done. Now."

"Forgive me, Your Majesty," de Ciutiis said. "But this is a delicate international situation that—I am sorry for the bluntness—simply does not involve you. These are governmental decisions."

"This does not involve me? My sister is a prisoner, thanks to the government. Somebody just tried to kill me and my wife, thanks to the government."

"And we are dealing with all of that."

The door to the Council Chamber opened and Westlake entered the room followed by Cassiopeia. Stephanie noticed that Westlake had shed the costume he'd been wearing in the photographs, now dressed casually.

Stephanie faced the king. "Your Majesty, this is Cassiopeia Vitt. She was there, in the arena, and interrupted the attack on you."

"Then I owe you a debt of thanks." The king glared at Westlake. "What were you doing there?"

"I thought I was helping find Lysa."

"You told us, quite clearly I might add, that you had no way of doing that."

"I was wrong."

The king gave a dismissive hand. "You disgust me."

"You need to hear what he has to say," Cassiopeia said.

"Hear what?" the king asked.

"The truth, Wilhelm," Westlake said. "A painful, hurtful fact that it is time you know."

CHAPTER 26

COTTON REACTED TO THE HAMMER ON THE GUN BEING CLICKED BACK, unsure if this man had killed the other three or not. But the fear in the eyes seemed to signal that was not the case.

"Jakob Elmore?"

"Who are you?"

Asked in English. He decided to take a stab. "I'm not with the people that came here and killed those three in the conference room."

"That is not an answer."

"Cotton Malone. I'm here on behalf of the palace."

"You are American intelligence?"

He nodded. "We are trying to find Princess Lysa. Who are the dead people?"

"My former associates. I want asylum."

He'd guessed right. "You're SVR?"

He nodded. "I want asylum?"

"From who?"

"Moscow."

"You mind lowering the weapon."

He complied, returning the hammer to its closed position. Elmore was definitely scared. Unusual for an embedded field operative. By definition those people had cool nerves and sharp minds, as they literally made it up as they went. But he'd seen this look before, the one when someone realized they were expendable. By their own people.

"Two men came half an hour ago and killed my associates," Elmore said.

"SVR?"

The lawyer nodded.

"Why were they killed?"

"I do not know. I thought the men were here to participate in the operation. But they came in and opened fire. I managed to avoid them by making it to the safe room."

Now they were getting somewhere. "This is a Russian operations center?"

"It was. Thankfully they could not gain access to the safe room and it's bulletproof. They gave up and left."

"What's the operation?"

"To stop the Swedish deal with the Czechs."

"Do the Russians have the princess?"

"I will tell you all about that when you have me safely away from here and inside the American embassy."

"You know that's not how this works. I can't grant you asylum."

"But you know who can."

The request was one he'd heard before. But every intelligence service was cautious about walk-ins—those who just appeared and freely offered information, out of the blue. They were usually defectors or asylum seekers, not people who had been seriously recruited or sought after. The Soviets hated them, and were notorious for chasing them away. America? Land of opportunity? You go with it. Walk-ins were not summarily dismissed. Instead, they were handled in a slow and deliberate process, far away from the mainstream. Never were they taken to a place where they could discover the identity of any intelligence or counterintelligence personnel. Never were they privy to anything that might prove useful to the other side. First requirement of a walk-in? Show some evidence of access to or knowledge of valuable material. James Elmore had just tossed that bait out. And a bit too quickly for Cotton's liking. History noted, though, that some of the best intelligence had been learned from people who just walked in and offered it in return for freedom. So he was keeping an open mind. Particularly considering the time crunch and lack of information he presently possessed.

"I can take you to the right people," Cotton said. "But first you have to convince me that it will be worth my while."

"I will tell you nothing until I am safe."

Typical demand, so he shrugged. "Then I pass. And I wish you all the best in surviving through the night."

"You have no idea, do you?" he asked.

He was troubled by the tone. As if there was something he definitely should know. Part of a sales pitch? Trying to reel him in?

Maybe.

"There is much more going on here," Elmore said. "More than you could possibly be aware of."

"You need to explain—"

One of the windows facing the front of the building in the secretarial area shattered. Broken glass rained down. High-powered rounds whined through the opening and found the walls and furniture. Little noise was associated with the shots besides soft, repeated pops.

Cotton dove to the floor.

Elmore was not as quick.

His body was peppered with bullets that twisted him around in a herky-jerky dance. The gun fell from his grasp and he dropped to the floor. Cotton belly-crawled over to him. Blood poured from multiple wounds. No way the man was still alive. A cacophony of more indiscriminate rounds tore through the building's interior. The bursts began to come in single rounds as the ammunition diminished. He grabbed the gun from the floor and focused on the problem outside, belly-crawling toward another window that faced the front where he managed to gain a look.

A man and woman, both with automatic rifles, were changing clips.

Heading his way.

CHAPTER 27

JOHN PICKED ONCE MORE THROUGH THE LAST THREADS OF HIS RAPID thoughts. He'd been contemplating this moment for a long time. Ever since years ago when he was accused of being a foreign spy. He'd had no choice, considering what was at stake, which included his standing in the business community and his reputation both in England and abroad. Monica had been quite clear.

"You will accept the fact that you have been implicated and take whatever punishment King Wilhelm wishes to privately mete out. Just accept it and move on. The good thing is nothing will be public."

"And if I do not?"

"You will be killed, and your death, a suicide by the way, will serve as proof of your guilt. So we are clear, we prefer you alive."

"Good to know."

"In return, you will be allowed to expand your business into Russia after, of course, an appropriate period of official denials and objections. And what do you care? The king has never liked you. There is no real loss here. Now you have a reason to never go to Stockholm again."

True. So he'd accepted the blame. Lysa, of course, had no idea. As with most things in her life, she remained oblivious to reality. Wilhelm was satisfied. The Swedish government was satisfied. Even the woman now standing across from him, Stephanie Nelle, was satisfied.

Everybody. But him.

His satisfaction was about to come. But he told himself to keep the face of a chess master waiting coolly for his opponent's next move. Revealing nothing until it was too late for the other side to respond.

"We are waiting," the king said. "For this so-called truth I need to hear."

"And you will continue to wait until I am ready to tell you," he made clear in a defiant tone, which felt great.

"You will not speak to me like that."

"I will speak to you however I see fit. I am not a Swedish citizen. And as you remind me every chance you get, I am not a royal either. I owe you nothing. You are a pompous, self-righteous fool. You have your crown simply because you were fortunate enough to be the firstborn in your family. You have done nothing to earn it."

"It is obvious you despise me. Is that why you were there at the circus, to kill me?"

"You cannot be that ignorant. Do you honestly think that the case? That I would shoot you? I am a billionaire twice over. If I wanted you dead, I could hire a professional to do it. I was there to find my wife. Unlike you, who wallows here in the luxury of a pampered life where everyone jumps at your command, I was actually doing something. The same woman from nine years ago, an SVR asset who calls herself Monica Butler-White, is here in Sweden. She's the one who led the assault on you, though I suspect it was not about a killing. More a message being sent."

"That says what?" Stephanie Nelle asked.

He'd been waiting for her to enter the conversation. She'd been carefully listening, gauging him, surely waiting for an inconsistency, anything she could use to trip him up. But he'd given this conversation a lot of thought. So he said, "Do. Not. Trifle. With. Us."

He fished from his pocket the two pieces of paper with the handwritten messages and handed them to Stephanie Nelle, along with the circus entrance pass and ticket. "One was delivered to my hotel room. The others were slipped into my pocket outside the arena."

Stephanie read them both, then glanced over at Cassiopeia Vitt.

"A bellboy took a message upstairs to his room," Vitt said. "And another man did bump into Westlake outside the building. I saw his hand go into a coat pocket. Which all seemed to be unexpected on Westlake's part."

"It was," he added. "I was being led. Once again. Only this time we have a witness to what actually happened." He glared at the king. "It is not just my word any longer."

"I am still waiting for that truth, *Sir* John."

"Nine years ago there was, indeed, a spy among the Swedish royal family. That spy is still here to this day. The SVR is quite good at manipulation. They find a weakness and exploit it. The asset they recruited was perfect, providing Moscow with a wealth of information while never suspecting they were doing so. Bits and pieces that, by themselves, meant little. But placed into context with other acquired intelligence? The information could be quite valuable."

"So you were not that asset?" the prime minister asked.

He shook his head. "I was not."

"Then how could you possibly know all that you are saying?" the king asked.

"Because I am married to that asset."

Stephanie caught the implications of the accusation and reminded herself that John Westlake was an accomplished liar. But the intelligence officer in her reminded her to keep an open mind. Listen. Evaluate. Then make judgments.

"I have known Princess Lysa for a long time," she said. "I've never seen or heard anything that would indicate she's been radicalized in any way. She is a lovely woman who never has a bad word to say about anyone or anything."

"Which makes her perfect," Westlake said. "Her naïveté was easy to manipulate. And why would there be signs? She has no idea she is being used."

She knew the game. Intelligence assets came in four distinct forms. Those who willingly elected to associate with a foreign power and betray their country. Those who worked for pure monetary gain, selling their secrets. Those who'd been blackmailed and forced into their role. And those who did not even know they were in the game.

The so-called useful idiots.

They represented the vast majority of assets. The best of the best of those were people well connected in their community. Above reproach. Never to be suspected. Like a member of the royal family who liked to talk.

"Lysa has no idea she is an asset," Westlake said again.

"How is that possible?" the king asked.

"It's actually quite easy," Stephanie said. "Most are unwitting. The trick? Finding the right handler to innocently manipulate them."

"And my wife has one," Westlake said. "Her closest friend in the world. A society woman who runs in some fairly high circles. She is an SVR sleeper in England. Lysa comes into contact with a wide assortment of politicians, royalty, and businesspeople. She hears a lot and, God love her, my wife loves to gossip. *Spilling the tea,* she calls it. It is a fault her handler has expertly exploited for a long time."

"And you allowed that?"

"I had no choice. Once all of you decided I was the spy and should be banished, I was told by the SVR to accept it or be killed. Even worse, they threatened Lysa's life too. So I accepted my fate and moved on. And frankly, every one of you deserved that outcome, considering how quick you were to blame me."

"I need a name for that handler," Stephanie said.

"And I will provide that. It is time all this ends."

"This is preposterous," the king said. "You are merely trying to divert attention away from yourself. You were the one in that arena tonight, not my sister, who is being held who knows where."

"And there it is," Westlake said. "That famous Bernadotte stupidity and arrogance. For once, you need to shut your mouth and listen."

Stephanie knew that Wilhelm was not without his faults. He was known to be sometimes misinformed, quick-tempered, and a bit too free with his comments. Through the years there'd been some serious PR missteps. He once critiqued the prime minister of Norway on her conservation policy, questioning how someone who could not take care of the seals could take care of Norway. Needless to say that comment had not been well received. After a state visit to Brunei a few years ago, he went out of his way to praise the sultan, despite Brunei's controversial human rights history. A similar incident happened during a visit to Saudi Arabia. Each gaffe hurt the king's popularity. But he'd always rebounded.

"Here is the reality," Westlake said. "Manipulate your subject enough and control becomes easy. Say the right words, paint the right picture, and the response is guaranteed. Lysa's handler is good at what she does. But Lysa makes it easy with her almost childlike naïveté. She's a good, decent person who just cannot keep her mouth shut."

"What are you saying is happening here?" Cassiopeia asked.

"The situation is more dire than you think. Lysa was not kidnapped. Far from it, in fact. She is a passive participant in what is happening. And she may be in real danger."

CHAPTER 28

COTTON WANTED AT LEAST ONE OF THE TWO WITH AUTOMATIC RIFLES alive. Didn't matter which one. And if they came bleeding with a bullet hole or two, he could also make that work. They were advancing inside. To make sure that James Elmore was dead? Maybe. Did they know he was here?

Of course they did.

A second chance to take him down?

He heard the back door open.

Too many lights were on. He started flicking switches, moving through the secretarial area, down the hall, to the conference room. Darkness dissolved the few bits of light that remained, offering him cover. A man appeared to his left where the corridor right-angled. He kept the gun he'd retrieved hidden and slipped into James Elmore's office. A rapid fire of soft pops signaled incoming rounds that obliterated the doorjamb.

He'd been seen.

The shots were all sound-suppressed. Nothing to draw outside attention. These people came prepared and were coming fast. He hustled to the desk and took cover behind it. When he was in the office a few minutes ago, he'd noticed that the desk was U-shaped, open in the center with drawers on either side.

He crouched down before one set of the drawers.

"I'm unarmed," he called out in English. "Please don't kill me."

Why not? Take a chance. See what happened. Would the guy think he had the advantage and keep advancing? Most would not. But these folks had taken aim from the outside, through a window, to get Elmore. Nothing subtle about them at all.

Here he was again. In the line of fire.

What was the saying? *Death is the number one killer in the world.* Damn right.

And so true. Why was he here? Easy. Because Stephanie had asked for his help. He would do anything for her. And he'd seen the concern in her eyes back in Italy when she'd asked him to come. A bit unusual. Emotion was something she stayed away from. At least with her subordinates. Still, he considered himself more than a former employee. They'd really bonded when she appeared in Copenhagen a few years ago. A tough time for them both. But they'd not only discovered the truth about her dead husband, they'd also found her lost son. And here he was again. Caught in the cross fire.

Helping Stephanie.

He heard movement, then he caught sight of the man with the rifle, peeking around the doorjamb.

"Stand up," the man ordered. "I need to see your hands."

"Okay. I'm here. My hands are up."

He stood and raised his arms, the right hand with the gun shielded by his head in the semi-darkness. The man snuck another peek and saw what he wanted to see. In the two seconds it took for the guy to swing around into the doorway, rifle cradled, finger on the trigger,

Cotton shot him in the upper chest. The round thudded into flesh and the body fell backward into the hall, not moving. Cotton wasted no time and headed for it, retrieving the automatic rifle to ready himself for the second attacker. The woman. He hoped someone heard the shot and called the police. His gun was not sound-suppressed.

The back door opened, then closed.

Careful. That could be a trap too.

He dropped low to the ground and worked his way down the partially lit corridor. All quiet. He kept going, passing the other offices, then the conference room, and finally the last turn toward the rear door.

No one in sight.

But if the woman was anywhere, she was around that corner.

He made his way to the edge and pushed the short barrel of the rifle past in the hope of enticing a response. Nothing happened. Okay. No choice. He snuck a quick peek. The corridor was empty. He rushed to the rear exit and slowly opened the door.

An engine roared to life.

On the other side of the building.

He turned and hustled back toward the front of the building. Outside he spotted the lights on a pale-colored Volvo speeding away. Was it the same one that had tried to kill him and Stephanie? He could not allow that car to flee. Something he recalled seeing earlier sprang to life inside his brain. He darted toward the conference room, grabbed a set of car keys off the table, and returned to the front door. Outside he hit the remote's lock button.

Lights flashed on a dark BMW.

He climbed inside and laid the rifle on the passenger seat. Elmore's pistol was tucked inside his belt in front.

He fired up the engine.

And raced off.

CHAPTER 29

CASSIOPEIA WAS WRESTLING OVER WHETHER TO BELIEVE WESTLAKE. The assertion that his wife was somehow complicit, however passively, in her own kidnapping bordered on the absurd. But why would the man toss out such an allegation to the prime minister and king of Sweden unless he could back it up? So she asked, "Why did you not mention this before now?"

"No one was ready to listen."

"You're saying you took the blame for her?" Stephanie asked.

"Not willingly. The SVR came to me, through Monica Butler-White. She told me that I had a choice. Go along and say nothing or be killed, and probably Lysa killed too."

Cassiopeia was curious. "The princess is totally unaware of what happened to you? How can that be?"

"She knows nothing. I was just always busy when she wanted to return here. On those occasions when I had no choice but to come, the Swedish government made sure I was carefully watched. And His Majesty here kept me at arm's length. Which was not all that unusual for us. Sure, Lysa knows there is tension, but she thinks that is related to me being a commoner."

"So the SVR has continued to use the princess?" Stephanie asked.

"To my knowledge they have, but I am not in any sort of information loop. Today was the first time Monica Butler-White has contacted me in a long time."

"And you were okay with your wife being used?" Stephanie asked.

"It mattered not to me. I just wanted her safe. Myself safe. And quite frankly, the way I was treated by all of you, I did not really care about the ramifications. I simply did as the SVR demanded."

"Why were you at the circus?" the king asked Westlake.

"I have explained that."

"Do it again."

"I was sent a note, which used a term of endearment that is only known to Lysa and myself. That was surely for authenticity. So I went. Once I saw that Monica was there, I had no choice but to participate in whatever she was doing. I learned a long time ago that arguing with her is useless. Once I realized what was happening, I did what I could to disrupt things. Ms. Vitt here witnessed that. Monica obviously wanted to implicate me once again, just like she did years ago, drawing me ever deeper."

"I saw her remove his mask," Vitt said. "She made a point to do it. It was like she wanted him seen."

"You could have come to the government," the prime minister said. "Told us the truth."

"Nobody would have believed me, and Monica would have put a bullet in my head to make sure their secret stayed safe."

"You were exposed by an active Russian operative," Stephanie said. "I was there when he was interrogated. He named you specifically as an SVR asset. You're saying that was planted?"

Westlake nodded. "Of course it was, all designed to protect Lysa. I was told that they used that defector to pass that information along."

Stephanie shook her head. "Then killed him?"

"Precisely. They pointed everyone at me, then silenced the source and left me to hang. Of course, I am sure that traitor thought he was doing what they wanted and would not be harmed."

The king's eyebrows bristled into lines of doubt. "My sister is not a Russian spy."

"Not knowingly. But a spy nonetheless. And let us be clear. All of you needed someone to blame. The Russians gave you that person. I was an easy choice since, *Your Majesty*, you despised me anyway. The SVR played to your fears. They tossed out the bait and all of you bit on the hook."

The room went silent with a long, uncomfortable pause.

Cassiopeia nearly smiled at the decisive manner in which Westlake had turned the tables.

This guy was good.

But there was one point he'd not explained.

STEPHANIE WAS TRYING HARD TO KEEP AN OPEN MIND ABOUT THE situation. Was it crazy? Maybe not. Princess Lysa had a flawless reputation. She'd raised millions for charity. There was even a yearly scientific research prize that bore her name. Her popularity with the Swedish people was unparalleled. Not a bad word was ever said about her. She ranked as a "must guest" for any social occasion. Her presence at the Nobel Prize festivities was never in doubt, an invitation to sit at her table the most coveted after the king and queen. On the one hand, she would be the last person anyone would suspect as a foreign asset. But on the other, that made her perfect for the job. Her access to people and information would be endless. And no one would suspect her. Sweden stayed on everyone's radar. Technically neutral territory, but both Russia and the United States maintained a constant presence. Having Russian eyes and ears so close to the royal family, the government, and society would be like intelligence gold.

Still.

"Is Lysa in danger?" she asked Westlake.

"She could be."

That grabbed the king's attention. "Could be?"

"I worry that she is becoming expendable. The Russians want results. When noon comes tomorrow, whether the Devil's Bible is turned over or not, it will be easy to put a bullet in her head just to prove the point."

"You think this Monica woman would do that?" Cassiopeia asked.

"I assure you, she is most capable. One thing I have learned is that Russians are dangerous and unpredictable when cornered. They do not want Sweden in NATO and, from my experience, they will do whatever it takes to achieve a result. Lysa has no idea as to why she is actually there."

"How did she get there?" the king asked.

"Yes," Cassiopeia added. "You have not explained that point."

"I have no idea. Which was another reason I went to the circus. I had hoped Monica would take me to Lysa. Hold me captive too. That did not happen. I fear my wife desperately needs our help."

"On that we agree," the king said. "We have to find her. She is my only sibling and I will not allow her to be sacrificed."

"Can you contact Monica Butler-White?" Stephanie asked.

Westlake shook his head. "I cannot. But she can find me."

"Are you sure about that?" Cassiopeia said.

"She will not be happy with what happened at the circus. She will find me."

"What do we do in the meantime?" the king asked.

"We wait," Westlake said.

And Stephanie was grateful for the time. Cotton had told her precisely what the old man said about the moment Princess Lysa was "taken." It all seemed far too cordial. But was that information correct? Or planted for Cotton's benefit? A way to spur him along? Get him underground in that cistern. Regardless, a point was still nagging at her. If Lysa was an unwitting ally, how had the Russians managed to get her to cooperate?

Stephanie glanced across the room at Cassiopeia.

Who seemed to be considering the same question.

She slowly shook her head, signaling that the issue should not be further explored.

Instead they would wait.

CHAPTER 30

COTTON GAINED ON THE VOLVO BUT INTENTIONALLY STAYED BACK SO AS not to arouse suspicion. The boulevard before him was busy with traffic, typical for a city that accommodated nearly two million people. The road cut a swath north to south through the city among a steady parade of trees and buildings. The rain had finally subsided, but the pavement remained soaked. He assumed the driver was the woman from the attack. He had to stay with her, as it was the only lead left. Somebody was systematically eliminating anything and everyone. That had to be intentional. What else could it be? This whole thing had turned chaotic.

A lot like his own life at the moment.

Not all that long ago he'd watched as Suzy Baldwin died in his arms. A woman from his past who reappeared in Switzerland with quite a revelation. A daughter had been born as a result of an affair they'd had twenty years ago, at a time when Cotton was married and a much different person. A young, brash JAG lawyer who cheated on his wife. Even after all the ensuing years, just to think about that awful reality hurt. Seeing Suzy had brought it back home.

Then she died.

Horribly.

But a secret from her past survived. A file that Suzy's employer had accumulated for whatever reason. Mainly field reports from an investigative agency that apparently had located a young woman. Three color images showed a lean figure in a simple red dress, her face sharp-featured and attractive. There had also been an order of adoption, issued by a Texas court. The petitioner, Susan Baldwin, noted as the natural mother. The adoptive parents' names had also been there, Evan Acree Wells and Kristie Restco Wells, with the court extinguishing all Suzy's parental rights in their favor. He knew what that meant. Even the birth certificate was changed so that Suzy's name disappeared. The child's new name? Jacqueline Suzanne Wells. The order also provided that the petitioner had sworn, under oath, that she had no idea as to the identity of the natural father.

He'd also seen a copy of the new birth certificate showing the adoptive parents now as mother and father, vested with all the rights as if they'd produced the child themselves. But it had been one other sheet that had grabbed his undivided attention. The original Texas birth certificate that noted the date of birth. Seven months after Suzy and he parted ways.

Did he have a daughter? Hard to say.

The jury was still out on that one.

Was there a twenty-year-old young woman out there who was biologically half his? Did she know she was adopted? That was a tough secret to keep. Had she wondered about her biological parents? But maybe she had no desire to know from where she'd come. Him finding her might not be welcomed. So many questions. So many doubts. He needed to make a decision on what to do, one way or the other, then stick to it.

But that was something for later.

His phone buzzed.

He answered the call, switching to speaker and laying the unit on the passenger seat.

"Tell me what's happening," Stephanie said.

"There are a bunch of dead bodies at that law office," he told her. "Somebody is cleaning house. And they wanted me on that list too."

"An attempt was made on the king's life tonight," she said. "It failed, and get this, Westlake now says Princess Lysa is a tacit Russian asset."

"Didn't see that wrinkle coming."

"Neither did we. The king is livid. But for some odd reason, I believe Westlake. To a point."

He listened as Stephanie explained the entire situation. Then he said, "So this whole thing could be a dog-and-pony show?"

"I'm not sure. This is not going to be as easy to reveal as it was for your Mr. Solomon."

He knew what she meant. A story he'd told her a long time ago. Of a local lawyer from Vidalia, where he grew up in Georgia, highly capable, with a quick wit, and a storied biblical name. Noah Solomon. Once Solomon had cross-examined a young man claiming damages for an arm injury caused by the negligence of a school bus driver. *Will you please show us how high you can lift your arm now?* Solomon asked. The young man raised his arm to shoulder level, his face agonized with pain. *Thank you*, Solomon said. *And now, could you show us how high you could lift it before the accident?* The young man eagerly shot his arm up above his head. The plaintiff, of course, lost the case.

"Nothing is ever that easy," he said to her.

"We have a serious mess here," Stephanie said, exasperation

in her voice. "It's possible the woman you're following is Monica Butler-White. We need her. Alive. It's the only way we're going to get to the truth here."

"I'll get back to you when I have something," he told her.

The Volvo shot forward and passed a car ahead.

Crap. "Gotta go."

He ended the call.

Another car coming in the opposite lane screeched its brakes and blared a horn as it scraped the Volvo's side. The Volvo came back into the right lane and accelerated.

Had he been made?

His gaze swept the road and he took his chances. Tires shrieked and burned off some smoke as he sped ahead, passing a couple of cars. Another car coming toward him swerved but still grazed him, causing a little fishtailing that he wrestled back under control. He kept the accelerator down, found traction, and kept going. The Volvo came to an intersection, slowed, then sped through as the traffic signal changed from red to green. He maneuvered around a car stopped in front of him into the opposite lane, then came back into his own lane and approached the intersection, intending to cross.

Headlights glared from his right.

Bright. Coming fast. Out of nowhere.

He tried to speed out of the way but the other car slammed hard into his rear passenger side, metal crunching metal, glass shattering, spinning the BMW around like a teacup at Disneyworld. The momentum sent him across the wet asphalt in a dizzying arc, but all movement stopped when the car slammed into something solid.

A harsh rattling breath hissed through his teeth.

Vertigo overcame him.

And the world went black.

CHAPTER 31

9:35 P.M.

STEPHANIE ENTERED THE KUNGLIGA BIBLIOTEKET, THE SWEDISH Royal Library, an impressive collection of eighteen million objects. As with the Library of Congress back home, Swedish law required that publishers of printed material send one copy of every book to the national library. Creators of music, film, radio, and TV were similarly required. The collections dated back to the mid–seventeenth century and the days of King Gustav, who acquired a multitude of books on a variety of subjects. Eventually they were expanded through seized war booty. Those treasures included the episcopal library of Würzburg, the University of Olomouc library, and the royal library of Prague, where the Codex Gigas, the Devil's Bible, was acquired.

In the beginning the royal book collections were kept in the old Tre Kronor palace. But after it burned to the ground in the late seventeenth century, changes were made. The current building, a masterpiece of stone and iron, was built in the nineteenth century, later remodeled and expanded. Two large underground stacks, built into the bedrock below the building, now contained the bulk of the collection, while library patrons, visitors, the main collection, and employees shared the space in the upper main building.

She'd come straight from the palace. The king and prime minister were still not convinced on the allegations made against Princess Lysa. *Outrageous*, was how the king kept describing everything. It was a hard pill to swallow, but she'd assured him that they would conduct a detailed investigation and find the truth.

But how?

She had a few ideas on that one. All of them made more complicated by the fact that Westlake was either lying, at least on parts of the story, or not telling them everything.

Tops on the list?

If Princess Lysa was a tacit accomplice, ignorant of the fact that she was being manipulated, how had they managed to get her to cooperate? The lack of an answer there advised caution when dealing with Westlake. She'd charged Cassiopeia with trying to find an answer, which would go a long way toward determining whether Westlake was worthy of belief.

Stephanie's task? Deal with the Devil's Bible.

She'd read the book Koger had supplied and learned quite a bit. There were 320 folios. More than a hundred lines of text on each page, each composed in a tight small script with colorful additions. All on vellum, which would have taken about 150 animal hides to create. That meant there'd been money behind its origins. Somebody had to pay for all that. In thirteenth-century Bohemia, that kind of wealth would have come from only two sources.

Royalty or the Church.

The story behind its creation was more legend than fact, most of it fashioned once the codex made its way to Sweden. Supposedly a monk, sometimes named Herman the Recluse, was sentenced to death by being walled up alive for breaking his monastic vows. As a last gasp for survival, he made a deal with his captors that he would create a single book filled with the world's knowledge in return for his life. The proposal was accepted, but his pardon from death would only be granted if the monk managed to complete the task in one night. The only way the monk could see himself completing that insurmountable endeavor was with the help of the devil. So he sold his soul, wrote the book in one night, and gained his freedom.

The reality of the Codex Gigas was far less intriguing.

It would have taken a single person, working continuously, maybe three decades to produce the wording and illustrations. That there was only one scribe seemed evident, as there was an amazing uniformity in the script from start to finish. It was known that the completed manuscript was pawned by the monks of Podlazice Monastery in 1295 in an effort to raise money. They'd wanted to repay the loan and obtain the book back but never did, and it eventually made its way to Břevnov, near Prague. The next mention of the codex was when the Bohemian Emperor Rudolf II acquired it in 1594. In 1697 a fire broke out at the Tre Kronor that devoured seventeen thousand books and more than one thousand manuscripts. The codex was saved when it was thrown out a window, but its binding was destroyed. It wasn't until the nineteenth century that it was rebound, becoming a central part of the Swedish Royal Library.

Where it had remained.

Until tomorrow.

She was led to an elevator and descended to the subterranean levels. Two weeks ago the codex had been brought down from its main-floor display case. It had long been kept inside a sealed glass container filled with nitrogen. No need to display the individual pages as every one of them had been photographed in high resolution, available on the library's website for public inspection. The staff here was aware that the book would be leaving, but was unaware the move would be permanent. There were almost certainly SVR eyes and ears everywhere, so she'd decided to use that potential liability to their advantage.

The library was closed for the night, only the few staffers readying the codex for transport were there. It lay atop a stainless-steel table, exposed to the air, waiting to be packaged in a nearby wooden crate. Its outer binding was made of wooden boards covered in leather, decorated with ornate metal guards and fittings. She wondered about its practical usage. Why create such an unwieldly tome? For anyone to even be able to peruse the folios, the codex would have had to be placed atop a reinforced reading desk. That effort alone would take several strong men to accomplish. So what was the purpose of a book, whose content was obviously intended for reading, that was physically impossible to read under normal circumstances? Hard to say. But perhaps its size was its main appeal. She imagined the effort it had taken to transport it the seven hundred miles from Prague to Stockholm in the seventeenth century.

No easy feat.

She introduced herself to the curator and asked where they stood relative to shipment. The prime minister had called ahead and told everyone to cooperate with her in every way.

"The plan is to crate the codex over the next few hours and transport it tomorrow morning."

The question remained, though, whether it would be headed to the airport for a flight south to the Czech Republic or be handed over to the kidnappers. Prime Minister de Ciutiis had made it clear that the government would like to move forward on the deal with the

Czechs. First and foremost because they did not cave to criminals. Even more important, if Westlake was telling the truth and Princess Lysa was in the slightest way complicit in her disappearance, whether consciously or not, all the more reason to proceed forward.

But the question remained. Was she?

"How will it be moved?" she asked.

"By van. With no escort. We do not want to draw attention. It's about a half-hour drive to the airport north of Stockholm. A private plane will then fly it to Prague."

She understood the need for discretion. Neither government wanted the scent of a quid pro quo to emerge in the press. The whole idea was to make the exchange seamlessly. The official story? Another loan of the book to the Czechs. It just would never return. Then a few months down the road Sweden would reapply for NATO membership and the Czech Republic would vote in favor.

All nice and easy.

Wrapped in a pretty bow.

Or was it?

CHAPTER 32

John had returned to the Grand Hôtel, along with his minder, whom he now knew as Cassiopeia Vitt. Stephanie Nelle had been emphatic. Vitt would stay with him 24/7. No big surprise there. Nelle had surely noticed the hole in his story. He'd be really disappointed if she had not. No one had pressed him at the palace for answers. Again, no real surprise. They were giving him a long leash. Plenty of rope with which to hang himself. But he at least knew that. They surely realized that he was the best conduit they had to the Russians, and Stephanie Nelle seemed intent on maximizing that fact.

But not without some safeguards.

Hence why he now had Vitt in tow.

"Was your father Arturo Vitt?" he asked her.

She nodded, and he connected the dots. A billionaire. Founder of Terra, one of the world's largest and most impressive conglomerates. Dead for a while. Which meant his daughter now owned it all.

"How does a woman of your means become entangled with Stephanie Nelle?"

They sat in one of the ground-floor lounges, filled with a late-night crowd, and he was enjoying a splash of twenty-three-year-old Pappy Van Winkle bourbon. A favorite. Always calming. Vitt nursed a soft drink.

"Call it a hobby?"

He smiled. "Really? There are other pursuits far less demanding."

She shrugged. "I like a challenge."

He sipped more of the dark liquid, which burned his throat in a familiar soothing way, and decided to get to the point. "Why is it so hard to believe that Lysa could be a foreign asset?"

"Perhaps because the allegation came out of nowhere, from someone with a clear motive to lie."

He shrugged. "It is not like I could have come forward with it any earlier. No one would have believed a thing I said."

"And British intelligence? You could not have told them?"

"The same problem existed, and I was told by Monica, in no uncertain terms, to keep quiet. So I chose to leave it alone, convincing myself that it was not my problem. Which it was not, by the way. It was only after I arrived at the palace today and learned of Lysa's disappearance that it all became relevant again."

"You sure about that?"

"What does that mean?"

"Are you not the least bit curious as to how your wife was taken? How she was convinced to participate in the charade? You had nothing to do with that?"

He decided to allow that question to linger. No need to answer immediately. After all, this was a game. So play it.

"I also still do not understand why Monica Butler-White decided to lure you to the circus," Vitt said.

"I suspect it was a way to trap me within her web once again. She is a devious person. If it matters at all, I do not think that she intended to harm the king."

"She went to a lot of trouble *not* to harm someone."

"Monica is a complex person. But she is excellent at what she does." He sipped more of the bourbon. "Ten years ago I was working hard to expand my business inside Russia. The politics then were much different from now. Russia was far more benign, even friendly to foreign investment. Franko had not, as yet, taken power. The SVR used my capitalistic desires to draw me in deeper with whatever they were doing with Lysa. Then they set me up to take the fall. It happened so fast, I had no idea how to fight back. Monica made it clear they could just kill me, then implicate me as a spy after I was dead. That particular alternative was not overly appealing."

"You never answered my question about your wife's cooperation."

"I have no idea how to answer that. I am at a loss. Just like you."

"How much money have you made from your Russian stores?"

He resented the question, but noted that she'd been following his words with varying expressions of interest. Which was good. She was listening.

So he decided to be honest.

"More than enough to soothe my battered ego."

CASSIOPEIA REALIZED THAT THE MAN SITTING ACROSS FROM HER was not to be trusted. Not now. Not ever. Stephanie had told her to stay close and try to find out more. Maybe Westlake would slip and reveal something. They desperately needed facts. Operating in the dark came with an assortment of obvious risks, the worst of which was that the other side could always stay a few steps ahead. Something told her that this man was miles past them.

"So you have lived for the past nine years on the promise that nothing about you or your wife would ever be revealed," she said. "Seems like the perfect situation for extortion." She was fishing, tossing out bait. Doing her job. "But instead you have greatly profited from your silence."

Westlake chuckled. "I assure you, no one has tried to extort me. Sure, I have paid the required bribes to many a Russian official. That is simply the cost of doing business there. But British intelligence is aware of all that. I file a regular report, with a detailed accounting, as required by English law."

"And your wife? Should you not have told her that she was being used?"

"I actually tried that once. She would not even entertain the possibility that her close friend was not her friend. So I let it go."

"And allowed her to keep providing information to the Russians?"

He shrugged. "None of that mattered to me."

"But, as you mentioned at the palace, your wife may now be in danger."

"Monica is hard to predict. She is impetuous and could use this opportunity to rid the SVR of a loose end."

"She gave you no indication when you were with her as to what was happening?"

He shook his head. "Not a word. I simply did what she said, hoping it might lead me to Lysa. But when all the shooting started, I decided to act."

"You still love your wife?"

He considered the inquiry for a few moments before saying, "I would not want to see her harmed."

Not an answer. But she'd not expected one.

"It is important that we find your wife," she made clear. "Alive. If she is a spy, she will be dealt with. No reason exists for you to accept the blame for her any longer."

"*It is a divine kind of madness, lovingly not to be able to see the evil which lies just in front of one.*"

"Your words of wisdom?"

"From a Danish playwright. I always thought them most applicable to my darling Lysa."

He emptied the tumbler in a final swallow of bourbon, then tabled the glass. A waiter hustled over to see if he wanted more.

Westlake waved him off.

His phone hummed and he checked the display. "A text. From Monica."

He displayed the message.

Call me. Now.

"I await your orders," he said to her.

"Do it."

"Let us walk outside."

CHAPTER 33

GENERAL HANS CHRISTOFF VON KÖNIGSMARCK DISMOUNTED FROM his horse and admired the exterior of Prague Castle. Impressive. One of a kind. Definitely fit for an emperor. He was the supreme commander of Sweden's famed flying column. A small, independent military unit blessed with rapid mobility, capable of striking fast with deadly firepower. He had led a successful attack on Prague, settling his men on the east bank of the Vltava River. That great meandering waterway divided Old Town, New Town, and the Jewish Quarter from the lesser town and castle, which stood here, atop a steep hill. Yesterday, July 16, 1648, one hundred of his soldiers successfully scaled the castle walls. They then managed to take the guards by surprise and were soon joined by three thousand more men. He wanted to take the entire town but had to settle for half, looting Prague Castle and the surrounding palaces and monasteries.

He was here on order of his queen, Christina, the sovereign ruler of Sweden. His mission? Find and obtain the great private collections of Rudolf II, once Holy Roman Emperor, king of Hungary, Croatia, and Bohemia, archduke of Austria, a member of the House of Hapsburg, dead now for thirty-six years. Rudolf may have been the greatest collector of his time. He also transformed a drafty, drab castle into a grand Renaissance residence.

Which von Königsmarck now controlled.

He was weary of fighting. The Thirty Years' War had raged across Europe, claiming countless lives, including Christina's father, King Gustav Adolph. Bohemia, the Palatinate, Savoy, Transylvania, Denmark, Norway, Prussia, Saxony, and the Heilbronn League fought for the Protestants. The Hapsburgs, Spain, Bavaria, and the Catholic League on the pope's side. About eight million people had died from battle, famine, and disease. Bohemia lost a third of its population. Germany half. Until 1635 the conflict was primarily a civil war within the Holy Roman Empire. But after 1635, when Denmark and Norway switched sides, the struggle became France and Sweden against the Emperor Ferdinand III and Spain. Both sides were depleted and exhausted. Everything had come to a climax here. Fitting that the war had started in Prague and should likewise end here. Negotiations were proceeding along in Westphalia, and the delegates were close to a peace. But Queen Christina had ordered one last campaign into Bohemia to loot the remaining collections of Rudolf II.

And he understood why.

To maintain Sweden's national prestige, a certain level of culture was required. But Sweden's treasures did not compare to those of any of its neighbors, let alone the rich lands of Spain and France. Plundering was a quick way to bolster the situation, though armies were expensive and a military victory was not always assured.

But here, in Prague, victory had come.

Rudolf had been, by all accounts, an enlightened man. Always reserved, secretive, and largely a recluse who did not like to travel or participate in the daily affairs of the state. He was fascinated by the occult, astrology, and alchemy. He methodically acquired paintings, sculptures, and objets d'art, both the sublime and the ridiculous, along with the inanimate and the living. All held in the famed Kunstkammer.

His chamber of art.

Von Königsmarck had already been told about some of what the chamber contained, especially the Caravaggio canvases and Dürer woodcuts. Drawings, prints, busts, statuettes, bowls, cameos, weapons, coins, precious stones, crystals, and assorted gems filled the rooms. More paintings lay in piles, one atop the other, hundreds of them. Musical, astronomical, and scientific instruments, along with clocks, were there mixed with a wide variety of the ethnographical, zoological, and botanical objects, all reflecting Rudolf's fascination with nature.

Now it all belonged to Christina.

Time for him to see it for himself.

"They are waiting," his aide said.

"Lead the way." He set out through the towering archway, entering the castle's main courtyard. The twin spires of St. Vitus Cathedral rose before him past the courtyard's southern side. Prague was a great, splendid, populous city. The capital of Bohemia. A wondrous place of countless spires and underground dungeons, of basilisks, rams, skeletons, stars, and other esoteric symbols, that reached its zenith with Rudolf II.

War had definitely ravaged its beauty, but not its charm.

He kept walking, entering the castle through a side portal and climbing one flight of stairs to the first floor. A long corridor stretched before him, one he knew connected Rudolf's private apartment to the south wing of the Spanish Hall. They approached a closed door with a Renaissance brass knocker. When its two sides were brought close, the stylized figures of a naked man and woman came together in an act of fellatio. Disgusting. It offended every bit of his Protestant sensibility. If he'd planned to stay in the city any longer, he would order the obscenity removed. But he, and his army, would soon be gone.

He approached the door, which was opened by his aide to allow him to enter an antechamber decorated with images of the four elements and a microcosm of the universe presided over by Jupiter. An open doorway led to where four long rooms spilled into one another in succession, a decorated vaulted ceiling overhead. Countless objects were everywhere, filling shelves, cabinets, and tables.

"It is overwhelming," he said to his officers.

"We were amazed that so much of it remains."

As was he. The pillaging had begun right after Rudolf died in 1612. The king's brother took many of the paintings. Bohemian rebels stole and sold the jewels. Maximilian of Bavaria carted fifteen hundred wagons full of booty back to Munich. Now the Swedish army was prepared for a final sweep to take what remained.

He stepped through the rooms. Most of what he saw had little to no value, but there was one object he'd been told to specifically target.

"Show me the book," he ordered.

They made their way to the fourth room. A hall more than a hundred paces long, sheathed in bright silver and decorated with various story depictions and paintings, most in gilded frames. Tapestries hung on the wall, woven from silk, gold, and more silver. Windows lined each side with panes of smoked glass. Books lay *everywhere on the side tables and stuffed onto dusty wooden shelving. Hundreds of them. Maybe thousands. The air smelled of old leather and aged vellum. Lying atop a sturdy oak table was what he'd been told might be here.*

"It is huge," he muttered.

"And quite heavy," his aide added.

Nearly a hundred centimeters tall, fifty wide, and about twenty thick. Perhaps the largest book he'd ever seen. He also knew the appropriate name by which many referred to it.

The Codex Gigas.

"Is the devil there?" he asked.

His aide nodded. "Folio 290. We have it marked. Would you like to see?"

CHAPTER 34

STEPHANIE STARED AT THE REFERENCE BOOK KOGER HAD SENT HER way, which featured not only a detailed account of the 1648 capture of Prague and all that happened afterward, but a photograph of Folio 290 from the Codex Gigas.

The devil was depicted as a monstrous figure taking up the entirety of hell, with large claws at the tips of outstretched arms, red-tipped horns, small red eyes, a green head, and two long red tongues. He was shown crouching between two large towers, wearing an ermine loincloth. Portraits of the devil were a common occurrence in medieval art, but the depiction here stood out for not only its size but also its grotesqueness. On the opposite folio was a full-page representation of the Heavenly City, shown in tiers of buildings and towers behind red walls. Its inclusion was most likely there to inspire the ideas of hope and salvation, a clear contrast with the evil nature of the devil. Taken together, the portrait and city probably were meant to be a reflection on what would await if you lived a good or bad life. There were many other illustrations throughout the codex, but

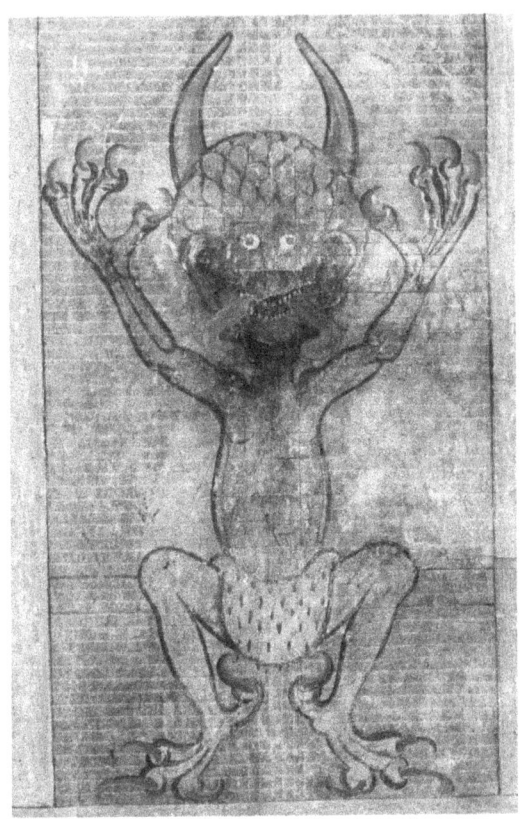

the devil and the Heavenly City were the only ones occupying full pages. A message of some sort?

Maybe.

From her reading she'd learned that the label Devil's Bible attached to the book sometime between its seizure in 1648 and the mid–nineteenth century, when it had become a Swedish fixture. People from all over the world came to see it. The whole thing would have fascinated her late husband. Lars so loved a great historical mystery. And if he could wrap around that some sort of conspiracy, no matter how far-fetched, then so much the better. She'd indulged his fantasies, which at the time seemed harmless. But one of those ultimately got him killed. Lars had been a dreamer who made the mistake of getting in over his head. He finally found a real-life conspiracy, with real-life consequences, and it cost him his life.

She'd returned to her hotel from the national library and settled down for a few minutes of quiet time. She was stymied until Cotton and Cassiopeia reported in. She'd learned a long time ago not to press her operatives. If people higher up the pole than her wanted fast results, it was her job to slow them down. She'd worked by one rule since the beginning. Hire the right people. After that they had to work at their own pace. If she did not like that pace, then fire them. But there were always distractions and obstacles along the path to finding answers. Cotton and Cassiopeia were pros. They knew what they were doing. So let them do it. In the meantime she decided to do a little more reading of the book that Koger had sent by way of Sandra Koss. A lot happened in Prague from July to November 1648. The Swedish looting of Bohemia went on for days. So much was taken.

And all in a deliberate plan.

The book noted that the issue of whether to return those spoils of war had been raised many times over the ensuing centuries. According to the most basic legal principles an act must be judged according to the law that prevailed when the deed was done. So it would be illogical to apply modern legal rules to crimes that were committed in the mid–seventeenth century. Perceptions of right and wrong shifted. What would be criminal today had not always been thought of in that way. How many European libraries and museums were full of stolen treasures, all acquired during times when looting, as a consequence of war, was considered lawful and justified? What was the general argument raised so many times? *All that loot had been given a new home where it could be preserved for much longer than otherwise might have been.* A stretch? Probably. Another argument was that returning spoils of wars could create unpredictable consequences.

Really? Like here?

Unforeseen seemed an understatement.

The Czechs obviously were serious about the return of their cultural treasure. Enough that they were willing to stop one of the world's great nations from gaining admittance to NATO. That showed fortitude. And importance. The deal the Swedes had made seemed like a smart move. The only entity on earth that would be opposed to that would be the Russian Federation.

No other suspects.

Just that simple.

She'd delayed long enough.

Time to call in some favors.

CHAPTER 35

COTTON WOKE.

The last thing he recalled was a car striking his and spinning him around, then hitting something solid. A streetlight or power pole? He shook the cobwebs from his brain and tried to focus. He was no longer in the car. Instead, he was inside a room. Small. Lit by a single lamp on a small table beside the bed upon which he lay. And the furniture. Antiques. Stylish. Old-style. Where was he?

He pushed himself up.

A wave of dizziness swept over him, which he allowed to pass. A concussion? Maybe. He needed to call Stephanie. He searched for his phone, which was not in any of his pockets.

The door to the room opened.

And a familiar face strolled in.

"You have a name?" Cotton asked.

"Call me Ivan."

The Russian accent lacing his English made the label appropriate, as did the man's appearance—short, heavy-chested, with grayish-black hair. A splotchy, reddened skink of a face was dominated by a broad Slavic nose and shadowed by a day-old beard that shone with perspiration. He wore an ill-fitting suit. They stood in a small plaza within the shadow of the Round Tower, a seventeenth-century structure that offered commanding views of Copenhagen from its hundred-foot summit. The dull roar of traffic was not audible this deep into the Strøget, only the clack of heels on cobbles and the laughter of children. They were beneath a covered walk that faced the tower, a brick wall to their backs.

"Did your people kill those two men back there?" he asked.

"They think we come to whisk them away. Big mistake."

"Care to tell me how you know about Cassiopeia Vitt?"

"Quite the woman. If I am younger, a hundred pounds lighter." Ivan paused. "But you do not want to hear this. Vitt is into something she does not understand. I hope you, ex-American-agent, appreciate the problem better."

"It's the only reason I'm standing here."

His unspoken message seemed to be received. Get to the damn point.

"You can overpower me," Ivan said, nodding. "I am fat, out-of-shape Russian. Stupid too. All of us are, right?"

He caught the sarcasm. "I can take you. But the man standing near the tree, across the way in the blue jacket, and the other one near the Round Tower's entrance? I doubt I'd evade them. They're not fat and out of shape."

Ivan chuckled. "I am told you are smart. A few years off job have not changed this."

"I seem to be busier in retirement than I was working for the government."

"This bad thing?"

"You need to talk fast, or I may take my chances with your friends."

Ivan chuckled. "This problem we have is serious."

He lunged forward, grabbed Ivan by his lapels, and slammed him into the bricks behind them. He brought his face inches away. "Where the hell is Cassiopeia?"

He knew the backups were most likely reacting. He was prepared to whirl around and deal with them both. Of course, that was assuming they didn't decide to shoot first.

"We need this anger," Ivan quietly said, his breath stale.

"Who is we?"

"Me, Cotton."

The words came from his right. A new voice. Female. Familiar. He should have known. He released his grip and turned.

Ten feet away stood Stephanie Nelle.

There were a lot of surprises that night in Copenhagen when he first met Ivan from the SVR. An unlikely field operative. He'd wondered then what could possibly have rankled the Russians to the point that they mounted a full-scale intelligence operation, dispatching a midlevel operative as overseer. Then, to thwart the Americans, the Russians brazenly shot two people dead in the middle of Copenhagen. Back then, when Danny Daniels was still president, Stephanie and the Magellan Billet were usually only called in when conventional intelligence channels no longer were viable. She'd been there that night.

And here they were again.

He, Stephanie, and—

"Good to see you," Ivan said, with a smile.

Then it occurred to him. "Did you have someone ram my car?"

"*Da.*"

He shook his sore head. "You're about to really piss me off."

"Like back in Denmark, we need your anger. Hitting your car was fastest, easiest way to get you here."

"With me unconscious?"

Ivan shrugged. "Work for me."

"I see your English is not any better."

"How your Russian?"

"I try and stay away from the country and its people."

"A shame. But all this necessary. I can explain."

"I really, really hope so. For your benefit."

"I much more important now than back in Copenhagen. High in command. We do good there, and in China. Changed things. Now here I am. Doing good again."

Cotton rubbed his temples and decided to be patient. Ivan, if nothing else, was competent. And the big man had gone to a lot of trouble for something. "Okay, tell me. What's going on?"

He knew this Russian liked to feign that he was not the brightest bulb in the box. But that was not the case.

Not in the least.

"I need to show you important things."

CHAPTER 36

Stephanie rode in the backseat of an unmarked palace car headed out of Stockholm for Uppsala. It sat about fifty miles north, Sweden's fourth largest city, long serving as the country's ecclesiastical center and the seat of the archbishop of the Church of Sweden. It also accommodated Scandinavia's largest cathedral, where every Swedish monarch up until the nineteenth century was crowned. She'd made some calls to people within the SVR, contacts she'd long cultivated. Friends? Not really. More professional acquaintances. Men and women who occasionally needed favors. Nothing treasonous. Just things their superiors demanded, and others could help deliver.

And what she'd learned surprised her.

They sat at a table in the Café Norden, nestled close to an open second-story window. She, Cotton, and the Russian, Ivan. Outside, Copenhagen's Højbro Plads vibrated with people.

"The tomato bisque is great here," Cotton told them both.

Ivan rubbed his belly. "Tomatoes give me gas."

"Then by all means let's avoid that," she said.

She realized that, to Cotton, her presence here, on this beautiful day in Denmark, signaled nothing but trouble. Which was not far off the mark. Her association with Ivan definitely compounded the situation. She knew Cotton's position on working with the Russians.

Nothing but trouble.

The café tables were crowded, people drifting up and down from a corner staircase, many toting shopping bags. Cotton had to be wondering why they were talking in public, but figured she knew what she was doing.

"What's going on here?" Cotton asked.

"I learned of Cassiopeia's involvement with Lev Sokolov a few days ago. I also learned about Russia's interest too."

"You killed those two men I was after so we'd have no choice but to deal with you," Cotton said to Ivan. "Couldn't let me learn anything from them, right?"

"They are bad people. Bad, bad people. They deserve what they get."

"I didn't know that would happen," she said to him. "But I shouldn't be surprised."

"You two acquainted?" he asked her.

"Ivan and I have dealt with each other before."

"I not ask you to help," Ivan said. "This not concern America."

"Cotton," she said. "Cassiopeia has involved herself in something that is much bigger than she suspects. China is in the midst of an internal power struggle. Karl Tang, the first vice premier, and Ni Yong, the head of the Communist Party's anti-corruption department, are about to square off for control. We've been watching this battle, which is rapidly escalating into a war. Like I said, I became aware of Cassiopeia's entrance a few days ago. When we dug further, we found Ivan was also interested—"

"So you hopped on a plane and flew to Denmark."

"That's my job, Cotton."

"This isn't my job. Not anymore."

"None of us," Ivan said, "want Tang to win. He is Mao again, only worse. You Americans nose into my business. Then want to tell how we do it."

"The other side may try to contact me again," Cotton said.

"I doubt that's going to happen," she said. "When Ivan decided to improvise, he may have sealed Cassiopeia's fate."

Cotton glared at Ivan. "You don't seem concerned."

"I am hungry."

The Russian caught the attention of a server and pointed toward a plate of røget in a glass-fronted case, displaying five fingers. The woman acknowledged that she understood how many of the smoked fish to bring.

"What do you want me to do?" Cotton pointed at Ivan. "Sergeant Schultz here knows nothing, sees nothing, hears nothing."

"Who says this? I never say this. I know plenty. And I love Hogan's Heroes."

"You're just a pain-in-the-ass dumb Russian."

The stout man grinned. "Oh, I see. You want to anger me. Aggravate, yes? Big, stupid man will lose temper and say more than he should." He waggled a stubby finger. "You watch too many CSI on television. Or NCIS. I love that show too. Mark Harmon is tough guy."

The server brought the five fish, smelling as if they'd just been caught.

"Ah," Ivan said. "Wonderful. You are sure you not want any?"

She and Cotton shook their heads.

Ivan chomped down on one of the fish. "I will say this concerns big things we do not want the Chinese to know."

She glanced outside.

Cotton's bookshop stood across the sunny square. People streamed in and out the front door, more swarming about like bees around their honeycombs. She knew he loved the store and his new career as a bookseller. Over the past two years he'd gained a reputation as a man who could find whatever collectible you wanted. Similar to the dozen years when he was one of her best agents. Always delivering.

"I'm going to Antwerp," Cotton said. "To find Cassiopeia."

Ivan was devouring another fish. "And what to do when you get there? You know where to look?"

"Do you?"

Ivan stopped chewing and smiled.

Bits of flesh had lodged between his brown teeth.

"Oh, yes. I know where Vitt is."

So much happened in Antwerp and later in China. The world changed. Enemies became friends and vice versa. The Café Norden was now gone. Out of business. She'd loved that place. Danny Daniels was no longer president. The current administration was no friend. Lots of hostility and mistrust. But all those years ago Cotton did his job. So had Cassiopeia. Both survived. And Ivan? Like Cotton had said, a royal pain in the ass. But he did his job too.

Now Ivan was here in Sweden.

"What is he doing here?" she'd asked her Russian contact on the phone.

"Under normal circumstances we would not even be talking. So I certainly would not answer a question such as that. But this is not a normal circumstance."

Nothing about that had sounded good, and the next words that had come to her ear seemed worse.

"Listen carefully."

CHAPTER 37

Cassiopeia recalled something Cotton once told her.

Another of his stories.

There was a criminal who committed a crime. But he was caught and sent to the king for punishment. The king told him he had two choices. He could be hanged by a rope or take what was behind the big iron door. The criminal quickly decided on the rope, and as the noose was being slipped onto his neck he turned to the king and asked, "Out of curiosity, what's behind that door?" The king laughed and said, "I offer everyone the same choice, and nearly everyone picks the rope." The criminal remained curious. "So what's behind the door? I mean, obviously, I won't tell anyone," he said, pointing to the noose. The king paused, then answered, "Freedom, but it seems most people are so afraid of the unknown that they immediately take the rope."

A good lesson. Also a reminder about the dangers of clinging to the familiar. So many people choose it. Too many are fearful about the unknown. Risk is foreign to them. She was like that once.

Not anymore.

"*My grandfather was a smart man,*" Cotton told her. "*He said that life is just one long try to resist the unknown. He taught me about making choices. To push past your fears and open the doors to the unfamiliar. Like he would say, 'When nothing changes, then nothing changes.' If you keep doing what you're always doing, you'll keep getting what you're always getting.*"

All good advice that she was practicing here. Choosing the door, and the unknown. Changing things up.

She and Westlake had left the Grand Hôtel and, out on the sidewalk, Westlake had called Monica. The conversation was brief.

"She wants to meet," he said to her, when the call ended. "What do you want to do?"

No choice. The familiar be damned. "We meet."

But she'd told herself to be wary.

What would Cotton say? *To get you have to give.*

She debated whether to go alone, but realized there wasn't much help she could call in. The locals were out. Cotton was off on his own line of inquiry. Stephanie had told her they had CIA backup, but she decided that would be more of a problem than a solution. This one was on her. The good thing? She was armed with a semi-automatic, its holster tucked tight at her belly beneath her shirt, two extra clips in her back pocket. The bad thing? The time was approaching 11:30 P.M. and she was tired, running on adrenaline. Nothing new there. Thankfully, she was a night owl. Westlake ordered an Uber and they left the city, heading north.

"I should warn you about Monica," he said as they rode. "She has little patience and is accustomed to having her way. She can be extremely unpredictable and dangerous. Spontaneous, even. It's another reason I chose not to challenge her."

"She knows I am coming?"

He nodded. "She wants you to take a message back to the palace."

Okay. That could mean a multitude of things.

She found her phone and sent a text.

STEPHANIE WAS CONCERNED.

And she had every right to be.

First she'd been headed to Uppsala to find Ivan. Her contacts in Moscow had provided an address. Then a text had come from Cassiopeia. Meeting set with Monica. Heading there now. So she'd pivoted with a change of plan, calling the number that Sandra Koss had provided and requesting immediate CIA assistance. Thirty minutes later a car intercepted them on the highway and she switched vehicles, sending the palace driver back to Stockholm. Earlier, she and Cassiopeia had activated the FIND ME applications on their phones so both would know the other's location. They hadn't been sure what would happen. Perhaps nothing. But just in case, they'd arranged a contingency plan. No way was she allowing Cassiopeia to enter that hornet's nest alone. The two men who'd been sent were local operatives the CIA routinely contracted with. Sandra had said they were at her disposal for as long as needed. The purpose of her late-night venture had been to find Ivan. Now that had changed with an opportunity to take Monica Butler-White into custody.

"Where are we headed?" she asked the driver, who had her phone and was following the tracker toward Cassiopeia.

"It seems to Sigtuna."

"And that is?"

"A small harbor town on Lake Mälaren. About halfway between

Stockholm and Uppsala. One of the oldest places in Sweden. Mainly a tourist destination now."

"How large?"

"Less than ten thousand people and definitely not a late-night place. All its cafés, restaurants, and shops will be closed."

"Speed up. We need to get there. Fast."

CASSIOPEIA STEPPED OUT OF THE UBER.

They were about fifty kilometers north of Stockholm in a quiet little village called Sigtuna. A single cobbled street ran down its center, both sides lined with colorful clapboard and shingled houses that held boutiques, shops, and cafés, each advertised by ornate iron placards that hung out over the street. The lighting was minimal, mainly from the backlit storefronts and a few streetlamps that threw out long streams of dull radiance. The place appeared old, but was most likely all of a more recent vintage. Off to the right, among trees, stood a church lit to the night, built of brick in the Romanesque style, which had definitely been there for a few centuries.

"Monica awaits us," Westlake said as he climbed from the car too.

The Uber driver left, the taillights receding. She looked around. No one in sight. Apparently Sigtuna was not a late-night place, even in summer. Westlake started walking. Absolutely nothing about this was good. More of what Cotton would say came to mind.

Make what you can out of a bad situation, even when it's really bad.

Like this.

CHAPTER 38

Cotton left the house, which was more like a colonial barn with a faded yellow façade. Two upper windows gave the impression of a happy house, like smiling eyes, the door below a sloppy grin. Some sort of manor house that occupied a skinny sliver of land. The address seemed to be outside of any town, neighbors far between, isolated by thick trees on a rise next to a lake. The night air loomed cool, which helped clear his humming head. Overhead, tendrils of fading daylight still lingered.

"This a place we use," Ivan said. "Out of sight. Out of mind."

"And the reason you are showing me an SVR safe house? A bit unusual, to say the least."

"Why not? Not like it breaks Moscow rules."

He caught the reference to a set of maxims developed during the Cold War by spies working in Moscow. Which was like the Holy Grail for field assignments. Everybody wanted it. But few could cut it. The rules had not been written down at the time, but were precepts of engagement that everybody who worked there lived by. Simple. To the point. Loaded with common sense. Cotton had visited the International Spy Museum in DC, where the rules were displayed.

Ten of them.

Assume nothing. Never go against your gut. Everyone is potentially under opposition control. Do not look back, as you are never completely alone. Go with the flow, blend in. Vary your pattern and stay within your cover. Lull others into a sense of complacency. Do not harass the opposition. Pick the time and place for action. And, most important, keep your options open.

He shook his head with an odd mixture of pleasure and reluctance. "Granted, it doesn't, but maybe there should be an eleventh rule. Never take the other side to your safe house."

Ivan chuckled. "Unless the other side has reason."

And he was sure this big man had one.

Like last time.

Cotton stepped off the NATO chopper at a small airfield north of Antwerp. Ivan followed Stephanie onto the tarmac. Stephanie had arranged the quick flight from Copenhagen. When they were clear of the blades, the helicopter departed back into the night sky. Two cars awaited with drivers.

"Secret Service," she told them. "Out of Brussels."

Ivan had said little on the trip, just small talk about television and movies. The Russian seemed obsessed with American entertainment.

"All right," Cotton said. "We're here. Where's Cassiopeia?"

A third car approached from the far side of the terminal, passing rows of expensive private planes.

"My people," Ivan said. "I must talk to them."

The pudgy Russian waddled toward the car, which stopped. Two men emerged.

Cotton stepped close to Stephanie and asked, "Do we have any independent intelligence on this?"

She shook her head. "Not enough time. It'll be tomorrow, at the earliest, before I have anything."

"So we're bare-ass-to-the-wind, flying blind."

"We've been there before."

Yes, they had.

Ivan stepped back toward them, saying as he walked, "We have problem."

"Why does that not surprise me?" Cotton muttered.

"Vitt is on the move."

"How's that a problem?" Stephanie asked.

"She escapes her captors."

Cotton was suspicious. "How do you know that?"

Ivan pointed at the two standing beside the car. "They watch and see."

"Why didn't they help her?" But he knew the answer. "You want her to lead you."

"This is intelligence operation," Ivan said. "I have job to do."

"Where is she?"

"Nearby. Headed for a museum."

Cotton's anger grew. "How the hell do you know that?"

"We go."

"No, we don't," he said.

Ivan's face stiffened.

"I'm going," he made clear. "Alone."

Ivan's haggard face cracked a smile. "I am warned of you. They say you are Lone Ranger."

"Then you know to stay out of my way."

Ivan faced Stephanie. "You take over now? You think I allow that."

"Look," Cotton said, answering for her. "If I go alone, I have a better chance of finding out what you want. You show up with your squad and you're going to get zero. Cassiopeia is a pro. She'll go to ground."

At least he hoped so.

Ivan jabbed a forefinger at Cotton's chest. "Why should I trust you?"

"I've been asking myself the same thing about you."

The Russian removed a pack of cigarettes from his pocket and clamped one between his lips. He found matches and lit it. "I not like this."

"Like I care what you like. You want the job done. I'll get it done."

"Okay," Ivan said as he exhaled. "Find her. Get what we want."

"Once I make contact, I'll call Stephanie. But I'm going to have to gauge Cassiopeia. She may not want help."

Ivan raised a finger and pointed. "She might not want, but she gets it. This matter is bigger than she thinks."

He did not plan to make the same mistake he made in Paris with Henrik Thorvaldsen. Cassiopeia needed his help and he was going to give it to her. Unconditionally and with full disclosure.

And Ivan could go to hell.

He hadn't thought about Henrik in a long time. His dear friend had been dead for a while. True, Cotton had made a mistake there, one he hadn't repeated in Antwerp. Nor did he intend to do so here. So he faced Ivan and asked, "What's going on? A lot of people died today."

"Those were our people. Not acceptable."

He was beginning to understand. "Somebody has gone rogue?"

"Seems that way. At least in part."

"And you need my help?"

"We need each other."

CHAPTER 39

John walked down Sigtuna's main artery. A lot of paths were about to cross. Scores to be settled. Things to be righted. They were coming to the point of no return. He'd thought of this moment for a long time, imaging how he would feel. Monica was here doing what she did best. Creating chaos. Keeping everyone off guard. What he'd not told the king or Stephanie Nelle was that he'd not been all that innocent nine years ago.

He'd had an affair. With Monica.

Hard not to find her brains, beauty, and energy attractive.

For the first few years he and Lysa had a reasonably solid marriage. But sadly, their relationship had always lacked intimacy. They were more like a couple of good friends than husband and wife. For a decade he just ignored the issue and quietly satisfied himself outside the marriage. Lysa was oblivious to any of that, so cheating had been easy. But with what happened nine years ago, stacked on top of a frigid wife, he'd recently decided he could ignore the situation no longer.

Sex for Lysa was nothing but a chore that occurred once every other month, at best. And with so many rules. Never after dinner. Or in the middle of the day. Or the day of or before a doctor or dentist appointment. Morning was preferable. Late afternoon better. And always after a shower and her makeup was applied. Never, though, if she had a lunch engagement or visitors expected for the evening. Their public displays of affection were nonexistent. She considered those unseemly. *I love yous* came rarely. True, they were kind and respectful of each other, but the relationship possessed not a hint of passion. He supposed a lot of that was her upbringing. Being raised in a royal bubble by strict Protestant parents came with its ups and downs. But humans were social animals and, as such, had a need to feel connected, to believe that they were worthy of someone's love and lust. Intimacy made you feel alive, like you'd been found, as if someone was finally taking the time to peer into the depths of your soul and really see you. With Lysa he'd always felt like she was looking right through him. Gradually he'd slipped away until finally considering himself just a roommate. Friendly and cordial, but a roommate nonetheless.

Which Lysa seemed to embrace.

But he grew to resent.

Monica was not the first "other woman," nor the last, but she had been the longest and most enduring of his extramarital relationships. Monica was different. They'd connected. On many levels, both physically and emotionally. She was a vibrant, alluring woman. Exciting. Daring. And bold. With a capital *B*. They'd long maintained a robust physical relationship, covert and secret, that was also coming to a point of no return.

Choices were about to be made.

Farther down the street a figure emerged from the shadows. The form and shape unmistakable.

He stopped.

"There she is," he said, voice low.

CASSIOPEIA STOOD HER GROUND BESIDE WESTLAKE.

Monica was about her height and size. Dressed similarly too. Jeans and a button-down shirt with boots. Her right arm hung free, but the left hand gripped a pistol, which she kept at her side.

Cassiopeia reached for her own weapon.

But Westlake stopped her, saying, "That would not be wise."

The buildings on both sides of her were packed tight, the street only about six meters wide, with alleys leading in and out. Lots of places for trouble to hide. The whole thing felt like a showdown from some American western movie. Two gunslingers facing off, but only one with a weapon drawn.

And the odds that Monica Butler-White was here alone?

Zero.

JOHN STARTED WALKING TOWARD MONICA. "OKAY, I CAME AND brought her, as you asked." He and Cassiopeia stopped a few meters away. "This is Cassiopeia Vitt. She was sent by Stephanie Nelle to keep an eye on me. She is working directly for the palace."

"With the American, Cotton Malone?"

"You seem to be remarkably informed," Vitt said.

"It is my job to be so."

"You have a message you want delivered?" Vitt asked.

"I do. The Swedes need to understand that we are not bluffing. We want that codex."

"A complication has developed."

"Really? Care to explain."

"Sir Westlake, here, says that his wife is an SVR operative. If that is true, no one is going to trade for anything."

CASSIOPEIA KEPT HER EYES ON MONICA'S HANDS, WHICH STAYED down at her sides, resisting the urge to reach for her own weapon. Westlake was right. It would only provoke this unknown commodity.

"Did you tell them that?" Monica asked Westlake.

"It is the truth."

"If the princess is compromised, even innocently, the government will make no trade," Cassiopeia made clear. "There will be little sympathy for her situation."

Movement on the peripheries from the side alleys caught her attention. Two men appeared. One left, the other right. Both armed. She could take one, maybe two. No way she'd take down both, plus Monica, before one of them shot her.

"Is the princess an SVR asset?" she asked.

Monica stepped close to Westlake and said, "You talk too much."

"Actually, I do not talk enough. I have stayed silent for nine years. Because of you."

Monica shook her head.

Then her left arm swung up fast and the butt of the gun she held smashed into Westlake's right temple. The neck whipped back and Westlake began to stagger. Cassiopeia moved to defend him but the two guys with guns leveled their weapons straight at her. She froze and raised her arms in mock surrender. Westlake collapsed to his knees, dazed, and reached up, rubbing the side of his head, but Monica was not finished. She slammed the weapon again into the other side of Westlake's head. His eyes rolled skyward. Mouth opened. And he folded to the cobbles, landing hard on his right shoulder.

Monica faced her. "He stays here. With us. Now we have two hostages."

"You plan to kill him?"

"Why do you care?"

"I don't."

"Let me be clear. Princess Lysa has, in fact, for many years supplied us with much useful information. We manipulated and used her, all without her knowledge. Sir Westlake here? He was someone we used to divert attention away from the princess. He's a greedy capitalist who was easily bought. Tell the Swedes that if we do not have the Devil's Bible by noon tomorrow, I will personally put a bullet in Princess Lysa's and Westlake's skulls. If they think I am bluffing, you can tell them what you just witnessed."

"How did you manage to get the princess to work with you?"

"Leave."

Cassiopeia stood her ground. She needed to learn what she could.

Monica fired a sound-suppressed round at the cobblestones. The bullet ricocheted away a few inches from Cassiopeia's feet.

"I told you to leave. I would like you to deliver the message but, if need be, I can shoot you dead and do it another way."

She decided she'd pushed enough.

So she turned and walked away.

CHAPTER 40

SHE WAS BORN MARIA CHRISTINA ALEXANDRA, IN STOCKHOLM, ON a cold December day in 1626. Her parents were the Swedish King Gustav Adolph, who later earned the moniker Magnus, and his German wife, Maria Eleonora. She was first thought to be a boy, as she was hairy and screamed with a strong, hoarse voice. Deep embarrassment spread among the midwives when they discovered their mistake. The king, who'd made no secret of the fact he'd coveted a boy, was surprisingly thrilled at the revelation, saying his daughter would make fools of them all.

Her childhood spanned a long European cold spell called the Little Ice Age and coincided with the Thirty Years' War, when Sweden sided with other Protestant nations against the Catholic Habsburg Empire. Her father's role in that war may have turned the tide from the Catholics to the Protestants. When her father was killed in battle, the six-year-old girl became Queen Christina. Lord High Chancellor Axel Oxenstierna ruled as regent until Christina was of age. But even during the regency, she followed her own mind. Against Oxenstierna's advice, she initiated an end of the Thirty

Years' War, culminating with the Peace of Westphalia in 1648. But not before she ordered the taking of Prague and the plunder of its castle.

She was intelligent and strong-willed, always happy to engage in political intrigue, a learned woman, fluent in Greek and Latin, studying philosophy, political science, mathematics, and astronomy. Alchemy fascinated her. Both a fine shot and a fine horsewoman, she particularly enjoyed winter sports. She was known for her maxims of wisdom. Fools are more to be feared than villains. Knowledge of the past is of great help for the future. It is good to remember that vain people can never be trusted. *She eventually acquired the nickname Minerva of the North, referring to the Roman goddess of the arts, and Stockholm became known as the Athens of the North.*

History noted her as one of Sweden's great rulers.

Lysa admired the canvas hanging in the bedroom.

It had stimulated her mind.

A wonderful collage with intermediate shades of warm orange-yellow, pale red, brown, and purple. Cooler tints came from green and shades of blue. A large, expansive scene from the seventeenth century where Queen Christina was signing a request for the privilege of opening a new silver mine. She sat at a long table decked with a dark-blue cloth, richly illuminated by candles. Before her stood a bowing mountain-captain. Behind her, mine employees, pressed against a wall, gazed on in awe. In the foreground work proceeded as usual with ore carts, horses, and men bearing torches. Most likely there to be an effective dramatic contrast to the grandeur behind them. A saying occurred to her. *Ars sina scienta nihil est.* Art without knowledge is nothing.

How true.

Sadly, there were no more monarchs granting mineral rights. The mine owners no longer strutted about dressed in black coats, knee breeches, and round hats leaning upon artistically decorated hatchet-canes. Mountain regiments fired no more cannon or musket shots. But for her that specially laden atmosphere, that rarefied air of the past, reminiscent of Sweden's former glory, would never fade. Christina had meant so much to the country. Her contributions should never be forgotten. But sadly, few now knew her name, and even fewer appreciated her greatness. Perhaps it was her end that made her less memorable. Inexplicably she converted to Catholicism and knew she could no longer rule a Protestant country. So she abdicated in 1654 and left Sweden. People should be mindful of Psalm 145:4. *One generation shall commend your works to another and shall declare your mighty acts.* But that was not always the case.

Far from it, in fact.

A knock broke the silence.

The bedchamber door opened and Monica walked inside. "You are up late."

"I never retire before midnight. John is the opposite. A devout morning person."

"Good news. Mr. Westlake is on his way here."

She smiled. "I am glad. I miss him."

"As I am sure he misses you."

"I heard some activity outside a short while ago," Lysa said.

"It was me, returning. I had to go out."

"Is John's business proceeding along?"

"It is. We should definitely be done by tomorrow afternoon."

"When will John arrive?"

"I would say within the hour."

She nodded. "That is good to hear."

"I will leave you now. I just wanted to make sure you were okay and knew that your husband was on the way."

"How thoughtful. I appreciate the gesture."

"Might I suggest you enjoy a warm bath while you wait," Monica said. "There is a wonderful Roman tub in your bathroom. Perhaps a little relaxation after an unusual day."

"What a lovely idea. I might just do that."

Monica excused herself and left.

The room around her was dignified with paneled walls painted a sage green. The house oozed an Old World atmosphere with warm parquet flooring, oil paintings, and tasteful furniture.

All of it quiet and calming.

On arrival she'd surmised that the house had been built in the mid-eighteenth century, its handsome exterior stained green with lichens. She assumed the location had been selected for its isolation, about eighty kilometers northwest of Stockholm, on a small island in Lake Mälaren, engulfed by forest. Surely a former hunting lodge of sorts. A snug, safe place resting from its labors. Outside the windows the woods were black and silent. Filled with threats? Doubtful. John would never allow anything to happen to her.

She stared again at the painting.

Christina had been one of the most erudite women of the seventeenth century, transforming both Sweden and Stockholm. She lived an unconventional lifestyle by her own rules. But her lavish spending and irresponsibility pushed Sweden toward bankruptcy, sparking domestic unrest. Pope Alexander VII described her as *a queen without a realm, a Christian without faith, and a woman without shame.* She eventually lived out her life in Rome, one of only a few women buried in the Vatican Grottoes. Proverbs 3:35 came to mind.

The wise will inherit honor, but fools get disgrace.

So true.

She walked to the bathroom door. Monica was right. There was a spectacular marble tub. She decided a warm bath would be a wonderful way to draw the day to a close.

John would be here soon.

Within the hour.

So why not.

CHAPTER 41

COTTON RODE WITH IVAN IN A RATHER UPSCALE SAAB.

"Nice car," he said.

"We maintain appearance in country. Blend in. And I like driving. Not many chances to do that in Russia."

They were alone. Just the two of them. He wondered what was going on. His one encounter years ago, in Belgium and China, with this burly man had been a mixed experience. Ivan had double-talked and betrayed both him and Stephanie every chance that came. Thankfully, though, it all worked out. Cassiopeia had been found and they'd averted a potential political disaster. But it had been touch and go the entire way. Now here he was again. With Ivan a few steps ahead.

"What is your position now with the SVR?"

"Deputy head of Directorate S."

His memory supplied what that entailed. The SVR was broken down into eight separate divisions, each autonomous within the larger entity. Directorate S dealt with the recruitment, preparation, and planting of agents abroad, along with finding foreign citizens to work for Russia. Sleeper Central, was the shorthand version he'd heard many times.

"Are you here because of John Westlake or his wife?" he asked.

"Both, I am afraid."

"Are you going to tell me what's going on?"

"Ever hear story of Koschei the Immortal?"

He shook his head. "Nope."

"Old Russian folktale. Koschei lucky. He had a spell which prevents him from being killed. So he hides counterspell for his death inside nested objects to protect it. Like matryoshka doll. One inside the other. Koschei was evil wizard who likes to steal beautiful women, especially those of noble birth. Many heroes went after him, but killing him hard. To do that a brave soul must find counterspell on unnamed island. One hero located tree. Under is a chest. Inside is rabbit. In rabbit is duck. Inside duck is egg. In egg is Koschei's counterspell for death."

"Sounds like a lot of trouble."

"Killing Koschei hard."

He was beginning to understand. "Somebody trying to kill you?"

"That would be too easy. My problem much worse."

They drove for a while in silence. He knew not to press. A road sign indicated they were headed toward Stockholm Arlanda Airport. A big international gateway. Ivan avoided the main terminals and drove toward the private aircraft facilities, parking in front of a partially lit two-story building.

They climbed out into the dim light of nearly midnight.

Ivan entered the building and walked through an empty lobby. Some sort of VIP lounge used by private jet passengers. Not busy tonight. They exited from a back door onto the tarmac and walked past an array of private jets, lined up like soldiers, each one dark and quiet. Maybe half a billion dollars' worth of aircraft. The play toys of the rich, industry, and governments. It had been a while since he last sat in a pilot's seat. The navy taught him to fly fighter jets. He'd been good at it. But his career took quite a different direction.

He'd come a long way.

Ivan led him around one of the hangars to the far side of the tarmac where an EMB 120FC Brasilia turboprop was being prepared by a ground crew. Bright lights illuminated the scene. He knew the plane. Held about thirty passengers, though this one appeared to be a cargo version with a side-loading ramp. Range? About a thousand miles. Ivan moved into another of the hangars, its massive doors open but the inside dark and empty.

"That plane out there. It will take the codex to Prague for Swedes."

"Private charter?"

Ivan nodded. "Keeps things secret. That book big, heavy. Hard to handle."

Which also made it hard to steal.

Cotton knew from Stephanie that the codex was being crated and readied for transport. Ivan was right. The book weighed nearly two hundred pounds and required either a lot of strong people or hydraulic assistance to move. Add in the wooden crate and it was one heavy, bulky item.

"Another plane on the way," Ivan said. "From Moscow. Will be here soon."

He understood. "How do you plan to get the Devil's Bible onto that second plane?"

"I do not plan that at all."

He was all ears.

"There is problem. Big one. The ongoing operation here involving the princess is not sanctioned by Directorate S. We have difference of opinion within Kremlin."

"Really, now. Do tell."

"Franko is idiot. He will be the end of Russia."

That was an interesting admission.

Konstantin Franko was president of the Russian Federation. In the last "election" Franko received eighty-eight percent of the vote. Which was ludicrous. Press reports indicated that rivals had been imprisoned or died in all-too-convenient accidents. The media had been bullied into toeing the line. Voters terrorized. Most Western intelligence agencies believed that Franko had ambitions to retake a huge chunk of the former Soviet Union, which was now all sovereign neighboring territory.

But Franko could not care less.

"He is dictator and fool," Ivan said. "Pushing power beyond Russia's borders will not be easy. America, NATO, they will not back down. If Franko pushes too far, he will plunge us into world war. Any allies Russia has will run from us. We will be left out in cold. Sanctions will wrap us so tight we cannot breathe. Economy will crumble. That is when oligarchs and mob will rise."

"You paint a pretty dim picture."

"It is truth. Sad. But true."

"So what's going on?"

"It simple. Franko does not want Sweden in NATO. But he not smart enough to think to take princess. That came from S Directorate. Stupid move. And there is problem."

Which seemed like an understatement.

"Oligarchs are involved. They have long reach within Kremlin. Franko lets them do as they want."

He connected the dots. "The oligarchs want Sweden in NATO.

Right? It aggravates Franko. Keeps him off guard. Directs his anger away. Which gives them even more freedom of movement."

Ivan pointed a stubby finger. "You still smart."

"Directorate S is in conflict?"

"To say the least."

"Is the princess cooperating in her kidnapping?"

"Not at all. Her husband got her there. Said he need her help. So, as his wife, she gave it. Woman has no idea danger she is in."

Stephanie's fears confirmed.

"Is she expendable?" he asked.

"It is possible. We have SVR person here. Monica Butler-White. She and Westlake know each other. If you get what I mean."

He did. "They're an item?"

Ivan nodded. "Like Sonny and Cher."

He chuckled. "Look at you. But those two eventually divorced."

"These two are up to some bad things. Westlake is working with Monica. I think he does not want to deal with divorce. I think he and Monica have other ideas, making him a widower and blaming us."

Cotton was not sure what to make of all that he was hearing. "Why are you telling me this?"

"SVR is in mess. A lot of problems. Some with Franko. Some not. Nobody really in charge."

Civil wars within, and between, intelligence agencies were not uncommon. Whether those be foreign or domestic. But the Russians were never noted for such chaos. Dissent was dealt with in a swift and decisive manner, so revolutionary thoughts rarely made it to reality.

"The oligarchs are using that division to get what they want. Not good."

"How bad is it?" he asked.

"Bad enough many people will die."

He watched as technicians continued to work on the EMB 120, readying it for flight.

"Westlake has implicated the princess as an SVR asset," he told Ivan. "An unknowing one, used for intel. He also says he has no idea how she was taken. If the princess is on your playbill, whether voluntary or not, the Swedes will have no sympathy for her. They will never make a deal for her release."

"She is definitely a tacit asset."

And Ivan would know.

"But she does not need to die," Ivan said. "We have to take the codex and not give it to the Czechs. America should keep the book and negotiate a deal to protect everyone."

He liked the sound of that, except that he was beginning to wonder if the Devil's Bible mattered anymore. He'd also caught the reservation in Ivan's voice and asked, "What are you not telling me?"

Ivan reached into his pocket and found a phone, which he handed over. "Yours."

He accepted the unit.

"I need you to make call."

He waited.

"To whoever can grant me asylum in United States. I want to defect."

CHAPTER 42

QUEEN CHRISTINA'S GAMBLE HAD PAID OFF. THIRTY LARGE CRATES had been sent from Prague down the River Elbe to Mecklenburg's Fortress Dömitz, where they wintered in 1648. In the spring they were transported to Wismar and reached Stockholm in May 1649. A thousand-kilometer journey that had not been without incident. Some of the spoils had been sold along the way by greedy soldiers.

Which was not uncommon.

Sweden had enjoyed great success at the military annexation of foreign lands, which had assured a steady influx of art and objects for the queen's collections. Rudolf II's plunder had proven spectacular. So many items. Tapestries with depictions of Alexander the Great and Caesar. Oddities like nails from Noah's Ark, a jawbone supposedly belonging to one of the sirens from Homer's *Odyssey*, even a live lion, which had been quite popular with the Swedish people. Of particular interest had been the Codex Gigas. No one had ever seen a book so large, so encompassing. So much mystery became attached to its purpose and creation. It eventually *acquired the label Devil's Bible from the many patrons who came to the royal palace and saw the image of the Trickster himself on Folio 290.*

Sweden's hold on the codex strengthened as chaos reigned in Bohemia. After 1526 the entire region came under Habsburg control. Between 1583 and 1611 Prague was the official seat of Holy Roman Emperor Rudolf II and his court. The Thirty Years' War further crushed any thoughts of Bohemian independence. The nobility and all of the local Protestants had to either convert to Catholicism or leave the country. Nobody cared about Sweden's plunder of Prague. From 1620 to the late eighteenth century a dark age enveloped Bohemia. One calamity after another. Disease and famine reduced the population by a third. Ottoman Turks and Tartars invaded. The end of the Holy Roman Empire in 1806 led to a further degradation when Bohemia became part of the Austrian Empire. Eventually, though, a Czech national revival began, slow at first, then gaining momentum in an effort to resurrect language, culture, and national identity.

In 1819 two manuscripts from the Swedish Royal Library were loaned to Bohemia. The Codex Gigas was not one of those. It was said at the time that the diplomat who came to claim the loans did not have the room to return with it. In January 1878 the codex itself was moved from the palace to the new Royal Library in Stockholm. The chief librarian brought the book across town on a sleigh, then displayed it atop a special desk in the center of a grand hall, where it became a showpiece.

All during the nineteenth century Czech scholars made pilgrimages to the Swedish imperial archives to view the books and art taken long ago from their land. Some used those cultural treasures to pen scholarly works. War constantly dominated their homeland from the late nineteenth century until 1945. Then the Soviets seized control and all went quiet until the Velvet Revolution of 1989, when the communists were rooted from power.

Interest in the Codex Gigas grew.

In 2007 the book finally returned to Prague, on loan to the Klementinum Gallery for five months. Good relations between the Czech National Library and the Swedish Royal Library helped make the loan possible. Political pressure came when two successive Czech prime ministers made the case for a permanent return.

To no avail, though.

The perfect leverage arrived when Sweden, breaking with centuries of neutrality, applied for NATO membership. Finally, the Czechs had real bargaining power.

That they did, Stephanie thought.

And good for them.

The Codex Gigas, the Devil's Bible, was Bohemian, not Swedish. It was war booty. Stolen. It should be returned, no matter that its acquisition violated no seventeenth-century law. But that was her personal opinion. Which had no place in the equation. She was here to find Princess Lysa and make the deal with the Czechs happen.

No more. No less.

She sat in the backseat of a car. She and the two CIA operatives were headed for Sigtuna. A text had come a few minutes ago from her son, Mark. Just a short message to see if she was okay and mention that he was looking forward to their seeing each other in a few weeks. She still recalled how she felt all those years ago in southern France. Disconnected from her life. A jumble of confusion, her anxiety hard to settle. So many demons from the past that finally had to be confronted. Both then, and now, she was the head of one of the most highly specialized units within the United States government. She dealt with crises on a daily basis. Like right now. True, none were as personal as that day, facing her supposedly dead son from across a room.

But she'd worked it out.

With Cotton's help.

Stephanie opened the door lock. Inside, Cotton flipped on a lamp in the den and immediately noticed a rucksack tossed into a chair that neither he nor Stephanie had brought.

He reached for the gun at his belt.

Movement from the bedroom caught his eye. A man appeared in the doorway and leveled a Glock.

Cotton brought his weapon up. "Who the hell are you?"

The man was young, maybe early thirties, with the same short hair and stocky build that he'd seen in abundance over the past few days. The face, though handsome, was set for combat—the eyes like black marbles—and he handled the weapon with assurance. But she sensed a hesitancy, as if the other man was unsure of friend or foe.

"I asked who you are?"

"Lower the gun, Geoffrey," came a voice from inside the bedroom.

The weapon came down.

Cotton lowered his too.

Another man stepped from the shadows.

He was long-limbed and squarely built with close-cropped auburn hair. He too held a pistol, and it took her only an instant to register the familiar cleft, swarthy skin, and gentle eyes from the photo that still angled on the table to her left.

"My God in heaven," she whispered.

Her body shook. Her heart pounded. For a moment she had to tell herself to breathe. Her only child, missing for years, was standing across the room. She wanted to rush to him, to tell him how sorry she was for all their differences, how glad she was to see him. But her muscles would not respond.

"Mother," Mark said. "Your son is back from the grave."

She caught the coolness in his tone and instantly sensed that his heart was still hard. "Where have you been?"

"It's a long story."

No shade of compassion tempered his stare. She waited for him to explain, but he said nothing. Cotton came toward her, placed a hand on her shoulder, and broke the awkward pause. "Why don't you sit."

That had been quite a day.

Her son, indeed back from the dead.

Thought gone forever.

But not.

Thankfully, she and Mark ultimately resolved their differences and grew close. He still lived in southern France as the prior in a long-standing monastery, his life happy and fulfilling. Her own? Both happy and fulfilling too. Definitely. She loved her job. There was nothing she'd rather be doing. Retirement was an option, but the prospect of not working any longer simply did not appeal to her. President Warner Fox would love to see her go. He was no fan, nor was she of him. Firing her had once been on the table but not anymore. The current attorney general seemed ambivalent. But he was a political appointee and his loyalty was to the White House. First, foremost, and always. She'd dealt with so many AGs. Some hot, some cold, most lukewarm.

Thinking of Mark had been happening more and more of late.

But nostalgia was a dirty liar, one that insisted things were better once than they seemed now. Change was the law of life. Unbending and certain. She'd come to learn that the past could not hurt you unless you allowed it. Memories can both warm your insides and tear you apart. Her late husband was the perfect example. But she'd learned from his mistakes, God rest his soul. Now she knew that you could either feel sorry for yourself or treat all that had happened as a gift. What had Cotton told her once? *There comes a time in your life when you have to choose to turn the page, write another book, or simply close it.*

He did love his book metaphors.

But he was right.

Which one should she choose?

She still harbored a private thought that she'd never shared with anyone. Nobody worked forever. Not even her. She would eventually retire, but she wanted to make sure that the Magellan Billet passed into good hands. Her dream for so long had been for Cotton to take the reins. He'd be perfect as director. He had the right temperament, had an uncanny ability to lead, and was totally results-oriented. He was also apolitical, which to her was an absolute prerequisite for the job. He would continue what she started while, at the same time, stamping it with his own unique perspective. Bottom line. She trusted him like no other. But she doubted that would ever happen. He was happy being a bookseller. And she was going to work forever.

Right?

The car eased through a succession of sharp turns, then stopped.

Time to focus. Get in the game.

She popped open the door and stepped out into the night. The two CIA operatives followed suit, each reaching for their weapons. No other cars were around, but their tracking said Cassiopeia's phone was here in Sigtuna. A figure appeared on the street. A hundred feet away. Walking with a familiar gait.

Cassiopeia.

"That one is with me," she said to the two men with guns.

They relaxed, but kept vigilant.

Cassiopeia approached. "Westlake was taken."

"Is Monica Butler-White here?"

"She was, and she confirmed what Westlake told us about the princess. She also said Westlake was innocent, but took him as insurance."

"And the question of the night?"

Cassiopeia shook her head. "I tried but got nothing."

She motioned and the two men headed to check things out. A few moments later they trotted back to the car and reported that there was no one to be found.

She stared up into a sky that was finally surrendering to night.

What a long day.

CHAPTER 43

COTTON COULD SEE THAT IVAN WAS SERIOUS.

This man wanted to defect. But the intelligence officer inside him urged caution. *Take it slow. Sort it through and be sure you're not being used or deceived.*

"The Czechs are playing the game correctly," Ivan said. "They wait until they in control, when they have the thing Sweden wants most, then apply maximum pressure. Moscow pleased by that."

"You mean Franko is pleased?"

"Correct. He encouraged the Czechs. But others do not see it that way. They oppose Franko in all he does. But not in the open. That is fatal."

He fully understood what *that* meant.

"Russia has changed," Ivan said. "I not know it any longer."

Konstantin Franko had definitely altered the landscape. And not for the good. It had once again become an aggressive military state with eyes on its neighbors and the consequences be damned. Repression of political opposition had returned as the norm. In response the West had imposed crippling economic sanctions but Franko remained unfazed. Any dissent was met with violence.

"The world is no longer what Franko thinks it be. He assumes he can do as he wants and that the army can conquer all. But our forces are weak. Disorganized. Putin and Ukraine showed that. Also still poorly led by men loyal to Franko. The best generals, the smart ones, he killed."

They remained within the hangar, alone, the cargo plane still being readied. Odd place to be having this conversation, but he thought it as good as any.

"You are a ranking member of Directorate S," Cotton said. "That's pretty high up the flagpole. You defecting is not going to be taken lightly by your bosses. They will come after you."

"No doubt."

"Do you have a wife? Children?"

Ivan shook his head. "Wife died five years ago. No children or other family for them to hurt. Just me."

Which made things easier. No question.

But it also made him even more suspicious.

Ivan pointed to his balding scalp. "This brain full of information. You can have it. I care not anymore. It is all pointless. Franko has to go."

Okay. So he asked, "Explain to me what is happening here in Sweden."

"That field officer I mentioned, Monica, pitched a plan to S Directorate. The princess for the codex. She and Westlake are close. She said he could deliver the princess and she would, unknowingly, work with us, just like she has for long time. The husband will make that happen. Some of us thought it too much. The risks too many. And all was good as it was. Princess runs in some big circles. Talks to lots of important people. They tell her things. She repeats them to us. You know the game."

That he did. "And you can learn a lot from someone who likes to talk."

"No doubt. She has provided good intel to us. Politicians love to brag. Make people think how important they are. Princess a good listener. No one would ever suspect she is foreign asset, especially since she has no idea she is. So they talk. I was told princess a good asset they want to keep. So the operation was denied. But others, higher in command, approved it. So Monica went ahead."

"Do you know where the princess is being held?"

"I do."

"Providing that location would go a long way toward establishing your credibility."

"I know, and once across that line, no going back."

He told himself to be careful. Defectors nearly always came with "salable stories," the more exclusive, shocking, or emotional the better. They also generally had done their homework and knew what the other side most wanted to hear. Sure, there were ways to confirm any information through cross-examination or by consulting other sources, but those took time. Most did not worry about small factual mistakes, so long as the big picture drew the right amount of attention. Here, Ivan knew what the big picture entailed. But the minutiae were vitally important.

"Getting to princess is but one part of this," Ivan said. "We have to secure codex too."

"Why can't we just let it go to Prague?"

Ivan shook his head. "You not understand. SVR is going to deal with codex. It will never reach that plane out there."

"And Monica and Westlake?"

Ivan shook his head. "They are working both sides. Playing all angles. They have different plans in mind. For them, this is personal."

Which was never a good thing. "Who is killing all the assets?"

"Oligarchs. They sent team here to eliminate SVR people. Will make it harder for them to be caught screwing Franko. Monica has been helping them."

"This is a friggin' three-ring circus."

Ivan chuckled. "Our circus has but one."

"This kind of anarchy is not something often seen within the SVR," he said.

"I suspect that be the whole idea. Stir it all up so much that no one can be blamed."

He was having trouble making an accurate assessment of this supposed defector. His previous dealings with this burly Russian were all dubious. But why would Ivan be lying? For what? To throw them off guard? Send them on a folly that led to nowhere? Possible. But not likely. Still, as someone once told him, life was like a jar of jalapeño peppers. What you ate from that jar today could burn your ass tomorrow.

So be careful.

"You do know I don't have the power to grant you anything?"

"But your old boss does." Ivan pointed to the phone he still held. "Make the call."

He tapped the screen. Stephanie answered quick and said, "I hope you have good news."

"I think I hit the jackpot."

CHAPTER 44

STEPHANIE TRANSFORMED HER HOTEL ROOM INTO A MOBILE COMMAND center. Cotton's call had changed everything. Ivan was in Sweden. She already knew that. Now she knew why. Her Moscow contact had not been wrong when he said this was an unusual situation. *Unprecedented* seemed a better description. Cassiopeia had returned to Stockholm with her, and together they were dealing with the evolving scenario. Sometimes, not often, but sometimes the breaks fell your way.

"We know all about Ivan," Koger said to her from the computer screen. They were on a secure video call. "His name is Dmitry Lut. A seasoned SVR operative who started with the old KGB. He's worked all over the world. And I don't have to tell you that, within the SVR, promotions come solely from longevity and who you know."

She was well versed with the Foreign Intelligence Service, whose focus was beyond Russia's borders. It conducted military, strategic, economic, scientific, and technological espionage in foreign countries. A massive entity. Understanding the SVR, and the role it played in supporting Moscow's geopolitical agendas, allowed for a better understanding of how Russian foreign policy was shaped and executed. So it was watched. Carefully. Every day.

Its list of greatest hits impressive.

Cozy Bear had been a specialized cyber unit within the SVR, responsible for conducting high-profile, state-sponsored internet attacks. Targets had included the 2016 Democratic National Committee, Homeland Security, AT&T, Microsoft, Cisco, and Deloitte. Every Russian sleeper agent around the world was recruited and managed by the SVR. It also worked closely with the Chinese through a secret cooperation treaty. Political assassinations were managed by the SVR, though publicly the Russians claimed no part in any of that. The murder of former acting Chechen President Zelimkhan Yandarbiyev, in Qatar, and the poisoning of FSB-officer-turned-defector Alexander Litvinenko were SVR operations. Disinformation remained an SVR specialty, designed to plant propaganda and fake news across the internet with the aim to promote a positive image of Russia, incite anti-American sentiment, and cause domestic unrest across the globe. Of late, with Franko in power, Russia had been making long-term investments in infiltrating and influencing key geopolitical countries. This was particularly true across the African continent, where Moscow had greatly expanded its presence and reach. Knowing and understanding the SVR was critical. And she also realized a fun fact. Never had the West turned anyone with the standing of Ivan. He could be a game changer.

"Does he have political connections?" Cassiopeia asked.

"Through his dead wife," Koger said. "Her father was high in the Kremlin, close to a lot of people under Putin who have risen to the top of the food chain under Franko."

"Any idea why he would want to defect?" Stephanie asked.

"I get it," Koger said. "I'm suspicious as hell too. It's way too convenient. Right when you need a break, one just drops out of the sky? Even worse, one you already know. It's like a Christmas gift all wrapped up with two big red bows."

"Tell me about it," she said.

"To answer the main questions," Koger said, "Ivan is old school in every way. Which means I doubt he's a Franko fan. Old schoolers hate the new Russia. They long for the Soviets. We get a defector or asylum request nearly every month. We work 'em. Test 'em. And reject ninety-nine percent. But, I will say, this guy is definitely different. He has my attention."

"He told Cotton where the princess is being held," Cassiopeia said.

"Which needs to be verified," Koger noted.

"It's tops on my list," Stephanie said. "He also confirmed that Westlake was the one who drew Princess Lysa into this. We suspected as much. Now we know."

"I don't have to tell you," Koger noted, "that those two things were exactly what we wanted to hear."

"I know," Stephanie said. "But Ivan helped save my butt a few years ago. He was a pain, but he eventually shot straight with us. Let's not judge him until we're sure." She hoped that was not wishful thinking on her part. "They want us to think they have two hostages now. But Westlake could be an active participant. We are going to get to the princess and Westlake. Hopefully, they are being held at the same location. I want them both."

"Who is *we*?" Koger asked.

"Me, Cassiopeia, Cotton, and your two helpers."

"You do know we have trained units on call to handle that."

"The Swedish government does not want an American military presence on its soil. They want us to handle it. Quietly."

"I want Sandra there."

"For what?"

"To keep me posted."

"You don't trust me?" Stephanie asked.

"I don't trust anyone. You do realize the whole thing could be a trap?"

"It's a chance we'll take."

"Let's not include Captain America," Koger said. "He's going to have to deal with Ivan. That man needs a full-time nanny watching him."

She could understand the wisdom in that.

"And he's going to have to deal with that codex," Koger said. "We have to control it to keep all these loose cannons in line. The Swedes, Czechs, and Russians. All of them. Like children in a sandbox, staking out their corners. Some leverage would be nice."

She agreed. "I came to that conclusion hours ago and have it under control."

"Care to explain?"

"Not really."

"Okay. But lockjaw toward people trying to help you is not good."

"I hear you. But I've got this one. It's better you don't know. What does Langley say?"

"They want what the White House wants. Sweden in NATO."

She got it. "They have no idea what's going on here, do they?"

"Not a clue."

She actually liked that. "Let's keep it that way, until we resolve it."

"I've always loved your optimism," Koger said.

And he ended the call.

Cassiopeia stared at her. No words were needed.

Koger had hit the nail right on the head.

"How ironic this is," Stephanie said. "Four hundred and fifty years ago the Swedes invaded Prague and looted the palace, stealing everything. They carted all that booty back to Stockholm. And kept it. Like a big middle finger to the world. Now Sweden's entry into a self-defense pact that could secure its borders and protect its citizens hinges on the return of some of that plunder."

"Throw in the United States and Russia and you have the makings of a total mess," Cassiopeia said.

"I agree. But Ivan may be correct. Something else is also happening here. Something outside of the politics. Ivan said Westlake and Monica were a thing. This could also be personal. Which comes with unpredictability. No matter, we move forward. Cotton will stay with Ivan and deal with the codex. We'll see about the princess and Westlake."

CHAPTER 45

JOHN DABBED A COLD, WET CLOTH TO BOTH SIDES OF HIS HEAD. MONICA had slapped his temples hard enough with the gun that he'd blacked out for a few minutes. They'd carried him from the street in Sigtuna to a waiting boat where, under cover of darkness, they'd sped across Lake Mälaren back to the island where Lysa was being held. Along the way he'd somewhat revived, his head spinning and sore from the two blows.

So far everything was proceeding according to plan. They'd made an attempt on Stephanie Nelle's life on the streets of Stockholm as a way to garner her attention. Then they used Vitt at the circus to establish that he was not part of the SVR—or at least create enough confusion that no one knew for sure—which had allowed him to stay on the inside and steer things along. On the call he'd made outside the Grand Hôtel, Monica had conceived the idea of bringing Vitt to Sigtuna and taking him off the board.

She was anxious. A bit unusual for her. Her oligarch friends wanted the deal with the Czechs to go through. Of course, not a one of them wanted to be openly attached with that effort in any way. *Not a single fingerprint.* So they were doing what they could to disrupt, including murdering active SVR assets. A fine line existed between an oligarch and a Russian mob boss. Money was no object to either one. Morality did not exist with either. And there were absolutely no rules that applied to anything they did.

Like dealing with so many devils all at one time.

The bedroom door opened and Monica stepped inside. "How is your head?"

"You hit me bloody hard," he said from the bathroom.

"It had to be real. You know that."

He had a knot at each temple that was sore to the touch. Monica came close and lightly took the rag from him, rinsing it in fresh cold water from the sink, then gently dabbing the bruises.

"Better?" she asked.

"For someone who can be so brutal when need be, you have a loving touch."

She kissed him softly on the lips.

In the beginning he'd thought of her as just another of his many dalliances, one more woman of little to no consequence, but she'd proved to be much more. When another SVR asset was caught by the Americans and revealed a link into the Swedish royal family, Monica had approached him with an offer. Take the blame and use the estrangement from the royal family as a way to end his marriage. He'd debated going to the authorities and reporting the whole thing, but Lysa would have been ruined.

So he played along.

Lysa was told his self-imposed banishment was to appease Wilhelm, who simply did not care for her husband. She'd not liked her brother's hostile attitude but, characteristically, kept her dislike to herself. It all should have led to a divorce. But Lysa, being the dutiful wife, had told him that was out of the question. She'd turned, like always, to the

Bible. Matthew 19:6. *So they are no longer two, but one flesh. What therefore God Has joined together, let not man separate.* Then 1 Corinthians 7:10–11. *To the married I give this charge: the wife should not separate from her husband, but if she does, she should remain unmarried or else be reconciled to her husband, and the husband should not divorce his wife.* And finally Luke 16:18. *Everyone who divorces his wife and marries another commits adultery, and he who marries a woman divorced from her husband commits adultery.*

Perhaps sage advice two thousand years ago.

But not today.

Lysa had been accommodating and conciliatory. Only she would return to Sweden from time to time. Alone. *We can live a wonderful life in England.* So he'd accepted the new reality of making money and having a Russian consort. The Swedes and Americans had been stymied regarding him, without proof. Then Wilhelm stepped in and demanded a secret resolution. Which happened. He was not prosecuted and Lysa kept listening and gossiping and talking, no one suspecting her of a thing.

"You do know, *Tomte*," Monica said, with a smile, "after today, we will be making some needed adjustments in our relationship."

"I was unaware of that."

She softly pressed the cold cloth to left side of his head and held it there. "Where before I tolerated your incessant need for sexual variety, that will no longer be the case. I will be more than enough woman for you."

"I never knew you to be the jealous type. And does this new rule apply both ways?"

"I have decided to devote myself to you alone. What about you?"

He did not immediately answer her.

She pressed the cloth hard into the knot on his head.

He winced in pain. "Okay. Just kidding with you. Of course, I shall do the same. You and you alone. This *tomte* is in total agreement."

She went back to softly dabbing his head. "I need to tell you some new information. We have an SVR operative here, in Sweden, who has made unauthorized contact with the Americans. My superiors fear that he may be defecting."

"That sounds serious."

"It is. The SVR does not tolerate traitors. They want him dead. But this defector could prove useful to us."

"What do you have in mind?" he asked her.

"I may be able to assist Moscow in finding this defector. That will not go unrewarded."

"And the codex?"

"I can help them with that too."

He caught the glint in her green eyes. "You have a source?"

"I do, which should be able to provide us a way to exit this scenario in one piece."

He was concerned. "Is where we are located now compromised by the defector?"

She shook her head. "I rented this on my own. It has no connection to Moscow. Just you, me, and the three men we have here know this place."

Good to hear.

She stopped applying the cold rag. "That leaves us with just one other issue to deal with."

He knew.

"Your wife is upstairs taking a bath. She expects you to arrive here soon. We both knew when this started what the end result would be. How we got there? That was flexible. But the end? That was a given. We are now at the end."

Yes, they were.

CHAPTER 46

MARK NELLE OPENED HIS EYES.

He was no longer eight thousand feet high in the French Pyrenees, wearing spike shoes and carrying a pick, hiking a rough trail. He was inside a room of stone and wood with a blackened beamed ceiling. The man standing over him was tall and gaunt with gray fuzz for hair and a silver beard as thick as fleece. The man's eyes were a peculiar shade of violet that he could not recall ever having seen before.

"Careful," the man said in English. "You're still weak."

"Where am I?"

"A place that has been for centuries one of safety."

"Does it have a name?"

"Abbey des Fontaines."

"That's miles from where I was."

"Two of my subordinates were following you and made a rescue when the snow began to engulf you. I am told the avalanche was quite intense."

He could still feel the mountain as it shook, its summit disintegrating like a great cathedral falling apart. An entire ridge had shattered above him, and snow had poured down as blood would from an open wound. The chill still gripped his bones. Then he recalled tumbling downward. But had he heard the man standing over him right?

"Men were following me?"

"I ordered it. As with your father before you, sometimes."

"You knew my father?"

"His theories always interested me. So I made a point to know both him and what he knew."

He tried to sit up from the bed, but his right side jarred with electric pain. He winced and clutched at his stomach.

"You have broken ribs. I too broke mine once, in youth. It hurts."

He'd noticed the white cassock and rope sandals. "This is a monastery?"

"It is the place you have been seeking."

He was unsure how to respond.

"I am master of the Poor Fellow-Soldiers of Christ and the Temple of Solomon. We are the Templars. Your father sought us for decades. You too have sought us. So I decided the time was finally right."

"For what?"

"That is for you to decide. But I am hoping you choose to join us."

"Why would I do that?"

"Your life is, I am sorry to say, in utter chaos. You miss your father more than you could ever voice and he has been dead a long six years now. You are estranged from your mother, which is difficult in more ways than can be imagined. Professionally, you are not satisfied. You have made some attempts to vindicate your father's unconventional beliefs, but have been unable to make much progress."

"What do you know of my father and mother?"

"I know much."

Stephanie recalled what Mark had told both her and Cotton all those years ago. A lot of unique information. Things she'd never known. A hesitant thought—what was said after he finished—crept into her mind.

As painful now as then.

"I stayed in a bed for three weeks," Mark said, "recovering from the avalanche. After, my movements were restricted to certain parts of the abbey, but the master and I spoke often. Finally, I agreed to stay on and took the oath."

"Why would you do such a thing?" Stephanie asked.

"Let's be realistic, Mother. You and I had not spoken in years. Dad was gone. The master was right. I was at a dead end. What I sought was there. So the master became a father to me. He was a kind, gentle man, full of compassion."

She caught the message. "Unlike me?"

"Now is not the time for this discussion."

"When would be a good time? I thought you were dead, Mark. But you were secluded in an abbey. You are as bad as your father."

"That's your problem," Mark said. "You never knew anything about what Dad thought. You believed everything he sought was a fantasy, that he was wasting his talents. You never loved him enough to let him be himself. You thought he sought fame and treasure. No. He sought truth. Christ has died. Christ has risen. Christ will come again. That's what interested him."

Stephanie collected her scattered senses and told herself not to react to the rebuke.

"Dad was a serious academician. His work had merit, he just never talked openly about what he really sought. People enjoyed reading about it in his books regardless of the embellishments. You were one of the few who didn't."

"Your father never found a thing. Never proved a thing. He only speculated what might be out there. Regardless, he and I tried to work through our differences."

"How? By you telling him he was wasting his life, hurting his family? By telling him he was a failure?"

"All right, dammit, I was wrong." Her voice was a shout. "You want me to say it again? I was wrong. I screwed up. Is that what you want to hear? In my mind, you've been dead five years. Now here you are, and all you want is for me to admit I was wrong. Fine. If I could tell your father that, I would. If I could beg his forgiveness, I would. But I can't."

The words were coming fast, emotion charging her, and she intended to say it all while she possessed the courage.

"I came here to see what I could do. To try to follow through on whatever your father and you thought important. That's the only reason I came. I thought I was finally doing the right thing. But don't shoot that sanctimonious crap at me anymore. You screwed up too."

She slumped back in the chair and realized the gulf between them had just widened.

A shudder passed through her.

Thankfully, they'd bridged that gap and created a second chance for them both. Her husband was gone. But her son was alive and well.

She sat alone in her hotel room, working the problem, everything funneling through her as the decision maker. With little to do at the moment, her mind had drifted to Mark. As it had more and more of late. Was that a sign of age? Maybe. She definitely needed to spend more time with her son. That second chance they'd both been offered had proved rewarding. No sense allowing anything to lapse. He was a good man, doing good things, and she was proud of him. She just needed to say that out loud a little more. Too often work and responsibility took precedence. If she retired, then that would not be the case. Another good argument for walking away.

But not at the moment.

She'd briefed the prime minister, who was keeping the king informed. The Swedes were allowing her to handle the matter. And she was doing just that. So far everything had been contained and they wanted to keep it that way.

She would be sixty-nine on her next birthday. She'd failed as a wife but had been granted a reprieve as a mother. How was she as a girlfriend? Hard to say. But Danny never complained. He was so different from Lars. But she was older now. More seasoned. Experienced. She'd dealt with so much. Presidents had trusted her with the most sensitive of problems. And she'd delivered, time and again. The cost? A husband, family, and, for a while, a son. Love? Companionship? Definitely.

Maybe it was indeed time to walk away.

And consider herself.

For once.

CHAPTER 47

Lysa lay in the marble tub and enjoyed the warm water. She'd found some expensive bath salts in the cabinet, which made the experience that much more satisfying. Thank goodness Monica had made the suggestion.

The bathroom was nothing special. But the tub. That was something else entirely. A solid piece of Carrara marble fashioned in the Roman style. Deep. Long. Like a miniature pool with enough wonderful hot water to submerge herself in. She was accustomed to luxury and pampering. After all, she was a royal princess. Their country estate in England was a seventeenth-century lodge that John had converted into a comfortable residence with a dozen bedrooms and even more baths. They loved to entertain and a constant stream of guests filtered in and out all through the year, especially during hunting season. John loved to hunt. And she enjoyed indulging him.

The hour was approaching midnight, but she was not tired. She'd always preferred late night to early morning. She seemed to come alive after the sun set. John was the opposite. But they both recognized the other's preference and worked around it, neither of them complaining. In fact, John never complained. Sure, they had disagreements. What married couple didn't? But rarely had they openly argued and never had they gone to bed angry. She was lucky to have a man like John. He was a mature adult, not intimidated by her royal status. Many of her friends were not as fortunate, their marriages unhappy unions with unfulfilled men. She'd listened to their endless list of things they did not like about their husbands. Adultery seemed rampant. She could not imagine how a husband could disrespect a wife in such a way. Thankfully, infidelity had never been an issue with them.

She settled into the steamy, sudsy water, her breath catching in hitches. A hint of a smile played at the corners of her lips as she bottomed out in the water. Towels hung from nearby ivory rods, ready for her use. A Bible verse occurred to her. *For all that is in the world—the desires of the flesh and the desires of the eyes and pride of life—is not from the Father, but is from the world.*

1 John 2:16.

So true.

She heard the bedroom door open, then close. Odd. Footsteps echoed across the hardwood floor. The bathroom door hung about three-quarters of the way open.

Who was this?

JOHN PUSHED THE BATHROOM DOOR OPEN.

Lysa lay inside a large tub, facing away from the door, the water clouded and bubbly. She turned her head, and he caught the relief on her face. Her hair was pulled back into a ponytail, the face still made up as if she were about to leave for the night.

"Darling," she said. "It is so good to see you."

He entered, approached the tub, bent down, and kissed her forehead. He knew the rules. Nothing on the lips was ever allowed once lipstick was there, though he wondered if that rule applied when taking a bath. This was the first time he'd ever approached her while she lay in a tub. More of her rules. Bathing was not something for husbands to see. The soapy water concealed her nakedness, and he could tell she was uncomfortable with the situation. Lysa had always been extremely modest. They'd dressed separately for years in their own bathrooms and closets.

"I was told you were here," he said.

"What happened to your head?" she asked, noticing the two welts.

"I am afraid I was a bit clumsy and lost my footing. I fell down a few stairs."

"Were you hurt?"

He heard the concern in her voice.

"Just my pride. This is a bit unusual for you. A bath so late at night."

"It was hard to resist this lovely tub. Is your business concluded?"

He knelt down close to her head. "Things are moving faster. By morning it will be finished."

"That is so good to hear. Perhaps we could have a late snack or meal? Could you ask them to prepare something?"

"Absolutely. I want you to know that I could not have done any of this without you."

"How lovely for you to say. It is the least I could do. After all, I do not get many opportunities to help with your business. Though I have no idea what exactly is going on."

She'd flown privately from England to Stockholm four days ago on a previously scheduled visit and followed his directions to the letter, cooperating with the staged kidnapping, even allowing her precious dog to participate. That animal went with her wherever she traveled and ate better than most humans on the planet. She'd named her Christina, after the Swedish queen from the seventeenth century, a personal favorite of Lysa's. Monica had been there to make sure the dog was returned to the apartment safely. That had been the one condition Lysa had imposed.

"I will explain it all to you over our meal," he said to her.

He studied her in the water. There was no denying that his wife was still an attractive woman. She'd aged beautifully. He read once that, contrary to popular belief, older people were happier and more romantically attached than their younger counterparts. What was the saying? *One is never too old to yearn.* So true. Hence the reason for his periodic affairs and his relationship with Monica. Nothing wrong with his libido. Did happiness and romance decline with age? For him it seemed the exact opposite.

Of late, as he began to realize that his years were numbered and he was now on the downside of life, his perspective had changed. The present became vitally important. No way he was going to allow maturity to run counter to novelty or excitement. But the past nine years, being a pariah at the Swedish royal court, regarded secretly as suspect and untrustworthy by various intelligence agencies, had taken a toll. As the Rolling Stones said, *You can't always get what you want but, if you try sometimes, you just might find, you get what you need.*

And what did he need?

Freedom.

And to worry less. To be optimistic. Harbor positive illusions. He thought of himself as a rich man among peasants, seeking solace. Both he and Lysa existed within defined social networks. True, he had many business associates, but precious few close friends. You would think that would mean, as their outer horizons decreased, they would deepen their own private relationship. But that never happened.

Just the opposite occurred.

Yes, they were friendly and respectful toward each other. Mainly thanks to him, as he'd learned long ago that arguing with her was counterproductive. He'd read once that, over time, people became accustomed to their spouse's negative traits. They learned to live with them while minimizing any harmful impact. Supposedly, when you realized that your time on this earth was running out, your alternatives decreasing, you were more likely to accept limitations and not pursue other more attractive options. Not him. He was rich and in good health. His life seemed an endless realm of possibilities.

And choices.

There were many positives about Lysa. She was an excellent companion for any party or event. Popular, well liked, respected. And she loved him. No. She worshiped him.

But the negatives. Oh, the negatives.

Her aloofness. Formalities. Lack of sexuality. The illogical dependence on religion. And the immaturity. That had become the most tiresome. Life was like a fairy tale to her. Understandable since she'd been born a princess and constantly pampered. Monica had told him that the SVR considered Lysa a valuable asset. One of their so-called level five covert sources. Sporadic, for sure, as the intelligence had to come to her as opposed to the other way around, and she took effort to maintain, but they were patient.

His patience, though, had run out.

Like Monica had said.

Time for this to end.

Behind Lysa he caught movement at the doorway. Monica. Who'd quietly entered the bedchamber when he had, staying outside for a few moments. Waiting. He gently ruffled the top of the water, the ripples masking Monica's approach across the tile.

"Now, John, you know better," Lysa said. "Let me finish my bath. You wait outside."

He ignored her plea, kissed her on the forehead, and said, "Forgive me."

"For what?"

Monica pressed her hands onto the top of Lysa's head, forcing her under the water. The tub was over half a meter deep, more than enough water to keep the head fully submerged. Her arms flailed. One hand found Monica's right arm and locked in a vise grip. Water poured out over the top edges, soaking the bathroom tiles. He stepped back, horrified at the sight but doing nothing to stop it. Lysa's feet came out of the water, her legs thrashing. Monica did not allow any opportunity for a breath to be grabbed. Lysa kept fighting. Longer than he'd anticipated.

He shut his eyes to the horror.

Then all movement stopped.

Nothing at all.

He opened his eyes.

Monica did not release her clampdown on the head. The limp arms and legs relaxed atop the edge of the tub. The soapy water remained agitated but continued to shield Lysa's nakedness. A part of him wanted to rush to her aid, yank her from the water, and revive her. But another part wanted her gone. Monica kept the head submerged a few more moments.

Then released.

Lysa lay still in the water. Monica lifted the head clear. The eyes were closed. Mouth open.

He stared at the dead face.

Finally. He was a widower.

CHAPTER 48

Cotton had always been a planner. There were those who flew by the seat of their pants, making it up as they went. And those who meticulously thought through every detail of an operation before acting.

Pantsers and planners.

Truth be told, he was a little of both, and the older he got, the more of a pantser he'd become. That was probably thanks to his early retirement from the Magellan Billet and the fact that trouble found him at the oddest times with little to no warning and no time to plan.

But here? He had the time.

So use it.

Ivan had told him all about the ongoing operation here in Sweden, spearheaded by Monica Butler-White. He'd also told him about a physical relationship between that woman and John Westlake, one the SVR had only recently discovered. But Cassiopeia had reported that Westlake had been beaten, then taken. Was that for real? Or just part of the show? What Monica would do next was the question. Ivan had provided the locations of all the SVR safe houses in Stockholm and its environs. Assets had been dispatched by Koger, and they were searching. One of them contained the princess. Finding her remained the top priority, and Cassiopeia was working that angle.

His job?

Deal with Ivan, who was the precise definition of a loose cannon on deck. The Swedes were determined now, more than ever, to make the deal with the Czechs. They'd agreed to wait until morning to make the transfer of the codex, providing a little more time to sort through things.

But there were two problems.

First, Stephanie was flying blind. Sure, she had Koger's help, but that was all unofficial. Neither the State Department nor Justice was involved, and no one at the White House had any idea what was happening. So command decisions were being made here, in a vacuum. Second was the Codex Gigas or, its more appropriate name given the circumstances, the Devil's Bible. The Swedes, the Czechs, and the Russians all wanted it, just for vastly different reasons.

"One thing is clear," Stephanie said. "We need to control that book. It's the only way we're going to be able to ensure things happen."

"You have a plan?"

"I do. I've arranged for you to fly the charter plane south. The Swedes liked the idea of us taking on that task. Keeps them more out of the mix."

"And Ivan?"

"I never mentioned him to the Swedes. I doubt they would care. But he goes with you. Get him out of here in one piece."

"You have a plan for that too?"

"Don't I always. But—"

"You need some deniability."

"Something like that."

"And you also think bringing Ivan home and turning him our way will forgive all?"

"Seems like a good bet."

But he wasn't so sure.

"Can this be done?" Ivan asked him.

They were back at Cotton's hotel, safe in his room.

He nodded. "It can. All we have to do is get in the air. Once up we'll go south, but not to Prague. We'll divert to Ramstein Air Force Base in Germany. That's U.S. soil."

A secure location.

In southwestern Germany. Headquarters for the United States Air Forces in Europe and NATO Allied Air Command. Over sixteen thousand military personnel, civilians, and contractors. Plenty of protection for the Devil's Bible.

And Ivan.

"What happens before we get in the air?" Ivan asked.

"That's the tricky part."

CHAPTER 49

JOHN WAITED ABOUT TWO HUNDRED METERS FROM THE HOUSE where Lysa had been held, enjoying the anonymity of darkness. The light of a lopsided moon dominated the heavens. Crickets filled the silence, throbbing in their own language. Monica stood beside him. They'd crossed the point of no return. The only path now was forward.

"Will they come?" he asked her.

"No doubt."

"How will they know where to come?"

"The defector will lead them, and I'll provide a beacon."

"Have you always been so ruthless?"

"I like to think of it as organized and efficient, without remorse."

He chuckled. "I have never heard it described that way before."

They'd left Lysa in the bathtub. No need to move her. Monica had dealt with the men on station in the house. Two downstairs, one up. Three bullets had taken care of the problem, all three bodies still lying where they fell.

Everything was so upside down.

Back in the 1960s people mainlined acid to make the world weird. Now the world *was* weird and people abused drugs to make it normal. So much had happened. He'd witnessed a lot. Been a party to a lot. But he'd come to wonder if anything was real anymore. Lysa's father, the former king of Sweden, had been an ardent anti-communist, opposed to anything and everything related to the old Soviet Union. He'd been highly outspoken about the evil of their hostile neighbor. That was back when Finland walked a fine line, officially embracing neutrality, but also avoiding any rhetoric or policy that could be interpreted as anti-Soviet. Now Finland was all in with the West, a member of NATO, no ties with Russia.

But it remained high on Moscow's interest list.

At last year's Nobel laureate dinner Lysa had an enlightened conversation with the Finnish president, one she'd told him all about, which he'd reported to Monica. Finland had the longest border with Russia of any NATO or European Union country. Its level of military preparedness was unequaled in the Western world. The president that night had felt comfortable in telling her that Finland had begun storing military equipment outside its borders, in both Sweden and Norway. They'd also finalized more than a thousand agreements with private companies to provide equipment and services in case of war. The president had said that the nation had stockpiles of at least six months' worth of major fuels and grains, and enough air shelters for its entire population. Almost a third of Finland's adult population were reservists, giving the country about five and a half million soldiers, one of the largest militaries in Europe.

That was precisely the kind of information someone in Lysa's position could easily obtain without raising a shred of suspicion.

Would Lysa's father be ashamed of her naïveté? Absolutely. But that old man had been another arrogant misogynist who inherited a title that he did nothing with. Kings possessed no power? That was wrong. Kings had the people, and the people had power. You just needed to know how and when to use it.

As with what just happened to Lysa.

He'd callously watched while his wife was murdered. Any regrets? Maybe a few. But he'd get over them. His marriage had ended long ago. The only person unaware of that fact had been his wife. Further, he could not care less if Sweden made it into NATO. The Devil's Bible? Burn it. Who cared? Politics and history held little interest, except when it affected his life or his business.

Which was the case here.

Damn Swedes.

They'd done nothing but antagonize.

The government had already agreed to serve as "host nation" to NATO forces without any official membership, a move that had infuriated Franko. In response there'd been a growing encroachment by Russian forces toward both Sweden and Finland, including a much-publicized mock air attack on Stockholm by Russian warplanes. A message? Definitely. Monica had told him that Sweden had also became the target of an internet disinformation campaign aimed at sowing domestic discord, fostering suspicion of NATO, and stanching criticism of Russia. Many fake news stories were generated. Forged documents circulated. In response conscription was reinstated by Sweden to bolster the army. A never-ending cycle of move, then countermove.

Like his own life.

At this point the Americans believed he was being held against his will. But he would reemerge. The death of his wife? That would be chalked up to the Russians. Moscow would deny everything, which would only bolster their guilt in the eyes of the West. And with Lysa dead there would be no worry about what she might say. That voice had been silenced. No more problems for him or the SVR. The Swedes? They would pin it all on Moscow but, sadly for them, there would be no proof. Not a single piece of evidence. And witnesses? All of the local SVR operatives involved had been killed, as had their help in the house. Monica had seen to that.

No one was left.

Wilhelm would be forced to handle his sister's demise in the same manner he'd handled John's supposed treason. Quickly and quietly. Everything should work.

Just one more thing.

Monica tapped her phone and sent a signal to a package she'd left behind at the house, attached to a large external propane tank.

A second later the house exploded.

CHAPTER 50

Wednesday, July 9
3:35 a.m.

Cassiopeia climbed from the boat cradling an assault rifle that had been provided by the Swedish military. She was followed by the two agents Koger had supplied, both also toting sound-suppressed rifles. All three wore military-grade Kevlar vests. A report had come in about an hour ago of an explosion and a building on fire. Lake Mälaren was huge, spanning about one hundred kilometers from east to west. Once its calm waters were the most efficient way to get around, so castles sprang up across the countless islands that became centers of royal dominion. Björkö Island lay toward the center of the lake, its landscape a combination of pine-clad rocky hills and moraine ridges dotted with fields and deciduous trees, mainly tall, bushy oaks. It stretched about three and a half kilometers wide and two kilometers long. The highest spot, about fifty meters above sea level, provided a great view of the lake and contained a former ancestral country estate.

Which was burning.

She led the way from the dock, plunged into the trees, and started up a mild incline toward the house. She'd been briefed on the locale. No full-time residents. The island privately owned. Used as a hunting and fishing retreat. The first building was erected in the fourteenth century. A fortified castle. It changed hands a number of times until the fifteenth century, when the Carthusian monks took title and made it a monastery. King Gustav Vasa confiscated the property in the sixteenth century and tore down the old stronghold, building a château that royalty enjoyed until the beginning of the twentieth century when it was bought privately. Currently, title was held by a Swedish national who resided in northern France. It was also on the list of sites Ivan had provided to Cotton.

She caught sight of the château.

Firefighters had arrived. Two pumper boats were anchored close to shore, but the house was too far inland for any water to reach. The structure itself was nearly gone. By all accounts the explosion occurred about ninety minutes ago. She'd been told the house was a couple of hundred years old, built of wood, which had burned fast.

Not much was left.

A group of firemen watched the smoldering ruins from a distance. Flames still lit up the night, consuming the last bits of fuel. She approached and introduced herself. Stephanie had worked through the prime minister's office and made sure the firemen knew to expect her.

"These old places were built solid," the man in charge said. "It will be a few days before this fully extinguishes. We will be here to make sure nothing spreads to the forest. But there is something you need to see."

She followed the man toward the conflagration, feeling the heat from the steaming embers. The two men who'd come with her stayed back and kept an eye on the situation. A three-story building that had survived the centuries was gone. Its footprint remained, along with piles of smoldering rubble.

"We found three male bodies," the fireman said. "Burned to a char. But toward the back we discovered something else."

They rounded the site to the rear where the house had collapsed down onto itself, much of it still burning, though the flames seemed to be receding. At ground level was what had once been the kitchen. Appliances and a refrigerator could be seen. Along with what appeared to be a large stone tub.

"It is marble and heavy. It sat on one of the upper floors but ended here after they collapsed. Incredibly, it fell straight down and did not flip over. The worst of the flames seem to have spared it."

She wondered what this was about.

The man led the way into the rubble. She followed. He clicked on a flashlight and illuminated inside the tub. She saw a body. A woman. Naked. Had she been taking a bath? Older. Her arms and legs had sustained burns, along with her torso. But the fireman had been right. The tub had apparently shielded the corpse from the worst.

She found her phone and typed in Princess Lysa's name, then clicked on IMAGES. Many pictures appeared on her screen of the princess in various poses and places.

Her skin pimpled into gooseflesh.

No mistake.

The corpse seemed reasonably intact. Like a message from the dead. Surely the idea had been to eliminate any trace of what might have happened here. On that count the effort had failed. She tapped her phone screen again a few times, then brought the unit to her ear and stepped away from the fire, walking toward the trees for privacy.

"I found the princess," she told Stephanie. "She's dead."

"Any indication as to how?"

"She was naked inside a tub, in the house that exploded. I'm not sure what conclusions can be drawn from that. The body is partially burned, but there was no sign of any bullet holes or knife stabs."

"Collect the body and bring it back. Keep things contained. I'll make sure the firemen at the scene are not a problem. I'll have an ambulance waiting when you get back. We need an autopsy."

"Got it."

"Everything just changed," Stephanie said.

"That's an understatement."

"Get back here. Fast."

CHAPTER 51

6:40 A.M.

STEPHANIE HAD TRIED TO REST, BUT SLEEP HAD PROVEN ELUSIVE. Instead she'd lain in bed and considered all the possibilities. Princess Lysa was dead. Had she been murdered? Impossible to say at this point. More than likely, yes. Cassiopeia had returned with the body, which was now at a Swedish military base being autopsied. That seemed the best way to keep everything contained. The firemen at the scene of the explosion had been sworn to secrecy. They knew there was a body, just not who.

And they'd only need a few more hours.

Why had the house exploded? The preliminary indications pointed to a propane tank. An accident? Or intentional. Impossible to say. That was being actively investigated by fire officials and the local police, given four bodies had been found in the ruins.

She ran through the list of players.

Princess Lysa. Dead by some unknown means. Was she an SVR asset? It appeared so, confirmed by not only Ivan but in Sigtuna by Monica Butler-White, who openly assaulted John Westlake. Had

Westlake been a spy? Probably, or at least a suspect, given his connections to Monica. Then there was Ivan, Dimitry Lut, who had interjected himself into the mix, demanding asylum. Was that real? Or another SVR ploy? No way to pass judgment on that point as yet.

The king was going to have to be informed. She was not looking forward to that task. The prime minister had been told about the body, but she agreed to keep that to herself until the cause of death was determined. Medical officials at the base had said they should know something more definitive in the next couple of hours. All in all a terrible situation. But she was at a loss as to what she could have done differently.

A knock came to the hotel room door.

A bit early for visitors. Only Cotton and Cassiopeia knew where she was staying. Cotton was off with Ivan. Cassiopeia with the princess' corpse. She rose from the bed, still dressed in yesterday's clothes, and approached the door, stealing a quick peek through the peephole.

Really? She opened the door.

"You look like crap," Derrick Koger said.

"And it's good to see you too. To what do I owe the honor of your presence?" She made no effort to hide her sarcasm. "At such an early hour."

Koger pointed. "We have a problem."

And him being here added one huge exclamation point to that observation. So she gestured for him to come in and closed the door.

"Are you watching me?" she asked, wanting to know how she was found.

"My people know how to find somebody."

Koger looked the same. Tall, with sparse ash-blond hair and candid brown eyes topped by bushy, almost amused, eyebrows. His midsection, which once toted a bit of a beer gut, was gone. He'd definitely slimmed down. She pointed. "You lose that belly on your own?"

"I did it the old-fashioned way." He flashed a cheeky smile and held out both arms in a mock welcome embrace. "The agency's European station chief needs to look his best."

She shook her head. "Like you care what anyone thinks."

"I care what you think."

That comment caught her off guard. Then it hit her. "Danny called you."

"I cannot confirm or deny that allegation. But I thought it necessary to put in a personal appearance."

"After the junior senator from Tennessee told you to get off your butt and come here?"

"I will say that instruction was not appreciated."

Just like she thought. She and Danny were going to have a serious conversation as soon as all this was over.

"Since you seem to be Johnny-on-the-spot," she said, "are you briefed on all that's happened in the past few hours?"

"Why don't you enlighten me."

And she told him what they'd discovered, then asked, "Why has the European station chief come here? It's not because a former president asked you to." Then it hit her. "Dmitry Lut."

Koger shook his head. "That's your problem. But the Russians know he's defecting."

Concerning. But not unexpected. "Are they making a move?"

"We're not sure. But they definitely know. Ivan left Moscow unexpectedly and without permission. I don't have all the details, but apparently he's been suspect for some time. A hanger-on, if you know what I mean. His inside track died with his father-in-law years ago. We suspect they are going to make a play on the Devil's Bible today, during transport, then take Ivan down."

"You have intel on that?"

He pointed to his belly. "Right here. In my gut. They're going to try and take that book. Count on it."

"I am, actually, counting on just that."

"I told Danny that you were way ahead of us."

She was still perplexed, though. "This whole thing makes little sense. Why kill the princess before the deadline expires? It seems like there are two different things happening here, neither of which relates to the other."

"I agree. The Russians have one objective. Monica Butler-White and John Westlake have another. I talked with an analyst who specializes in Monica Butler-White. She has quite a record. An experienced field operative. So they had a lovers spat? Right in front of Cassiopeia, after specifically asking for Cassiopeia to be brought there? A little much, don't you think?"

She agreed. "Monica has to be running the whole thing. First she kills the old man Cotton found. Then takes out those sleepers at the law office, who most likely had been working with her. Finally, she kills Princess Lysa and all the men there, then torches the evidence. Everything is gone. Which makes it easy to blame it all on the SVR. Who will, absolutely, deny the allegations, which only makes them look more guilty."

"But you have a body, which they did not count on."

"A lot of good it does us. We just know she died, not why or by whom."

"The Devil's Bible is not all that important anymore, though the SVR hasn't forgotten about it. But what they really want is Ivan dead."

She understood. Completely. Still, "You said we have a problem."

"I need to run a canary trap."

She was surprised. "You have a security leak?"

He nodded. "One I inherited from my predecessor who was too blind to take a good look. I've been looking at this carefully."

She wanted to know, "Your security leak and what's happening here are related?"

"I'm about to make them related. Give a person a fish and you feed them for the day. Teach a person to use the internet and they won't bother you for weeks, months, maybe years."

She smiled. "And the relevance of that wonderful piece of wisdom?"

"We need to keep the other side busy. Do you think the SVR has the national library under watch?"

"I hope so."

A gleam came into the big man's eyes. "I knew you were way ahead of them. Two great minds, thinking alike. We need to bring them, and my mole, out into the open. But to do that we're going to need Cotton's help." He paused. "Big time."

She caught the use of a name instead of a catchy label like Captain America. "That sounds both serious and extremely dangerous."

"It is."

CHAPTER 52

JOHN LIKED BEING OUT OF THE LINE OF FIRE.

If but for a short while.

He and Monica had fled Björkö Island. They were now kilometers away, at a new location on Lake Mälaren, where they could rest and ready themselves for the final push.

"Pass me the berries," Monica said to him.

The time was approaching 7:30 A.M. They were enjoying breakfast, Swedish-style. Yogurt, boiled eggs, oatmeal, crispbread, fruit, and smoked sausages. Surprisingly, he was hungry.

Success had that effect on him.

Months ago Wilhelm had confided in Lysa, telling her about the deal the government made with the Czechs, thinking the secret safe within the family. The king had not been happy about losing the Codex Gigas, which he considered Crown property as it had been his ancestor, Queen Christina, who'd secured its possession. But as was customary, he'd kept his objections to himself, realizing that he had no real say in the matter. John told Monica, who reported the matter and gained approval for a limited operation. Monica had conceived the idea of a "kidnapping," using Lysa as bait. His job? Convince Lysa to participate while revealing nothing about the true objective. She would be kept in isolation the whole time to prevent her from learning more. Lysa had been thrilled to help, especially since he'd convinced her they were working together on something important for his business. Thankfully, Lysa was completely self-absorbed, thinking their marriage the perfect union. He'd fed that illusion by essentially doing and giving her anything she wanted. Nothing at all to indicate any problems. Divorce was definitely out of the question. Too much involved. A lot of exposure. So Monica developed a plan to use the "kidnapping" operation to rid himself of a wife. The explosion should wipe away any and all evidence that might have existed. The trail should grow cold fast.

He handed her the bowl of berries.

Her phone rang and she answered the call instead of taking the food. He held the bowl and watched as she listened to what was being said. Then she said a few words in Russian and ended the call.

He knew better than to ask. But she offered, "I have learned some particularly pertinent information. Something Moscow does not know, but desperately wants to."

"And how is that relevant to us?"

"It will be our ticket out."

He liked what he was hearing and gestured with the bowl. "Still want those berries?"

COTTON WATCHED AS THE WOODEN CRATE WAS LOADED INTO THE rear of a dark Mercedes van. The vehicle was nondescript and unassuming, perfect to blend in with other traffic headed for the airport. Cassiopeia would be driving. He'd ride shotgun. The plan, as explained to the library staff, was that at the airport the crate would be loaded onto a chartered EMB 120FC, and Cotton would fly the turboprop south to Prague.

"You got this?" Stephanie asked.

They stood on the loading dock outside the national library.

Stephanie said, "It's a forty-minute drive and early in the day. I was told traffic should be light heading out of the city."

"Are you sure this is a good idea?"

"It's the only play we have."

"And the king?"

"He hasn't been told that his sister is dead. We are going to wait until the codex is in the air before informing him."

"And when the Swedes realize you double-crossed them?" he asked.

"It's going to be a problem."

"The White House is not going to be happy either. Sweden is an ally."

"They'll get over it," she said. "At least this way we'll have control. Fox will love that. And the Russians will be out of the picture. We, of course, have no definitive proof the princess was murdered, much less by the SVR. The preliminary autopsy report was inconclusive. No evidence of foul play. The fire masked a lot of markers."

"That's a problem."

"I can't help but think that her body surviving the explosion was a mistake. But it may not be one we can capitalize on." She paused. "We will eventually complete the deal and make the Swedes and the Czechs happy. So that should get us out of the doghouse."

Cassiopeia walked over. "You ready?"

"Always," he told her with a smile.

"Calm down, big boy."

"The question is, are *you* ready?"

"Sleep is really underrated."

He faced Stephanie. "Are my toys inside?"

She nodded. "Just as requested."

"Nice to have friends in high places."

"Even better to have friends willing to put their butts on the line, just to prove a point," Stephanie said.

He knew what she meant. He'd listened as Stephanie had told him everything Koger had said, or at least everything she'd deemed necessary to share. Koger had a problem and a plan. Granted, it was a big ask. Tons of risk. But that could be the shorthand description of Cotton's entire life, from the navy to the Magellan Billet and then into a supposed retirement. His answer, though, to the original question—*are you ready*—was never in doubt. "We've got this."

"You always say that," Stephanie said.

"I always mean it."

The attendants finished loading the crate into the van and strapping it in with adjustable nylon belts.

"Koger's right," he whispered to her. "This is the only way." One thing, though. "For this to work there have to be SVR eyes and ears here."

"I've made no effort to keep any of this secret."

"Let's hope they see, hear, and report," he said.

"It's not going to work unless they do. Be careful. This could get real, real tricky."

"Thankfully I've become quite the pantser when it comes to planning."

He was making light of what was definitely a dangerous situation. It was never fun being the fox in the hunt. But at least he and Cassiopeia knew the hunters were coming. He'd given her a choice as to whether to participate. *It's your call.* But her answer was never in doubt. *Where you go, I go.*

He motioned and Cassiopeia headed for the driver's side. He hopped into the van's passenger seat as the rear doors were slammed shut.

"Okay," he said. "Let's do it."

CHAPTER 53

STEPHANIE FOCUSED ON THE VAN UNTIL IT DISAPPEARED AROUND A corner. The staff and some of the curators joined her on the library's loading dock. They'd all worked hard to get the crate safely inside the van, their task over. It would be up to Cotton and Cassiopeia now. She said her goodbyes and headed back through the main building and out the front door. The weather today was much better than yesterday, the sky overcast but lacking rain clouds. The temperature felt like Atlanta in the fall, but she realized that heat and humidity were not so common this far north. She didn't like sending Cotton and Cassiopeia directly into the line of fire. They both meant the world to her. If anything happened to either one, she would never forgive herself. True, she was an experienced professional and dealt with life and death daily.

But this was different. They were rolling some really dangerous dice.

All she could do now was wait.

She checked her phone. Earlier, she'd received a text from her son. That was their main form of communication considering the differing time zones in which each of them lived. She was generally a twenty-four-hour-a-day person, her job literally never ending. Mark lived in a cloister monastery that adhered to strict religious rule. Though he was in charge of the facility, he too had to adhere to the same regulations that governed all of the other brothers. Texting seemed the easiest and quickest way to stay connected. His message had confirmed that she was welcome to visit the monastery in a few weeks. They'd been talking about a face-to-face, which they hadn't managed in a while. She'd quickly replied and said she would be there. But his reply surprised her. He'd told her to bring Danny along, if she would like. Her choice. Her late husband, Mark's father, remained a sore spot between them. But both of them had admitted they'd been wrong about him. Mark with his unrealistic admiration, and she with her bitterness and resentment. Her son knew about her relationship with Danny. She'd decided that there would be no more secrets between them. Mark had been receptive to the situation and now, with the extended invitation, he seemed to even be welcoming.

Her phone vibrated in her hand.

She found the unit and saw the call was from Danny.

"Were your ears burning?" she said to him. "I was just thinking about you."

"Hopefully in a good way."

"Always."

And she meant it. Good to hear his voice. "How are things in the United States Senate?"

"No deferring for you, Ms. Nelle. What have you got yourself into there?"

"Your babysitter came to see me."

"I don't look at the chief of the European station as a babysitter."

"More a pain in my ass." She stepped away from the library's entrance and found some privacy beneath the trees that fronted the building.

"The White House has called and demanded to know what you're doing over there."

"How high up the pole?"

"The friggin' national security adviser. Who I don't even like."

"And what did you say to her?"

"That you are a grown-ass woman who does not report to me your every act."

She smiled. "Good answer."

"They said you have a defector on your hands. A big fish on the hook."

"Is that all they mentioned?"

"Yep. That means there's a whole lot more going on that you don't want them to know about."

"Not yet."

She wondered how they knew about Ivan. Koger? Doubtful. Then it occurred to her. "Which intelligence agency flagged the defector?"

"CIA. They received some intel out of Russia. The SVR is not happy."

"How unhappy?"

"The they-are-willing-to-do-anything kind."

"It's under control," she said to him, trying to keep the conversation as uninformative as possible, as they were on an open line.

"I'm sure it is. But I worry. Occupational hazard."

She appreciated the gesture. "Cotton and Cassiopeia are both here. I'm fine."

"I have no idea why you're there. None of my business. But what is my business is you. Let them handle the heavy lifting. Stay out of the field."

"I intend to do just that."

"When will you be back?"

"By the weekend."

"I'll meet you in Atlanta."

"That would be nice."

And she meant it.

"Congress is out for two weeks. Summer recess. And you keep avoiding the issue."

She'd been around a long time, served presidents from both parties, so she knew the game. White House advisers did not call just to chitchat. Especially this White House and its advisers. The current administration was proudly ultra-conservative. Though elected on a pledge of bipartisan cooperation, its attitude had been unbending. It wasn't their-way-or-the-highway, it was their-way-and-only-their-way. Foreign policy had been particularly hardcore and happenstance. The lingering conflict in Ukraine was still not resolved, and American troops were now deployed to even more tight spots throughout the world. Southeast Asia was heating up, as was western Africa. Nobody knew if the war on terrorism was being won or lost. The White House liked to proclaim that the tide had turned, but she knew that, privately, many officials were concerned about the lack of progress. Compounding all of that was the fact that she was not one of President Warner Fox's favorites. Two efforts to replace her had fizzled. Maybe because nobody wanted her job? Not much glamour in working out of a nondescript Atlanta office, away from mainstream politics, out of sight. Careers were woven from much thicker thread. More than once she'd asked herself why the White House kept her around. Easy.

They feared her.

Maybe she'd write a tell-all book, or end up on CNN as their resident intelligence expert, spouting catchy twenty-second zingers that pointed out the administration's stupidity. Warner Fox would hate that. He liked a uniform message. His message. No variance. One voice. So they tolerated her. *Keep your friends close and your enemies closer.* That sort of thing. She was hoping that no one at Justice or the White House knew a thing, but now she'd materialized on somebody's radar screen, and at a high level too.

"Stephanie," Danny said. "You know that this administration's foreign policy is fairly basic. You either love us or not. There's no middle ground. And they hate Russia. Any opportunity to stick it to Moscow, they are going to take. No matter the consequences. Do you have this under control?"

"Cotton can handle himself."

"It's not him I'm worried about."

"I know, and I appreciate it."

"I would never tell you what to do, nor criticize your decisions. Just remember that bad luck seldom comes alone."

"You read that from a fortune cookie?"

"Actually, I've lived it all my life."

"Here's another one for you," she said. "Even if you fall flat on your face, you're still moving forward."

"The problem with those words of wisdom is that you're still flat on your face."

"I hear you. I'll watch myself."

"And I got your back here."

He'd told her, on more than one occasion, that he would always have her back. Not to tell her what to do, or say I-told-you-so or, God forbid, try and fix things. Instead, as he put it, *If you fall, know I'll be right there on the ground, ready to cushion the impact.*

Which she loved.

"I'll see you in a few days," he said to her.

CHAPTER 54

CASSIOPEIA DROVE THE VAN, STAYING TO THE POSTED SPEED LIMIT, and followed the E4 highway north to Stockholm's main airport. Yesterday's storm had blown itself out, but ragged bands of black clouds still hung in the morning wind. So far the trip had been uneventful. Lots of trees and greenery and moving lines of cars that sparkled under the morning sunshine, traffic moderate on the four-lane, median highway. Cotton glanced back into the cargo bay, most likely taking a quick inventory of his "toys." She'd already checked. Resting safely inside a plastic bin were two automatic rifles, spare clips, and two automatic pistols with extra magazines. They'd also asked for a few incendiary ordnances.

"Enough firepower?" she asked.

"More than plenty."

She checked the rearview mirror again. "I think we have company."

Three motorcycles were closing fast. One accelerated in the left lane, a machine so low-slung the driver's knee could almost touch the pavement during turns. It was green and white and seemed built for speed, the engine screaming from the strain. It drew up beside them, and the helmeted man on it held a gun in his right hand, along with the handlebars.

She kept the van steady on the road.

A second motorcycle, this one orange and black, approached from the shoulder on Cotton's side, another gun wielded from a hand on the handlebars. A quick check of the speedometer showed 120 kilometers an hour.

"Make it tough for them," Cotton said.

"With pleasure."

She swerved and the orange-and-black cycle took a direct hit, wobbling hard to the right, then bouncing off the shoulder, ejecting the rider skyward.

"One down," he said.

"There's also a car behind us," she told him. "Keeping pace."

"That will be the real trouble," he said.

He found one of the rifles, released the safety, and prepared to fire. He then rebuckled his seat belt and made sure the shoulder harness was tight. Hers already was snug. She swerved to the left and popped the green-and-white cycle, sending it skidding on its side, twirling in circles, also ejecting its driver.

"That's going to really make them mad," he said.

A new sound, a big throaty rumbling, caught her ear as a gleaming chrome giant of a motorcycle slid into view in her outer mirror. It had been following the car on their bumper. She saw that it was ridden by a large man with blond hair, wearing black gloves with the fingers cut off. The cycle swung out to the left lane and sped up parallel. The urge was to floor the accelerator and break free. But that was not the plan. So she allowed the cycle to draw parallel.

"Keep that rifle ready," she said, watching both their front and rear.

The man on the cycle lifted a hairy arm and gestured that she should pull over. She shook her head, and he motioned again.

"Make him work for it," Cotton told her.

She pressed the accelerator. The Mercedes' engine revved as they shot forward, gaining on the cars ahead. The cycle to her left dropped back and she watched from the outer mirror as the man reached beneath his leather jacket, produced a gun, and fired. A loud bang signaled that one of the tires had blown. Left rear. Then another shot and a second tire exploded. The van dropped down at the rear. The steering wheel twisted hard right. She grabbed tight and tried to yank the wheels back. But the van veered off the highway, past the shoulder, into the grass on the other side. A sloping embankment filled with ferns and greenery inclined downward before trees started that lined the right-of-way. The van clunked along but the laws of physics could not be ignored. For every reaction there was indeed an equal and opposite reaction. Forward momentum and the unstable surface flipped the van to the passenger side, and they started sliding down the incline. She gripped the steering wheel in a death grip. The crate in the rear also held to its moorings and stayed put.

They kept sliding.

Then stopped.

"You okay?" Cotton asked from below her.

"I've parked better before."

"Look at you. Being funny."

She knew what to do and released the seat belt, working the door lever, kicking the panel out and open. No way to exit from Cotton's side. There'd only be a few moments to act. The motorcycle and car would have to do some backtracking. Cotton handed her a rifle and she pulled herself out of the van. Up the incline at the highway the motorcycle returned, along with the car. She hopped off the van. Cotton followed her out, tossing her one of the handguns.

"Let's make our shots count."

She understood. Careful with the ammo.

They both retreated to the side of the van away from the road, using the upturned vehicle for cover. Three men stood above with guns, which they fired their way. Bullets pinged off the van.

"Thirty meters to the trees behind us," she told Cotton.

"I'll give you cover to go first. Then it's your turn for me."

No sense arguing, so she readied herself to run. Cotton aimed the rifle and sent a burst of rounds upward. The three men scattered, disappearing backward out of sight. Cassiopeia raced to the trees and made it there without incident.

She knew what to do.

The three men reappeared and were about to fire again.

She sent more bullets their way as Cotton made his escape to the trees.

They both directed their aim and attention to the road above. Silence reigned for a few moments, and they waited like prey for the hunter to move in. Then one of the men drew close to the edge and she saw that he toted a shoulder-launched weapon. RPG-7. Russian through and through. The most widely used anti-armor weapon in the world.

"They came ready," she said.

Two of the other men fired their way, but the distance and angle made it tough to zero in on a target. The rounds whizzed away overhead. Cover fire. So the man with the launcher could do his job. There was a bang, then smoke as the high-explosive warhead roared from the barrel and traveled the fifty meters down to the van. It impacted with force, then exploded. The van ripped apart with a blast of light, sound, and heat. The incendiary devices they'd brought along and the fuel in the gas tank joined in the eruption, obliterating the van. A sprouting black cloud of smoke blossomed skyward. They used the trees for shielding and watched as the men above retreated to the car and cycle, leaving in a hurry.

The van continued to burn.

Crate and all.

CHAPTER 55

COTTON WHEELED UP TO THE GATE THAT HUNG OPEN. BEYOND LAY A small private airfield about fifty miles northwest of Stockholm. He'd been driven over by one of the palace security men, while Cassiopeia was taken to Stephanie. They'd both fled the accident scene before the police arrived in a car Stephanie had arranged.

Waiting for him here were two things.

The first was an EMB 120FC Brasilia turboprop, identical to the one at Stockholm's international airport, with the same circular cross-section fuselage, T-tail, and low-mounted wings.

Koger and Stephanie had anticipated that the Russians were closely watching everything related to the Devil's Bible, so they'd carefully staged the entire transfer of the codex by loading a crate onto the Mercedes van and driving off with it from the national library. But instead of the codex, the crate held about 150 pounds of scrap bundled paper. The switch had been made in the wee hours of the morning, with Cassiopeia and the two CIA operatives handling the work. All three had been snuck into the national library and given access to the vault where the codex had awaited transfer. The entire switch had taken less than half an hour. Nobody was around except for two library guards, who were taken into custody, released only after the attack happened. There'd been no way to know when or how the Russians would strike, but it was a safe bet that they would do it during the transfer, and that whatever they did would entail wholesale destruction. And they hadn't been disappointed on either count.

The second thing waiting for him was Ivan.

He'd been taken there earlier by Koger's acolyte, Sandra Koss, who'd kept a close eye on him while everything played out during the staged transport.

The codex itself had been transported here by the two CIA operatives Koger had made available. No big fancy wooden crate, though. Just wrapped tight in bubble wrap and polyurethane, then loaded into the back of an SUV. Low-tech for sure. But it would have to do.

He drove through the gate and headed for a small hangar that sat before a concrete runway. The turboprop waited outside. Ivan stood nearby with a woman, whom he assumed was Koss. He wheeled up, stopped the car, and emerged into the bright morning. The sky above had cleared, now peppered with low-level clouds, plenty of blue peeking out here and there. It had been a while since he'd last sat in a cockpit. But flying was second nature to him. He'd read up on the EMB last night, trying to familiarize himself with the cockpit layout. Normally there would be two pilots. Not today. Just him and Ivan.

"I see you still in one piece," Ivan said as he approached.

"Can't say the same for that crate."

Ivan chuckled. "Moscow will be really mad. They do not like to lose."

"Hopefully they are reveling in their supposed win." He faced Sandra. "Is everything ready?"

She nodded. "Flight plan filed for Prague. That's for anyone who looks. But there are a lot of planes in the air right now, so just blend in and keep going south, then make a detour. You're cleared into German airspace."

As he'd told Ivan hours ago the idea was to land at Ramstein Air Base. Officials there were already alerted, ready for their arrival. It would be important to preserve the codex, so a chamber had been readied where it could be stored in a pure nitrogen atmosphere, as it had been at the Swedish national library. Ivan would be taken into custody and quickly transported to the United States. No wait. No delay. Off one plane and onto another. Hopefully all that would happen before the Russians discovered anything about his whereabouts.

"All the flights are ready to go in Germany?"

Sandra nodded. "I personally oversaw everything. It's ready."

"You ready?" he asked Ivan.

"To get out of here? Definitely. Too many people want me dead."

Cotton faced Sandra. "How will communications work?"

"The plane's radio button is set to the frequency we will be monitoring. It's off the usual scale, so maybe it won't be noticed. We'll keep radio silence unless absolutely necessary. But Stephanie will be right there with you, in your ear. Ramstein will also use the same frequency as you approach for landing."

All good to know.

He stared at the plane. Flying was in his blood. No denying it. Odd considering his father had been a submariner. But spending months at a time undersea, encased within a steel tube breathing recycled air, had never appealed to him. Give him the wide-open spaces flying fighter jets, strapped into an ejection seat that could shoot you up and out into the sky just by pulling the right cable. A constant stream of fresh oxygen running into your face mask. The canopy offering 360-degree views of the world around you. Every movement the plane made could be felt, going from cruising to high-speed G turns in an instant. Every move had to be precise. The tight turns, near-vertical climbs and drops, and everything in between. The best part? Due to all the different forces and the endless sky in all directions, and the fact that the only things you really concentrated on were breathing and staying conscious, most times you had no idea when you were upside down, normal, or going vertical. Flying navy jets for a living, and getting paid to do it, had always brought a smile to his face. Would today's flight be uneventful?

Only one way to find out.

He made a quick preflight check of the exterior, studying the wings, flaps, gears, and all the other things pilots checked before climbing aboard. Before doing that he asked Sandra, "Is someone standing by?"

"As you requested, a pilot familiar with the EMB Brasilia is at Ramstein on the assigned frequency to offer any assistance you might need. They will be in your ear, with Stephanie."

"I appreciate that."

"Should I be worried?" Ivan asked.

"You could stay here."

"No. I cannot."

And Ivan followed him to the plane.

CHAPTER 56

JOHN STUDIED THE MAN WHO'D ARRIVED AT THE HOUSE WHERE HE and Monica were hiding. He was tall and thin with a nearly Spartan vigor. His hatchet-like face was clean-shaven and seamed with wrinkles. The teeth were abnormally white, the eyebrows crescent, the skin spotted with café-au-lait, as if someone had spilled coffee with milk. A battered felt hat covered a nearly bald pate, a few tufts of gray fluff sneaking out at the edges. There were no introductions, but after a knock at the door Monica whispered that he was known as Aleks, top-level SVR, and key to their survival.

"Moscow is not happy," their visitor said with a thin contained voice, in perfect English, surely for John's benefit. "This entire endeavor is a fiasco, beyond comprehension, and needs to end."

"But you got what you wanted," she said. "The codex has been destroyed."

"That is the only saving grace to what is otherwise an embarrassment. The Americans are now making official inquiries. People in the Kremlin are wondering what is happening here. How long will it be before Franko himself becomes involved? That is never a good thing. A member of the Swedish royal family is dead."

"An unfortunate occurrence."

Aleks' voice seemed carefully controlled, the face like stone. "Unfortunate? That seems an understatement. Your exploding the house accomplished nothing. The body survived the fire and is now in the possession of the Swedish military."

News to him. "Lysa was not burned?"

"Not enough to matter. They have her corpse."

Monica seemed unfazed. "But they have no evidence of anything. She was drowned with no marks, and everyone associated with the operation is dead."

"I have been instructed to add the two of you to that list of casualties."

"That would be a grave mistake," Monica said.

John admired her courage. She was not backing down.

"You and I have worked together a long time," Aleks said. "You are a competent and aggressive operative. Sometimes reckless. But never stupid. So please, explain yourself."

John stepped to the window and glanced past the sheers. Four men stood out on the grass beneath the trees. None looked friendly. Aleks had not come alone. *Yes, Monica, do explain yourself.*

"Princess Lysa has been our asset for over a decade," she said. "Her husband, that man right there, took the blame for her actions nine years ago so we could continue to use her."

"And he has been handsomely rewarded for that gallantry."

"It was time that our association with the princess ended," she declared.

Aleks shook his head. "That was not your decision to make."

"I disagree." He watched as Monica's face tightened into a determined look he'd seen before.

"I needed to be rid of my wife," John said.

"Really? Are there not less violent means of accomplishing that?"

"None with such finality."

Aleks apprised him with a hard stare, then said, "By my count three of our operatives are dead, along with a freelancer that was used to impersonate an old man. Three more outside contractors are likewise dead. I am not sure why any of that was necessary, save for, of course, the personal motivations that seem to be at work here."

"Are you a hunter?" John asked.

"Not of animals."

"I am. I quite love it. In the Russian Far East, sandwiched between China and the Pacific Ocean, caribou and wolves roam free. It was once a nearly perfect habitat for Siberian tigers. Amazing creatures. Five hundred pounds. Ten feet long nose-to-tail. With impressive agility. Years ago there was a poacher out there who shot and wounded a tiger, then, foolishly, stole part of that tiger's recent kill for himself. A caribou, I think it was. Incredibly, that injured tiger hunted the poacher down, staked out the man's cabin, then waited for the man to come home. This was not an impulsive response. The tiger held that idea in his brain for almost forty-eight hours. When the poacher finally appeared, the tiger killed him, dragged the body into the bush, and ate him."

"Sounds like the tiger was out for revenge," Aleks said.

"In reality, the tiger was just being a tiger. Unfortunately, the tiger was hunted down and shot. To do that hunters had to anticipate what the animal's next move would be, then get there first. Think about it. Human beings and tigers hunting for the same prey in the same territory. There are bound to be conflicts, and if the tiger had not been wounded by the poacher, there would have been no story to tell."

"You are the tiger?" Aleks asked.

"In a manner of speaking. You stole my life. For nine years I have done as you asked. Now here we are, hunting for the same thing."

Aleks motioned at Monica. "I am told that you two are romantically involved."

She nodded. "I too am tired of chasing shadows and fighting ghosts. I want more from life. I want out. What has occurred here over the past two days was designed to make that happen."

"Really? This whole thing seems at an end. Except, of course, for the death of the two of you."

"You are forgetting the story," John said. "To kill the tiger, the hunters had to anticipate what the next move would be, then get there first."

"And you are ahead of me?" Aleks asked.

"By leaps and bounds," Monica said. "First off, your information is flawed. The codex was not destroyed. It was not even inside that van. The Americans made a switch at the national library."

"And you know this, how?"

"I received a call a little while ago that informed me of the deception. I was also told that the codex was taken secretly to a regional airport where it is about to be flown away."

"To Prague?" Aleks asked.

"Doubtful. The Americans did not go to all that trouble just to give the book away. My guess? They are going to keep it, along with the defector." Monica's lips formed a thin smile. "Human beings and tigers hunting for the same prey in the same territory. We both hunt for the defector. But I found him. I am assuming his elimination is far more important than my or John Westlake's errors."

The wiry Russian stood silent for a moment before saying, "The princess' British handler was arrested during the night."

Monica shrugged. "Thanks to your defector. He pointed them that way. I know that for a fact too."

"Your source is credible?"

"Beyond reproach. I can tell you where the defector and the codex will be in the next hour. It will be an easy matter to eliminate both at the same time. All I want—"

"Is your freedom."

"Precisely. Seems a simple trade for such a great service to the motherland."

Aleks turned toward John. "And you?"

"We are a package deal," he said. "I am out too, but my businesses are left alone. Everyone gets what they want. Moscow should be thrilled."

Aleks pinched back the sleeve of his shirt and read his watch. "I will need to make a call."

"You do that," Monica said. "But do not take long. What you want will soon be gone, and your opportunity to act will be gone with them."

CHAPTER 57

COTTON SETTLED IN BEHIND THE CONTROLS, IVAN IN THE COPILOT'S seat. He gave the instrument panels a quick once-over. Not all that dissimilar to other aircraft he'd flown while in the navy.

Occasionally back in Copenhagen he would charter a plane and fly out over the Baltic just to feel the air beneath him and practice his skills. He'd even considered buying a small single-engine aircraft but had just never gotten around to taking the time to shop for the right one. He could certainly afford one. The jobs he'd taken on over the past few years had paid solid. Not that he'd billed anyone. But Stephanie had always insisted that he be compensated. He lived a basic, no-frills life, so all that money had been banked and invested. Probably time to spend some of it.

Maybe. One day.

He donned the radio headset, pressed the brake pedal, flicked the right switches, and fired up the two turboprops. The blades began to spin, faster and faster, coming up to speed. He eased off the brakes and taxied out to the runway. The airport was tiny with only a single landing strip. No other planes or aircraft were in sight. Sandra had told him there was no need to check in with any air traffic controllers. Just squawk. The Swedish military had already cleared him for both takeoff and the trip south out of their airspace. Once out over the Baltic, Germany would assume control.

He came to the end of the runway and stopped the plane. A quick check of the gauges showed nothing of concern. Ivan was watching him with an intense gaze that seemed to question his ability to handle the controls.

Oh ye of little faith.

He released the brake and pushed the throttle forward. The engines revved to full speed, and they started to roll out. It took about five thousand feet to reach airspeed. He pulled back on the yoke and rotated. The wings caught air and the plane lifted, slow and steady, into the late-morning sky. The controls responded to his commands, soaring them upward.

High, hot, and heavy.

He banked left and adjusted course toward the south, which would take them past Stockholm, then down toward the Baltic. The controls were tight and responsive and felt good in his hands. The landscape miniaturized with altitude. He focused on the instruments but said to Ivan, "Take a look at that chart."

Stephanie had followed his instructions and provided a map of northern Europe.

"We're going to ground-track our way there," he said.

"Assuming chart is correct."

He smiled. "It is."

He kept climbing, wanting to reach around forty-five hundred feet for a cruising altitude. Below stretched Lake Mälaren, a panorama of islands and inlets that fanned out from Stockholm. On one of those Princess Lysa had died. Murdered? More than likely. Ahead the terrain was mostly flat. Lots of potato fields and apple orchards. Mountains rose far off to the west. His plan was to parallel Sweden's rocky east coast, then cross the Baltic into Danish, then German, airspace, all NATO-controlled. They should be fine there. The trick was getting there without anyone noticing. Thankfully the skies north of Copenhagen, out over the water, were familiar.

"I can't ask you to do this," Stephanie said. "It's far too dangerous."

She'd just explained what she and Koger wanted done. Originally, they were going to switch out the codex and fly it quickly to Germany. The new plan called for adding a passenger to that flight. Ivan. The problem? Koger had a security leak that he wanted to plug, and the current situation offered the perfect opportunity to accomplish that.

"It makes sense," Cotton told her. "To catch big prey, you have to use big bait. If Koger's hunch is right, the source will report the flight, and the Russians will act."

"And fighters will be heading your way to shoot you down," she said.

"Let's deal with that when we get there. It may not happen."

"The Russians will throw caution to the wind. Franko's people will not care about protocol."

"Hopefully, Koger is wrong about the leak."

"Unfortunately, he has great instincts."

He knew that about 250 miles lay between here and the city of Malmö at the southernmost Swedish coast. From there it was a quick hop over the busy Øresund Strait to Denmark. Except for some wind, the day seemed perfect for flying. He liked what one of his instructors once said. *Everyone could take a lesson from the weather. It pays no attention to criticism.* He scanned the instruments one more time. Everything normal. The timbre of the turbos sounded strong and uniform. The skies, as far as he could see, were devoid of other planes.

"I certainly hope you're worth all this," he said to Ivan.

"Being a traitor not something I thought I would ever be. But my country is lost. Franko will rule until he dies, which will be long time. Sadly, he is quite healthy."

"Unless someone puts a bullet in him."

"It has been discussed. But would be hard to do. Better to just get away from Russia."

He kept a light grip on the yoke as the plane slid through the midday air. "Is it that bad?"

"My country is lost. The place I knew is gone. We are doomed. Better to bring it all down."

"I admire your courage."

"But am I being foolish?"

"No more than the two of us, up here, in this plane."

"Are we a target?"

He hadn't explained any of what Stephanie had told him about them being bait to reveal a spy. No need for Ivan to be aware of that.

"Let's just hope no one knows we're here."

CHAPTER 58

Cassiopeia faced King Wilhelm.

She'd come to the palace to show him the photographs and answer questions as Stephanie passed on the terrible news that his sister was gone. The king had stood silent for the past few moments, absorbing the devastating news.

"We were close, as children," Wilhelm said, regret in his voice. "But as we grew older, we drifted farther and farther apart. Not estranged. Just a coolness."

"From her marriage?" Stephanie asked.

"I never cared for Westlake. Just a man with money and an attitude. I tried to like him but never could."

"There is something else," Stephanie said.

The king waited.

"We have confirmed that your sister was a tacit asset for the SVR. She had a handler, in Britain, whom we arrested a few hours ago. That woman confessed. She also confirmed that Westlake was not involved."

"That cannot be true."

"Unfortunately, it is. Westlake is now missing too. But we're unsure of his motives and intentions. It could all be planned."

"And the Codex Gigas?"

Only Koger, Cotton, Ivan, Sandra Koss, Stephanie, the prime minister, and she herself knew the details. The two CIA operatives were also aware of the switch, but not where the codex was headed.

"Unfortunately, I cannot share that information," Stephanie said.

"The arrangement with the Czechs is proceeding?"

"Again, I cannot say. But I can say that the prime minister has been fully informed as to everything."

"So the government gets what it wanted. The Czechs get what they wanted. America gets what it wants. And my sister is dead. What. Will. Be. Done. About. That?" With each word he slapped the back of his right hand into the palm of his left.

"Do not be naïve," Stephanie said, her voice firm. "Your sister unwittingly passed on valuable intelligence to the Russians for over a decade. Her actions were foolish and reckless, no matter the lack of criminal intent. And as much as you and I detest Westlake, he was framed to take the blame. That is the reality."

"As is her death. Who will be held accountable for that?"

"No one," Cassiopeia made clear. "There is no evidence that points to any specific suspect. Granted, the Russians are at fault. But we have no way of proving that."

"We have her body."

"Which, so far, has yielded nothing."

"Can we not find and capture this Monica Butler-White? Would that not offer up some possibilities?"

"That would," Stephanie said. "And we are actively searching for her. But my guess is she's long gone from Sweden. In her mind this operation is over."

"And Westlake?"

"Gone with her, most likely," Stephanie said. "There is an indication that the two of them are romantically connected."

"Good God. My sister died for nothing," the king muttered with a sigh, the voice filled with sorrow and disbelief.

"Not true," Stephanie said. "Sweden's national security is on the line. The security of every one of your subjects is on the line. Serious issues involve serious actions, and there are always, and I mean always, consequences to that. Your sister simply had no idea how deep she was in."

Wilhelm's back stiffened. "I resent your tone. We are old friends, and you are here because I asked for your help. But that does not give you the right to denigrate my sister and speak to me as you please."

STEPHANIE LEARNED A LONG TIME AGO THAT POWER RESPECTED power. So she stiffened her spine and said, "I am not a Swedish citizen. You are not my king. True, I owe you a measure of respect. But that works both ways. You called me here to help. So we helped. It's a partial win, for sure, but a win nonetheless. In my business we take all of those we can get, however we can get them."

"And my sister be damned?"

The hostility had faded from the king's face, and he suddenly looked old and tired.

"She was my friend too, Wilhelm. I mourn her. But she was an unfortunate victim of her own mistakes."

"And Westlake?"

"Nine years ago he was forced into an untenable situation. The SVR could easily have killed him to protect their asset's identity.

Instead they went down another path, and Westlake chose the lesser of two evils, accepting the blame, staying silent about Lysa. I'm not saying I agree with that. I just understand how that choice could have been made. Now? He's a co-conspirator. Unfortunately, unless we can find people willing to talk, we have no evidence to prosecute him."

The intelligence business was dangerous.

Without a doubt.

Cassiopeia took risks when she went to meet with Monica Butler-White. Cotton was, at this precise moment, taking a huge risk flying Ivan and the codex away from Sweden. Sometimes it all seemed so pointless, so repetitious, until she reminded herself that it mattered. She hated being disrespectful to the king. Not her style. But she was tired of his blind arrogance. *Yes, he's royalty. But let's get real. So what? Who cares?* His kingship was a ceremonial position based on heredity. Still, she should be conciliatory and was about to apologize when a knock broke the silence.

The door opened and a gloved, uniformed aide entered and handed her a folded sheet of paper before leaving. Interrupting this royal audience meant something important. She read the message, her eyes closing for a moment in despair as she absorbed the bad news.

Dammit.

She motioned with the paper, indicating that Cassiopeia should read it too.

TWO RUSSIAN FIGHTERS HAVE LEFT CHERNYAKHOVSK AIR BASE, HEADED WEST OUT OVER THE BALTIC. NOT ON THE SCHEDULE.

She knew that base. In Kaliningrad Oblast, a wedge of Russian territory that sat between Poland and Lithuania, which provided air support for the Russian Baltic fleet.

And she also knew about the reference to the "schedule."

Both NATO and the Russians kept each other apprised on any flights over the Baltic. A courtesy that helped keep the peace and prevent some trigger-happy missile operator, or an enemy fighter pilot, from starting a world war.

But no notice had been given for these two.

"Is he in trouble?" Cassiopeia asked.

"What is happening?" the king asked.

"Reality, Wilhelm," she said. "It has a terrible tendency to never let up."

CHAPTER 59

Cotton rattled off in his brain the EMB's specifications. Maximum speed, 328 knots at 20,000 feet. Cruising speed, 300 knots. Really important, stall speed, 87 knots with flaps down. Range, 1,090 miles. Service ceiling? 29,806 feet. But he was going nowhere near that altitude.

No need.

The plane bumped through a line of turbulence.

Total distance from Stockholm to Ramstein Air Base was right at eight hundred miles. So they were pushing the plane's range with only a couple hundred miles to spare. The coast below had a crazed outline with craggy juttings. He spied the blue expanse of the Baltic ahead, its surface dotted with ships. An alluring pocket of waning wheat fields and apple orchards stretched for miles. Smoke belched from the chimneys of fishing hamlets nestled close to the water.

"I appreciate this," Ivan said. "They would kill me."

"They may still."

"I have faith in red, white, and blue. You protect me."

"What are you going to do with your life? You'll always be looking over your shoulder."

"Nothing new there. But I would like to live in Texas or Arizona. I read about those places. Lots of desert. I tired of the cold. No more for me."

"Arizona would be a nice place to live. But you better like red sand. There's a lot of it."

"Americans take freedom for granted. You expect it. Demand it. But I doubt many understand its meaning. Have it taken away. Then you will understand. Russia now is awful place to live."

They sat in silence for a few moments, and he left Ivan to his thoughts. Flying had always been therapeutic. The perfect place to clear your head. This had to be tough for the burly Russian, no matter how negative he felt about his homeland. Leaving your home forever was never easy.

"My wife would love this," Ivan said. "She was good woman. Hated Franko. I do this for her. She once told me a story. I have thought of that many times since she died."

He needed a distraction. "Tell me."

And he listened as Ivan explained that, once upon a time, there was a colorless horse. All of his shades were grays, blacks, and whites. His lack of color had made him so famous that the world's greatest painters came to his barn to try to add color. None of them succeeded, as the tints would always just drip off his skin. Then along came Pigger, the crazy painter. A strange guy who traveled about, happily painting with his brush.

But that was the thing.

He never actually applied paint to the brush.

He just moved the bristles about in the air as if to paint. So when he said he wanted to color the horse, everyone laughed.

But Pigger was serious.

He entered the horse's stable and whispered in the animal's ear, moving his dry brush up and down the body. To everyone's surprise the skin started to take on a vivid chestnut color. He then spent more time whispering to the animal, and the result was beautiful.

Everyone wanted to know his secret.

Pigger explained that his painting was meaningless. Instead, he managed to bring out the horse's color with a phrase he kept whispering in the animal's ear.

In just a few days you will be free again.

Seeing how sad the horse was in his captivity, and how colorful and joyful the prospect of freedom seemed, his owner set the horse free, where never again would he lose his color.

"My wife wise," Ivan said. "Freedom is what gives life color. That should never be forgotten."

He could not argue with any of that. But unlike the horse's situation, here there was no one to have pity on the oppressed and set them free.

Just the opposite in fact. Which did not bode well for Ivan.

The sun shone through scattered clouds, reflecting a glare from one of the metal window frames. Off the tip of his port wing he saw they were passing Gotland Island to the east with its flat lush countryside. He caught a glimpse of the wooden windmills on the closer Öland Island, with its long sandy beaches.

He ticked off more of the geography learned from the chart.

The narrow Øresund Strait separated Sweden from Denmark, draining north into Kattegat Bay and south into the Baltic. Three islands dotted its choppy waters. Copenhagen's international airport sat on the largest of those. He'd have to angle to the southwest toward Bornholm Island and avoid its restricted airspace. Surely the air traffic controllers had noticed his presence, but he assumed the Swedes had alerted them.

Or at least he hoped so.

The EMB's wings skipped air.

Engines sputtered, then quickly refired.

What the hell?

The right wing sheared from impacts and the ailerons went loose. The plane arched right as the starboard side failed to respond to commands. He compensated by working the yoke.

"What was that?" Ivan said.

The answer came as a jet roared past overhead. The sound of high-performance engines tore through the air and a gentle rumble shook the sky.

"Cannon fire," he said.

The fighter's delta-winged triangle disappeared in the distance, but a vapor trail indicated a turn for another approach.

"That's a Russian fighter," he said.

He worked the rudder and used air speed to regain some semblance of control. The EMB's engines screamed at each other like an arguing soprano and baritone. One thought rushed through his brain. The EMB was little match for modern avionics, cannons, and radar-guided missiles.

But they'd had no choice.

To upgrade would have drawn suspicion, alerting the Russians, and the whole idea was to bait the trap and flush out the mole.

Back in the navy a target like the EMB was called a grape.

Because it was so easy to squash.

CHAPTER 60

STEPHANIE STEPPED INTO THE COMMUNICATIONS CENTER LOCATED on the ground floor of the palace's north wing. She and Cassiopeia had left the king and come straight here. Wilhelm had wanted an explanation but she'd politely declined. There'd been enough security breaches for one day. Prime Minister de Ciutiis was already there, standing before a desktop monitor.

"We are patched through to our air defense command," the prime minister said. "Two Sukhoi 30 fighters have intercepted your people and are engaging."

The canary trap had sprung.

No doubt now.

Koger had a serious security leak.

"Where are they?" Stephanie asked.

"Just north of Malmö, still in our airspace."

"And the Russians fired on them?"

De Ciutiis nodded. "I know. Bold. NATO is responding. Two F-16s are being sent out of Holland. They will be there in ten minutes."

Which was an eternity. That EMB turboprop was no match for an advanced military fighter jet. True, the Russians were using interceptors that dated to the 1990s. But they came with cannons and missiles, and it would be an easy matter to shoot the EMB from the sky. A radar image filled the desktop monitor showing the EMB's flight path south along with two other blips moving west, then turning back to the east.

"They made one pass and are coming back for more," de Ciutiis said.

The room was empty except for the three of them. Stephanie had requested the communication link be established so she could monitor Cotton's progress south, hoping no one would intercede.

"Any idea how they knew to be there?" Cassiopeia asked.

Cotton had requested that Cassiopeia not be told about what Koger had proposed in using him as bait. She would have insisted on going along, and he was not going to hear of that.

"That's a question for later," Stephanie said. "Right now, we have to help them survive the next ten minutes."

COTTON HAD BEEN AROUND ENOUGH FIGHTER PILOTS TO KNOW HOW they think, no matter the nationality. This was a hawk challenging a pigeon—easy prey. The pilot would be focused on his firing radar, trying to get a lock on the EMB, deciding when to pull the trigger. Best guess? The Russian would wait until he was close before firing. Why not? No danger of any resistance.

Just another grape.

He'd caught enough of a glimpse to know that his enemy was a Sukhoi 30. Twin-engine two-seater, fast and super maneuverable. Developed in the old Soviet Union. A multi-role fighter for all weather. An oldie but goodie, still in operation. And loaded with a 30mm autocannon and air-to-air missiles.

"Cotton, can you hear me?" Stephanie's voice said in his ears through the headphones. "You have two visitors."

Both capable of about 1,100 knots at low altitude, while he chugged along at less than 350.

"One has already let us know he's here."

"You have help coming. Less than ten minutes out."

Which could not have been dispatched sooner so as not to alert the Russians.

"Okay. I know what I have to do."

He spied ahead out the forward windshield and saw rivers, lakes, some brooding forest, and a stunning archipelago. Beyond was the blue water of the Baltic. Denmark was in sight on the other side of the narrow strait. So was the Øresund Bridge that ran for five miles from the city of Malmö on the Swedish coast to an artificial island, Peberholm, where it ducked under the water into a two-and-a-half-mile-long tunnel to the Danish coast.

An engineering marvel.

But maybe their salvation too.

CASSIOPEIA WAS SCARED.

Cotton was in trouble. And there was nothing she could do to help. She also saw the concern on Stephanie's face. De Ciutiis stood silent but clearly troubled too.

Stephanie's phone buzzed.

She answered, then switched to speaker mode. "Colonel, repeat what you just told me. The Swedish prime minister is here."

"NATO planes are in the air and should be there in about seven minutes. Let's hope the Russians don't want to engage any further. I have no authority to return fire."

"Can you get it?" Stephanie asked.

"That would involve revealing what's happening here. Since I don't know what that is, it will be hard to explain to my superiors."

"It's a CIA and Justice Department joint operation."

"That's not going to be enough to justify starting World War III."

She was well acquainted with Russia's central command units. They were ultra rigid, and the people closest to the action were not the ones making the decisions. That came from farther away and higher up the food chain. The U.S. was different. The guys on the ground had a much bigger say. But there were limits. Rules of engagement. That had to be obeyed. This colonel was only the operations officer of the day for the Baltic air region, stationed in Holland.

And one other thing.

The CIA was surely listening to all of the radio chatter in the Baltic. That was standard operating procedure. The presence of the two Russian fighters had surely garnered their attention. So none of this was staying secret.

"Let's hope our fighters' presence is enough," Stephanie said.

"I'll keep this line open and will be here," the colonel said.

"Have you made inquiries with the Russians as to why they are in our airspace?" de Ciutiis asked.

"We have. They have not responded. Any idea, Madam Prime Minister, why that is the case?"

De Ciutiis gave them both a look that said, *We cannot go there.* Stephanie shook her head in agreement, then said, "We'll be right here, Colonel. Where are the fighters?"

"Five minutes out."

CHAPTER 61

COTTON KNEW ALL HE HAD TO DO WAS AVOID THOSE FIGHTERS long enough for help to arrive. One would be tough to shake. Two? Nearly impossible. But he had an idea. With the Baltic approaching, the wind had noticeably picked up, buffeting the plane, especially its damaged wing. The Øresund Strait churned with long rows of whitecaps. He knew from experience that white tops came from at least fifteen-knot winds. The Russian had only grazed them with the initial cannon fire, surely trying to damage the plane enough to knock them down as opposed to openly shooting them down. But everything was still playing out in the sky for all to see.

So let's give them something to watch.

He eased the yoke forward and dropped altitude. He checked his airspeed. A little under 130 knots. He recalled what his flight instructor had taught him. *Nobody ever collided with the sky. Altitude is your friend.*

Except when it wasn't.

Like here.

"He will be back here soon," Ivan said.

He hoped the EMB could handle what he was about to do. The starboard control surfaces were severely damaged, but the port side and tail rudder seemed okay. Most important, the engines were working, though there was now a noticeable difference in their timbre.

He engaged the lever and lowered the landing gear. He heard the hydraulic noise of the gear doors grinding open and the spinning of the wheels' reverse rotation. He then angled the flaps down, slowing their speed dramatically.

Flying dirty. Which ate up altitude. Fast.

He had to get low. Real low. For two reasons. First, those capping waves would create clutter for the fighter's firing radar. Second, and even more important, the Russians would have to go dirty too. But fighters were not low-altitude machines. They worked best in the stratosphere, not near the ground where computers and engines could be tapped to the max. They would also be sucking fuel at an alarming rate to stay aloft at their breakneck speeds. And for two hostile aircraft far from their base, that was a disadvantage he had to exploit.

He waited another two seconds, then pulled back on the throttle and pushed on the yoke. The plane dropped faster.

Tracer rounds rocketed past as their altitude decreased.

Two thousand feet.

Fifteen hundred.

One thousand.

The fighter shot past above them, its turbofans leaving a trail of black smoke.

"My stomach is in my throat," Ivan said.

"I had to do something he wouldn't expect."

He focused through the windshield. Another Sukhoi loomed in the distance toward the north. Stephanie had said there were two.

One was circling, watching, waiting, the other engaging. He realized either fighter could easily shoot them down with air-to-air missiles.

Another navy lesson flashed through his mind.

Learn from other people's mistakes.

"We're going to the water," he said.

STEPHANIE'S MIND RACED.

Everything was happening fast. No time to be afraid. Cotton's life was in real jeopardy.

"Colonel," she said to the phone. "You still there?"

"I am. We are three minutes out."

He'd anticipated her question and provided the correct answer.

"Can't they do something to let those fighters know they're not alone?"

"I have no authority to fire air-to-air missiles at Russian aircraft."

"Colonel, you don't know me. But I am the head of the Magellan Billet, a covert intelligence agency of the U.S. Justice Department. What's on that plane is vital to our national security. I need you to protect it."

She was throwing a little weight around hoping it might generate some action. Not usually her style. But there was nothing about this that was usual.

"I can't fire on that plane, ma'am."

"Can you fire and miss?"

COTTON FIGURED HE HAD ABOUT THREE TO FOUR MINUTES LEFT BEFORE the cavalry arrived. So he decided to use the two things he had.

Low altitude and the Øresund Bridge.

Built a quarter century ago to connect Denmark to Sweden, the abovewater portion of the span ran five miles from Sweden to Peberholm Island before dipping below the surface into a tunnel. The span supported a roadway and rail line, along with data and communications cables. It was held aloft every 450 feet by concrete piers rising from the water. At the center of the main span, two pairs of freestanding, cable-supported towers suspended a fifteen-hundred-foot-wide opening over the water, allowing ships to pass beneath. Most important was the height from the bottom of the span to the top of the water. Maybe a couple of hundred feet? Going to be tight for a fast-moving aircraft.

But that was the whole idea.

He reduced their speed further. The outside air seemed capricious and inconsistent, which only aggravated the lack of full control. He dropped the left wing and slipped into a slow bank, the controls straining from the damage, the airplane sluggish in the turn. After another slow turn, he angled the nose and leveled off at eight hundred feet above the water.

"You see the jet?" he asked.

Ivan's head spun in every direction possible out the windows. "*Nyet.* But that mean nothing. He could still have us in sights."

A fact he realized. He struggled to keep the wings level, as the starboard side control surfaces were ignoring his commands. Luckily, it seemed the codex was safe, strapped down behind them, not moving.

A rush of wind shoved them to the right.

He held the nose high and angled straight for the bridge, dropping to a hundred feet above the water. A small container ship was coming toward them from the other side, lined up to pass beneath. He knew that usually the ships avoided the open span and passed unobstructed in the Drogden Strait that ran above the tunnel. Nothing to hit there. But he'd spotted the ship as they'd approached and decided to use it too.

"I see fighter," Ivan said. "There."

He followed Ivan's pointed finger and caught the glint in the sunlight ahead and above them. Coming fast. The Russian had chosen a frontal assault. A game of chicken? Okay. He could do that.

But where was the other fighter?

The bridge offered the perfect distraction from any incoming rounds. All that metal would play havoc with firing radars. As would the container ship, which was literally a floating pile of steel boxes. The unknown? How far were the Russians willing to go to kill Ivan?

Missiles from afar?

He held the yoke steady and could already tell depth perception was going to be a problem. He would have to judge the distance correctly, both up and down and right to left, and make sure airspeed was perfect. He was worried about stalling. Luckily, no crosswind blew, or at least none he could feel.

But like he'd been told.

Gravity never loses.

CASSIOPEIA WATCHED THE MONITOR.

Cotton had dropped to just barely above the surface. The two Russian fighters were overhead, one in front, the other looping around to approach from the rear. He seemed to be flying straight for what the monitor identified as the Øresund Bridge.

The screen suddenly split.

One side showed the radar, the other a view from one of the F-16's cameras down to the water.

"I've sent a live feed through Swedish military command," the colonel said from the phone.

"We have it," Stephanie said.

They could see the bridge and a small container ship approaching from the north headed south. The EMB was flying low just above the surface, south to north, headed under the bridge, straight for the ship, to its right.

"What's he doing?" she muttered.

"Surviving," Stephanie said.

The radar image showed something moving away from the Russian fighter in front of the EMB.

"They fired a missile," the colonel said through the phone.

Another image emerged from one of the American interceptors that had just come onto the screen.

"We fired too," the colonel said. "At the higher fighter to the rear."

"Why not to the one who fired first?" Cassiopeia asked.

"That one is for Cotton to avoid," Stephanie said. "They're trying to give pause to the other to not join in the attack."

COTTON HOPED THERE WAS ENOUGH ROOM.

They were a hundred yards from the bridge, the ship to his right, and he was flying barely above the uppermost containers stacked tall, which was taking about half the space beneath the bridge out of play. The Russian fighter was nowhere to be seen.

Off to the south, a flash appeared.

An instant later a vapor trail snaked a path across the morning sky.

He knew what was happening.

Incoming air-to-air missile, its fire-and-forget active radar zeroing in on them. He kept the EMB on course and decided to use the ship to maximum advantage. The bad part? He had no electronics, nothing at all to track the approaching danger.

They were now no more than fifty feet above the water.

It looked like the ship, the missile, and the EMB would all arrive under the bridge—

At the same time.

CHAPTER 62

JOHN SAT IN THE SMALL PARLOR AND LISTENED AS ALEKS AND MONICA renewed their conversation. Aleks had excused himself and retreated outside to make a call. He'd stayed there for nearly half an hour, on and off the phone.

Apparently, Monica had struck a nerve.

First rule of making a good deal? Know what the other side wanted most. Second rule? Get control of it. Monica had done just that. The Russian had returned with the same scowl on his face, as if he might be constipated. Was it all an act? If so, it was a good one.

"We agree to leave you both alone, in exchange for accurate intelligence on the whereabouts of the defector."

"Forgive me," Monica said. "But your word can be...fluid."

"That it can. But I am assuming you have a dead man's switch in play."

"Look at you, all current with your spy slang."

"You were always careful. Until the past few days."

"What can I say? Sometimes an operation can be fluid too."

"Do you have a switch in play?"

"I do. I know a great deal. I have no intention of ever speaking of any of it. I am loyal to the motherland. That would change only if something happens to me or John. We just want to be left alone."

"And you will be. Now where is Dmitry Lut?"

Monica told Aleks about the American's deception with the codex, that its destruction had been anticipated and accomplished nothing, and that the book and the defector were on a plane heading south for Germany. Aleks quickly excused himself, and both he and the four men who'd stayed outside left.

Gone. Just like that.

"Are we truly done with them?" he asked Monica.

"You are never done with the SVR. But they are not without logic. They know I can hurt them. I would assume they will leave us alone until they need me again one day. We can deal with that when, and if, it happens."

He asked, "And what does the future hold for us?"

"First, I plan to remove from your residence all of the hideous clothing that your wife loved to wear and donate it to charity."

"And her jewelry?"

"We will auction it off for charity."

He liked that.

"You can start over," she said, "by dazzling me with extravagant purchases. Outrageous things. I will give you a list. Thankfully, you can afford them."

"And what will you give me?"

He saw the twinkle in her eye. "Whatever you want."

"You have apparently given this a lot of thought."

"We will also be redecorating. It baffles me how someone with all the culture, education, and training that your wife possessed had such awful taste in furniture and clothes."

He chuckled. "You do realize that I never gave a damn. I simply allowed her to do as she pleased."

"I hope I will be extended the same courtesy."

"Are we to be married?"

"After an appropriate time of mourning. As you have long wanted, your connection to the Swedish royal family will be over. You will be Sir John Westlake, billionaire, entrepreneur, philanthropist. Your reputation in England is impeccable. Any implications that you are a spy have been resolved and your name cleared. No one will be paying you, or us, any attention."

"Surely they know of you and your SVR connections. Ms. Vitt was a good messenger for all of that."

"Of course. But they have no proof of anything, and my statements to them will be that we both wanted out once we realized they intended to kill the princess. Moscow will say the opposite and confusion will reign. Nobody will be able to do anything."

Made sense. "And our wedding?"

"A lovely affair, in the English countryside, with select friends. Neither of us have anything that resembles a family."

"Black tie?"

"Of course. What else?"

"How silly of me to think otherwise. Forgive me, but do we not have to get out of this country first? Alive. Past not only your Russian associates but also the Swedes and the Americans, who are not going to be happy when I reappear. Stephanie Nelle is quite determined." It was approaching lunchtime and he was hungry. So he asked, "Could we also, perhaps, leave this island?"

"I suspect that my former employer is going to keep a close watch on us both until the information I gave them is confirmed. Maybe we should stay in Uppsala, not Stockholm, until all is resolved."

"How will we know if everything works out?"

"Simple. We will still be breathing."

Nothing about that sounded comforting.

"But I assure you," she said. "Killing you or me will not be easy for them."

And he believed that.

She checked her watch. "They have surely discovered that the information about the plane was correct. It would have been an easy matter to do. My guess is they are acting on that intelligence right now."

STEPHANIE WATCHED BOTH THE RADAR AND THE LIVE FEED, HER heart pounding.

Two missiles were in the air.

One from the Russians headed toward the bridge and the EMB, the other from us toward the second fighter that was off to the west. Smart move on the colonel's part to order that the second fighter be the target of his intentional miss. It should be enough to keep the other Sukhoi at bay.

Giving Cotton only one problem to deal with at a time.

COTTON KEPT THE PLANE LEVEL AND IN A TIGHT PATH.

The EMB was set to pass beneath the bridge just before the container ship, which had apparently noticed him and was sending out long, loud blasts of its horn. The Sukhoi had fired one of its air-to-air missiles to take down the EMB, which was closing in on the target.

But they were now so close to the surface that the water, the ship, and the bridge would be obstacles.

Air-to-air missiles fell into two groups. Short-range were designed to optimize agility and used infrared guidance. Movies and TV called them heat-seeking missiles. Medium- to long-range missiles relied on radar. Both liked open spaces where their computers could work unimpeded. But this was a visual war. Everything was happening relatively close. The Russian missile was going to have to find him amid a multitude of radar clutter. The ship. The containers. The bridge. The choppy water.

Clutter was his friend.

They roared past the container ship.

An explosion erupted from the top of the ship. Large. Violent. Taking out the top row of steel containers. The missile had locked onto the largest and closest target its infrared guidance could find.

They flew out the other side of the bridge.

Cotton pushed over on the yoke and added thrust, sending the EMB seeking altitude as they passed over Saltholm Island. Flat chalk meadowlands and a rocky shore stretched below, the ground loaded with geese that also filled the air above. He had to be careful with that. Too many planes had been brought down by birds.

He banked as they climbed and headed back north for the Swedish coast. Copenhagen loomed off to the south. The starboard control surfaces were barely working and he had to force the plane into the turn. The landing gear was still down. The Russian fighter that had fired the missile was ahead of them, coming in fast. But he also caught sight of an F-16 on the Sukhoi's tail.

Thank goodness.

Hopefully the other fighter had been similarly engaged. The Sukhoi ahead of them kept coming but surely knew he had company, which meant that no more missiles would be used. He pushed the throttle forward and increased speed, accelerating their climb. The Russian raced toward them.

Tracer rounds came from cannon.

Then more fire.

Straight at them.

CHAPTER 63

JOHN KNEW THAT HIS LIFE WAS NEVER GOING TO BE THE SAME. HARD to believe that Lysa was gone. He'd imagined what this day might feel like, not necessarily with her death, but definitely with them parting ways. Sadly, their relationship was a failed one. Truth be told he had no interest in anything his wife might have thought or done. Never once had he been physically or emotionally abusive, but never had he cared either. He stopped long ago being her lover. True, he remained kind and thoughtful. But over the years he just slowly faded away, his voice becoming quieter and quieter in their relationship. Lysa simply was not an important part of his life. Looking back, it had been the little things at first. Like where to have dinner, who to invite to gatherings, where to go on holiday, but those disagreements eventually became more significant. Finally both Lysa and her opinions had no place in his life. He'd known from the beginning that Lysa would not survive this operation.

"Are you okay with that?" Monica had asked him.

"You speak of murder as if it was just a business deal."

"It is, in my line of work. People die all the time."

"She is my wife."

"Whom you could not care less about. You are the one who said you want out of the marriage, and that you cannot divorce her. I am simply offering the means to make that happen, while someone else does the deed and others shoulder the blame."

"What do you want me to say?"

"How about thank you."

He'd managed to get himself in really deep. But Monica seemed to have it all under control. He'd come to know that the greatest burdens borne in life were lost opportunities. Never have too many "if only" stories. He'd always possessed the ability to identify opportunities and take advantage of them. How else could he have amassed billions in wealth? Missing an opportunity could change the direction of lives. And almost never did the same opportunity come twice. Which explained, more than anything else, why he'd agreed to assume the blame for Lysa's mistakes all those years ago. The Russians offered an opportunity not otherwise available, and he'd taken it. Miss that and he'd have been forced to wait for another chance.

Which might have never come.

Yes, life was full of opportunities. But the trick was to know when to take them and when to pass. He once read something the Greek philosopher Heraclitus said. *No man ever steps in the same river twice, for it's not the same river and he's not the same man.* Water never flowed backward, so the water from the river the man stepped into was gone forever. The goal? Allow the river of lost opportunities to flow away with that inexperience, so you can step back in wiser and better. Here he was. About to step back into that river. And what had he learned? To not push his luck. To take what he'd gained and move on.

Monica had disappeared deeper into the house that was their new refuge half an hour ago. He heard her returning to where he'd stayed in the front parlor.

"They found the defector and the codex," she said to him. "Exactly where I said they would be."

"Is that good for us?"

"Hopefully. But we will proceed with caution."

"How did you know where to find the defector?"

"I had inside information at the highest level. One of my assets passed it on to me."

"How fortunate."

"It's time we leave this country," she said. "Back to England."

"Do I not need to resurface? If Lysa's body has been recovered, there will be a funeral that I would be expected to attend."

"Of course. And you will. I think you should make your reappearance today. I will leave and meet you back in England, after the funeral."

His head still hurt from the pounding she'd administered.

Both temples were swollen and sore.

"How will I resurface?"

"I have that all planned out."

CHAPTER 64

COTTON COULD FEEL THAT SOMETHING WAS WRONG WITH THE EMB besides the initial damage to the starboard-side wing. He'd brought the plane out of the sharp bank and leveled off at two thousand feet just over the Swedish coastline, heading north.

"Cotton." Stephanie's voice in his ears. "The F-16 reported that your right rear landing gear is damaged badly."

So that's what the Russian had been firing at. A parting shot. The look of concern on Ivan's face said that he'd heard the bad news too. So he anticipated the question, *Can we land?* and said, "I don't know. Not yet, anyway."

Okay. Time to *aviate, navigate, and communicate.*

The pilot's three rules in a crisis.

He'd already aviated and reviewed the plane's status, the gauges all fluctuating. He worked the control column and kept the altitude gyro even. He also knew exactly where he was and where he wanted to be.

Time to communicate.

"I need a place to land," he said into the radio.

"Karup Air Base is close. About 120 miles west."

Which he knew. Located in the central part of Denmark's Jutland peninsula about two miles west of Karup. Built by the Luftwaffe during the German occupation in 1940 and used for offensive operations against England. The Royal Danish Army took control of it after the war. Midtjyllands Airport, which serviced Karup, shared the base's runways. A busy place. Lots of flights. Now home to several wings of the Royal Danish Air Force, including helicopters, a flying school, and fighter jets. He'd visited there a couple of years ago and had flown over it several times on his recreational outings. Sweden was closer. Definitely. But he knew what Stephanie was going to say. *Get Ivan and the codex to a place we control.*

"I'm declaring an emergency," he said into the radio. "Have Karup clear us a path."

That meant he would keep flying by using the ground to show the way. Air traffic controllers would take that declaration to heart and divert every plane out of his way, making the airport all his.

"How about the Russians? They gone?" he continued.

"Cut tail and ran when our guys showed up."

Good to hear.

He banked the plane left and turned west, heading back out over the Øresund, just north of Copenhagen. The track to Karup was familiar. They would need to cross Zealand Island over Roskilde, then back out to open water past Samsø Island, then northwest to the Jutland peninsula and Karup. Short hop. Luckily, the engines sounded reasonably okay. But half the control surfaces were gone, the other half sluggish and barely responsive.

"I need that guy you have at Ramstein," he told Stephanie. "The EMB expert."

"Already have her patched in."

Her? "My apologies."

"We can let that go," a new female voice said. "Captain Andrea Malarkey, U.S. Air Force. You seem to have your hands full."

"You could say that, Captain."

"Call me Andrea. We have you headed northwest, three hundred degrees, straight to Karup at two thousand feet."

"Okay, here's the deal. I have a good nose gear and one good main, the other is badly damaged. My starboard flight controls are nearly gone. Good news? Engines are working, but keeping this thing level is becoming increasingly difficult."

"We can take a look at that gear when you get to Karup with a fly-by. You still flying dirty?"

"I thought it best to not clean it up. I slowed to 150 knots. We need to burn fuel. I'll also need your help to dump the rest before we head down."

"Never flown one of these before?"

"Can't say that I have."

"Lucky for you that is not the case with me."

"That is lucky for me."

STEPHANIE REALIZED THE SITUATION WAS DIRE.

Cotton was flying a severely damaged plane that he had to land without hurting either himself, Ivan, or the codex. The Russians had done their worst, and there'd be hell to pay for those actions. But a man like Konstantin Franko could not care less what Sweden or the United States thought or did. In fact, he seemed to go out of his way to provoke whoever he could whenever he could. She could see that

Cassiopeia was concerned too, though she was trying, like herself, not to show it.

"Colonel, are you still there?" Stephanie asked her phone.

"I'm here. I've been in contact with Karup Air Base. They're preparing for the arrival. The runway will be fully foamed with fire retardant, and all emergency vehicles will be standing by. The other runways are closed to all traffic."

"Sounds like they're ready. It's important that this plane survive in one piece. No fire."

"That's always the goal."

"Make sure Captain Malarkey stays with him. Cotton might have a tendency to not ask everything he should. Part of that navy macho."

"She's one of our best pilots. She'll get him down."

But Stephanie was not reassured.

And neither, it seemed, was Cassiopeia.

COTTON KEPT A LOOKOUT AHEAD AS THEY PASSED ZEALAND ISLAND and headed over Århus Bay. He held the plane as steady on the horizon as he could. He could see the Jutland peninsula to the west, in the distance. Karup not far beyond that. He had maybe twenty minutes to get ready for a controlled crash landing. He'd practiced those in the navy, but only in a simulator.

There were two kinds.

Gear up or gear down.

He'd decided to go with gear down, forgoing any cycling of the undamaged gear up, then back down. No sense pushing their luck and losing the other two. Just leave things as they were. Bad enough that the starboard flaps were gone and the plane was flying like an eighteen-wheeler with half its tires flat. There was also banging and clanging. Lots of stuff loose below. None of which boded well for what lay ahead.

"Can you do this?" Ivan asked.

He wasn't sure, but he knew that was not the right answer. So he smiled and said the obvious, "I'm all we've got."

CHAPTER 65

COTTON PREPARED HIMSELF FOR WHAT LAY AHEAD AND ASKED INTO the headset, "You there, Andrea?"

"Right here."

"We need to use the next few minutes to test how bad this is going to be."

"My thoughts too."

He gripped the yoke in a tight hold and banked right fifteen degrees. Sluggish. Slow. More clanking came from underneath. He straightened back out and tried a move to the left. Same thing. But he got there and back.

"Left to right is dicey. Let's see up and down." He pitched up five hundred feet, then back down to two thousand. "Elevators seem okay, but the flaps are responding slow. There's a delay. Things aren't controlled. The drop is going to be quick."

Which was why they were practicing. To eliminate surprises and see how the aircraft would handle at landing. There was a definite delay from inputting a command to seeing the result. That meant the glide slope down to the runway was going to be steeper and faster than normal.

He tried the flaps. One set was gone, the other worked. The drag generated a lot of vibration. Definitely more lift on the left wing than the right. He was going to have to compensate for that with the yoke and the engines. It was going to be a rough ride down.

"I been in tough spots before," Ivan said. "But this one is top of list."

"This is not as bad as you might think."

"You bad liar."

"I just need a long straight runway to get this thing on the ground."

More clanking and the right engine sputtered.

His gaze raked the dials and stopped at fuel. The levels had dropped. A slow leak? Damn. What else could go wrong?

"We're pissing fuel," he said into the radio to Andrea. "Slow, but steady."

"Will you have enough to get to Karup?"

"We should. We had full tanks when we took off. I estimate we're about ten minutes out."

"Then it's not a problem. Let's worry about what is."

He liked her attitude.

"The control tower is ready to have a look at your underbelly," Andrea said. "Bring her in low and slow for a pass. In the meantime, we need to lose even more fuel."

"Tell me which switches to flip."

STEPHANIE WAS REGRETTING GOING ALONG WITH WHAT KOGER HAD wanted Cotton to do. The whole thing, baiting a canary trap for an informant, had been fraught with danger. True to his nature, Cotton had seen the need to take the chance. So they'd selectively passed along information on the switch of the codex, along with the change of flights that included Ivan's exit from Sweden.

And it had made its way straight to Moscow.

Koger had been right. The SVR would throw caution to the wind, not taking the time to care about protecting its source. Instead, they would immediately act on the intel and deal with their source later, most likely just eliminating it to avoid any further complications.

But that was not the problem of the moment.

COTTON STARED DOWN THROUGH THE WINDSHIELD AND SAW KARUP Air Base and its long landing strip. Vehicles moved back and forth across the pavement spraying fire retardant foam. He pulled back on the throttle and slowed their airspeed. The EMB shook with strong vibrations that rattled the cabin. He'd already acted on the instructions Andrea had provided and ditched ninety percent of the fuel left in the tanks.

Which had been tricky with the damaged control surfaces, trying to keep the plane level. The yoke had bucked in his hands hard, but he'd managed to rid it of the excess fuel. Or at least enough to not have a huge fireball on landing. He lost more altitude and prepared for the flyby so the control tower could take a close look at his landing gear. He tilted the wings and dropped to about a hundred feet, coming in low and slow across the airfield. The plane bucked and rattled as they flew past the tower.

"They got a good look and some video," Andrea said. "The front and left rear gear are okay. The right one is gone. Its pieces are just hanging there. So you have nothing supporting the right wing."

He'd been hoping there might be something there.

He flew past the end of the runway and powered back up to a thousand feet, swinging north about twenty miles from the base. He needed a long glide slope to maneuver down.

"You ready?" Andrea asked him.

"Let's do it."

"Just handle it like you did that fighter and missile. That was some good flying," she said.

"Even a blind-eyed squirrel finds a nut now and then."

"Let's find another one."

She was definitely cool under pressure.

"I have a live video feed," she told him. "I see you."

He swung the plane back to the east for a downwind run and lined up with the runway in the distance. The yoke held steady, but there was a lot of shimmy. He wondered if the right wing was going to hold together under the stress.

"You need to run through it with me?" Andrea asked.

He knew what she meant. "Obviously, I have to keep the right wing off the deck as long as possible. Once it dips the props are going to shatter and send shrapnel everywhere."

"Keep the nose up until the wing stalls," she said.

He agreed. Then it would just collapse onto itself. Which might or might not be a bad thing. But shrapnel. That was the danger.

He could feel more lift on the left than the right and he was using the yoke and what few control surfaces remained to compensate, along with working the engines.

"Strap in tight," he said to Ivan. "This is going to get rough."

"I'm ready. Get us down."

He glanced at Ivan. "There's going to be a lot of spinning once we hit. So hold tight until we come to a stop."

They were about five miles out and he could feel they were coming in too fast, but there was nothing he could do. The control surfaces were barely responding.

"Mr. Malone," Andrea said in his ear.

"I know. Too fast. It's going to be a hot navy landing."

The joke was an old one. Navy pilots liked to hit the deck hard and fast, part of being able to land quick on a carrier deck at sea. Air force pilots touched down on smooth concrete runways with a gentle kiss of their wheels and plenty of room to stop.

He reduced power and the vibrations escalated.

The entire plane shook as if in a convulsion, the yoke vibrating violently in his hands. They drifted left, then right, coming back and forth off the center of the foamed runway.

"By the way, Captain," he said. "That last name of yours. I bet you catch hell for it."

"I've heard every malarkey joke there is. How are you doing?"

"Trying to hold it together, but we're falling fast."

Emergency vehicles were parked to one side, waiting, their lights flashing.

At once comforting.

And disturbing.

CHAPTER 66

COTTON COULD SEE THE GROUND RUSHING UP TO MEET THEM AT AN alarming rate. He kept raising the nose to lose airspeed. He could not stall early. That would be disastrous. Normally you eased down. Not this time. *Just fly it into the ground.* What did the flight manuals say? *A controlled crash involves landing in an unplanned location, often with compromised control of the aircraft.* Really? That was an understatement, to say the least. More of the manual flashed through his eidetic memory. *The primary goal is minimizing damage to the aircraft and ensuring the safety of passengers and crew. Three main steps are involved. First, identify a suitable landing site, as flat and obstacle-free as possible.*

Done.

Next, manage speed and descent so as to touch down as gently as possible.

Still working on that one.

Finally, configure the aircraft with flaps and landing gear down.

Done, or at least as best he could under the circumstances.

The good news?

This was doable.

Everyone knew about US Airways flight 1549, the "Miracle on the Hudson," when Captain Chesley "Sully" Sullenberger struck a flock of geese shortly after takeoff, causing both engines to fail. Sullenberger then executed a controlled water landing on the Hudson River, saving all 155 passengers and crew.

More of the flight manual came to mind.

A controlled crash is a testament to the skill, training, and composure of the pilot. Through quick thinking and decisive action, pilots can transform a potentially catastrophic situation into a survivable event.

Good to know.

Thankfully, the EMB was a modern aircraft, designed with multiple redundancies and fail-safes. It had a reinforced fuselage, energy-absorbing seats, and advanced avionics. All of which increased their chances of walking away.

He tightened his grip on the yoke, bracing himself for the coming impact. The plane's vibrations grew stronger, rattling his teeth, blurring his vision. The plane tilted left, then jerked back violently to the right. He fought to keep the wings level. More wisdoms from the past flashed through his brain.

Nothing more worthless than air above you or runway behind you.

You got that right.

Timing was everything.

They were less than a hundred feet from the ground and he tilted the plane left, trying to use the good main gear to cushion the initial impact.

He cut the engines and feathered the props. The plane swayed from side to side as it drifted over the runaway, then bottomed out with a jolt. The left wheels hit the concrete with a bone-jarring thud, skipping and bouncing on the foamed surface. He fought to keep the nose high but, as friction stole speed, the plane slowed and the nose gear kissed the runway.

Sparks flew as metal scraped against the tarmac.

The screeching sound was deafening.

The EMB shuddered and groaned in protest. The props from the right engine shattered into pieces. They careened down the runway, the emergency vehicles growing larger in the windshield. Firefighters and medics were poised and ready to spring into action. The plane began to slow, the vibrations lessening.

And they spun. Round and round.

Staying on the runway, plowing through the foam, the EMB seemingly reluctant to give up the fight. They continued to spin, the plane's belly screaming off the concrete.

A final shudder, and they came to an abrupt stop.

Then silence.

His adrenaline rush began to fade, replaced by a profound sense of relief and fatigue that mixed with palpable tension. He turned to Ivan, who seemed equally drained but managed a weary smile.

"If you ever go to Disneyland," he said, "now you know what an e-ticket ride feels like."

The Russian nodded. "That was more than enough."

Outside, emergency crews swarmed the EMB, assessing the situation as others sprayed the plane with more foam. He unfastened his harness and stood. His legs felt like jelly, but he steadied himself and made his way to the exit door. A quick glance back and he saw the codex was still safely strapped down, unharmed.

He released the latch, opened the exit door, and stepped onto the runway, his feet sinking into the foam. Emergency personnel rushed toward him, their faces masked by respirators, their eyes scanning for any signs of injury.

He shook his head indicating he was fine.

Ivan joined him.

They moved away from the wreckage.

The EMB, though battered and bruised, had held together with no fire, no explosion.

And they were alive.

STEPHANIE WAITED AN ETERNITY FOR A REPORT ON THE LANDING. HER face was a mask of worry, her eyes searching for any confirmation of safety. The feed from the F-16 had stopped and all communications to Cotton had likewise been severed. He was either down with no power or they'd crashed.

"Colonel," she said to the phone. "What's happening?"

"They're on the ground, in one piece. No fire. I'm told they are exiting the plane."

She heaved a sigh of relief.

As did Cassiopeia.

Cotton had displayed extraordinary composure and expertise, turning what could have been a catastrophe into a manageable situation. But Stephanie knew that they owed their safety not just to his skill, but to everyone who had supported the mission.

"Thank you, Colonel, for all you did," Stephanie said. "And to you too, Captain Malarkey."

"Our pleasure," the colonel said.

She ended the call.

Prime Minister de Ciutiis had stood silent during the entire event. No surprise. A person in her position faced life-and-death decisions every day. But she knew what was on this woman's mind.

"The Czechs are expecting the codex to be delivered," de Ciutiis said.

"And it will be. Once we deal with the Russians."

"That was not the arrangement."

"It is now."

"This is a serious break of protocol. I would have never agreed to this if I had known your true motivations."

"I have no motivations, besides the fact that one of my own was nearly blown from the sky. Only a handful of people knew that plane was there, you being one of those."

"Are you implying I did something improper?"

"Not in the least. We know exactly the source of the leak, and that has to be dealt with before we release the codex."

"The Czechs will not be happy."

"They'll get over it. We are not Sweden. I doubt they are going to challenge Washington."

"It seems we have no choice, do we?"

"That is incorrect. Finally, through this whole mess, we actually do have a choice."

CHAPTER 67

CASSIOPEIA LED COTTON OUTSIDE INTO THE BRIGHT AFTERNOON. They strolled back down a shaded lane, toward the car park and her castle construction site.

"When finished," she told him, "a thirteenth-century castle will stand exactly as it did seven hundred years ago."

"Quite an endeavor."

They entered the construction site through a broad wooden gate and strolled into what appeared to be a barn with sandstone walls that housed a modern reception center. Beyond loomed the smell of dust, horses, and debris where a hundred or so people milled about.

"The entire foundation for the perimeter has been laid and the west curtain wall is coming along," she said, pointing. "We're about to start the corner towers and central buildings. But it takes time. We have to fashion the bricks, stone, wood, and mortar precisely as was done seven hundred years ago, using the same methods and tools, even wearing the same clothes."

"Do they eat the same food?"

She smiled. "We do make some modern accommodations."

She led him through the construction area and up the slope of a steep hill to a modest promontory, where everything could be clearly seen.

"I come here often. One hundred and twenty men and women are employed down there full-time."

"Quite a payroll."

"A small price to pay for history to be seen."

"Your nickname, Ingénieur. Is that what they call you? Engineer?"

"The staff gave me that name. I am trained in medieval building techniques. I have designed this entire project."

"You know, on the one hand, you're quite arrogant. On the other, you can be rather interesting."

"I realize my comment at lunch, about what happened with Henrik's son, was inappropriate. Why didn't you strike back?"

"For what? You didn't know what the hell you were talking about."

"I'll try not to make any more judgments."

He chuckled. "I doubt that, and I'm not that sensitive. I long ago developed a lizard skin. You have to in order to survive in the intelligence business."

"But you're retired."

"You never really quit. You just stay out of the line of fire more often than not."

"So you're helping Stephanie Nelle simply as a friend?"

"Shocking, isn't it?"

"Not at all. In fact, it's entirely consistent with your personality."

Now he was curious. "How do you know about my personality?"

"Once Henrik asked me to be involved, I learned a great deal about you. I have friends in your former profession. They all spoke highly of you."

"Glad to know folks remember."

"Do you know much about me?" she asked.

"Just the thumbnail sketch."

"I have many peculiarities."

He stared down at the construction site. "The sign out front said it'll take thirty years to finish."

"Easily."

She was right.

She did possess many peculiarities.

That day in France, a few years ago, always remained in her thoughts. Then, she and Cotton had not been close. In fact, they'd been extremely antagonistic toward each other. It had taken time and a lot more close calls for them to even like each other, much less love.

But they'd accomplished that.

For the past hour she'd tried hard to keep her thoughts to herself, but her face had betrayed the troubling emotions that had bubbled below the surface. She'd never really thought about a future that did not include Cotton. But what had just happened in the air over the Baltic had brought that awful possibility into sharp focus. And she did not like it. The prime minister had left the communications center.

Not happy.

"Okay, it's just you and me," she said to Stephanie.

The computer monitor, which had served as their eye to the world, now blank.

"I asked you earlier if you had any idea how the Russians knew to be there. You said that was a question for later. It's later."

"We baited a trap," Stephanie said.

"I know. I was part of that bait."

"No. There was more. When we let it be known where the codex was taken, we also let it be known how it was leaving the country."

"You put Ivan and the codex on that plane to draw them straight to it?"

"We put him on that plane to draw out a traitor. Koger needed to find out who. Now we know."

She was shocked. "Cotton agreed to that?"

Stephanie nodded. "I know he didn't tell you. That was on my order."

"Nice try. He chose not to tell me."

"Can you blame him? It was better you didn't know. You going along with him might have raised unnecessary questions. And by the way, we could have been wrong about a leak and nothing could have happened. No fighter jets would have been sent."

"But you weren't wrong."

She and Cotton had a rough patch a while back, even breaking up for a short time. But when they made up and reconnected, they'd agreed to no more secrets. None. Yet here was one.

A big one.

"Cut him some slack," Stephanie said. "You would have done the same thing."

Yes, she definitely would have. But that was irrelevant. "Who's the spy?"

"That's what you and I are about to deal with."

CHAPTER 68

JOHN ENTERED A TOP FLOOR ROOM AT THE HOTEL VILLA ANNA in Uppsala. It filled an olden building from the nineteenth century that sat within sight of the cathedral. The room was spacious with a king-sized bed and Swedish designer furniture, which cast an austerity that he'd never really cared for. But there was also a flat-screen television, mini-bar, and electric kettle. Not the Grand Hôtel in Stockholm, but few places could compare with its opulence. They'd opted to come here instead of Stockholm simply to stay out of the way. He was not a known commodity throughout Sweden. He'd been out of the limelight for the past decade. Few knew his face, even fewer knew his association to the royal family. No one at the reception desk gave him or Monica a second look.

"Do we have any idea if the defector is dead? The codex destroyed?" he asked Monica.

"We have this."

And she showed him a text message on her phone.

Carolina Rediviva. 2:00 p.m. Be There.

"Aleks sent that before we left the island," she said. "That location is here in Uppsala."

He was concerned. "What does he want?"

"Not to kill us. He would have just done that, not sent a text. My guess is that something went wrong and he wants a loose end cleaned up."

"Why you?"

"Because it is my loose end."

"You do not seem surprised."

"Why should I be. It is the SVR. What do you expect?"

COTTON POLITELY WAVED OFF THE OFFER OF A STIFF DRINK AND OPTED instead for a glass of ice water. He and Ivan were inside a secure facility at the Karup Air Base. The emergency crews had done their jobs and prevented any fire from breaking out in the destroyed EMB. He wondered who was going to pay for the loss of that multimillion-dollar aircraft. The Devil's Bible had been removed and was now being loaded into another plane that would take both it and Ivan south to Ramstein Air Base. No danger existed from any more Russian fighters, as not even Franko would risk another attack. Out over the Baltic and international waters was one thing, but to try it over German airspace right smack in the middle of NATO? That was another matter entirely.

"Here's where we part ways," he said to Ivan. "I need to get back to Stockholm."

"You did good up there. I appreciate it."

"Make it count for something and give them plenty of intel."

"I owe Franko nothing. He made big mistake trying to kill me."

"The CIA will take good care of you. Maybe even get you that house in the desert."

"That would be wonderful. My old bones are tired."

He extended a hand, which Ivan shook.

"You good man, Cotton Malone. Be careful out there."

STEPHANIE SHIFTED FROM CRISIS TO DEFENSIVE MODE. COTTON WAS safe. Ivan and the Devil's Bible were on their way to Germany. Russia had been thwarted. Only one problem remained to be resolved.

She faced Cassiopeia. "Koger has a security leak. A big one. His predecessor left it for him to find and solve. So he did. With Cotton's help. We fed the source inside intel that said where and when to be."

"And the source took the bait?"

"Hook, line, sinker, the whole damn boat. It's a deep sleeper agent who managed to stay in place for a long time."

Recruiting spies was an art. A cat-and-mouse game. If done properly, as with Princess Lysa, the asset would not even know it happened. There was indeed a fine line between persuasion and manipulation. Though the Magellan Billet was not in the business of recruiting foreign assets, she knew the drill. A targeting officer started the process, trolling for people who would want to work with America. Nowadays they checked social media and any public information sites both before and after approaching a target. If those raised no red flags, then a deep dive happened. Was the target happily married? Had they achieved a reasonable amount of success in their career? Did they have any hobbies? All these offered opportunities for the recruiter to wrangle an invitation into the target's life, without seeming obvious. The more well-rounded a CIA officer was, the easier it was to connect with a target. They even had a catchy name for it. You, Me, Same Same.

Common ground was essential. It implied trustworthiness. The targeting officer was not just a smiling stranger. They were a friend, a peer. Development could take months, even years, depending on the target, their country, and how difficult an operation might be. The danger zone came once the courtship ended. How could you be sure the potential asset would not report everything to the authorities? What had a CIA case officer once told her? *Most normal people are not going to propose to someone unless they know they are going to say yes. The same can be said of espionage.*

But why would people betray their country?

Money, more often than not. But some spied for ideology, others were coerced, and a few just needed an ego boost.

Done right, nothing ever seemed manipulative. Just a natural progression in an ongoing relationship. People skills were the biggest weapons in a handler's arsenal. More of what that CIA handler had told her came to mind. *Make it something that they want to do. Something that they've been destined to do.* But what happened when an asset stopped providing worthwhile intelligence? Or was no longer needed? Or became a security risk?

That's where they were at the moment.

"They acted fast on the intel we fed them," Stephanie said to Cassiopeia. "No effort made to hide anything. That means the source is now expendable."

"The source does not know they are in trouble?"

"Overestimating your importance is an occupational hazard of a traitor."

"Only six people knew about that plane and Ivan. I'm going to say the prime minister can be trusted. That leaves five, four of whom are me, you, Cotton, and Koger. So the leak is obvious."

"That's right," Stephanie said. "Time to find Sandra Koss."

CHAPTER 69

John and Monica entered the Carolina Rediviva, the main building of the Uppsala University Library. The name meant "Carolina Revived," given in remembrance of the old Academia Carolina building, which had functioned as the university library for most of the eighteenth century. Now it was the oldest and largest university library building in Sweden. The time was approaching 2:00 p.m. and they had arrived a few minutes early.

But so had Aleks.

The wiry Russian stood in the entrance hall.

He and Monica approached.

"So you would not feel threatened," Aleks said. "I came alone."

John shrugged. "How thoughtful."

"I assume since we are meeting something went wrong?" Monica asked.

Aleks motioned to a set of glass doors to their left. "Shall we."

Obviously he wanted them to go inside. John glanced at Monica who nodded, so he pushed through the doors into a small exhibition hall. A placard told visitors that the most important objects in the library were displayed here for public viewing. He knew about this place. It held precious maps and manuscripts, including illuminated Ethiopian texts and the first book ever printed in Sweden. But the star of the show was the Codex Argentus, the Silver Bible, written in gold and silver ink atop purple vellum.

Aleks paid the admission fee for all three of them, and they walked into the dimly lit gallery. Temperature- and humidity-controlled glass cases lined the walls displaying treasures, and in the center a larger one held the codex. Ambient light cast a soft glow on the fragile pages.

"This book was created in the sixth century for the Ostrogothic King Theodoric the Great," Aleks said. "Eventually, Rudolf the Second acquired it and the Swedes, during the Thirty Years' War, pillaged it at the same time they stole the Devil's Bible. It has been here, in Uppsala, since 1649."

John took a moment and admired the codex through the crystal-clear glass.

"They often open it to a particularly splendid page," Aleks said, "allowing viewers to marvel at the intricate Gothic script and the shimmering silver inks that have, amazingly, withstood the test of time."

"You seem to know a lot about this book," Monica said.

"I like to think of myself as a student of history. But this book is most interesting. Aside from being beautiful, it is linguistically the most complete existing document written in the Gothic language. That is somewhat amazing."

"What happened today?" Monica asked, changing the subject.

"Your information was correct, but we failed."

"How does that concern me?"

Aleks shrugged. "Did you know that this library contains books stolen from Poland in the seventeenth century by the Swedish

Army? According to the Treaty of Oliwa all those books should have been returned in 1660. Yet Sweden has given back only one-tenth of one percent. In the same vein, they have not returned this treasure here to the Czechs."

"What do you want?" Monica asked.

"I want you to arrange a meet with your source." Aleks' voice had lowered. "Immediately."

"You want to know if that source has been compromised."

"I want the source gone."

John heard the finality in the voice.

Monica said, "I can provide you the name, and you can do it yourself."

"I know the name."

"All the more reason you do not need me."

"We need to end our association with your source. This entire endeavor, like the return of all these treasures, has been fraught with failure. I need you to arrange the meet."

"And once this meet is set?"

"Be there. Then get out of the way. I will take it from there. And please tell the source I will be present. Stress that I want to speak to them personally and offer my sincere thanks."

John stayed out of the conversation. It really did not concern him. But Aleks had deliberately included him. Why? He decided to do a little fishing himself. "Why do you think the Czechs did not want this Silver Bible back? They had the leverage to get whatever they wanted. So why not ask for this too?"

"Why would you ask me that?"

"You seem to know a lot about something that is not all that relevant to our current situation."

Aleks pointed a finger. "Details are always important. Many times they supply the answers we seek. This book? It was stolen by Queen

Christina at the same time as the Devil's Bible and has been held here for nearly four centuries. A precious artifact. One of a kind. But it is flawed. Only 187 of the original 336 folios survived. So perhaps the Czechs considered it incomplete. No longer belonging to them."

He caught the message. The same could be said for both him and Monica.

"The Americans may know they have a leak?" Monica said.

"I considered that possibility, but doubt that to be the case. They sent the plane up with the defector and the codex inside. If they knew we knew, why would they have done that and risked losing both? Your source confirmed that Ivan and the codex were on the plane?"

She nodded. "Personally witnessed."

"So they have no idea of your source. Please arrange the meet before they do discover that fact. We cannot afford any more defectors to go free."

"Can't the SVR handle this?" John asked. "You know the source's identity."

"Believe me, you do not want me to involve them any further. Nobody in Moscow is pleased with anything that has happened here. There will be ramifications from all of this. Unpleasant ones. I am simply trying to minimize those."

"He is right," Monica said to John. "I have to do this."

"And what of my reemergence?" he asked.

"That can occur after we get this done," she said. "The source needs to be eliminated before anyone realizes it exists. I can get her there."

He could see her mind was set.

So he simply nodded.

In agreement.

CHAPTER 70

STEPHANIE STOOD INSIDE HER HOTEL ROOM WITH KOGER AND Cassiopeia. A call had been placed to Sandra Koss by Koger, telling his subordinate to be here at 2:00 P.M. Things were happening and he needed all hands on deck. A knock at the door and Koger opened it, inviting Sandra inside, closing it behind her.

"Good to see you again," Sandra said to Stephanie.

"Please, have a seat," Koger said, his voice light and friendly.

The recalcitrant subject of an intelligence interrogation must be broken, but broken for use like a riding horse, not smashed in the search for a single golden egg.

Wise advice from the CIA interrogation manual.

The arrest should take the subject by surprise and should impose on them the greatest possible degree of mental discomfort, in order to catch them off balance and deprive them of the initiative. It should take place at a moment when the target least expects it and when mental and physical resistance is at its lowest.

This scenario, about to be played out, definitely qualified.

Each interrogation is carefully tailored to the individual subject. It is a battle of wills in which the turning point is reached as the subject realizes the futility of their position.

Sandra sat in one of the chairs.

"Look," Koger said, his voice turning hard. "We can go through the whole bullshit interrogation procedure, following the manual and slowly beating you down until you break. I've done it many times in the past. I'm actually really good at it."

He walked to the bed, grabbed a pillow, then reached beneath his jacket and removed a pistol. He nestled the gun into the pillow and brought it close, aiming it straight at Sandra. She tried to get up but Koger motioned that she should stay put.

She stopped resisting. Her face filled with fear.

"I'm going to ask you some questions. God as my witness, Sandra, I will blow your damn brains out if you lie to me. We're in a no-rules situation here. And I really, really love no rules."

Terror now filled Sandra's face. True, she was CIA. But she was administration, not operations. She hadn't worked the field in a long time. And surely she'd never had a gun pointed at her before, especially by an extremely agitated individual whom she'd betrayed. She had to know that Koger never bluffed.

"Question one," Koger said. "Do you know Monica Butler-White?"

Sandra stayed silent, surely trying to ascertain how bad things were. How much did her boss know? Was he fishing? Could she lie her way out?

The most difficult subject is one who will not talk at all. But a silent prisoner may find it hard to revert to complete silence if caught off guard. The device of starting with questions easy for the subject to answer is useful with many whose replies to significant questions may be hard to elicit.

"Let me clarify," Koger said. "For me, silence is the equivalent to lying."

Another few tense moments passed. The gun never moved off her.

"Yes, I know her," Sandra said.

"Question two, did you sell us out about the flight south?"

The gun stayed aimed.

Everything possible must be done to impress upon the subject the unassailable superiority of those in whose hands they find themselves, and therefore the futility of their position.

"I can't...Derrick."

"You can. If not, I will shoot you right here, right now, with not a hint of remorse or consequences. You're an enemy of the state. A traitor. Your life has zero value."

The questioning itself can be carried out in a friendly, persuasive manner, or from a hard, merciless, threatening posture, or with an impersonal and neutral approach. At all times the interrogators must show an attitude of assurance and unhurried determination.

"I will give you to the count of three, then I'm going to end you and deal with this another way. One."

Except as part of a trick or plan the interrogator should always appear unworried and complete master of the situation.

"Two."

In the arduous examination of a stubborn subject one must guard against showing weariness and impatience.

He moved the pillow closer to Sandra, never taking his eyes off her.

"Yes. I did," she quickly said.

Koger stood silent, gun still aimed, staring without a blink.

Sometimes a long period of silence will unnerve the subject.

Finally, he asked, "Why?"

"Why not?" Sandra said.

Was that defiance in her voice?

"I've worked for the CIA nearly twenty years. You know what that gets me?" She paused. "Nothing. Not a thing, except a paycheck once a month and an occasional good job mark in my personnel file. But it's all meaningless. There's nowhere to go in my job. Nobody cares whether I'm there or not. You included. If I leave, I'll just be replaced by another nobody who no one will care about either."

Interrogation is a probe for an opening. Once found, however small, every effort should be concentrated on enlarging it and increasing the subject's discomposure. At this stage they are allowed no respite until they are fully broken and resistance comes to an end.

"You did this for recognition?" Stephanie asked. "For ego?"

"I did," Sandra said. "And each time I felt wanted. Important. Somebody who was needed."

Koger lowered the pillow and the gun. "You're a fool. A stupid, idiotic fool. They just used you."

"No more than you did. No more than the people who were my bosses before you did."

"It's over, Sandra," Stephanie said. "All that remains is what will happen to you. You're headed to federal prison for the rest of your life."

"They want to meet," Sandra suddenly said. "I was called earlier."

Interesting. Stephanie had not seen that coming.

"Where and when?" Koger asked.

"The Vasa Museum, 6:30 P.M. I chose the spot."

"Why is that?" Stephanie asked.

"A public place with metal detectors. So no weapons."

"Will Monica be there?" Koger asked.

Sandra nodded. "She asked for the meet."

In order to achieve results it may be necessary to use as many as three different approaches to an interrogation. First, the cold, unfeeling individual whose questions are shot out as from a machine gun, whose voice is hard and monotonous, who can be threatening showing no compassion.

Koger had played that part perfectly.

Second, the naïve and credulous questioner who seems to be taken in by the prisoner's story, making them feel smarter than the interrogator, building a false confidence that may betray them.

Stephanie had tried to play that role.

Finally, the kind and friendly person, understanding and persuasive, whose sympathetic approach is of decisive importance at the climactic phase of the interrogation.

"Do you know what they want?" Koger asked.

Sandra shook her head. "You never know that until you get there."

"Then get there," Koger made clear.

"If I do this, I want immunity. No jail."

"You're in no position to bargain."

"I disagree."

Stephanie glanced at Cassiopeia, her eyes saying, *Your turn. Be kind and friendly.* Cassiopeia had stood silent, watching, but she stepped across the room and stood before Sandra. "Do you realize what's at stake here?"

Sandra said nothing.

"Do you know how critical this is?" Cassiopeia asked.

Still nothing.

"Princess Lysa is dead. John Westlake is missing, presumed dead. What's happening here is vital to not only Sweden, but the United States and NATO as a whole. This woman, Monica, is responsible for all the bad things that have happened. Not you. She's in charge. You say you feel underappreciated. Unimportant. Here's your chance to do something really important. In fact, you're the only one who can."

"I don't want to go to jail."

"Then let me ask you this. If you did not go to jail, would you tell us, at some point, all that you have told them. All that was passed on. That way we'll know what they know."

Sandra nodded. "I can do that."

Cassiopeia smiled. "That would be wonderful. But today, in the here and now, we need you to go to that meet so we can arrest Monica. To protect your cover, we will arrest you too. That way it does not seem you are cooperating with us. Does that sound okay?"

"And will I be credited for doing this? Will Langley know I helped make it happen?"

"Without a doubt. You will be fully credited for everything you did."

Sandra Koss seemed pleased. But was she that naïve? That low on self-esteem? Koger stayed silent, doing what they'd agreed he would do. Be himself and scare the crap out of Sandra.

Then Stephanie and Cassiopeia would reel her in.

All by the book.

CHAPTER 71

COTTON WAS FLOWN DIRECTLY BACK TO A SWEDISH AIRBASE OUTSIDE of Stockholm, then driven into town. He caught up with Stephanie, Cassiopeia, and Koger around 5:30 P.M. at the Vasa Museum, outside the public areas, among the museum's back spaces inside the security office. He caught the initial look of relief on Cassiopeia's face, then the annoyance. Like Lucy Ricardo. He'd have some explaining to do. But later. Not now.

"You okay?" Stephanie asked.

"All is good. Ivan is gone and the codex is safe."

"We have to finish this," Stephanie said.

And he listened as they brought him up to speed.

"We have Sandra under watch," Koger said. "She's making her way here."

Cassiopeia still had said nothing. So he decided to preempt the problem. "I know I did wrong. But you would have done the same thing." She opened her mouth, and he raised a finger to stop her. "Before you chew me out, tell me I'm wrong."

She hesitated.

He waited.

Then she said, "You're not."

"So can we let it go? I'm here. In one piece."

"It was still reckless."

"I would say it was a controlled risk."

"Now that peace has come in our lifetime," Koger said, "can we work on the problem at hand."

"That was actually kind of important," Cotton said. "How's Kristin?"

Kristin Jeanne worked for the Eidgenössische Finanzmarktaufsicht, Switzerland's Financial Market Supervisory Authority. She'd been helpful recently, and they'd all learned that she and Koger had an interesting past.

"Actually," Koger said, "she's doing just fine. Thank you for asking. Now we need to focus."

JOHN CHECKED HIS WATCH: 6:15 P.M.

Monica had done as Aleks asked and contacted her source, who'd chosen another public place for meeting. The Vasa Museum. Open from 10:00 A.M. to 8:00 P.M. It sat on Djurgården Island, inside Stockholm, home to the *Vasa*, an awe-inspiring relic of seventeenth-century naval engineering. Commissioned by King Gustav Adolph to bolster Sweden's maritime supremacy, it met an untimely fate in 1628 on its maiden voyage, capsizing and sinking just a few nautical miles from where it had sailed out of Stockholm harbor. Over three centuries later the ship was rediscovered and meticulously salvaged, emerging from the Baltic in an unprecedented feat of maritime archaeology. He'd visited the museum before. Several times. Once during an official function with the king, one of the rare times during the past decade they'd been in the same room.

He and Monica had arrived ten minutes ago, parked in a lot with about twenty other cars and one large tourist bus. Aleks had provided them a vehicle.

"You stay here," she said. "I'll make the introductions, then get out of there and let Aleks do whatever it is he intends on doing."

"How bad is this going to get? Would he kill her, right here?"

"He could. They want to send a message to the Americans. Get at least one win. It is all part of the SVR's institutional mentality."

"If I practiced that in business, I would be broke. Seems a reckless and unnecessary action. Much smarter to take your losses and walk away."

"Like we are doing?"

"Precisely."

"The SVR is not noted for walking away."

"And you? Will they leave you alone?"

"I am sure they would love to end me too. But that will be far more difficult. And Aleks knows that."

CASSIOPEIA RECOGNIZED THAT WHATEVER IRRITATION SHE POSSESSED with Cotton had to wait until later. They needed to finish this. He'd taken a huge chance going up into the air. That flight may or may not have been compromised. Only one way to find out, and he'd done that like a pro.

Now it was her turn.

They'd retreated to the building's security office, and she took a moment to study the bank of wall monitors. The good news? Everyone was required to pass through a metal detector before entering, which reasonably assured there would be no weapons. Visitors milled about admiring the ship, its grandeur towering above them. There were three more levels that rose upward, wrapping the ship at varying heights, offering closer views. The museum's dimly lit interior enhanced the mysterious aura of the vessel, almost daring visitors not to stare. The whole thing was so odd. A ship inside a building, balanced atop a steel cradle, seemingly ready to set sail. There were also a wealth of exhibits that showcased the construction, sinking, recovery, and conservation, along with detailed insights into life aboard during the seventeenth century.

None of which interested her today.

"I want you two out there," Stephanie said. "Stay back, out of sight. The third level should give you the best vantage point."

"Stephanie and I will be here. Thankfully, the place is loaded with cameras. We'll communicate through these," Koger said, handing over two small walkie-talkies with ear fobs. "And you'll also need these." Koger produced two 9mm pistols, handing one to each of them, along with a spare magazine. "Time to arm up."

"You expecting trouble?" Stephanie asked.

"I was an Eagle Scout. Always prepared."

"I want Monica Butler-White alive," Stephanie made clear. "That's really important. We still have a dead princess and a missing British billionaire who may be in this up to his eyeballs. Somebody has to be held accountable, and Monica is the most likely suspect."

"Understood," Cotton said. "We'll get her."

"And Sandra Koss?" Cassiopeia asked.

"I want her," Koger said, "alive. We need to know how much damage she's done."

CHAPTER 72

John sat in the car.

The expansive lot was less than a quarter full, and he was concerned. So many variables were at play. All out of his control. The only thing that brought him any solace was that the location was surely secure. Every place had metal detectors, especially public museums. That should minimize the risk of weapons making their way inside. Hopefully, Aleks' interests were confined to Monica's source and not to her.

He hated everything about the spy business. Loyalties were paper-thin and changed by the second. He firmly believed that the only reason the Russians had left him alone for the past nine years was visibility. Being rich came with benefits, one of which was that a lot of people knew who you were. Moscow had apparently decided that those benefits were not worth challenging. Just leave well enough alone. All that changed, though, when he and Monica decided to thrust him back into the limelight and onto the SVR's radar.

A car entered the lot beneath the tall trees, thick with their summer foliage. It parked closer to the front doors than where he sat. He heard car doors open, then close, and wondered if this might be Monica's source. He glanced back to see Aleks and two of the men who'd been with the Russian earlier out on the island. He shrank down in the front seat out of sight. The two men toted backpacks and headed off across the lot, avoiding the main entrance and rounding the building.

Where were they going?

Aleks walked straight for the glass doors and entered the museum.

STEPHANIE STOOD BEFORE THE BANK OF CLOSED-CIRCUIT MONITORS. Thankfully, the museum's interior was well covered, and they were able to easily watch as Monica Butler-White passed through the metal detector. Cassiopeia had supplied a detailed description that fit the woman perfectly.

Monica made her way into the center of the museum and seemed to be admiring the *Vasa*'s intricate seventeenth-century carvings and robust framework. There were also a variety of exhibits, meticulously arranged, and Monica moved from one to the next, surely assessing the geography, trying to fit in, studying the huge ship and the museum's upper levels—all visible thanks to the building's open design. Not a lot of places to hide. But so many vantage points. Something on one of the other wall screens caught her attention.

"You see that?" she asked Koger.

"Yeah. We just got a whale in the aquarium," Koger muttered.

She knew the face of the man walking through the metal detector and collecting his wallet and cell phone. A seasoned SVR operative high up in the command chain. Rarely seen in the field.

"Grigory Vaino," she said. "Code name Aleks. I've dealt with him before."

"So have I."

They'd intentionally kept this entire operation to corral Monica and Sandra close, involving no one outside their immediate working circle. That had been done for a number of reasons, primary among them the fact that this whole thing was off the books, with no official sanction. Also, they had at least one leak in Koger's camp. Were there more? The White House had been informed of Ivan's defection, but they knew nothing about Sandra or anything else. Langley was another matter. Koger had told her that inquiries had come and that he'd just ignored them. Nothing unusual there. The hope was to get Ivan and the codex away safe, and Monica and Sandra in custody, all of which would go a long way toward smoothing over the rules and regs that had been broken. But—

"This just took a new turn," Koger said.

"I agree. The Russians know we know about Sandra. He's here for a reason, and it's not good."

"So let's get him too. Just one thing."

She knew.

He almost certainly had not come alone.

COTTON WAS UP ON THE SECOND LEVEL, STAYING BACK FROM THE RAILings. Koger had just told him that Monica was in the building, on the ground floor, along with another man, whose description was provided.

A Russian SVR big deal, code name Aleks.

"We'll keep a close watch on them," Koger said in his ear. "But new plan. We want all three."

No problem. The good thing? Neither of the two below were armed, as they'd both made it through the metal detector unscathed. And both he and Cassiopeia carried weapons. But this was not his first rodeo.

"Did he come alone?" he asked Koger.

"Unknown. But not likely. Do we need the cavalry?"

"Not yet," he whispered. "Let's see if we can keep this party contained. Any sight of our leak?"

"Not yet. But I'm told she'll make her appearance shortly."

CHAPTER 73

CASSIOPEIA CAUGHT SIGHT OF MONICA BUTLER-WHITE ON THE ground level. She motioned to Cotton, who was at the far end of the second-level pathway that led around the stern of the *Vasa*.

He understood her perfectly.

That was their target.

And he confirmed that with a nod of his head.

"The guy approaching Monica," Koger said in his ear, "is Aleks. And Sandra has just arrived."

STEPHANIE KEPT HER EYES GLUED ON THE MONITOR AS SANDRA entered the main area of the museum and approached Aleks and Monica.

"Do we have audio," Stephanie asked.

Koger switched on the receiver for the wire Sandra was wearing now that it was in range. That had been a non-negotiable point, but Sandra had not objected. More of the stuff that really seemed important to her. She'd actually been thrilled to finally be back in operation, no matter the risk she was taking.

"Do you think she knows her life may be in danger?" she asked Koger.

"Not a clue."

"You care?"

"Not in the least. You play with fire, you get burned. She's a traitor."

A hard truth, but the truth nonetheless. Sandra's fate would be a jail cell for the rest of her life. True, they would debrief her ad nauseam, extracting every piece of information they could, but none of that would forgive what she'd done. Unlikely the Russians would ever trade for her. That was the problem with turncoats. The one you turned on hated you and the one you turned to never trusted you.

"You and I both know that a bullet to her head would be merciful," Koger said.

Another hard truth.

The door to the security room opened and one of the uniformed guards stepped inside. Koger walked over and they spoke in whispers while she kept watch on the screens that filled the wall before her.

The guard left.

"Two men have entered the building through a rear exit," Koger said. "One of the custodial staff let them in, thinking they were here on business. The security people want to know what we want to do. I told him we would handle it."

He activated the walkie-talkie. "Okay, listen up."

COTTON REACTED TO KOGER'S INFORMATION.

We have two uninvited visitors back in the work areas. Probably headed your way. Find them.

He hustled forward, past the *Vasa's* bow, to a metal door marked in Swedish and English.

EMPLOYEES ONLY.

And eased the door open.

CASSIOPEIA WAS TOWARD THE *VASA'S* STERN. COTTON WAS TO HER right on the third level with her, but more toward the bow. The three targets remained at ground level on the ship's port side, currently out of view. But Koger and Stephanie were monitoring what was occurring there. Cotton was dealing with one problem, heading through a metal door. She had to deal with the other, so she stepped to a metal door marked EMPLOYEES ONLY.

And turned the lever.

COTTON STEPPED THROUGH THE DOORWAY AND ALLOWED THE PANEL to quietly close behind him. He stood in a small corridor that surely led to the back bowels of the museum, where staff and maintenance people toiled out of sight of visitors. To his left a staircase led up and he heard the peppering of footsteps ricochet off the concrete-block walls.

One of the men?

He started up, careful with his feet, staying quiet.

He heard a door open and close.

Then silence.

He hustled up the risers that right-angled their way toward the museum's roof. Before reaching the top he came to a small landing where another metal door led out. No choice. He had to risk a peek. He gripped the handle and carefully twisted it open, exposing a one-inch view of the world beyond, which opened out into the museum and the bow of the ship. Right past the door was a metal catwalk attached to the inner stone wall. Some sort of service area for the stage lights that illuminated the ship. Wrought-iron screening formed a waist-high railing that blocked any views of below. The door moved to the outside left and he was afraid to open it any further, which meant there was no way to see to the far left where the catwalk stretched.

Then he heard it.

A zipper being worked.

Somebody was out there to the left of the door.

He eased the door closed.

"Got mine in sight," he whispered into the mic.

CASSIOPEIA ALLOWED THE METAL DOOR TO GENTLY CLOSE.

She'd climbed a set of metal stairs and found herself at a small landing with an exit door, then a final flight of stairs that led up to the roof. She'd already risked a look past the door and determined that someone was out on the catwalk. Cotton had one of the intruders toward the bow of the ship. She had the other at the stern. Both of whom had sought out and taken the highest ground in the room.

"Got mine too," she whispered. "Now what?"

CHAPTER 74

STEPHANIE ASSESSED THE SITUATION.

The two intruders were under close watch. Monica, Sandra, and Aleks were still at ground level. Their conversation so far had been more about the *Vasa* than anything else. Aleks had been admiring the ship that towered up above them. Sandra had stayed relatively quiet, as had Monica. Aleks was clearly stalling, allowing time for his men to get into position.

"I think I will leave now," Monica suddenly said. "You two can talk privately."

"I would prefer you stay," Aleks said. "As I am sure Ms. Koss would too. After all, she does not know me."

"She does now."

"I insist," Aleks said.

And Monica had not challenged that.

"I wanted to personally meet you," Aleks said to Sandra. "You have been a valuable asset. We appreciate your work."

"Were you able to intercept the plane?" Sandra asked.

They'd intentionally not included Sandra in the need-to-know circle about what happened over the Baltic.

"Oh, yes," Aleks said. "We located it."

"May I ask what happened?" Sandra said.

Aleks motioned to Monica. "Tell her."

"We were able to take the plane down," Monica said. "Thanks to you."

"Did you know that the creation of this ship is taught in business management schools," Aleks said. "Even in Russia. Its construction was a fiasco of inefficiency and error. One mistake after another was made, yet the builders continued on, never correcting a thing. The result was inevitable. The ship rolled over and sank twenty minutes out from where it set sail. Just a light gust of wind toppled it right over. All thanks to it being incredibly top-heavy. It is a lesson in how human problems in communication and management cause projects to fail. It even has a name. The Vasa Syndrome."

"He's still stalling," Koger said. "With bullshit."

"You think?"

"An organization's goals must be appropriately matched to its capabilities," Aleks went on. "Here there was an overemphasis on pleasing the king with elaborate ornamentation and firepower. Not enough on more critical issues such as stability and seaworthiness."

"They're going to take Sandra out, right here, in public," Koger said. "And my guess? Monica too."

"Hence why he wanted her to stay and why there are two intruders," she said. "Monica is surely aware of this. She's a pro."

"But a trapped one, at the moment." Koger hit the button on his walkie-talkie. "Okay, you two, take those men down. Now."

"You want them alive or dead?" Cotton asked.

"Surprise me."

COTTON SHUFFLED THROUGH THE POSSIBILITIES.

Of course they would want to get these guys with minimal disturbance and the smallest possible amount of gunfire. There were people below visiting the museum, not to mention their three targets whom they definitely wanted alive. But the door was the problem. It opened the wrong way. To get a shot he would have to swing the metal panel all the way out. Which would alert his target.

And the response would be immediate.

"You have door issues over there too?" he whispered into the mic.

"I do," Cassiopeia said. "And it's hollow metal. Not much there to stop a bullet."

"I say kick it wide open and get the jump."

"Ready when you are."

JOHN WAS UNSURE JUST EXACTLY WHAT HE WAS SUPPOSED TO DO. Monica had told him to stay in the car. But Aleks had not come alone. Should she be told? Of course, but he was no operative. Just a businessman who had the bad luck to be married to a woman with a big mouth who caught the attention of a foreign power. Then he caught the eye of an SVR operative looking to protect her asset and things became really complicated.

"We have an opportunity, in Sweden, to rid ourselves of several problems at once," Monica had said to him a few weeks ago. *"I am going to give you the chance to be done with your wife, clear your name, stick it to the king of Sweden, and get me in the process."*

Hard not to admire her confidence.

He was told once about what confident people said to get what they wanted. Things like, *I value your opinion, but I trust my instincts on this one.* Or something a bit more negative. *That's kind of you, but I'm not interested. I respect your beliefs and opinions, but I need to stay true to my own.* Or, *I appreciate what you're saying, but I see it differently.* Then there was the outright pushback, *Your ideas are appreciated, but they are not a good fit in this situation.* He always preferred a more positive approach. *I am confident that I can do this, thanks. I have it under control.*

He could have told Monica any one of those things. He could have also rejected her offer. *I'm not interested in trying that, but thank you. That doesn't sound like something I'd find enjoyable, but I wish you the best.* Or something even simpler. *I'm sorry, I can't do that.* But he'd not said any of that. Now he was beginning to wonder if he'd made a mistake.

But it was far too late to second-guess things.

He stepped from the car.

And headed for the museum's entrance.

STEPHANIE CONTINUED TO WATCH AND LISTEN TO THE CONVERSAtion that was happening out on the museum's ground floor.

"Once they make their move on the two shooters up high," Koger said, "those three are going to make a run for the exit. I plan to be waiting for them outside."

"Alone?"

"I just texted the two men who've been helping out here, the guys who went to Sigtuna with you. They are on-site now. I also have the other exits for the building covered, in case the two on the catwalks make a run for it. Nobody is leaving this place."

"And the reason you did not have all that help on station twenty minutes ago?"

"You know the answer. I wanted to see how far the SVR is willing to go."

"There are civilians inside that museum."

"And the two men with guns are currently in our sights. Nobody else has a weapon. We've got this." Koger headed for the door. "I'll leave you the walkie-talkie. I have one too, in my ear. Keep a watch over everything and let us know what's happening."

The big man left the security room.

She refocused on the monitors and noticed the visitors milling about. A small tourist group with a guide lingered on the second level. Aleks, Monica, and Sandra were still at ground level about midship. She could hear their conversation through the receiver's speakers. Some shop talk, mostly small talk, with Aleks continuing to compliment Sandra. Then something caught her eye at the security checkpoint.

John Westlake. Passing through the magnetometer.

"Lazarus back from the dead," she muttered.

But why was he here? Only one explanation.

He was with Monica.

A rage swept through her at his incredible gall, the kind that hammered home that she, and everyone else, had been played for a fool. Westlake was guilty of everything they'd ever believed about him. Koger had been right. Whatever happened in Sigtuna had been, as Cotton would say, a dog-and-pony show for Cassiopeia's benefit. Her initial instincts from a decade ago had been right.

No question.

Enough. More than enough, actually.

This had to be dealt with.

Now.

She grabbed a third pistol that lay on the desk and stormed from the room.

CHAPTER 75

COTTON SAT ON THE CONCRETE FLOOR WITH HIS GUN READY. The idea was to stay low, bang the door open, and catch his target off guard. He'd already told Cassiopeia to do the same thing. Since it didn't matter whether the two men came out with or without holes, he'd leave it to them to determine their fate.

"Ready," Cassiopeia said in his ear.

"Do it."

He leaned back on his butt and slammed the soles of his shoes into the metal door, which flew out and, with nothing to stop it, opened to 180 degrees, slamming into the museum's inner wall, then rebounding. He used that moment to come to a crouching position, staying low, ready to engage. He heard three soft pops and bullets smacked into the metal door. Two of the rounds blew out on his side and whined away. The door returned to the jamb, which he stopped with his hand before the latch engaged.

"Nowhere to go," he called out.

Two more rounds hit the door as he moved it outward. The

impacts sent the panel back his way. He shoved it open, stayed low, and swung out, aiming his weapon down the catwalk and firing two rounds. His weapon was not sound-suppressed so his shots banged through the museum's cavernous interior. The bullets struck nothing and careened off the inner stone walls beyond the catwalk.

He risked a look.

Twenty feet away the guy with the gun was leaping off the railing, propelling himself outward toward the crow's nest at the top of the *Vasa*'s foremast. It was a good twenty-foot leap out and down. The man still held the gun in his left hand, arms extended, and he hit the shroud hard, searching for a grip with his right hand, which he found. The guy held on to the shroud's thick hemp with one hand and fired a shot back toward Cotton with the other. He ducked beneath the screened metal railing and the bullet flew high into the wall behind him.

No choice now.

He came up and shot the man as he scrambled down the shroud.

The guy cried out in pain and released his hold on the ropes, falling downward into a space between the ship's forward deck and the viewing levels, finally smacking the tile floor at ground level.

CASSIOPEIA WAS PINNED DOWN FROM SEVERAL SOUND-SUPPRESSED rounds that came from the man on her catwalk. Cotton was still dealing with the threat at the bow. Things were not progressing. She needed to end this guy, but she did not want to shoot him unless she had to.

"How about you put your gun down and come with me," she called out.

His answer came with three more bullets that whizzed by the open doorway. The bad angle worked both ways, making it hard to shoot each other.

But enough.

Finger on the trigger, she stuck the gun out the jamb, pointed down the catwalk, and fired twice. Then she swung herself close to the jamb and grabbed a peek. The man was trying to escape, pivoting up onto the iron railing and attempting a leap down to the *Vasa*'s stern deck.

She shot the guy midair.

The body slammed into the railings that lined the top of the quarter deck. The gun released from his grip and fell all the way to the floor at ground level, clattering about.

Then the body settled onto the deck.

Not moving.

JOHN MADE HIS WAY TOWARD THE CENTER OF THE *VASA*, STAYING OFF to one side among the exhibits. He caught a few shrieks of excitement from children enjoying themselves. He glanced up at the ancient hull, then the tall masts and riggings.

Two pops echoed throughout.

He stared up past the ship to a catwalk that ran near the top of the towering inner walls toward the bow. A door was swinging from open to closed. He heard more shots toward the *Vasa*'s stern, then saw a man leaping from another of the catwalks where a woman stood, gun pointed.

The man slammed into the *Vasa*'s deck.

Chaos erupted on the various viewing levels. Voices rose. People on the ground floor began to rush toward the main entrance and the other fire exits.

He decided to head the opposite direction.

And ran through the exhibits.

Toward the gun that had fallen to the ground.

COTTON COULD NOT SEE WHERE ALEKS, MONICA, AND SANDRA were standing, even though he was high, as the ship blocked his view to the ground floor on its far side. Cassiopeia had been forced to deal with her problem in the same manner he'd been compelled to employ.

Both intruders were surely dead.

Threats eliminated.

CASSIOPEIA WAS ABOUT TO FLEE THE CATWALK AND HEAD DOWN TO where their three targets were positioned, but before she turned to leave she saw John Westlake, twenty feet below, rounding the ship's stern and snatching the gun from the floor. His appearance was both a surprise and a concern. Where had he come from? Why had no one alerted them?

And he was now armed.

No time to backtrack and use the stairs.

So she stuffed the gun at her waist, planted her right hand on the iron railing, and pivoted up and over.

Down to the *Vasa*.

CHAPTER 76

COTTON WATCHED AS CASSIOPEIA LEAPED FROM HER PERCH DOWN onto the ship. He was sixty feet away, equally as high as she had been a few moments before.

"What are you doing?" he said into the microphone.

"Westlake is down there and he has a gun."

Alarm swept through him. Then, below where he stood, he saw a woman grab the gun the man he'd shot had dropped. She turned and headed back around the *Vasa*'s bow.

"Monica just got a gun here off the floor," he said.

"Stop her. I'll deal with Westlake."

The bad guys on the floor being armed changed everything. He tucked his own gun at his waist and leaped down, finding the shroud at the *Vasa*'s bow that the other guy had likewise located. He gripped the thick hemp and inserted his shoes into the spaces formed by the crisscrossing rope, working his way down to the deck. He then stepped over the petrified ancient planks to the port side and glanced down. Monica reappeared from the starboard side of the ship and started firing. Visitors were racing to get out of the building. To his left, fifty feet away from Monica, John Westlake appeared.

Holding a gun.

STEPHANIE HUSTLED FROM THE SECURITY OFFICE AND HEADED through a maze of corridors, finding a door that led out to the museum's public spaces. She'd left the walkie-talkie in the office.

Big mistake.

She should return and get it.

Then she heard muffled bangs from inside the museum.

Gunshots?

Keep moving.

She opened the door ahead of her.

JOHN WAS NO STRANGER TO WEAPONS, MAINLY RIFLES AND SHOTguns. Handguns? Not his thing. But he knew how to handle one, having learned in the military. He checked to make sure the safety was off and that there were still bullets in the magazine.

Six rounds.

Good to know.

Monica appeared about thirty meters away, around the bow. She never hesitated or lost a step in her stride. The first shot found its mark in Aleks' body, which shuddered from the impact. Two more also found flesh. A fourth shot was to another woman who had to be Monica's source. Both dropped to the floor and blood poured from the limp bodies, pooling on the tile.

So much was happening so fast.

"John," Monica called out. "We have to go."

CASSIOPEIA STOOD TEN METERS ABOVE WESTLAKE, WHO MOVED IN and out of view thanks to the *Vasa's* bulging hull.

She needed to get down there. Fast.

But it was too far to jump.

So she hopped the railing and grabbed hold of a carved decorative post that extended upward on each side of the quarter deck. Two overhangs extended from the hull planking, shielding windows that opened into the two lower decks. She used them like steps and slid down from the top one to the bottom one, holding on to a wooden rail that projected beneath the overhang's length. The wood was petrified, but she kept reminding herself that it was also four hundred years old and had spent the majority of its time at the bottom of the Baltic. The jump now from where she was perched to the second level was about five meters.

She leaped.

COTTON WAS HIGH ON THE *VASA'S* BOWSPRIT.

A lot was happening thirty feet below at ground level. Two people were down and Monica was calling out to Westlake. So much for taking Aleks and Sandra alive. But Monica and Westlake? They were still in play. Off to his right at the main entrance he saw Koger entering the building, shouldering his way against the wave of people making a hasty exit.

He could not take a shot at Monica. Bad angle.

Then, to his left, back toward the ship's stern among some of the exhibits, he saw a familiar face.

"Stephanie, what are you doing here?" he said into the mic.

No reply.

"What do you mean?" Koger said.

"Stephanie is on the playing field. With no radio and a gun."

JOHN SAW CASSIOPEIA VITT JUMP FROM THE SHIP'S STERN TO THE second-floor aisleway. What was she doing here? Was this a trap? Monica was right. They needed to leave.

"Westlake."

He whirled to the left at the sound of his name.

Stephanie Nelle was twenty meters away, marching with a stern determination.

Right for him.

With a gun.

COTTON HAD NO WAY OF GETTING TO GROUND LEVEL.

The distance from the *Vasa*'s deck down to the tile floor was a solid fifty to sixty feet. A bone-breaking drop. He could still see Stephanie, but not Monica or Westlake. Everything was happening fast. Koger was at least another sixty feet to his right.

"Cassiopeia, where are you?"

"Coming down the stairs to ground level. I'll be there in a moment."

Stephanie was now in view, storming across the ground floor among the exhibits with brisk, sturdy steps. He decided to try to find a better vantage point.

"Take Monica," he said to Cassiopeia. "I'll deal with Westlake. Stephanie is down there. Armed. But no radio."

He heard the expletive Cassiopeia muttered into the mic and agreed, as he moved across the main deck toward the stern.

"Stephanie," he called out. "Take cover."

STEPHANIE REALIZED THAT SHE MAY HAVE MADE A MISTAKE. THERE was a lot of gunfire happening, and though she was armed, this was not her forte. She heard Cotton yell her name and the warning to *take cover*, but the next few seconds happened in an instant.

One moment she was moving toward Westlake, raising her weapon and demanding that he surrender himself. The next she heard a bang, then felt the impact of a bullet that tore into her chest.

COTTON COULD NOT SEE WESTLAKE.

The man was below him, and the *Vasa*'s curved outer hull was shielding him from any view. To his horror he saw Stephanie stop her advance, her body jerking back in the distinctive move of somebody who'd been shot. He tossed caution to the wind and followed what Cassiopeia had done, rushing to the stern and hopping the top rail, using the layers of external carvings, there for decoration, as handholds as he worked his way downward.

He made it as far as the top of the rudder and spotted Westlake below, aiming his gun at Stephanie and firing again with another loud bang.

He held tight with his left hand and dangled his body out, the drop down a good thirty feet. No need to let go.

Just fire.

JOHN DID NOT AT FIRST REALIZE WHAT HAD HAPPENED.

Something had slammed into his right shoulder, then into his chest. Which hurt. Bad. He'd shot Stephanie Nelle twice and saw her fall to her knees. Reacting on instinct he squeezed off his last two shots so fast the explosions blended together.

But the bullets scattered off toward the ceiling.

Another bang filled his ears.

His head exploded. Then he heard nothing.

And the world vanished.

CASSIOPEIA TURNED ON THE LANDING AND HEADED DOWN THE LAST flight of stairs to the museum's ground floor. She'd heard more pops and bangs. Cotton was dealing with something.

"Find Monica," Cotton said in her ear. "Take her down."

She searched and found the woman toward the *Vasa*'s bow heading around and moving toward the stern where Westlake now lay on the floor. Monica seemed focused on him and did not react when she came down the stairs. Cassiopeia never hesitated. She stopped, aimed, and called out Monica's name.

The woman turned.

And Cassiopeia shot her twice in the chest.

STEPHANIE WAS TRYING TO ASSESS THE DAMAGE.

The first bullet had stopped her mid-stride and caused her legs to buckle at her knees. A second round set her chest on fire.

Westlake had shot her.

She tried to raise her own weapon, but her arm would not respond. She saw Cotton, high up on the *Vasa,* firing down, shooting Westlake and ending the threat. She opened her mouth to speak, to call out, but a spasm ruptured something in her throat. Her chest felt warm. Almost comforting.

A calm swept over her.

Then as straight as a falling tree, she pitched forward.

And fell onto her face.

CASSIOPEIA LOWERED HER GUN.

Westlake, Monica, Aleks, and Sandra Koss all lay on the floor. Dead. Which mattered not. Her focus was on Stephanie and she ran to where she lay. Cotton remained dangling from the *Vasa*'s stern.

"How bad is it?" he called out.

Stephanie lay face down.

She rolled her over.

Blood poured from two chest wounds. Breathing was short and shallow, the chest rising and falling in waves. A rattle filled the throat and the arms and hands trembled. She was alive, but a fluttering, sinking feeling hit her. This was not good. Then, nothing. No more breaths. No movement. The eyes fixed open, unblinking.

She checked for a pulse.

None.

Her eyes closed at the hard realization. Then she glanced up to Cotton, shook her head, and said, "She's gone."

PRESENT DAY

EPILOGUE

Atlanta, Georgia
July 23
2:30 p.m.

Cotton stared up and watched as a breeze rolled the clouds north in tumbling waves. The rain had dwindled to almost nothing and the sky had regained color. Cassiopeia had stood beside him while he thought back to all that had happened. His mind swirled with confused mists of anger, racked with regret that assaulted him from a host of directions.

The authorities had been called to the Vasa Museum, along with representatives from the American embassy. A lot of diplomatic wrangling had occurred. It was a lot to take in. A high-up SVR commander was dead. Monica Butler-White, also dead. John Westlake, a British citizen, dead. The sister of the king of Sweden dead. A confirmed CIA traitor dead. And worst of all, the head of the Magellan Billet, a longtime veteran of the American intelligence community, dead.

He and Cassiopeia had stayed with Stephanie's body as it was transported to a local hospital, where an autopsy confirmed that she'd died from two gunshot wounds. He'd delayed a few minutes to gather himself, then made a call to Danny Daniels, which had been one of the hardest things he'd ever done. Danny had listened in silence then, after a long pause, finally choked out, "Bring her home."

It had been three days before the diplomats had sorted everything out and the body was officially released. Russia, of course, denied any knowledge of anything that Aleks or Monica had been involved with. Officially, they were two rogue agents who were working outside official parameters. Everyone knew that was a lie, but there was no evidence to the contrary.

Princess Lysa's death could not be confirmed as a homicide. Was that the most likely thing? Absolutely. But proof was lacking. The king of Sweden had been beside himself, both angry and crushed, refusing to speak to anyone in Washington, including the president of the United States. Prime Minister de Ciutiis had done what she could to smooth things over with the State Department, but in the end she had to support her king, at least publicly.

Ivan made it to Ramstein Air Base and was immediately placed aboard a private jet and flown to the United States. Where was he now? That was way above Cotton's pay grade, but he hoped it was near a hot, arid desert.

With all that ultimately happened, the decision was made to send the Devil's Bible on to Prague, so it was flown south and turned over to the Czechs. Cotton assumed that at some point, after an appropriate interval, any and all objections to Sweden's NATO membership would be dropped.

Both the White House and Langley reacted harshly. True, reeling in Ivan and outing a mole helped, but somebody had to take the fall. Stephanie was gone. Cotton and Cassiopeia were civilians. That left Koger. Who'd been severely reprimanded, then demoted and transferred out of Europe. He hadn't been fired, as they had not wanted him on the outside pissing in. Better to keep him close. Amazingly, the big man had taken his lumps with his mouth shut.

Where was he now? Nobody knew.

The funeral had been three hours ago, attended by an array of people from the intelligence community, along with Danny, who'd sat stoic during the service, never saying a word. He'd also refused a request to speak, preferring to keep his thoughts to himself. The graveside service had been more private. Only Cotton, Cassiopeia, Danny, and Stephanie's son, Mark, who flew over from France, had been present. It had been good to see Mark again. No minister muttered hollow words about heaven and salvation. Instead, Mark spoke from his heart. Once the ceremony ended Danny and Mark immediately left the grave and drove off together. He and Cassiopeia lingered. The cemetery sat amid a lovely wooded glade north of Atlanta. Danny had chosen it for the seclusion. There'd been talk of a more formal funeral in DC, but Danny and Mark both nixed that idea.

Which was the right call.

Stephanie had never sought the limelight in life. Why should she in death? Where she lay right now, inside a white coffin, was the perfect final resting place. Workers were busy preparing to lower it into the ground. A backhoe was driven over to scoop the dirt that had been kept dry under a tarp nearby. Cotton had not wanted to leave Stephanie alone. It hadn't seemed right. So he would stay right here until she was sealed underground.

Danny had insisted that her headstone be made without delay and, being the former president of the United States, he was provided exactly what he wanted. A lovely slab of pink marble waited to adorn the grave with a matching headstone that quoted a particularly apt biblical passage.

2 Timothy 4:7.

> I HAVE FOUGHT THE GOOD FIGHT,
> I HAVE FINISHED THE RACE,
> I HAVE KEPT THE FAITH.

Danny had chosen the words, as Stephanie had never been religious. Just the opposite in fact. She'd made a career for herself trying to live on good terms with everyone, her pragmatism legendary. Her skill and patience enviable. Many a difficult situation had been resolved thanks to her. She'd always spoken to everyone on a footing of equality, adding civility and paying attention. Her eyes could be like shattered emeralds, her emotions just as jagged. And the voice. Which many times seemed sharpened by razor blades. But it was the boldness of any undertaking that excited her. He always said there was a little lion there, but a lot more fox. True, she liked to maintain perfect command over herself, but yes, she made mistakes. A big one in Stockholm, rushing into the fray. As she'd said on more than one occasion, *It's the mistakes that will get you killed.*

Yes, it was.

Age had always been a sore subject for her and, even in death, it remained a mystery. Danny had honored that lifelong quirk with a headstone that only recorded her name and the epitaph. No date of birth or death was noted.

Cotton stared over at the marble awaiting placement above the grave. "She was a remarkable woman who changed my life."

He squeezed Cassiopeia's hand, which he hadn't released for the past twenty minutes. Waves of sorrow swept through him, his vision blurring. He'd been fighting back useless tears of frustration all day, but finally one streaked down from his left eye. Thankfully, the rain masked its presence.

"It all seems unreal," Cassiopeia said. "Like it never happened."

"But it did."

On the flight home and during the service he'd thought a lot about the past and the first time he and Stephanie Nelle crossed paths. Inside the Duval County jail, in Florida. After a long day helping out a friend. Until that moment he'd never once struck someone in anger or harmed another person. But that day he shot a woman who'd killed her husband, then tried to kill him.

And he'd been arrested for felony aggravated assault.

He was led to a brightly lit, windowless space, not a cell but an interrogation room, equipped with a long metal table and six chairs. A woman waited. Middle-aged, thin, attractive, with short, light-colored hair and a confident face. She wore a smart-looking wool-skirted suit. His first impression of her was never in doubt. Law enforcement. Not local.

"My name is Stephanie Nelle," she said.

The corrections officer left, closing the door behind her.

"What are you? FBI?"

She smiled and shook her head. "I was told you were intuitive. Give it another shot."

He tried to think of a clever retort but couldn't, so he simply said, "Justice Department."

She nodded. "I came down from DC to meet with you. But an hour ago, when I showed up at your post, your commanding officer told me you were here."

He was in his second year of a three-year tour at Naval Station Mayport. The base sat a few miles east of Jacksonville, Florida, beside a protected harbor that accommodated aircraft-carrier-sized vessels. Thousands of sailors and even more support personnel worked within its fences.

"I'm sure he had nothing good to say about me."

"He told me you could rot here. It seems he considers you nothing but a problem."

Which, in all honesty, he'd tried hard not to be.

He slid one of the chairs away from the table and sat. The sleepless night was catching up to him. His visitor remained standing.

"Nice shooting out there," she said. "You could have killed her, but you didn't."

He shrugged. "She didn't appreciate the favor."

"Your first time shooting someone?"

"Does it show?"

"You look a little rattled."

"I watched a friend die."

"That would do it to anyone. The woman you shot wants to press charges against you."

"Yeah. Good luck with that one."

She chuckled. "My thought too. I was told you can handle yourself under pressure. It's good to see the intel was correct. You flew fighters, right?"

He nodded.

"I read your personnel file," she said. "You specifically requested flight training, and your skills were top-notch. Mind telling me why the shift to law?"

He trained his eyes on her like gun barrels. "You already know the answer to that question."

She smiled. "I apologize. I won't insult you like that again."

"How about you get to the point."

"I have a job for you."

"The navy has first dibs on my time."

"That's the great thing about working for the attorney general of *the United States, who works for the president of the United States. Jobs like yours can be changed."*

Okay. He got the message. She was important.

"The job I have in mind requires skill and discretion. I'm told you possess both qualities. But the question is, do you live up to that advance billing? Your CO doesn't think so."

Screw that idiot. He was an ass-kissing paper pusher and always would be. A career officer focused on doing his twenty years, then retiring out with a pension while he was young enough to double-dip in private practice. That path had never interested him.

Now here was an opportunity.

What did he have to lose?

Everything, actually. Including his life. But he took the chance and went from a JAG lawyer to a Magellan Billet agent.

And the world changed for him.

Stephanie had never been casual about risking either her own life or her agents'. But sometimes your luck ran out and the odds shifted away from your favor. And if you also made a mistake?

That was fatal.

One hundred percent of the time.

So much had happened in the past two weeks. All so unexpected. Shocking. Unforgiving. He'd been left with a nagging feeling that there may have been something he overlooked, something glaringly obvious that he'd failed to notice. But there was nothing. Stephanie's death was not his fault. Not anyone's fault beyond Stephanie's herself. He was tired, his mind cluttered, his thoughts tripping over one another. All the adrenaline inside him had fled his system, leaving him weary and disjointed. Even worse, anxiety had settled as a ball of burning pain that clawed at his stomach.

A fresh breeze brought the smell of sweet pine.

Which urged him forward and made him think about something else that had plagued him for the past few months. Ever since Morocco. Stephanie had been mortal. He was mortal. Death was no longer a stranger. In fact, that Grim Reaper had made its presence known by taking Henrik Thorvaldsen, Stephanie, and Suzy Baldwin. So why wait any longer? Why even question whether he should or should not? None of that made any sense. Not anymore.

A reassuring thought broke into his consciousness.

"I've made a decision," he said to Cassiopeia.

"You're going to do it?" she asked, reading his mind.

He nodded.

"I'm going to find out if I have a daughter."

WRITER'S NOTE

For this novel Elizabeth and I visited Stockholm, Uppsala, and Sigtuna. We stayed at the Grand Hôtel (as does John Westlake), there in late fall, everything coated in fresh snow. Darkness came about two o'clock each afternoon, the sun barely rising in the sky before disappearing. For a couple of southerners who have always lived in the heat, those were wondrous sights indeed. If you ever have the chance, I highly recommend a visit.

Time now to separate fact from fiction.

The various locales within the story are faithfully depicted. Those include: Stockholm, including its famous old town; the quaint village of Sigtuna; Uppsala; Lake Mälaren and its many islands; Sweden's national library; the royal palace; the Grand Hôtel; the Vasa Museum; and the Øresund Bridge, an engineering marvel connecting Europe to upper Scandinavia, the narrow straits between Denmark and Sweden some of the busiest shipping lanes in the world.

One of the premises of this story hinges on Sweden's admission into NATO. In real life that happened on March 7, 2024 (during the writing of this story), after Turkey withdrew its repeated opposition. A unanimous vote is required from all NATO members before a new nation is allowed to join the alliance. Of course, in Cotton's world none of that ever happened, and Sweden's fictional application was blocked by the Czech Republic.

King Wilhelm I and Princess Lysa are my creations, but the Swedish monarchy is one of long standing (chapters 2 and 10). It traditionally maintains a low profile and has been relatively scandal-free. Here's an interesting side note. In the story Princess Lysa disappears while walking her dog on the backstreets of Stockholm, near an iron memorial of a sitting boy. As noted in chapter 12, it's called Järnpojke. Iron Boy Looking at the Moon. Some also call him Olle. He represents the children of Stockholm who worked hard many centuries ago. You leave a coin or treat, or just touch his head, to find good luck. Stealing coins means bad luck as, according to legend, Olle sees everything and forgets nothing. While in Stockholm I saw one of King Carl XVI Gustaf's sisters walking her dog at the same memorial.

Sweden's government is a bit convoluted (chapters 3 and 7) with decision making and responsibility widely diversified. There are a lot of peculiarities to its parliamentary system, but to its credit, it has long provided stable leadership. The information about former Prime Minister Olof Palme, including his tragic death, is true (chapter 8). In this story his murder is solved. In reality it remains an open case, though the Soviets were a prime suspect.

Operation Ghost Stories (chapter 13) happened in 2010 and resulted in the FBI arresting ten Russian sleeper agents across the United States and one in Cyprus. The Russians remain experts at recruiting, training, and planting sleeper assets (chapter 68).

The Stockholm metro is accurately depicted, including its amazing underground stations, each one a spectacular work of art (chapter 13). It is no ordinary subway system and worth a look. The Vasa Museum in the Royal National City Park (chapter 71) houses the

WRITER'S NOTE

Vasa, a fully assembled seventeenth-century Swedish warship, raised piece by piece in 1961 from the waters off Stockholm, where it sank on August 10, 1628. It is a remarkable sight and made for a perfect backdrop for the novel's conclusion (chapters 71–76).

Nisses and *tomtes* are part of Scadinavian folklore. We might call them gnomes, and there are countless stories attached to them, a few of which are noted in chapter 11.

Queen Christina (chapter 40) was a remarkable monarch. All the history and background noted about her is accurate, including her fascination with the Codex Gigas. She did indeed send her troops into Prague in 1648 (chapter 33), toward the end of the Thirty Years' War, to take not only that codex but also the famed Silver Bible (chapter 69) and all of what remained of Rudolf II's legendary collections. Most of that Bohemian war booty still remains in Sweden.

The Codex Gigas is central to this tale. As noted in chapter 6 it measures three feet tall, nearly two feet wide, and nine inches thick with 320 vellum folios. It is the largest and heaviest medieval illuminated manuscript in the world, weighing an impressive 165 pounds. Where did it come from? Best guess? It was created sometime in the early thirteenth century in Bohemia, now the Czech Republic, inside one of its many monasteries (chapter 5). Each of its folios is penned with impeccable precision and relentless attention to detail, all with colorful illustrations, precise borders, and highly stylized letters. It supposedly contains the then-world's volume of knowledge through authoritative, ancient, and commonly recognized texts. The Swedes bestowed upon it a more popular label thanks to a highly unusual, nineteen-inch color drawing of Satan (chapter 34) that appears on Folio 290.

The Devil's Bible.

No other manuscript from that time period contains such a

provocative illustration. The Swedes invented the legend of a monk walled up, making a deal with the devil, and producing the manuscript in a single night to gain his freedom (chapter 31). In reality it would have taken decades to complete. Even more remarkable, it was written entirely by one person (as the handwriting is the same throughout) without a single mistake.

It has an interesting backstory, all of which is detailed in chapter 31. Through the years it has been loaned out to other nations (chapter 42) but always returned to Stockholm. The Swedes consider the codex theirs, though the Czechs have made repeated requests for its return. Negotiations continue to this day. If you're ever in Stockholm, stop by the national library and have a look as it rests inside its sealed display case. Also, on the website for the Swedish national library, there are hundreds of high-resolution images of every folio.

And finally, a word about Stephanie Nelle's swan song.

This is the twentieth book in the Cotton Malone series and Stephanie has appeared in all of them, starting with *The Templar Legacy* (2006). Only once before have I ended a main character. That happened in *The Paris Vendetta* (2009), when Henrik Thorvaldsen was killed. Sad, for sure, to see a character go, but there comes a time when a writer has done all he or she can do with that particular personality. You change, adapt, and modify, but eventually, just like in real life, you reach an end. It came to that point with Henrik and now with Stephanie.

Along the way in this story we revisited scenes and characters from *The Templar Legacy* (2006), *The Emperor's Tomb* (2010), and *The Bishop's Pawn* (2018). Moments that were particularly relevant to Stephanie's evolution, and to the introspection that occurs during this story. For those of you who may not have read those novels, I invite you to check them out. The idea was to complete the circle and give her a fitting farewell. Her demise opens up an opportunity for something new and different to drop into Cotton's world and, I assure you, that storm is most definitely headed his way. He also has to wonder. What of his sideline career in the intelligence business? Is that over? No more favors or assignments? Does he retire to his bookshop and fade away? Or is there something else? Something he simply cannot see coming.

At least not yet.

Stay tuned to find out more.

For Stephanie Nelle, she had a great fictional life. I named her after the feminization of my first name and my youngest daughter's middle name. She definitely left her mark and will never be forgotten.

May she rest in fictional peace.

As a final tribute, which Danny Daniels had chiseled into her headstone, 2 Timothy 4:7 says it best.

> I HAVE FOUGHT THE GOOD FIGHT,
> I HAVE FINISHED THE RACE,
> I HAVE KEPT THE FAITH.

ACKNOWLEDGEMENTS

My sincere thanks to Ben Sevier, senior vice president and publisher of Grand Central. To Lyssa Keusch, my editor, whom I've greatly enjoyed working with. Then to Allison Schuster and Rachel Rodriguez for their marketing expertise; Staci Burt who handles publicity; and all those in Sales and Production who make sure there is both a book to read and that it is available for sale.

A deep bow goes to Simon Lipskar my agent and friend, who makes everything possible.

A few extra mentions of thanks: Simone de Ciutiis, who guided Elizabeth and me across Stockholm then out into the Swedish countryside; Patrik Granholm, who provided invaluable information on the Devil's Bible; Ray Simmons for help with the aerial scenes; Katie Gledhill for some advance photo reconnaissance; and Benji and Jillian Stein, who are the best research assistants.

As always, to my wife, Elizabeth, who remains the most special of all.

Here's a fun fact. For every novel, this one included, there's at least one trip to a locale for research. Over the past twenty years, for me, those trips have been arranged by a lovely lady from California, Yvonne Governor.

ACKNOWLEDGEMENTS

What's the saying?

A good travel agent is hard to find. So true. He or she has to not only be organized and efficient, but patient and intuitive. All of us have our travel ideocracies. Mine include only aisle seats on planes, plenty of hotel space, room service, and at least two hours to change flights domestically and three on international flights. Not to mention locating the various cars and drivers, along with the specialized guides I always utilize. But Yvonne has handled all of that with grace and style. Nothing seems to faze her. She just gets the job done. Dedicating a book to her is long overdue and that is entirely my fault.

This one's for you, Yvonne.

Thanks for all the wonderful trips.

RAISING READERS
Books Build Bright Futures

Dear Reader,

We'd love your attention for one more page to tell you about the crisis in children's reading, and what we can all do.

Studies have shown that reading for fun is the **single biggest predictor of a child's future life chances** – more than family circumstance, parents' educational background or income. It improves academic results, mental health, wealth, communication skills, ambition and happiness.[1]

The number of children reading for fun is in rapid decline. Young people have a lot of competition for their time. In 2024, 1 in 10 children and young people in the UK aged 5 to 18 did not own a single book at home.[2]

Hachette works extensively with schools, libraries and literacy charities, but here are some ways we can all raise more readers:

- Reading to children for just 10 minutes a day makes a difference
- Don't give up if children aren't regular readers – there will be books for them!
- Visit bookshops and libraries to get recommendations
- Encourage them to listen to audiobooks
- Support school libraries
- Give books as gifts

There's a lot more information about how to encourage children to read on our website: **www.RaisingReaders.co.uk**

Thank you for reading.

---

[1] OECD, '21st-Century Readers: Developing Literacy Skills in a Digital World', 2021, https://www.oecd.org/en/publications/21st-century-readers_a83d84cb-en.html

[2] National Literacy Trust, 'Book Ownership in 2024', November 2024, https://literacytrust.org.uk/research-services/research-reports/book-ownership-in-2024